Lynne Graham was born in Northern Ireland and has been a keen romance reader since her teens. She is very happily married to an understanding husband who has learned to cook since she started to write! Her five children keep her on her toes. She has a very large dog who knocks everything over, a very small terrier who barks a lot, and two cats. When time allows, Lynne is a keen gardener.

Lorraine Hall is a part-time hermit and full-time writer. She was born with an old soul and her head in the clouds—which, it turns out, is the perfect combination for spending her days creating thunderous alpha heroes and the fierce, determined heroines who win their hearts. She lives in a potentially haunted house with her soulmate and a rumbustious band of hermits in training. When she's not writing romance, she's reading it.

Also by Lynne Graham

His Royal Bride Replacement
Shock Greek Heir

Billion-Dollar Bride Swap miniseries

Unveiling the Wrong Bride

Also by Lorraine Hall

A Wedding Between Enemies
Pregnant, Stolen, Wed
Unwrapping His Forbidden Assistant

Babies for Royal Brides miniseries

Secretly Pregnant Princess

Discover more at millsandboon.co.uk.

BOUND BY A SECRET

LYNNE GRAHAM

LORRAINE HALL

MILLS & BOON

All rights reserved including the right of reproduction in whole or in part in any form. This edition is published by arrangement with Harlequin Enterprises ULC.

This is a work of fiction. Names, characters, places, locations and incidents are purely fictional and bear no relationship to any real life individuals, living or dead, or to any actual places, business establishments, locations, events or incidents. Any resemblance is entirely coincidental.

Without limiting the exclusive rights of any author, contributor or the publisher of this publication, any unauthorised use of this publication to train generative artificial intelligence (AI) technologies is expressly prohibited. HarperCollins also exercise their rights under Article 4(3) of the Digital Single Market Directive 2019/790 and expressly reserve this publication from the text and data mining exception.

® and TM are trademarks owned and used by the trademark owner and/or its licensee. Trademarks marked with ® are registered with the United Kingdom Patent Office and/or the Office for Harmonisation in the Internal Market and in other countries.

First published in Great Britain 2026
by Mills & Boon, an imprint of HarperCollins*Publishers* Ltd,
1 London Bridge Street, London, SE1 9GF

www.harpercollins.co.uk

HarperCollins*Publishers*, Macken House, 39/40 Mayor Street Upper, Dublin 1, D01 C9W8, Ireland

Bound by a Secret © 2026 Harlequin Enterprises ULC

Her Two Greek Secrets © 2026 Lynne Graham

King's Heir Ultimatum © 2026 Lorraine Hall

ISBN: 978-0-263-41820-0

03/26

Printed and Bound in the UK using 100% Renewable Electricity at CPI Group (UK) Ltd, Croydon, CR0 4YY

HER TWO GREEK SECRETS

LYNNE GRAHAM

MILLS & BOON

CHAPTER ONE

A­RISTIDE R­OMANOS, BILLIONAIRE ENTREPRENEUR, was relieved when his senior PA, Georgio, contrived to give him a slight smile from his hospital bed. 'Only one more scan to go and I'll be free to leave, sir.'

Aristide winced. He wasn't always the most considerate employer but even he was not about to drag an employee with a broken ankle straight out of hospital. 'No, you won't be. You'll stay here until a medic tells you to leave and then only to return to the hotel where you will rest.'

A car crash in the airport car park had taken out Aristide's entire personal team of six. Three were down with concussion, one with a broken arm and another with a mix of injuries. Currently, Georgio was the only member of his staff to remain in full possession of his wits.

'But, sir…what will you—?'

'I will proceed to Traxis.' Aristide paused to enjoy Georgio's look of disbelief. 'I *can* work alone. I will do a tour and meet senior personnel. Another team will arrive to assist me tomorrow. Relax, Georgio, you're on sick leave.'

Aristide knew that his PA didn't find it any easier to relax than he did. Georgio, like Aristide, was a driven type-A personality. Ignoring the attention that his six-foot-four-inch, well-built frame and sleek, dark good looks garnered from the female staff, he strode out of the private hospital and back into his limo, directing his driver to his destination. Another takeover, another day, he reflected wryly, but, undeniably, work was the spice of life to him.

He scanned a text from a former lover and without hesitation asked her to lose his number. He was only twenty-eight but he didn't do repeats with women, never had, never would. Sex was just sex, a necessity for a male of his appetites, but it could still be controlled within certain boundaries. An entire weekend was as close as Aristide got to commitment. He was a shameless playboy, fashioned that way from growing up with a father who couldn't resist women. Ex-wives, ex-partners and discarded lovers and children had littered his father's life.

That kind of background left scars that Aristide was fully aware of having. But, even so, he simply didn't want female drama in his life: no broken hearts, no accusations of infidelity, no jealous scenes, no betrayals, no lies. Aristide could not imagine having only *one* woman in his life and he was even less keen on the option of ever fathering a child of his own. Without a doubt, his last will and testament would spread his wealth across the best of his many relatives.

One month later

Tabby checked the test and imagined her eyes shooting out wide on stalks like a cartoon character telegraphing fear and alarm. Her blood ran cold in her veins, shock rippling through her. She was *pregnant*. She sucked in a deep breath to ward off the dizziness assailing her. How on earth could she have been so stupid? So reckless? She, who prided herself on her intelligence and self-discipline, had just utterly messed up her life *and* her poor sister's. At the eleventh hour, she would have to back out of the business marriage she had contracted to complete and her twin, Violet, would have to take her place.

And that was only the *first* of the mistakes she had made, she acknowledged wretchedly. She had messed up so badly that she was horribly ashamed of herself. Furthermore, now she would have a child to raise alone, a baby who would be totally dependent on her currently useless self!

How on earth had she contrived to sink so low, so fast?

And the memories began to flutter back in a series of episodes like some ghastly soap opera…

It had started with their mother, Lucia's illness, persistent cancer, which had dogged her for many years and right then their beloved mum had been at her last post. Her sole hope for survival was a new experimental drug on a clinical trial in the USA. But it cost money to get a place on such trials and one thing Lucia and her two daughters had never had was surplus cash.

Indeed the only wealthy person they even knew, and they scarcely *knew* him, was their grandfather, Tomaso Barone, he of the hard heart who had cast off their mother when she was a teenager who chose to marry the wrong man. And regrettably, Sam Blessington, their father, had been very much the wrong man, a feckless artist with a taste for booze, violence and other women and no interest at all in his twin daughters. Throughout their childhood there had been sobering experiences like bailiffs, homelessness and hunger and, on several occasions, Lucia had begged her father to help them. But not *once* had he come through for his estranged only child. So, when Violet and Tabby had made an appointment to meet Tomaso and ask for his financial assistance to enable their mother to get on that trial, they had not been optimistic.

It had been a huge shock when Tomaso had looked across his giant office desk and said, 'Yes, I will help your mother *this* time...if in turn one of you does something for me.'

'Anything!' she and Violet had promised simultaneously with no idea whatsoever of what he had been about to propose: a marriage with the heir to his rival competitor's company to cement a business deal.

'As your sister has a child, it will obviously be you, Viola, who takes up this wonderful opportunity,' her grandfather had insisted. He wasn't even aware that she was called Tabitha because her drunken father had bungled registering their birth names. On paper she was Viola Tabitha but in actuality she had always gone by her middle name.

Of course, there had been no choice but to agree, not when he had been dangling the bait of that all-important cash for their mother's benefit. The very belief that his grandchild would get to wed the super-rich heir to Renzetti Pharmaceuticals and carry on what he somehow deemed to be *his* legacy had delighted the older man. Neither Violet nor Tabitha had guessed that, when it came to actually handing over the money, he would welch on the deal with the excuse that they had to wait longer for it.

Only they hadn't *had* time to wait when their mother was so frail and instead Tabby had had to ask her future husband's lawyers for the sum as conditional on her signing the pre-nup before the wedding. And in return, she had been asked to reduce the five-year marital term to three instead and of course she had agreed, not wanting to have her own life derailed for any longer than necessary.

Consenting to marry a male who couldn't even be bothered to meet her prior to the wedding had freaked Tabby out. It had felt as though every one of her personal choices was being stolen from her: she was to marry a stranger and live in his home and put up with whatever he chose to throw at her for three long endless years. A prison camp had sounded more appealing than that, especially after she had read the clause relating to her personal behaviour, which barred her from meeting any men or consorting with them in any way.

Why? Tabby had never had a man in her life or particularly *wanted* one. Her father had for ever soured her on the male sex but, even so, she still hadn't liked being a virgin at almost twenty-two. She'd seen that as a rite of passage into adulthood that she hadn't wished to wait another three years to experience. A mere physical thing, a bodily thing, and not something to make a big deal about, she had decided, in her innocence.

And that decision, Tabby recognised, and that rash attitude had brought her to her current crisis of having conceived an unplanned child. It should have been something she could celebrate and she blamed *him* for the fact she couldn't because *he* had already accused *her* of trying to set him up when the condom failed. What kind of madness had possessed her when she'd thought that she could have a simple one-night stand as other women did? Well, for her, it had gone badly wrong and she blamed inexperience and her ignorance in bedding such a dreadful choice of a guy for the consequences.

Certainly, the day it had happened, she had had no idea of what lay ahead. It had begun as a normal shift in her office temp job in a large insurance company where she worked for Ed Stokes, a harmlessly inefficient middle manager, who was, nonetheless, related to the CEO, who absolutely never showed his face in the building.

'Julian…' aka, the CEO of Traxis '…suggested that I look after this senior audit chap coming in,' Ed had explained. 'But I want you to do it instead because you have a degree in accounting and I work in sales.'

There had been no point reminding Ed that Tabby hated accounting and had learned that any day she preferred general office admin to perusing profit and loss figures. Ed was the boss and she had an easy job as long as she took care of all the many things that intimidated mild-mannered, socially awkward Ed, like meeting new people or dealing with senior staff. He shunted off everything he disliked onto Tabby and he got away with it too because he was on first-name terms with the big boss.

Tabby had hung about Reception awaiting the arrival of the VIP accountant with nothing but the name of the company he worked for in terms of information: Millwright and Sons.

A very tall, commanding male with a shock of cropped black curls had entered and the receptionist had greeted him while Tabby had hovered uncertainly by her side, sheltering behind the desk the more she noticed about the new arrival. The fabulous custom fit of his black suit, the unusual formality of the silk tie and closed collar on his shirt, the reality that he was so tall she had to crane her neck and tip her head back even to steal a look at his lean, bronzed face.

'Mr Millwright?' the receptionist asked hesitantly.

The reference to his London audit team, who wouldn't be arriving until the next day, relaxed Aristide into the belief that he was expected.

'No, I'm Aristide Romanos,' he announced.

'I'm Tabitha Blessington, Mr Romanos…' another voice interposed and he turned his proud dark head to look at her. 'My boss asked that I show you around.'

Aristide was taken aback that the CEO was not in place to greet him but, as a male, he was immediately captured by the angelic fairness of the speaker. Aristide liked blondes, he always had, but rarely had he met one quite so beautiful, who had not plundered every cosmetic trick in the box. This one had flawless translucent skin like fine china and not even a trace of lipstick on her sensually plump lips. Not to mention huge blue eyes, perfect features and a mane of pale blonde hair that looked as natural as a child's. She had an unspoilt look new to his experience and it grabbed his interest, which would at best be...fleeting, he assumed without a doubt of that in his handsome head. An arrogance taught by countless very willing ladies in his past.

He didn't view her as an employee. He owned dozens of companies. He took them over and sorted out their issues before installing trusted executives. He might well never visit Traxis Insurance again, so he didn't consider himself bound by any rules of the workplace.

'Miss Blessington,' Aristide returned as she extended a slender hand to his much bigger paw, the size differential between them making his shapely mouth quirk with amusement. She was small and unexpectedly slight with fewer curves than was usually his preference but his interest abated not a jot.

'Tabitha...or, er... Tabby will do,' she heard herself say like a woman in a dream because he was truly the most gorgeous male she had ever met and she felt overwhelmed by his presence. As if that were not bad enough, a sensation like an electric shock tremored down her arm as their fingers barely brushed. Static electricity, she gathered, but that unnerved her even more. Her hand retreated, fingers curling back in on themselves to drop to her side.

'Where would you like to start, Mr Romanos?' she asked shakily, refusing to look back up at him again, eager to get moving, to do anything other than be forced to concentrate her eyes on him a second time.

First off, she had collided with dark eyes as impenetrable as black glass and then he had tipped his strong jaw a little as she looked and those eyes had flashed to glittering gold in the sunlight. After that, brain power had kind of receded while he stood there, perfectly at ease and assured, and simply studied her in brooding silence from beneath straight ebony brows and lush black thick lashes. She had worried that she had greeted him wrong or somehow done something he took amiss and nervous tension had almost eaten her alive

'Top floor…obviously,' Aristide told her somewhat drily as he took the lead in heading for the lift, punching the button with an impatient air. 'Tell me about yourself…'

'I'm a temp,' Tabby admitted, hoping that any mistakes she made would be excused on that basis because this male struck her as unlike any accountant she had ever met and she had met a lot while studying and training. 'I work as a PA for Mr Stokes in the sales department—'

'Why am I being welcomed by a temp?' Aristide enquired, watching a flush of colour wash her dainty cheekbones, wondering if she coloured up like that as she came and wholly resolved to find out. It was an instant attraction, he reckoned, an attraction stronger than anything he had felt in quite a few years. He didn't want to recall the last occasion it had happened to him and he blocked off the recollection fast, determined not to revisit that time when he had been young and trusting and really pretty naïve about women and how manipulative they could be when the prize was big enough.

'I don't know, Mr Romanos. I was just asked to come down here. I think it was a request from our CEO—'

'And what's he like?'

'I've never met him,' she said honestly. 'But I think he goes on holiday a lot because he sends photos to my boss...you know the sort of thing. Skiing in the Alps, deep sea diving in the Caribbean, so I assume he's one of those men's men, who like to get physical.'

'As do we all,' Aristide purred, thinking that she could be a mine of information even if it was only common gossip. 'How long have you worked here?'

'Six months. My contract keeps getting renewed, probably because my boss likes me—'

An ebony brow hitched. '*Likes* you?'

Tabby went pink. 'Oh, not like *that*, for goodness' sake! He's a married man with a load of young kids—'

'That doesn't stop a lot of men from straying,' Aristide said with cynical bite. 'My own father was never happier than when he was playing away...'

'Mine too,' Tabby muttered helplessly, quite unsure as to why they should be discussing such things when they had only just met but encouraged by his confidence into giving her own.

Aristide clamped his lips closed, unnerved by how personal he had got with her. He never verged on spilling secrets with his lovers and remained a closed book to all of them. That was a very deliberate policy. He didn't create common ground, he didn't *relax*. But there was something about Tabby, something uniquely warm and inviting and, curiously, she had caught him off guard for a moment.

'Where is everybody?' he asked as they stepped out onto the top floor where he had expected to find the senior staff assembled for his arrival.

'Give me the name of whoever you wish to speak to and I will get him or her for you. Our finance director is on the floor below,' she told him expectantly.

Aristide had nothing to say to a finance director who hadn't even made it to the top floor in a business that was failing from lack of vigour and direction. 'You can give me a general tour instead,' he told her. 'While you tell me more about yourself.'

Women loved to talk about themselves and rarely realised how much they were revealing in so doing. He had learned that as a child while carefully navigating the stony pathways and fresh rules laid down by every new woman who entered his home. It was second nature for him to explore a woman's background and goals while remaining on the emotional sidelines. All he had to do was plant the occasional encouraging word and he found out about her mother's fragile health, her sister, Violet's bakery and the child her twin was adopting. Clearly they shared very close family ties and he wondered vaguely what that would be like to experience. He heard about how she had gone to university to study accountancy because that had seemed to offer the best hope of a decent career.

'Only I hated it,' Tabby told him.

'Then, why didn't you change your subject?'

'I had already acquired a student loan debt for that

year and I didn't want to add to that by dropping out, so I stuck with it and qualified,' Tabby admitted. 'But I think now that I'm working, I should've changed. That's life, isn't it? You don't have a crystal ball to see into the future—'

'Some day you may have your own business and you'll be glad of it then,' Aristide forecast.

Tabitha blinked, not quite sure she wanted to sign up for her own business as she knew her sister worked unbelievably long hours running the bakery. If that was what it would take, she wasn't sure she was ambitious enough to make that jump to greater responsibility. In time, perhaps, but at not yet twenty-two she had ample years ahead in which to create new goals.

Aristide suggested a view of the office space prepared for him. She took him down to the next floor to the empty office right next to the finance director and bustled off to provide him with refreshments. He had no complaint to make about her attitude but she definitely hadn't grasped who he was, he acknowledged. And in a twisty way he kind of enjoyed that ignorance and liked her for not being flirty and all over him as females generally were in his radius. It was oddly refreshing to see the way she looked at him with that warm smile in her eyes that he had never received from a woman before.

But then, he was like all men, he told himself cynically. She was beautiful and he wanted her. Naturally that had to be affecting his judgement. She was sincere and naturally friendly and Aristide was most definitely not accustomed to receiving purely friendly vibes from a woman. Of course, he had immediately wondered if she already had a man in her life, but he also reckoned, with an inner smile, that he would already have heard about such a man if he existed because Tabby didn't keep much to herself.

She just chattered like a stream wending its difficult way through a complex labyrinth but strangely it didn't irritate him, nor did the sudden conversational jumps. He wasn't used to chat with the women he took to bed. He was usually gone too soon after for such frills. Had he been missing out on something? Was it because she was a few years younger than most of the women he met? What was different about her? That lack of visible vanity? That easy laughter? That soothing silence that fell when he hitched a brow and she paused to see what he wanted from her. She was being professional to a superior, not encouragingly submissive.

Out in the tiny kitchenette, Tabby was brewing coffee and her mind was all over the place as though an avalanche had recently engulfed her... *Aristide*. She was totally convinced that she had found the guy she would accomplish that one-night-stand challenge with. He was so beautiful that she had had to force herself to stop staring at him. Her attraction to him was off-the-scale intense and she had never met with that before. He was considerate and interested in her as a person. Perhaps, best of all, he would just be passing through and she wouldn't see him again once his new team of auditors arrived the following day. He had to work for a very large firm because he had mentioned the accident at the airport and if that firm could muster another six employees that fast, they had to be big and important.

'Mr Roma—' she said, flushed from her current thoughts as she walked back into the office carrying a tray.

'Aristide,' he corrected, disconcerting her. 'Will you have dinner with me tonight?'

Her lower lip parted from the upper and she felt his shrewd dark gaze welding to hers, lifting her chin to say, 'I think I would like that—'

Me too, Aristide was tempted to say, watching the tip of her tongue steal out to moisten her full lip, suddenly rigid with sheer lust to a degree that shook him. With her that reaction was instant and he didn't like anything that felt that uncontrolled grabbing a hold of him. It was always *just* sex for him, never anything more, and maybe it was the dreamy deep blue of her eyes that affected him or the softness of her highly feminine face but he still heard himself murmur the warning, 'It will only be one night...'

And to his total surprise, she gave him a huge smile and nodded. 'Perfect,' she told him, while pouring his black coffee and offering him a selection of biscuits, which he ignored. If only all her sex were so practical, he reasoned, while wondering how on earth she could be wholesome one minute and coolly rational and cynical the next. *Perfect?* Women usually wanted and expected a whole lot more from Aristide than one night. In truth, it stung a little that she appeared so content with that likelihood.

He watched her eat three biscuits in succession while

he thought about that oddity. In between times she told him about the pervy employee none of the young women would get into a lift with, the executive PA madly in love with her boss and the security guard with the sick wife at the front, who brought her fresh vegetables from his allotment. She gave no names. Even so, she was…indiscreet but warm and entertaining, he decided with a generosity that would have astounded his hospitalised team because he had never tolerated gossip and lighter moments during his working day.

At noon, having seen even the basement service level of the building, Aristide informed Tabby that he had a meeting elsewhere and took his leave of her in the foyer. 'If you give me your address I'll pick you up tonight at eight,' he murmured lightly.

And she did, stumbling a little over the syllables, far more excited by the idea of a date than she felt she ought to be. After all, no one knew better than her how untrustworthy men could be. Of course, she had met exceptions to that rule, hadn't allowed her father's cruelties to turn her into a man-hater. She did have occasional dates, although none had amounted to much because she had never been attracted enough to get closer to a guy or to take that risk on catching feelings that weren't even wanted.

But the knowledge that she was to marry a stranger in six weeks and do without socialising or having sex if *she* wanted sex was a restriction her pride and self-respect could not accept. This night with Aristide would be *her* choice, her chance to assert her rights over her own body while she still could. There was no way she was running the risk that her stranger husband might be expecting bed privileges into the bargain and that he would then become her *first* lover. No, that little detail would be taken care of off stage and prior to that stupid marriage when nobody would even know about it.

And then, if her mother required some very expensive further treatment to continue her life, as the wife of the wealthy Tore Renzetti, she would be easily able to afford to cover the costs. Why else would she continue agreeing to the marriage after their grandfather had virtually refused to pay up for his daughter's care? With the number of health crises their mother had suffered in recent years, Tabby knew that she had to be aware of the risk that more might lie ahead.

Tabby adored her mother, even if she hadn't always been a mother she could respect as a woman. Lucia Blessington was a very caring, compassionate person and endlessly supportive of her twin girls. Even though her daughters had had a very unhappy childhood while their father was still around, Tabby and Violet had forgiven Lucia for giving their horrible father too many chances to reform.

Now that their parents were divorced and they had no further contact with Sam Blessington, their lives had become calm and peaceful. Now there was no man coming home in a drunken rage and lashing out with his fists or frittering away their mother's earnings. Now Violet and Tabby between them could look forward to keeping their mother out of those low-paid jobs that had been all she was able to get while they were still children.

'Julian's flying back early from his break in Cuba,' Ed informed Tabby worriedly when she returned after lunch. 'He told me that Traxis has been taken over. We'll just have to hope that it's not to one of those asset-strippers, keen to throw us all out of work and sell the building!'

Tabby got back to the flat she shared with several other girls that evening and went straight to her room to trail out her wardrobe and decide what to wear. But it wasn't *really* a date, she reminded herself. He had been quite clear about what it would be and she was fine with that, wasn't she?

The stirring of unease within her warned her that she was less confident than she would have liked about her decision. After all, here she was heading for twenty-two years of age and no *right* male had come along. She hadn't fallen in love and contrived to share a bed in the more natural way. She hadn't even been insanely attracted to a guy until that very same day. So, Aristide was simply the best available option. That was all the evening would be.

It would be like a date, Aristide was thinking with a frown while he showered. And he didn't *do* dates. What was it about Tabitha Blessington that knocked him off balance? As a rule, he met women at events, in businesses or through friends. He didn't ask them out anyplace, he just took them home, whether that be to a hotel or one of his properties. Dinner engagements didn't enter the proceedings. But he had had the suspicion that she would say no if he framed his desire any more frankly. And he hadn't wanted that. No, he hadn't wanted that at all. *Thee mou*, when had he last been this worked up about being with a woman? It was nonsensical and out of character.

By the time the door buzzer went, Tabby was dressed and ready, clad in a casual blue mini dress and a pair of high heels. She hadn't bothered with make-up. After all, it wasn't some romantic date, she reminded herself, opening the door to a middle-aged stranger.

'Mr Romanos is waiting in the car for you, Miss Blessington.'

Romanos, *that* was his name. She hadn't quite caught it when she'd first met him and then hadn't liked to ask him to repeat it lest he think she was pretty incompetent. 'And you are?' she queried quietly.

'His driver...'

Tabby followed the older man down the stairs, her brow furrowed. His *driver*? Who had a driver in London where most travelled by public transport? Only very well-off people. Possibly he was a director in the accountancy firm, she reasoned uncertainly.

She was extremely rattled to find the door of a silver limousine falling open for her arrival. Aristide folded out to his full height and gave her a slashing smile. In that moment, he looked so heart-stoppingly handsome and charismatic that her mouth ran dry and her wits might as well have been dandelion clocks floating in the breeze.

'You look amazing,' he murmured huskily, ushering her into the limo while his driver hovered, openly disconcerted by his employer's presence on the pavement.

No regrets about making the dinner date, Aristide was already thinking as he sank in beside her. The blue of her eyes matched the dress or maybe the blue of the dress heightened the colour of her eyes. He blinked, wondering why he was abstracted enough to think such a thing while simultaneously acknowledging that she was even more beautiful than he remembered her being only hours earlier, pale hair like rumpled silk lying across her narrow shoulders, a heart-shaped silver locket at her delicate collarbone. Somehow his brain conjured up an image of sapphires there instead.

'So, it seems that I've misunderstood who you are somewhere along the way,' Tabby remarked stiffly, intimidated by the level of opulence in the big vehicle. 'I believed that you worked for Millwrights—'

'No, I own Millwrights. They run audits for me,' Aristide told her casually. 'I did wonder what was happening this morning when nobody appeared for my benefit, but your charming company was a plus and I let it go.'

Tabby breathed in deep and slow, steadying her nerves. 'Then may I ask why you were at Traxis today?'

'I bought it over—'

'Traxis?' Tabby gasped in surprise and consternation because it was an international company. 'You *own* it?'

Good heavens, had she allowed herself to be chatted up by her new employer?

'If you're my boss, I shouldn't be here with you!' Tabby exclaimed in dismay. 'If you stop the car, I'll get out here—'

Aristide studied her in wonderment. 'Are you mad? I'm not your boss. I won't be taking much of an active part in running Traxis. My role is behind the scenes. I buy companies, reorganise them and then move on to the next,' he explained levelly.

Her heart still beating very fast at the belief that she was not only way out of her depth with such a guy but also doing something wrong in going out with him, Tabby stared back at him anxiously. 'I'm still not sure I should be with you—'

A big lean brown hand closed over hers where she had braced her own on the seat. 'Relax, *angelos mou*,' he urged. 'Of course you should be with me tonight. It's what you want…and what I want. Why should anything else come into it?'

CHAPTER TWO

'IT'S WHAT YOU WANT...*and what I want.*'

That was the indisputable truth, Tabby conceded. But Aristide made it sound so simple, although wasn't it simple? she asked herself. Two young people surrendering to an attraction and getting together, two people unlikely, it seemed, to meet again. It was just he wasn't the more ordinary salaried guy she had assumed he was, no, he was evidently quite wealthy. But ought she to hold that difference against him? My goodness, Violet would enjoy this story...

Only as soon as Tabby thought that, she reddened, knowing that there was no way she would be sharing this particular story with her sister. She suspected that her twin would be a little shocked by what she was about to do, not judgemental, of course, but definitely surprised. It was more likely a tale she would tell somewhere down the road after this fake-marriage nonsense was behind her and life had returned to normal.

Aristide was still holding her hand, she registered, and she liked that, liked that quiet connection so much that it was a disappointment when he freed her fingers and the limo stopped and it was clear that they were about to leave the car.

A faint darker line of colour scored Aristide's cheekbones as he curved a guiding hand to her slender back on the way into the exclusive restaurant. Once again he was wondering what was wrong with him because it was a challenge to keep his hands off her, even in a non-sexual way. What was that about? Maybe he would find out what she was doing over the weekend, extend their future. No, he told himself harshly, that would be getting into relationship territory and he wasn't going in that direction *ever again.*

As they were greeted at the door like important people and led through the packed tables, her companion acknowledging several comments, Tabby felt severely underdressed for the first time in her life. Her little cotton sundress didn't cut the mustard amongst company that wore glittering jewels and cocktail-type frocks. Cheeks warm, she sank down at the secluded table, grateful they weren't in the centre of the dining room where she had already spotted a couple of famous television actors.

Aristide could read her expressive face as easily as a book. The surroundings intimidated her and he should've put more thought into their location. Since he hadn't, he endeavoured to tease and entertain her while she perused the menu. Before very long, her easy smile was back and she was laughing. He couldn't take his attention off her and it felt too intense for him and a shard of uneasiness pierced him afresh. He didn't want to be involved, he didn't want to *get* involved and he was handing out the wrong signals, wasn't he? One night or even two was his limit and he didn't wish to mislead her. Striving to cool his attitude, he became quieter.

Tabby was mesmerised by Aristide, the ease of his manners, the witty edge to his conversation, the way his attention never once strayed from her even though there were two very beautiful, well-dressed women at a nearby table. And when it was time to leave and she only then thought of what lay ahead, she found herself getting nervous and quieter as well.

She knew that she could say that she wanted to go home and Aristide was unlikely to say anything, she reckoned. He had been way too kind to her to suddenly turn nasty, she reasoned. The only problem was that she didn't *want* to leave Aristide behind, didn't want to backtrack and never know what it would be like to *be* with him. And that seemed to be telling her that, for her, he was the right guy.

'Where are we going?' she asked uncertainly as the limo drove off again.

'To my home here. It's an apartment,' Aristide imparted, releasing his belt and leaning closer. 'I'm not sure that I can contain myself that long. I want to kiss you—'

A faint scent of cologne assailed her nostrils, reminding her of icy forest nights and, beneath it, the aroma of clean, husky male. He smelled so good she wanted to bottle him and sniff that scent like an addict. 'Go ahead,' she framed raggedly, meeting eyes like dark beaten gold in the lights flickering through the tinted windows of the dark streets outside.

His mouth closed over hers and she was electrified

from that first moment. It was that connection she had sought and waited for and never found. Her heart was beating so fast it seemed to be in her ears. He kissed her breathless, his tongue delving deep, teaching her other longings, other needs, spurring a building tightness between her slender thighs.

'We're here…'

Aristide was, once again, unsettled as he had forgotten where they were. He climbed out, hugely aroused, struggling not to recall that the last time he had kissed anyone like that, he had been about sixteen or so. And his first thought, a kneejerk reaction, was 'send her home'. It was followed by the awareness that there was no way he could do that without discovering what it was about Tabby Blessington that sent him into a tailspin. He would find out that it was simply a stronger than usual case of sexual attraction, he told himself soothingly.

'My goodness, how long were we doing that for?' Tabby mumbled as he ushered her into the lift.

'I don't care,' Aristide admitted, reaching for her again to cover her kiss-swollen lips with his own.

Feeling his lean, powerful physique sealed to hers unleashed another whole set of effects in Tabby. He virtually carried her through a door into the apartment and she was blind and mute, seeing nothing, saying nothing, only wanting the taste of him back on her lips and the feel of him against her.

Aristide scooped her up into his arms and carried her down to his bedroom. They had finally got there and he could hardly hold his libido back. Never had he felt such impatience, such eagerness.

Tabby surfaced from that mindlessness that had gripped her from the instant he'd touched her and gazed at him with concealed wonder. She was feeling what she had always dreamt of feeling, physically and emotionally and, even though she had told herself that there was nothing emotional about what she was about to do, she ignored that self-warning.

Aristide cast off his jacket, yanked at his tie, kicked off his shoes. He was struggling to hold back, to pace himself, stay in control. 'I find you incredibly attractive,' he confided in a driven undertone.

Tabby followed his lead more awkwardly and slid off her heels, pausing, not quite sure whether she should be stripping, which she was a little too shy to do for the first time with a man. Should she be waiting for him to undress her?

He came back to her and kissed her again and she felt his hands at her shoulders. Taking courage, she stepped back and lifted the dress off over her head, which was the only way to remove it, leaving herself bare but for her bra and panties. He pulled her back to him and then she remembered the one thing she had sworn she would never forget, and she pulled free to run back and grab her little envelope purse and dig into it for the item there she had been carrying round for just such a purpose for years. Cheeks scarlet, she pressed it into his hand and said shakily, 'Use this...'

A woman had never in Aristide's entire existence handed him protection to use before because he always used his own. It was a weird request, he thought, but everyone had their quirks and possibly this was hers.

He tossed the condom down on the bed and embarked on unbuttoning his shirt. His hands weren't quite steady because any kind of control when she set him on fire was a challenge.

He hadn't argued and Tabby was hugely relieved but, ever since being warned that there was an occasional man who damaged protection because his private kink was 'breeding' from a woman or because he was keen to pass on some unmentionable disease, she had been determined that such a thing would never happen to her. Not that she thought Aristide was of that ilk, yet how could anyone know such a thing if only one night was to be shared? Better safe than sorry, she reflected, glad that that moment of embarrassment was already past.

The shirt dropped to the floor and revealed Aristide's breathtakingly male physique. Her admiring eyes roamed over prominent pecs, an indented torso, strong biceps and the legendary V muscles disappearing below the waistband of his trousers. He was so beautiful, top-to-toe beautiful like a pin-up, and she marvelled that she had never before seen a male in that light.

Aristide surveyed her slender frame with fierce hunger roaring through him. She was sort of hovering beside the bed, giving him the vibe that she hadn't as much experience as he might have thought, but that was no deal-breaker for Aristide, who had once fallen intensely in love with a woman simply because he'd believed that she had chosen him to be her first lover. The treacherous betrayal that had followed a few years afterwards still bit deep.

Ever since then, the concept of virginity had turned him off. It was a social construct, an out-of-date expectation that had once wowed his ancestors, not something he would ever seek on his own behalf. It certainly didn't mean that that virgin would magically be pure of heart and faithful.

'You seem nervous,' Aristide commented as he closed his arms round her again, still finding it difficult to disconnect from a need to touch her continually. More than just lust, more than he would allow himself to *feel*, he finally recognised. He would handle it, of course he would, by being sensible, by walking away afterwards as he always did.

A tight smile curved her lush pretty mouth. 'I haven't done this much,' she muttered apologetically.

For the first time in his life, Aristide wished he could've said the same and as soon as that bizarre thought occurred to him, he shut it down fast, tugging her into his arms and kissing her, before lifting her and bringing her down on his bed.

'I want you so much, *angelos mou*,' he husked, detaching her bra with a skilled hand.

'Me too,' she managed unevenly, stretching up to taste his mouth again, already addicted. 'What language is that?'

'I'm Greek, born and bred.' Aristide was distracted by the small, pretty breasts he had unveiled, dipping his head to catch the hard little button of a pink nipple between his lips and dally there.

Tabby writhed, that first touch more than enough to set fire in her already overheated body. Long fingers tugged at the peaks of her sensitive breasts and her hips rose, catching her breath suddenly a challenge, her heart racing. And then he traced the heart of her, scoring the tender flesh still shielded by her panties, setting a flickering flame to the tingling nerve endings there.

'I need to be inside you,' Aristide groaned half under his breath, wildly impatient as he could never remember being before. He skimmed off her last garment, exploring the delicate damp flesh, teasing her clit and inserting a finger. By then, she was gasping, twisting and turning under the onslaught of more delightful sensation than she had ever dreamt would feature in her first experience.

And then he was reaching for protection, tearing it open with his teeth, leaning back from her to use it and she really could not help seeing that there was rather more of him than she had expected. She tensed, bracing herself even though she knew she should relax, and then he was sliding over her, lifting her up to him and her whole body was screaming with impatience for his next move even though she was nervous.

He eased into her slowly, with more care than she could have hoped to receive, but still it burned a little, stung as that part of her stretched to accommodate his invasion.

'*Thee mou*...you're so tight.'

As he lifted her to him, he plunged his hips and a stark jolt of pain raced through her, disconcerting her, startling her, and she gave a little gasp between clenched teeth, thinking that *that* had hurt more than she had been prepared for. She tucked the knowledge away fast, fighting to get back into the moment and still savour the other feelings.

Like being so close, so connected to him and she liked that. And the worst was over, past, she reckoned, a truth proven by the reawakening of those sensitive sensations at her core as he shifted position and with one ruthless twist of his agile hips sent a current of pure pleasure shooting through her whole being. Brilliant dark golden eyes assailed hers in a collision she felt to her very marrow. Her heart pounded and then he was moving. Sensation raced through her in ever surging waves until she was straining frantically to reach some distant peak of perfection.

But before she could reach that peak, he eased off her and flipped her over to change position. A little whimper of complaint escaped her because she would have dragged him back by force had he dared to walk off at that point. Every fibre of her was pleading for that ultimate end goal. He drove into her again. Hard. Deep. She was struggling to catch her breath, her heart banging so hard she was afraid it would burst and then suddenly it was happening for her, every sensation merging into a wondrous whole that blew her away. Fireworks detonated low in her belly and blissful pleasure washed through every nerve cell. Shaken by everything she had felt, she felt him reach completion as well.

She slumped down on the bed and then slowly eased round onto her back again.

Aristide vaulted off the bed in a rage. The condom had split, the condom *she* had insisted he use. He snatched up the discarded wrapper and checked the expiration date with a vocal growl of disbelief. 'You *gave* me an expired condom to use! What sort of a scam is this?'

In shock at the angry words, Tabby emerged from her stupor, suddenly feeling very naked and exposed. She slid off the bed to grab up her dress, putting it on over her head fast to feel covered again. Covered, the way you wanted to be when under attack. And that was how she felt: under *attack* at the least likely moment, when she was completely unprepared for the development.

'Expired?' she repeated chokily as he tossed the wrapper down on the bed between them rather as an official would produce Exhibit A in a courtroom. She lifted it and saw that he was correct from the date stamp. How long had she carried that item in her purse? Evidently longer than she should've done and she was only now recalling that she had invested in that box while she was at university. 'I'm sorry... I should've checked,' she muttered awkwardly, discreetly retrieving her bra and panties, digging the first into her bag and sliding into the second because she refused to travel home bare beneath her dress.

'And on top of that, you were a virgin too, weren't you?' Aristide prompted tautly.

Tabby paled. 'I don't think that has any relevance here but, for the sake of clarity...yes, I was.'

'I don't aspire to sleep with virgins,' Aristide informed her with scorn. 'And between the expired protection and your virginity, you've pretty much got the market covered when it comes to suspicious circumstances.' He studied her with hard dark accusing eyes as if they had not been as intimate as two people could be only minutes earlier.

His attitude in the aftermath of that intimacy was like a slap in the face, only she suspected it hurt more than the slap would've done. 'I didn't realise,' she said with determined dignity, 'that being a virgin was a hanging offence.'

'You could've told me. A normal woman would've warned me but you chose not to and that silence, combined with the expired safeguard, would make any man doubtful of your motivation!' he condemned angrily.

Tabby raised a dark blonde brow. 'I'm afraid I can't imagine what possible motivation I could've had other than the obvious…having sex with you,' she completed coldly, getting her armour on now, beginning to recover from her rude awakening to his opinion of her.

'You're not that naïve, nobody is, not these days!' he shot back at her. 'I'm a very wealthy man and I refuse to be a target for women who wish to enrich themselves at my expense—'

Tabby's rarely roused temper flared up in white-hot flames of fire inside her chest because she had had more than enough of his toxic assumptions about her character. 'Oh, if that's what you're worried about, I can free you of your fear,' she assured him almost sweetly. 'I'm getting married in seven weeks to a man who's… I assume…just as rich as you. I don't need to trade my virginity like a commodity, Mr Romanos, or run the risk of pregnancy to entrap any man. Rather an old-fashioned accusation that, don't you think? In fact if the contraceptive mishap *were* to result in consequences, I'd be the one in a serious fix!'

Aristide listened in growing disbelief. He couldn't believe what he was hearing! She was getting married, she was engaged to marry some other man in a few weeks and yet she had let *him* take her to bed? None of that made sense to him. If she was engaged, why had she still been untouched? He was shocked, appalled, and he was so angry as he pulled on clothes that he was shaking with the force of his emotions.

'So, you're a cheat as well as everything else,' he breathed tightly.

'Goodnight, Mr Romanos. Can't say it's been nice because, like other men I've met, you're not quite what you seem to be on the surface,' Tabby fired back at him with hot cheeks and a strong desire to push him fully clothed into the nearest weed-clogged pond.

'I'll take you home...' Aristide addressed her rigidly turned back as she reached the front door.

'No, thanks.' And with that calm retort, Tabby walked out of his penthouse apartment and finally felt able to breathe again.

'Tabitha...'

She turned her tousled head and arrowed glacial blue eyes back at him as she awaited the lift.

'If there *should* be consequences—'

'Forget it,' Tabitha murmured pleasantly. 'I wouldn't come begging to you if I was down to my very last penny and *starving*. That's a promise.'

Aristide strode back indoors and closed the door

quietly when he wanted to slam it. What the hell was Tabby Blessington playing at? Well, he intended to find out. Pulling out his phone, he texted her name and address to the private investigation agency he used and requested a full report on her. He was angry, frustrated and, yes, there was dissatisfaction too at the manner in which he had discovered her true nature. She had cheated on her fiancé with him. Acknowledging that reality, he told himself that he should be grateful to be made so swiftly aware of her capacity for deceit.

Tabby travelled home on the Tube, had a shower and went straight to bed. She longed to phone her twin and tell her what had happened but she cringed at the image of her having made an outsize fool of herself. There she had been, all sentimental and romantic about Aristide Romanos in spite of the fact it was only meant to be a one-night stand. No, she decided, she would take those short-lived girlie dreams to the grave with her. She had *asked* to be hurt, she told herself with self-loathing, she had turned out to be much more vulnerable than she had ever believed herself to be.

And why, when he had insinuated that she was after him for his money, had she responded with the news that she was due to marry another rich man in seven weeks? Why hadn't she foreseen that he would naturally assume that she was a faithless cheater into the bargain? He hadn't wanted to be her first lover either. There was something insulting about that, but it would be perfectly understandable if he simply preferred more experienced partners. And she had naïvely supposed that he wouldn't notice her innocence!

No, Aristide had been a disaster, but at least she had accomplished her goal. She squirmed in her bed, still aching, telling herself it served her right. She would probably confess all to Violet in a few months, once the crushing humiliation of her encounter with Aristide had faded a bit.

And the condom had let them both down. She had to worry about that as well, she reminded herself. But she brushed off that concern because she literally could not even begin to imagine being pregnant. Why borrow trouble when she was in a big enough mess as it was with a stranger bridegroom-to-be to meet at the altar in only seven weeks' time?

CHAPTER THREE

Turning full circle back from those memories and returning to the present, Tabby stared down at that positive pregnancy test and tossed it in the bin. The deed was done, the wondering at an end and full reality had set in.

That very same morning she had had an appointment with her future husband's lawyers to sign the pre-nup. She had forged her sister's signature in Violet's usual scrawl and shame covered her from head to toe because she had let her twin down badly. She was the single one of the two of them, free of dependants and a business, and naturally it would have been easier for her to make that commercial alliance. Now Violet, with the baby daughter she was adopting and a very demanding bakery, was about to be thrown in at the deep end to marry Tore Renzetti instead and, of course, Tabby felt terrible about that. Her unfortunate sister would be forced to make many more compromises than would have been demanded of Tabby, whose life had been more fluid and free of responsibility.

Tabby followed that act up with a visit to her twin, needing to confess her sins as soon as possible. She greeted her twin's childminder, Joy, who was also Violet's tenant, who told her that her niece, Belle, was down for a nap, having eaten. Tabby told Joy that she could leave early, leaving Tabby free to pace the floor in the tiny lounge.

Before Violet had even adjusted to her unannounced visit, Tabby had to dart off to the bathroom in haste where she was sick, an ever increasing reminder of her condition, she reflected unhappily.

'It's not a bug,' Tabby revealed tautly when she reappeared, her lovely face troubled and embarrassed. 'I wouldn't be visiting if I had anything contagious. No, the truth is that I'm pregnant.'

'Pregnant?' Violet gasped in disbelief. 'But *how*? I mean—'

'Not a virgin any more,' Tabby cut in somewhat bitterly. 'You have to remember me saying that there was no way I was going into this marriage a virgin and staying that way for another three years!'

'So, if you're pregnant, who's the father?' Violet asked worriedly.

Tabby grimaced. 'Someone I met at work who I believed was just passing through. I thought he would be perfect as I'd never see him again but the birth control let me down.'

Her twin studied her with sympathy. 'What are you going to do?'

'It's more a question of what *you* are going to do,' Tabitha stated, turning the question back on her sister. 'After all, I can't marry Tore Renzetti now that I'm pregnant. It would be a breach of the contract I signed and I can't hide it, so I'll have to 'fess up and then the marriage won't go ahead and that means we don't get the money upfront to cover Mum's clinical trial.'

Like Tabby, Violet was horrified by that idea because everything they had agreed had been for their mother's benefit to enable the older woman to get further treatment unavailable in the UK.

'I've already committed you,' Tabby admitted with a grimace of apology. 'I signed the pre-nup in your name. We can't take the risk at this stage that Renzetti will back out—'

'But *would* he? He must want those shares pretty badly to agree to this in the first place. And how am I supposed to pretend to be you when I'm six inches shorter and as dark-haired as you're fair? His legal team *has* seen you,' Violet reminded her in dismay.

'For the wedding, we'll stick you in high heels and a blonde wig with a veil on top. We can swing it if we try hard enough,' Tabby declared with characteristic fortitude.

The worst of her challenges accomplished, Violet's forgiveness for the bride swap freely given and gratefully accepted, Tabby returned to her shared flat. Her sister had already suggested that she move in with her because her tenant, Joy, was moving out. And Tabby could then easily take over running the bakery when Violet was absent.

The offer had only reminded Tabby that she had no permanent employment, no security. Not a good place to be in with a child on the way, she acknowledged, but she didn't want to be a burden on Violet, who had quite enough on her plate now with that horrid marriage ahead of her in less than two weeks. Three years at the mercy of some guy who neither of them knew a thing about. He was very good-looking too, likely slick and a womaniser, Tabby assumed, having already done her social media exploration on the father of her child.

There was nothing good to be found out about Aristide Romanos online. He was never seen with the same woman twice which said it all, she thought grimly. Surely only a rampant playboy would be worrying about a virgin scamming him with a faulty contraceptive? Or had some unsavoury event turned Aristide bitter and suspicious? It was a struggle but she was trying to be fair, trying not to hate and demonise the guy who had turned a single wild night, as it were, into a mere hour of humiliation. She wouldn't forgive him for that in a hurry, even if he *was* going to be the father of her child. She didn't care how rich and successful he was. That wasn't an excuse.

At work several weeks later, she received a call back from the doctor's surgery for another visit and groaned out loud. Being pregnant certainly seemed to run up the medical attention she required, although if they were able to give her something to combat the terrible nausea with which she was already suffering she would decide to be grateful. Now that she had taken over managing the bakery, she was surrounded by the fumes of food all day and it exacerbated the morning sickness.

That same evening, feeling like death warmed over, she was on her way out to keep her medical appointment when she walked out of the door of the flat and was confronted by the sight of Aristide in the flesh at the top of the stairs. 'Oh!' she gasped in panic, taken aback by the disconcerting sight of him when she had never expected to see him again.

'Tabby...' he positively purred, the benevolent tone ill matched to the slanting tension of the smile he dared to accompany it.

'What the heck are you doing here?' Tabby demanded sharply, in no mood to pretend that he could ever be a welcome visitor. 'I don't want to see you... I don't want to speak to you either!'

'Whatever else I may be, I'm responsible,' Aristide informed her, falling behind her as she clattered on downstairs, ignoring him. 'Obviously I need to speak to you again to address what happened between us last month.'

Although, in truth, Aristide was thinking that he probably wouldn't have bothered had it been any other woman in the starring role. But this was Tabby, Tabby the curiosity, whom he still couldn't get out of his mind, even if it was very possible that she was a gold-digger. How did he know? How could he even find out without seeing her again? So, it *was* a case of acting responsibly, he assured himself.

'Not as I see it,' Tabby said breathlessly as she headed down the next flight of stairs.

'I need to know if you're all right,' Aristide bit out impatiently.

All right? Being sick all the time and tired every hour of the day was all right?

'No, I'm *not* all right!' Tabby snapped back without thought or any more patience than he had. 'I'm pregnant and that is definitely not all right with me!'

Aristide was stunned, frozen to the spot as she disappeared ahead of him. By the time he reached street level there was no sign of her and frustration swelled inside him, threatening to overflow like a tidal wave. How could she just drop *that* on him and then disappear without another word? What sort of woman was she?

A young woman of twenty-one without anyone to fall back on for support, his sane mind recalled. He now knew almost everything there was to know about Tabby Blessington. He didn't know the details of the planned marriage she had flung in his teeth two months earlier but, more importantly, he knew that the wedding had gone ahead *without* her as the bride. He was also aware that she had quit her job as a temp and was in the process of moving out of her current accommodation into her sister's apartment above the bakery, which she was currently running.

Tabby submitted to another blood test at the health centre with poor grace. The nurse mentioned the need for her to make another doctor's appointment to see if anything could be done to help her with the morning sickness. Tabby made that appointment at the desk but she was really running on automatic pilot because everything after Aristide's appearance had taken on the oddest sense of unreality.

Aristide, standing there as if he had stepped out of a dream, looking exactly the same as he had looked that day they first met. Ridiculously tall, impossibly handsome, black hair a little ruffled and long enough to start curling, something she suspected he usually curbed by keeping it shorter. Nothing had changed for him but *everything* had changed for her. And it would've been a lie to deny that she was somewhat bitter and resentful over the truth that a woman suffered more than a man when she fell pregnant. A glimpse of Aristide, untouched by all the chaos that had engulfed her, had infuriated her and betrayed her into an honesty she would never have given him in any other circumstances. So, now that he knew there had been *consequences*, she wouldn't see him for dust, she assumed with satisfaction.

Aristide was in shock and grateful not to be in the middle of his working day. Tabby's fertility and his own had run a coach and horses through his life plan. Life had a habit of wrecking such ideas with the unexpected, he reasoned, straightening his spine. A baby... there was going to be a baby. But the minute he thought that, he realised that he didn't know even that for a fact. She might not be planning to go ahead and actually have the baby. He could not afford to make such an assumption when on that score the future was hers to choose. Sobered by that reflection, Aristide poured another strong drink and he sat down to consider matters he had once hoped to *never* have to consider again. He also reached conclusions that shook him rigid and contributed to another sleepless night.

The next morning, Tabby arrived at the bakery in a rideshare with her cases, reaching them out as fast as she could, toting them one by one across the pavement. She stowed them inside the street door of Violet's apartment upstairs and went into the bakery next door to start her working day. She had taken over the running of the bakery for her sister's benefit. She couldn't do the baking, for which Luca, an Italian pastry chef, had been hired, but she could handle the shop, the staff and the payroll.

In the tiny closet of an office space, Tabby checked the rotas, dealt with a salary query and made notes on the daily special orders for Luca's benefit.

'When I have my break at eleven, you'll join me for coffee,' Luca declared with warm dark eyes resting on hers.

'Whatever…' Tabby was weary of fighting off the Italian's come-ons, past caring if he forced her to the stage of saying an outright no. If he took offence, on her head be it even though the bakery couldn't function without his skills. Did he truly fancy her or was he merely under the impression that a female manager had to be convinced that he did? She couldn't believe his attraction to her was real when she knew that she was looking less than her best with pasty skin and dark circles below her eyes. And even her hair was going awry while her hormones seemed to be going into overdrive with her pregnancy.

Later, Luca snared her from behind the counter to share morning coffee with him and Tabby was trying to head him off at the pass, as it were, before she decided to simply be honest. 'Luca, I've just discovered that I'm pregnant,' she admitted awkwardly. 'So, really this is a case of bad timing—'

'Is the father with you?' Luca enquired with startling immediacy.

'Er, no,' she muttered with a grimace.

'Then we can be friends, if nothing else,' Luca told her with the easy English he had acquired while working in New York for several years, his dark eyes continuing to gleam with warmth and acceptance as he laid his hand down on hers in a soothing gesture.

And a friend worked for Tabby at that moment as nothing else could have done because, as well as Luca being very easy on the eye, Tabby had no friends in whom she had confided her secret. Why? The majority of her uni pals would have suggested a termination for an inconvenient, uncommitted pregnancy and that wasn't what she wanted, so she would've been out of step with them.

Aristide strode into the bakery with his bodyguards in tow like an invading Viking horde and froze in his path when he paused to take in the sight of the *mother* of his child having her hand fondled by another man, clad in chef whites. For a split second, he hovered in an uncharacteristic act of hesitation.

Tabby saw him straight away. Really, there was no chance of *not* noticing Aristide, the sheer height of him in a fancy dark suit, his gorgeous dark curly head held high, his keen dark golden eyes scanning the shop while the couple of males accompanying him fell back to the wall to watch him. Whoa, Aristide had a security team, she registered, wondering where they had been the day he visited Traxis.

'Excuse me,' she said to Luca as she rose from her seat. 'I'll see you later.'

Tabby stalked over to Aristide, attitude in every stressed line of her small, slender frame. 'What are you doing here?'

'Are you serious?' Aristide enquired in disbelief at that greeting. 'We need to talk.'

Tabby thought through several incendiary replies and discarded them because she already knew that Aristide was stubborn, impatient and possibly even a little dramatic. She didn't need him or any of that in her life but she hadn't yet contrived to tell him that, so she could accept that, after her announcement that she was expecting his child, a further conversation had to be had. 'Yes,' she conceded, feeling generous. 'But right now, I'm working—'

'You're the manager,' he reminded her and she wondered how he knew that.

'But this is a very busy shop and if I take time out to talk to you, something may come up,' she pointed out while thinking, to her annoyance, that he had the most breathtakingly beautiful eyes of anyone she had ever met, liquid gold like a burnished sunset and surprisingly eloquent even when he wasn't speaking. She sensed his urgency even though he had said nothing to express the feeling and it changed her mind.

Spinning round, she told the bakery's senior sales assistant that she was in charge until Tabby's return and, escorting Aristide back out onto the street, she unlocked her new front door again, apologising for the cases in their path.

'You shouldn't be lifting anything heavy up a staircase,' Aristide told her unnecessarily, because she was already painfully aware of all the shoulds and shouldn'ts in her immediate pregnant future.

'Are you going to take care of my luggage?' she asked snarkily.

'No, but my employees will,' Aristide asserted smoothly.

'Didn't think you'd be doing it,' Tabby commented snidely.

'I'm not ashamed that I pay others to take care of the necessities of life,' Aristide countered. 'My talents lie in other fields.'

'Not with the right word at the right time, if my experience of you can bear witness,' Tabby told him tightly.

'What transpired between us is entirely another story,' Aristide replied with a hint of defensiveness, sufficient to compress her lips on further provocative remarks. After all, she had nothing to gain from arguing with Aristide, indeed it might even convince him to stay longer and she didn't want that to happen.

Upstairs, she showed him into the tiny sitting room, smiling with relief when her cases were piled at the door, one after another.

'Where's your bedroom?' Aristide asked suddenly. 'I'll move them there.'

'The room at the end of the corridor,' she supplied while thinking that she would be occupying her sister's bedroom, sleeping in *her* bed with *her* sheets and that nothing around her actually *belonged* to her. Now that her sister was married, she no longer had much use for the apartment.

For the first time that was a rather deflating acknowledgement of the truth that, in getting pregnant and losing her independence, she had kind of become her twin's dependant. She reddened, knowing her sister would argue with such a statement but feeling it all the same as she was the elder twin, the one who had been born first, the one who liked to think she was the leading, protective half of the pair. Only not any more...

Tabby was shaken to appreciate, when she emerged from those pointless thoughts, that Aristide had moved her luggage down to the bedroom all by *himself*. It struck her that he was on his very best behaviour and that she would be rude if she offered him less. 'Would you like coffee?' she asked him as he reappeared, annoyingly looking not the least creased or out of breath from that physical effort.

'No, thank you,' he breathed, striding the small distance to the window, turning at the sight of the heavy traffic on the road outside and facing her again, dark eyes narrowed. 'I need to ask you, but it may not suit you to respond right now. Are you planning to have this child?'

Shame engulfed Tabby in a heated surge and she coloured. It hadn't occurred to her to think that he might be interested in asking such a very basic question. And yet it was an obvious question in today's world. Aristide had more layers than she had allowed him to have in her imagination, where she had demonised him. 'Yes. I will be having the baby,' she told him rather woodenly because, ironically, it felt like a very personal question from him that she didn't really want to answer even though common sense was warning her that it would be his baby as well.

Unexpectedly, Aristide appeared to relax at that admission and he smiled, moved to the armchair beside him and folded his big athletic frame down. 'Then, if it's not too late to change my mind, I would like coffee—'

Feeling a little dizzy at the surprise of that smile on such a subject, Tabby ducked into the kitchenette and then winced as the cupboard came up empty on the coffee that her twin rarely drank. 'There's no coffee...' she muttered in the doorway.

Aristide shrugged a wide, strong shoulder. 'I was only trying to be polite—'

'Is it that much of an effort for you with me?' she sliced in, unable to still the words on her tongue before she voiced them and then suddenly raising both hands. 'Forget I said that! Possibly I'm in a hostile mood—'

'Understandably. I assume this development has changed your life a huge amount because you didn't marry Tore Renzetti,' Aristide stated, disconcerting her with the sheer level of his knowledge about her.

'You've had me investigated...or something,' she muttered without surprise, reckoning that such caution and precision went with his sharp-edged, ruthless personality.

'Guilty as charged. I had to know what was going on and I'm afraid I still don't understand that relationship,' Aristide declared.

'It was supposed to be a business alliance. I'm not sorry to have missed out on marrying the guy—I mean, I never met him—but I'm *very* sorry and guilty that my sister had to marry him instead.'

'None of my business,' Aristide forced himself to say when really he wanted every tiny detail of that arrangement because he had an overriding need to know everything about her. However, he had heard enough to know that the heir to Renzetti Pharma would not be hovering on the sidelines of Tabby's life even though he had married another woman. Truly, that was the only angle, the sole possibility, that had still concerned him. If she had never met the man, there was no relationship to be considered. And if the sister had got him instead, that was even better.

'I really don't understand what you're doing here. I'm newly pregnant,' she pointed out uncomfortably. 'Now that you know I'm going to have this baby, you can—'

'I want to take you to see a good obstetrician and have you fully checked over,' Aristide announced without hesitation. 'It will be a private appointment in hospital. You are not obliged to agree to the idea but I would be grateful if you did.'

'Why do you want to take me to see a doctor?' Tabby was astonished by the suggestion.

'According to one of my cousins, pregnant women glow,' Aristide murmured wryly. 'You're still beautiful but you're not glowing.'

'I'd forgotten how charming you could be...saying all that instead of just biting the bullet and telling me the truth that I look like hell right now!'

'It's not like that—'

'It's exactly like that,' she interrupted impatiently. 'How soon could you set up the appointment?'

His luxuriant black lashes lifted on surprised dark golden eyes. 'As soon as you like?'

'I have to wait more than a week to see my GP, so it would suit me very well to visit a specialist sooner,' Tabby confided in a rush. 'I'm suffering from terrible nausea and maybe something could be done to alleviate that.'

'I gather being pregnant hasn't been a fun experience so far,' Aristide remarked, still carefully choosing his every word with a caution that irritated her. It struck her that she preferred Aristide relaxed and outspoken because anything else felt fake.

'Not so as you'd notice,' she agreed. 'So, if you organise this obstetrician, we should exchange phone numbers.'

Getting the message that she wanted to return to the bakery, Aristide vaulted upright again and dug out his phone, reminding himself that he had gained more than he had expected from this first visit. She hadn't abused him, assaulted him or refused to speak to him. She was feisty but she could also be reasonable, logical. He would count the meeting a win, a crucial first step on the route he had chosen.

As they reached the street where his bodyguards awaited him, Aristide turned back to her. 'I have one question but it's controversial—'

But Tabby guessed what that question would be, following on from their clash at his apartment that first night. 'Was I prepared to marry Tore for money?' she whispered back to him. '*Yes*, but probably not for the reason you assume.'

Aristide was taken aback by that accurate guess and he still wanted to know more. 'Maybe you'll tell me about it some day,' he teased, amused at the way she was playing him and holding back on giving answers. He could not recall when that had last happened to him with a woman.

CHAPTER FOUR

The specialist's waiting room was plush and comfortable and Tabby was so disconcerted by the immediate keen attention their arrival received that Aristide had accompanied her into the consultation before she had had the chance to consider leaving him outside. She hadn't objected to his presence during the blood test and, being of a practical bent, saw no reason why he shouldn't learn the extent of her woes.

Mr Chapman was a middle-aged male in a smart suit and he wasted no time in informing them that her blood test had revealed a surprise, without revealing what that surprise was. In short, he was a showman and it was Tabby's job to mention how very sick she had been feeling while he nodded without clarifying anything. She went into the room next door to lie down for the ultrasound with the deflated feeling that she would go back to her sister's apartment knowing no more than she had when she had arrived at the hospital. The consultant joined her and Aristide.

'Do you want me to leave?' Aristide asked, taking her aback with that consideration.

'No, my tummy isn't a sensitive area,' she chuckled and then she closed her eyes while the technician fiddled with the transponder wand, clearly unable to begin without the doctor's prompt.

'And this is why you're feeling sick,' she was informed and she opened her eyes.

'There's two of them!' Aristide exclaimed with all the drama of a male told she was hosting an alien invasion in her stomach.

Tabby suppressed a sigh of concern. Two babies instead of one was an even larger challenge to accept but she was determined not to get anxious. 'I'm a twin...'

'You didn't tell *me* that your sister was a twin,' Aristide complained, but it seemed a moot point as he was asking Mr Chapman questions about what he could see on the screen. She almost contradicted him because she had told him early on when he probably hadn't been listening with much interest.

They emerged from the hospital, both of them sort of shell-shocked in their own different ways.

'In two days, we'll know what we're having,' Aristide proclaimed with unconcealed awe at the blood test that would eventually reveal all facts to them. 'Boys, girls, a mix...'

'New tech is amazing,' Tabby agreed, shaken once again by his attitude, so foreign to her every expectation of him. It occurred to her that it was almost as though Aristide Romanos would welcome the birth of a child in spite of his manwhore reputation. Of course, the one did not automatically exclude the other, her brain warned her. He *could* be a playboy who loved children, couldn't he be?

'You'll have to move into my London apartment,' Aristide told her without stopping to draw breath.

'I beg your pardon?' Tabby queried with a dropped jaw as she clambered into the limo awaiting them.

'Well, obviously, you're not likely to be in a position where you can manage alone,' Aristide countered.

'The consultant didn't say anything like that,' Tabby protested.

'He said you were likely to suffer more severe side effects to being pregnant than other women,' Aristide reminded her. 'Which means that you will need more support to remain healthy and you haven't got any support right now with both your mother and your sister out of the country. Naturally, as the father of the children, it is my responsibility to help—'

'No, I don't see it that way at all,' Tabby argued vehemently as she fastened the seat belt he had helpfully threaded round her as if she couldn't find the belt for herself. 'I don't need anyone's help. I have a job and a home—'

'Your sister's home,' Aristide slotted in grimly.

'Yes, my sister's home *and* a job. I don't need *anyone*—' least of all you, went tactfully unsaid '—to take responsibility for me. I'm completely content managing alone.'

'But you're underweight and sick all the time—'

'Heavens, I shouldn't have let you *be* in the same room with the consultant!' Tabby told him in complete exasperation. 'You sucked all that info in and swallowed it like it was the Holy Grail or something! Let's be realistic here. Some women breeze through pregnancy like it's nothing, others have it less comfy—'

'Yes, but there are valid reasons for you to be less comfy, as you put it...you are carrying *two* babies, not just one. And you are more at risk of complications as well,' Aristide overruled without hesitation.

'But that's nothing to do with you!' Tabby shot back at him furiously. 'Me and my body are not your business!'

'You are going to be the mother of my children,' Aristide contradicted with his perfect measured diction, guaranteed to set her teeth on edge. 'How can that be none of *my* business?'

'Well, it's not!' Tabby assured him in fierce rebuttal. 'We're not a couple, we're not in a relationship—'

'If not a relationship, what is this?' Aristide cut in heatedly to demand.

Tabby pondered. 'A hate fest,' she pronounced with satisfaction. 'We don't even like each other, Aristide. So please do not ever refer to me again as the future mother of your children.'

'I do not hate or dislike you, *angelos mou*.' Aristide breathed in deep and long and resisted the temptation to admit that right now she was irritating the hell out of him. She was being insulting. Of course, she would be the mother of his children. That was going to happen whether she liked it or not and he wasn't going anywhere. Was her outlook tit for tat? He had accused her of unsavoury behaviour that one and only night, *that night* that had been the hottest experience of his life, they had been together. All he had wanted to do since then was repeat the experience, an idea that logic warned him would be as welcome as a rockfall on her in the mood she was in.

'Well, I'm afraid I can't say the same,' Tabby bit out, feeling the backs of her eyes sting with tears, hating the surging hormones that seemed to be making her so uncharacteristically touchy, short-tempered and overly emotional. It was an irony to accept that she could have dealt with Aristide much better without those extra hormones.

Aristide breathed in deep and slow a second time. 'I owe you an apology for the manner in which I behaved that night. We had, I thought, moved past that but I can see that was far too optimistic a belief in these circumstances—'

'Or maybe you just don't like saying sorry,' Tabby cut in before she could bite her tongue and swallow that unnecessarily provocative response. Couldn't she even allow him to apologise?

'You're correct. I don't. But I am sorry about what I said and how I behaved,' Aristide conceded grimly, sounding as if the very words were strangling in his throat.

'Shut up,' she muttered. 'You're just annoying me more—'

'That would seem to be a mutual affliction,' Aristide framed, suddenly closer than ever, leaning over her, evidently having released his seat belt.

He lifted a lean long-fingered brown hand and slowly tucked a hank of pale blonde hair behind her ear, fingertips grazing the top of her delicate ear. And it shouldn't have felt erotic but somehow it *was* erotic, particularly with those smouldering dark golden black-fringed eyes locked to hers. 'Aristide?' she mumbled unevenly, her heart pounding like crazy inside her, liquid heat pushing up between her thighs.

His sensual mouth came down on hers like a silencer that burned her alive with passion. It wasn't like the other kisses he had given her weeks earlier, it was infinitely more hungry, urgent and *fierce*. A flame seemed to spark low in her belly and suddenly, literally, between one moment and the next, she couldn't get enough of him. Her hands clutched at him on a frantic surge of feeling that pushed out everything that had happened before it. There was only that moment, her fingers spearing into his luxuriant black curly hair, a fever beat of insane responses thumping inside her head. *I want you, I hate you, I want you.* And yet the whole time, she was aware of nothing but the sheer burning glory of his mouth on hers, his body weighting her down, the thrill of that connection setting every nerve ending and skin cell alight.

With an effort, his breathing fractured, Aristide wrenched himself away from her again and flung himself back to his corner of the seat. He didn't have sex with women in the middle of an argument—he didn't *have* arguments with women, didn't get involved enough for that. Yes, he was lost and adrift in this entirely new scenario and it was *brutal*, he decided, awesomely aware of the throbbing pressure behind his zip, the tightness of the constraining fabric. Angry conflict consumed him and plunged him into brooding silence.

Tabby blinked like a sleepwalker roused without warning and only then registered that she was lying full length along the limo passenger seat. How had he achieved that without her noticing? Did it matter? Why was she acting like the sort of woman who said yes and then changed her mind when she *hadn't* changed her mind? For several moments—and she didn't know how many—she had wanted Aristide with every bone and sinew in her body. *Not* her brain. In fact her brain had had nothing whatsoever to do with it, she conceded in dismay.

'That wasn't a good idea,' Aristide murmured tautly.

'You're telling me!' Tabby scoffed in agreement, although his comment had surprised her. What had he truly intended when he had said that she should move into his apartment? A weird platonic relationship and nothing more? It was strange how wounding that suspicion was, she acknowledged. Somewhere in the turmoil of her buzzing thoughts, it seemed, it had proved oddly comforting to be able to believe that Aristide still saw her as desirable even though she was now pregnant and looking less than her best.

Instinct told Aristide to back off but there were other question marks darkening his horizon like storm clouds. He genuinely did not want the mother of his unborn twins to be financially dependent on Tore Renzetti. And yet, that was what would happen if Tabby became reliant on her newly rich sister. But those would be his children, nobody else's, and Aristide could not abide the concept of anyone else taking care of what was most definitely *his*. He needed to lure Tabby fully across to his side of the fence *before* those kids were born. And there was only one stratagem likely to lead to that conclusion. Just as Tabby had once condemned a pregnancy entrapment as an old-fashioned trick, Aristide's solution was an equally dated stratagem.

'I still want you to move into my apartment. It's not even as if I'm always there. I travel a lot. I own properties in other places. If you don't want to live in my apartment, let me buy you a house in your own name to give you and my children basic security,' he breathed in a raw undertone.

Tabby's head was banging with the sheer tension they had both unleashed inside the limousine. She lifted both hands in a desperate silencing motion. 'You're barking up the wrong tree with all of this, Aristide,' she muttered awkwardly. 'Please don't think that I'm not grateful for your willingness to be so generous. But the truth is, I don't need you right now in *any* way! I may be young but I'm not stupid. I'm single and educated and I already have a roof over my head and employment. I appreciated the specialist visit today for the sake of my pregnancy and health. Thank you for organising that for me but anything *more*—'

A hand closed over hers as the limo drew back up outside the bakery. 'Tabby...you're not listening to me—'

Tabby snatched her hand free. 'No, because I don't *need* to listen to you. I don't *need* contact with you either until the twins are born. And, you know, when you start laying down the law in that so bossy style of yours, I'm freakin' grateful I don't have to listen to a word you say!'

'You're being unreasonable,' he snapped back at her.

'And you're being impulsive and not thinking facts through,' Tabby condemned, by now standing on the pavement and looking down into the car to answer him back. 'We're nothing to each other, ships that were meant to pass and then wrecked on each other instead,' she fumbled, conscious they could be overheard now for the first time and lowering her voice.

'But I want *more*,' Aristide bit out with wrathful emphasis.

'Aristide...' Tabby dealt him a pained appraisal. 'You've got women raining all round you—'

An ebony brow hitched. *'Raining?'*

'It's a stupid song reference... OK? But it fits your lifestyle,' she argued. 'Twins *won't* and neither would I, so don't try to suck me into some situation that can only become messy. Do us both a favour. Forget my name, my number and my condition and get on with your own freedom-loving life!'

'Are you trying to say that you won't even accept me *keeping* my own children?' Aristide growled as he swung out of the car, once more in attack-force mode, lean bronzed face taut and clenched hard. He infuriated her by following her to the street door of the upstairs apartment and her teeth grated together. She wanted someone to call him off, deal with him for her before she exploded on him with rage. Unfortunately, Aristide Romanos had probably been born refusing to take polite hints.

He was so stubborn and strong-willed that he made her want to tear her hair out and scream. If he didn't hear what he wanted to hear, he kept on at her. He had no off switch, no concept of personal space or restraint. In every way, Aristide was anathema to her and yet, for some strange reason, she still understood his frustration with her, his inability to realise where she was coming from. She reckoned that he had never met with a brick-wall rejection from a woman before. Without a doubt, he was hugely popular with women. Her online snooping had revealed that as fact. Aristide had it *all*. The looks, the wealth, the charm…when he sought to use it.

'Isn't that my choice?'

'No, it's not. Men have legal rights over their children too—'

'But we're not married!' Tabby objected, surprise at his contention flickering through her.

'We don't have to be in today's world.' Aristide smiled down at her with sudden amusement. 'You didn't know that?'

'How would I know it? I don't have kids or married friends or even friends who have children. There's only my sister, who is adopting,' she conceded uncertainly.

'I will want shared custody rights,' Aristide told her almost conversationally.

Tabby swallowed hard on that enervating warning. All of a sudden he was making parenting with him a challenge she had not expected to have to meet and she was blaming herself for not consulting the law beforehand.

'Pushing me away won't get rid of me,' Aristide warned her.

'Could we talk tomorrow or the next day?' Tabby's courage had petered out the longer he talked because he was so poised, so assured of his rights and legal status, while she knew nothing. 'I have to work both days but my evenings are free.'

'As you like,' Aristide conceded, although he was not in the mood to give way on any point she had raised, but he did see that giving both of them a breathing space could be a good idea. 'Where, the day after tomorrow?'

'Perhaps we could meet at your apartment?' Tabby suggested, keen not to entertain him upstairs again. 'If you give me your address, I'll meet you there at...?'

'Eight,' Aristide decreed.

And that was that. Aristide strode back to his vehicle and she breathed in deep and tried to go on with her working day without dwelling on the shocks that had come her way.

Twins, *two* babies instead of one. Her heartbeat quickened and her insides softened as she remembered the little flashing dots and dark shapes onscreen. And the sheer surprise of learning that Aristide Romanos evidently intended to play the committed father. No, she hadn't expected that, no, she hadn't expected that ambition at all from a male like him. Naturally, that discovery made her less hostile towards him. Nobody knew better than Tabby what a resentful, angry didn't-want-to-be-a-father felt like.

A couple of days later, Violet made a brief visit, Tore and her having suffered a temporary falling-out. Tore Renzetti arrived hotfoot in her wake, clutching a magnificent bouquet, and Tabby left them to mend fences in privacy. Her sister had fallen for the guy and, seemingly, he was all in too. That relieved much of Tabby's guilt on her twin's behalf. The business marriage that Tabby had dreaded had worked out beautifully, it seemed, for Violet.

That evening, clad in the same dress she had worn to their dinner date, Tabby arrived at Aristide's apartment. The garment was loose and comfortable and that was sufficient for her at present when every other decent outfit seemed to be getting too tight round the waist or across the bust. For the first time in her life, she had breasts that were large enough to be noticeable.

Aristide's apartment was much swankier than she had taken the time to appreciate the night she had accompanied him home and that recollection made her face flush red. A manservant greeted her at the door and showed her into a big, open space with a fabulous view of the London skyline and the River Thames.

As she accepted a glass of water and stood admiring the view, Aristide joined her. He wasn't wearing his usual formal business suit. Instead, his lean, muscular physique was sheathed in tight jeans and an open-neck black shirt, a combination that made him look younger and more approachable.

And incredibly sexy, she acknowledged inwardly, taking in the full effect of his lean bronzed features as he smiled at her and her whole body was engulfed in what felt like a hot flush. Perspiration beaded her short upper lip. She glanced hurriedly away from his ripped, powerful physique, sipping her cooling water while promising herself that she would stay in full, unimpeded control of both her body and her swirling emotions. That was the way forward for her and Aristide, she reasoned. They would make sure that they respected each other's boundary lines and, in that way, keep the peace.

'Take a seat,' he urged.

Having spent most of the day on her feet, Tabby sank gratefully down into the nearest armchair. 'Let's try not to fight this time,' she murmured wryly.

'Something tells me that we were born to fight,' Aristide countered. 'We're both determined and we both like our own way better than anyone else's.'

'Maturity has made me more flexible,' Tabby declared.

What maturity? Aristide almost dared to joke as she sat there, slight and small as a child in the seat. 'You seem tired.'

'The delights of early pregnancy,' she quipped ruefully.

'You don't *have* to work—'

'Yes, I do. This is my life, not yours,' Tabby reminded him gently. 'I'm perfectly content for you to take an interest *after* the children are born, but anything more at this stage falls under the heading of interference...and I don't appreciate that approach.'

'I have a suggestion to make,' Aristide informed her.

Tabby tensed, reckoning that a suggestion from Aristide would ultimately prove as serious and immovable as a royal command. She lifted her chin, striving to seem as though she were a receptive audience when she didn't feel as if she could be.

Aristide stalked over to the window, bred-in-the-bone fluid grace edging his every lithe movement. He swung round, brilliant dark golden eyes pinning her in place. 'We need to get to know each other better. We can't be at each other's throats while we are trying to raise children together,' he told her grimly.

'Well, I certainly hope it won't be as bad as that.' Tabby swallowed with difficulty at that challenging opener of a dialogue. 'I think you're talking about a scenario that happens in an ideal world but unfortunately we don't live in that version,' she completed uncomfortably, unable to comprehend getting to know Aristide better in their current non-relationship.

'But if we are *both* willing to make the effort to become accustomed to each other, it *is* achievable.'

While we're trying to raise children together. That single phrase sounded like the bell of doom clanging in Tabby's delicate ears. She wasn't ready to establish *any* kind of togetherness with Aristide. She expected to have to consult him about matters relating to their children and that would be that. His expectations, however, clearly were higher than her own.

'For that reason I suggest that you accompany me to Greece for a couple of weeks, meet my family, learn the lie of the land in my home,' Aristide drawled casually. 'Our children *will* be spending time in Greece.'

Tabby's head flipped round, her blue eyes very wide in sheer shock and surprise. 'My word, I wasn't expecting that invitation! It's a lovely idea *but*—'

'I don't want to hear why you can't do it... I want to hear that you can and will make that effort.'

Tabby winced, her teeth gritting. 'Right now it isn't possible. With the best will in the world, I'm taking care of my sister's business—'

'And I could put a manager in there tomorrow...or *she* could,' Aristide sliced in without hesitation. 'Take that responsibility away and there is no longer anything tying you to the UK for the immediate future.'

'I couldn't let you do that—'

'Why not? You're exhausted. You need a break. Your health and well-being should come first right now,' Aristide told her unarguably.

'I believe that it could be very awkward meeting your family for the first time when I'm pregnant and I'm not even your girlfriend,' Tabby pointed out in a strained and stiff undertone, keen not to offend him.

'Then we should present ourselves as an engaged couple. That's the conventional answer to our predicament. Surely that would make you feel more comfortable and less ill-at-ease?'

Tabby was stunned by the concept. '*Fake* an engagement, you mean?'

'Why not? A fair proportion of engagements don't make it as far as the wedding,' Aristide countered with glancing cynicism. 'I don't see any harm in a pretence of that nature while we're in Greece. We can let the arrangement die away naturally a few months down the road...but in the short term, it would strengthen your position in my life. Family and friends respect ties of that nature.'

In a sudden movement, Tabby stood up tall and studied him with accusing blue eyes. In her own mind's eye, she saw herself transformed from the foolish young woman who had had a one-night fling with Aristide and, unfortunately from his point of view, managed to conceive, to a young woman in control of her life. It was a seductive image even though she knew it wasn't and wouldn't be genuine or real. She compressed her lips, deciding that his intelligence had a positively Machiavellian turn. 'You turn me inside out,' she muttered accusingly. 'You actually have me considering this crazy idea!'

'It's not crazy. You're simply stuck in your little groove and refusing to consider more promising options.'

Tabby ground her teeth together at the reproof but held her tongue. But *was* that how he viewed her? As too conventional and distinctly unadventurous? Her pride was stung. 'All right,' she said curtly. 'If we can get the bakery covered in time and Violet is happy with that decision, I'll go to Greece with you.'

Aristide's dark eyes glittered like gold ingots in strong sunlight, satisfaction winging through him in an intoxicating wave. He knew that he was being manipulative and he really didn't feel an atom of regret. Within days, he'd have a ring on her finger. A man could not afford to baulk at a solid wall of resistance, he had to get across it any way he could. A sapphire, he had decided, a gorgeous sapphire to match those stubborn, sparkling blue eyes. 'Phone your sister and tell her what you want to do and seek her approval,' he advised smoothly. 'I'll concentrate on drumming up replacement managers.'

Refreshments were served. Tea, for her, coffee for him and tiny delectable sandwiches followed by a selection of pastries. Tabby ate with appetite. Her anti-nausea medication was keeping her sickness at bay while encouraging her to eat a little more. She phoned her twin and brought her up to speed while she paced in Aristide's airy hall.

'Greece?' Violet squealed in astonishment. 'Gosh, this is so exciting—'

'No, it's not,' Tabby contradicted. 'It's a pretend engagement, *not* a real one, which is why I decided not to tell Mum about it.'

'I'm not sure I see the point,' her sister disappointed her by admitting. 'I mean, it's not like an engagement ties either of you down legally in any way—'

'It will make me feel better...as if I have some actual status in his life when I meet his family,' Tabby whispered, but only after checking that the door back into Aristide's presence was fully closed. 'But it's all smoke and mirrors this way, isn't it? He knew exactly how to get me fully onboard.'

'I thought you hated him—'

'Well, I do...sometimes,' she adjusted in growing embarrassment.

'Just not *all* the time?' her twin prompted with audible amusement.

'He's right on one score. Neither of us need any added stress or drama right now.'

'Twins!' Violet squealed in sheer anticipation.

'One of whom is definitely a boy,' Tabby reminded

her sister, 'but I still have to tell Aristide that I got the call about the blood test today.'

A boy and a girl, one of each, she rather hoped, thinking that that mix would be company for each other as she and Violet had been while each pursuing their own interests.

'A boy,' Aristide repeated minutes later, when she told him the results of the blood test. 'So, I will have possibly two sons or a son and a daughter. When will we know for certain?'

'In another few weeks. I'll need another ultrasound,' she explained, her attention locked to his lean, strong features and the interest unhidden there in the vibrant gleam of his expressive eyes. 'Be warned that you *can* get an erroneous result. The process isn't foolproof.'

Nobody knew that better than Aristide but DNA was unarguable fact. And *this* time, he knew, he knew for certain that he could not entertain for even a second the suspicion that those two babies would not be of his blood. He didn't care what sex the twins were, only that they were Romanos children. 'My relatives will be shaken by this development and I will warn them in advance of our arrival.'

'Shaken?' Tabby queried that choice of word, smothering a yawn at the exhaustion already creeping up on her again. These nights she always ended up in bed much earlier than had once been her habit.

'A long time ago, I swore that I would stay single and have no children,' Aristide admitted after a pause for thought, finally deeming it acceptable to tell her that much, even if he had no plans to tell her the rest of that sordid little story.

Her smooth brow furrowed. 'Why on earth would you make such a far-reaching statement at what must've been such a young age?'

Aristide shrugged a broad shoulder. 'Maybe I'll tell you some day. I'm not someone who looks back with regret. I prefer to look forward and I *was* still a student when I first reached that decision. Now let me see you safely home.'

And he did and she crawled into bed. She thought about his admission that he had once decided to remain unmarried and childless. She frowned, wondering at the past unhappy relationship that must surely have dredged such a declaration from a young man. He had got hurt once, badly hurt, she suspected with a pang of belated sympathy.

For the first time Tabby was feeling a little less alone. Her mother was excited and simultaneously worried about her elder daughter's pregnancy. Naturally the older woman was more preoccupied with her treatment plan. In addition, phone conversations were no replacement for talking face to face, Tabby conceded. Violet's main focus in life was Tore and Belle, her own little family.

But Aristide was different. He was focused solely on her. He was trying, she could see that, and he deserved that she made an equal effort. So, she resolved, no more sniping, no more eying him up like a steak dinner, either. But she still slid into sleep fondly remembering Aristide's smile at the prospect of a son and daughter or any combination of children and marvelled at his enthusiasm. She was lucky, she told herself. Unlike her own father, Aristide truly *wanted* children. In comparison, Sam Blessington had felt trapped and diminished by fatherhood and domesticity.

The following few days were exceptionally busy. Interviews, which Violet joined, took place and a female replacement was chosen and deemed suitable to start working immediately by Tabby's side.

At the start of the next week, Aristide sent his car to waft her to his apartment again to look at the engagement ring. Tabby couldn't understand why she should even see it in advance as a ring would only be an accessory that she would naturally return to him when the fake engagement concluded. Aristide pointed out that she was the party who would have to wear it and her text protests died down.

You argue about every little thing

Thinking that he was getting his own way enough that she could expect him to understand her reservations, Tabby arrived at his apartment, flushed and annoyed. Straight away she was ushered into the lounge where a jeweller and a security guard were hovering in readiness. A small box was set and clicked open for her perusal. It contained a dazzling blue ring in an unusual setting, an oval in a stunning diamond surround. It was breathtaking.

'Try it on for size,' the jeweller remarked with enthusiasm as he removed it from the box, gave it an unnecessary polish and extended it to her. 'A sapphire from Kashmir, rare and much appreciated by all who know their gems.'

Aristide watched the ring he had selected for her glide onto her slender finger in a perfect fit. 'It's the same cornflower blue as your eyes,' he told her.

'It's different and very elegant,' Tabby said, a little breathless as the sunlight accentuated the colourful depth of the precious gem and it shone, holding out her hand, daring to smile for the first time at him.

A slashing smile of appreciation illuminated his lean dark face, emphasising his stunningly handsome features. The level brows, high cheekbones, cut jaw line and brilliant charismatic dark golden eyes. And for a split second, time froze for Tabby while she stared back at him, involuntarily fascinated by all that set Aristide apart from other men.

'The stylist is waiting for you in my guest room,' he informed her in an aside.

Conscious of their audience, Tabby assumed that he wanted to deal with the business of buying the ring with her elsewhere and she said nothing about the sudden reference to a stylist, who presumably styled, whatever that entailed.

Bare minutes later, Tabby was surrounded by rails of clothes and the extrovert stylist was dragging out and holding clothes up for her scrutiny while her assistant proffered accessories and other combinations of garments, both women chattering volubly at the same time. All the garments were acceptable in cut to act as early maternity wear, she was assured.

'You can't buy me clothes,' she declared acidly to Aristide in the aftermath. 'I was ambushed.'

'That was the plan. Like the ring, they're mere props,' Aristide proclaimed dismissively. 'To act like my fiancée, you have to look as though you belong in my life...and unless you're happy to play Cinderella for your audience, you can't do that in unadorned cotton.'

CHAPTER FIVE

Ushered onto the private jet, Tabby attempted not to gape at the gorgeous pale pearl leather upholstery or the number of hovering staff who had greeted her as she climbed the steps to board.

She looked the part of a passenger on such a luxury flight, she reckoned with relief, well aware that her smart green dress and light jacket, which were cut to flatter the increase in her bust and waist measurements, would look stylish in any company. Even walking through the airport, she had registered that a mere flash of her dazzlingly noticeable engagement ring was sufficient to make her conspicuous to many people.

'You look terrific,' Aristide drawled with quiet approval, revelling in her newly found poise. 'I also feel a little less likely to be accused of cradle-snatching!'

'I'm almost twenty-two!' Tabby objected.

'And I'm almost twenty-nine. It's enough of a gap to cause comment,' Aristide told her, veiled eyes roaming slowly over her as she sank into the seat opposite him, slender, shapely legs set at a graceful angle to one side.

'Did your family comment?'

'Only to tease me about younger women,' he acknowledged with amusement.

'I think it's time you tell me who makes up your family,' she responded nervously. 'I only have Mum, Violet and Belle in my corner and you already know all about them. My grandfather doesn't really count because Violet and I've never got to know him…and what we do know isn't good.'

'My only really close relative is my father, but he has several brothers and sisters, who have given me a squad of cousins. My father's on his fifth marriage and my stepmother, Andy, has stood the test of time, unlike her predecessors. They've been married ten years now.'

'Andy?' she questioned.

'It's short for Andromeda. She's a darling, who would've made a great substitute mother for me, had she been around when I was younger and still needed one,' Aristide confided. 'I'm fond of her.'

'What happened to your own mother?' she asked uncertainly.

'She was my father's first wife,' Aristide informed her ruefully. 'She died from a fall on the stairs when I was only a few months old.'

'I'm so sorry,' Tabby muttered with a wince, blue eyes awash with sympathy. 'Do you have any memory of her?'

'None whatsoever,' Aristide admitted with regret. 'My earliest memories only relate to nannies, stepmothers or my father's temporary lovers.'

Her brow furrowed. 'Temporary?'

'The lovers, even the other wives, were all of a temporary ilk until my father met Andy. Dad's liaisons lasted weeks or a couple of months but, sometimes, only days,' Aristide related with a pained look of recollection stamping his lean dark face. 'My father is or *was* a dysfunctional man when it came to the women in his life. But he's settled now and content in his marriage.'

Tabby nodded. 'That's good. What about siblings?'

'None. I'm still an only child but I do have a few stepsisters and stepbrothers, whom I still view as family members. Some of their mothers were rather unreliable and my father maintained close ties with them, no matter how bitter the break-ups were.'

'What's your relationship like with your father?' Tabby was enjoying herself, delighting in Aristide's new openness with her and his willingness to satisfy her curiosity.

'At times, it's been troubled,' Aristide admitted, his shapely mouth compressing as he spoke with yet more honesty than she had expected to receive from him. 'For a long time I blamed Demetrius for the unstable home I grew up in with all those different women coming and going. I was a very pious teenager.' He grimaced at the memory. 'At one point, we didn't speak for several years. But adulthood made me less judgemental. He did fall for some truly horrendous women, however. He also cheated on some decent ones. Maybe he just wasn't ready to fully commit again until he met Andy.'

'And how does he feel about this pretend engagement of ours?' she steeled herself to ask.

'Nobody but us *knows* that it's fake,' he reminded her in stark reproof. 'He's shocked and surprised but very excited about the prospect of two grandkids. The stepchildren are all younger than I am. You will be the first in the family to reproduce. Now tell me about *your* father.'

'He's a creep,' Tabby admitted without hesitation. 'He never wanted children and if he'd had a choice, it wouldn't have been what he referred to as "whiny" daughters. I haven't seen him since the divorce and that's six, no, seven years ago. He tied Mum up in court for months because he fiercely resented being expected to support us and he didn't want further contact with either of us. We're just grateful that he's out of our lives now.'

'You're making me appreciate that I could have had it a lot worse. Demetrius has always loved and defended me. Whatever else he was, he has always been a great father. Clearly, I was fortunate, *angelos mou.*'

'Better the devil you know,' Tabby teased, watching that smile like summer sunlight flash across his lips, elevating his cheekbones and lightening his eyes to scorching gold enticement. She saw the approaching stewardess perform a double take at his sheer masculine appeal in that moment. Colouring on her own behalf for her hyper-awareness of Aristide, she listened as a wide variation of refreshments was offered.

As she collided involuntarily with his eyes, a little shimmy of heat currented down from her belly, making her squeeze her thighs together, much as if she was afraid of that sexual response somehow escaping her. It was little wonder that she was so susceptible, she reasoned. Aristide was drop-dead gorgeous, particularly with his lean muscular physique shown to advantage in beige tailored chinos and a dark purple shirt open at his strong brown throat. Naturally she was still attracted to him. Nothing that physically intense magically evaporated like mist.

'So, where in Greece are we heading?'

'Anthos, the island where my mother and I were both born. Her family has always been based there,' he explained. 'My father has made Anthos his home too.'

Somewhere in the aftermath of a light lunch, Tabby shifted as Aristide lifted her into his arms to carry her on board a helicopter, where he fixed headphones to her head and fastened her seat belt for her before sitting down.

'Where are we?' she mumbled, barely opening her heavy eyes.

'Almost at our destination,' he promised.

The jolt of the helicopter landing again woke her and she surfaced in a tizzy, peering out of a window to note the sprawling white house on the hillside below the hot blue sky. It was massive, an undeniable mansion in size, and people were already gathering on the spacious front veranda. In dismay she sat up and dug into her bag to search frantically for a comb and a lipstick. A cool, restraining hand covered hers. 'You look great,' Aristide told her soothingly, and he was telling her the truth because she might look rumpled and a little sleepy but she was still indisputably beautiful. 'There's no need for you to primp when we've been travelling for hours.'

'This is my property,' Aristide told her quietly as he vaulted out onto the grass and reached back to lift her down by his side in the sunlight. 'Demetrius and

Andy host family parties here because I have more space. Their own home, my former childhood home, is on the other side of the island, so there is no need for you to feel like a guest here.'

As they walked down a grassy path, Tabby noticed many of the guests standing outside disperse back indoors at a small, bustling brunette's instigation. Aristide, she realised, was the very image of his father and how he might look twenty or thirty years down the road. Demeterius was tall, straight, his black hair winged with grey, undeniably handsome and fit, the very image of a silver fox. By his side, his wife, Andy, was a curvy, scarlet-clad brunette with lively dark eyes and an irrepressible smile of welcome.

'Oh, it is *the* ring!' Andy exclaimed in excitement as she caught Tabby's wrist lightly in hers to grab a closer look at the sapphire. 'It's absolutely tremendous, gorgeous!'

'Thanks. I love it,' Tabby admitted with a smile.

'I'll show you up to our room. You can lie down if you like,' Aristide interposed.

'Again?' Tabby stressed with amusement, thinking that he needed to spend a little longer with his father and stepmother. 'I slept most of the way here. I can surely stay awake long enough to meet some people.'

'If that's what you would prefer—'

'Maybe you're gasping to look after an invalid,' she teased with a roll of her eyes. ''Fraid that's not me. All you've got here is one pregnant lady, who's feeling chirpy after so much rest. My nausea is definitely subsiding now. If you were to offer me food—'

'I can help there.' Andy cupped an arm to Tabby's elbow and walked her off into a grand room where a splendid buffet table and a collection of people awaited them. 'I slept the clock around when I was pregnant and I ate regular snacks to stave off the sickness,' she told her. 'Do you realise that Aristide has never brought a woman here with him before?'

'I didn't know that,' Tabby said non-committally, all too well aware that she was visiting because at some stage their twins would be visiting with their father and it was her job to pave the way for that future.

As she was filling a plate, various casual introductions were made. A welter of middle-aged uncles, aunts and more youthful cousins followed. A skinny teenaged girl with bright red hair darted past them to throw her arms round Aristide as he appeared in the doorway.

'Melody, one of my husband's former stepkids,' Tabby's companion explained. 'She and her two brothers lived with Aristide for weeks after their mother left them alone in London, where they attend school. They knew him when they were very young and contacted him when they ran out of money. I think they'll be spending most of the summer with us.'

'I'm glad he stepped in,' Tabby remarked, watching two tall teenage boys join their sister's animated conversation.

'He's good with children,' the brunette said cheerfully. 'Particularly teenagers. We're getting a little too old to be seen as cool.'

'Aristide can be surprising,' Tabby admitted with a sudden smile, suddenly grateful that she had come to Greece to meet his family even if she was a fake fiancée. It was reassuring to be somewhere Aristide could relax and shed his remote and detached business persona.

Making some more food choices with Andy's encouragement, she was soon sitting down and socialising.

'So, tell me about her,' Demetrius Romanos invited his son.

'Not right now. I know how you work. The more I tell you about her, the more suspicious of her you will become,' Aristide countered, knowing his parent of old and too respectful of him to comment that he considered his father one of the last people he would listen to advice from when it came to a woman.

'She *is* a real beauty,' his father conceded. 'But so was the last one—'

'Don't bring Imogen into it,' Aristide sliced in grimly. 'That's old history.'

'She's on the island right now,' his father warned him impatiently. 'I was furious when I was told but her grandfather is dying and she's entitled to visit. However, you own their properties—'

'I've no intention of being that petty,' Aristide parried, his lean, strong face taut. 'Let sleeping dogs lie.'

'As long as the dog doesn't start barking and upset her replacement—'

'Tabby's *not* a replacement. Tabby's an entirely different kind of woman,' Aristide murmured with innate assurance. 'If you take the time to talk to her, you will realise that.'

In between conversations, Tabby sipped her tea and watched Aristide with his father, wondering what they were discussing because she could see Aristide's hackles rising and his parent's unapologetic stance.

'They argue...frequently,' Andromeda Romanos whispered in rueful warning. 'But I've only once seen it come to an exchange of blows—'

'Oh, my goodness...' Tabby's eyes rounded in dread.

'I shouldn't have mentioned it,' the older woman said equally quickly. 'It only happened that once and tempers had become very frayed, I'm afraid. That incident separated them for years, so it won't *ever* happen again. They're far too fond of each other to risk it.'

'I'm relieved to hear that because I grew up in a violent home. My father drank and he often took his temper out on us,' she confided.

'How on earth did you and your mother cope?'

'Well, ultimately we didn't. They divorced years ago.'

Shortly after that exchange, Aristide retrieved her and offered to show her round the house. Some visitors were leaving, a few were staying over until the following day and some, like the former stepchildren, were staying at his father's house.

'It's a huge house,' Tabby commented as they stood in the giant hall with its contemporary limestone floor and modern paintings. 'Did you inherit it?'

'No. I built it during the period my father and I were at odds,' Aristide confided with a wince. 'I was only twenty and I was showing off—'

Tabby grinned as he directed her towards the glass

and stone double-flight staircase. 'You? Showing off? I don't believe it!' she mocked.

'It's far too big and unless I have half a dozen kids, I'll never fill it. It doesn't have much character either—'

'So why did you build it?'

'It was petty,' Aristide said wryly. 'But I was reminding my father that I was totally independent. I inherited my mother's wealth and this island on the day she died. I've never had to fight or ask or struggle for anything, which is why I went into business. I needed the challenges.'

Tabby sighed. 'My life has been so different from yours. Growing up, we were always struggling for money. Mum wasn't well enough educated to get a decent job and what she did earn my father tended to take off her. He was always moaning about how his family sucked his artistic soul out of him,' she muttered with a curled lip. 'But I don't believe he had an artistic soul. That was his excuse for ignoring the bills for rent, electricity and food and all the rest of the stuff you need to cover to survive.'

'No wonder you were willing to marry a stranger for cash!' Aristide said, startling her rigid with that assumption.

'Oh, good heavens, no, is that what you think? But that wasn't why I was willing to marry Tore Renzetti. No, *that* was to pay for Mum's clinical trial in Massachusetts and cover her costs while she was there. It's taken every penny of it too because Violet and I wanted to know she would be comfortable,' she explained. 'And she hasn't known what it is to be comfortable very often since she left my grandfather's home to marry my father.'

In receipt of her explanation, Aristide froze into stillness on the landing, his lean, powerful frame suddenly rigid with tension as he vented a harsh exclamation in Greek. 'Why the hell didn't you tell me about your *mother's* need to pay for her treatment weeks ago?' he demanded in raw disbelief.

'It wasn't relevant to us...and anyway, Violet ended up having to marry Tore instead, so it wasn't really my story to tell any more,' she proffered uncomfortably. 'And I hope that I can trust you to keep those facts quiet. Now that my sister and Tore have fallen for each other and are staying together, I shouldn't think either of them would want that original story told.'

'I'm not going to discuss it with anyone,' Aristide declared curtly. 'I'm just furious that you threw Renzetti's existence in my face that night and you all but encouraged me to think the very worst of you!'

Tabby shrugged a slight shoulder, not quite sure why he was so annoyed with her. 'Well, I had to throw back something with all the accusations you were hurling,' she reasoned defensively. 'And I believed that telling you I was to marry Tore and that *he* was wealthy would relieve you of the fear that you'd been specially targeted by me for some sort of profit venture—'

'But it also made me believe that you were a cheat!' Aristide flung back at her in condemnation. 'And I don't like people who cheat on their partners!'

Surprised by his vehemence and the fierce burnished gold of his gaze, Tabby flinched and spread her hands slowly in a soothing gesture. 'I've never cheated on anyone. I'm sorry if I misled you but it was accidental—'

'If you hadn't misled me, I'd have been in touch with you far sooner than I was,' Aristide shot at her, faint colour now edging his hard cheekbones while emotion still flared like a storm warning in his dark golden eyes, his annoyance and embarrassment visible. 'Sometimes, you really can be a piece of work!'

'I've apologised,' Tabby reminded him flatly. 'Have the grace to accept it and move on...'

Aristide closed a hand over hers and stalked down the long landing to the double doors at the foot, throwing a door wide. 'This is the master suite for our use.'

'Our?' Tabby questioned, kicking off her shoes that were pinching a little and stepping back to take in the full impressive span of the spacious bedroom and the selection of doors that opened off it. It was a really lovely room done in masculine shades of silver grey and dark blue, but the giant bed festooned in silvery drapes and crisp white linen would have delighted any princess in search of a suitable setting.

'Well, obviously we're sharing,' Aristide pointed out.

Tabby had assumed they would be sharing a bedroom and had refused to think about what that would be like. But now Aristide had started criticising her behaviour and had riled her up into a mood. *'Obviously?'* she stressed out of badness and as Aristide's eyes flamed like torches, she lifted a brow. 'There's a very nice couch over there. You could use that.'

'Like hell I will!' Aristide fired back at her.

Tabby gave him a tight little smile and rested her hands down on her hips for emphasis. 'Right at this minute, you have made me so mad with you that you're condemned to the couch—'

'I'm not sleeping anywhere but in that bed *with* you!' Aristide framed.

'Andy mentioned dinner and that I could change into something more relaxed,' Tabby announced, ignoring that statement as she shifted the subject. '*After* you unzip my dress…'

The grudging hint of an appreciative smile tugged at the corners of Aristide's sensual mouth. 'Turn around,' he instructed.

Tipping off her jacket, Tabby acquiesced. The zip ran down, the edges parted, cooler air brushing her heated skin. Lips pressed in a brief, light salute to her slender spine and she gasped, an electrified shiver running through her entire body. He set her back from him and murmured in a husky undertone, 'Don't pretend that you're not feeling the same things I'm feeling, *angelos mou*.'

In instant denial of the charge, Tabby spun round. 'The couch is still yours,' she countered.

'I need a shower,' Aristide breathed in a driven undertone. 'This room has separate bathrooms and dressing rooms, enabling both of us to have our privacy.'

And she needed a shower too, Tabby reflected dizzily, reliving the chemical charge of his carnal mouth on her warm skin, another reflexive shiver rippling through her taut and aroused body. Because there it was, that ferocious attraction that she would have denied but that honesty made her admit… She wanted to rip his clothes off, pin him to that bed and have her thoroughly wicked way with him. But surely that phase of their relationship was over and done with, wasn't it? Why was it that she had waited for so long to have a sexual relationship and the minute she tasted the flavour of sex with Aristide, she wanted more, more, *more*? It mortified her to feel like that around him.

In the bathroom he showed her, she found her toiletries already arranged and she smiled in surprise, realising that while she had been downstairs someone had unpacked her luggage for her. She stripped and walked into the shower to freshen up, drying herself on a fresh fleecy towel and reflecting that the life of a jet-setter certainly offered its comforts. With a touch of gloss on her lips and mascara, she was done. Carefully wrapped in the towel, she ventured into the spacious custom-built dressing room next door where her clothing selection for her two weeks in sunny Greece looked ridiculously tiny. She picked a casual long skirt and a tee that skimmed forgivingly over her no longer flat midriff.

Aristide, clad in well-fitted jeans and a tee, surveyed her as she emerged. 'Classy and simple. That's your style and it suits you,' he murmured, disconcerting her. 'And you really don't appreciate the damage you did to my opinion of you when you allowed me to believe that you were a money-grabbing cheat.'

'I didn't care that night,' Tabby countered, lifting her chin. 'As far as I was concerned, I was defending myself the only way I could and back then I still believed that it would be me who had to marry Tore. It wasn't until I realised that I was pregnant, which broke the contract I'd signed, that I thought it would have to be Violet who married him instead.'

'You should always care about what you reveal about yourself,' Aristide censured. 'Even if you're simply trying to score points and particularly if it paints you in bad colours.'

'I didn't give two hoots about your opinion that night, not after what you had said to me!' Tabby flipped back without apology, her head high. 'I have my pride too, Aristide. Why would you suddenly start imagining that I was the kind of woman who would set you up for some sort of a pregnancy trap? Who would want you for your wealth rather than who you are as a person?'

Aristide looked grim, his lean, strong face etched in hard lines. '*Why?* Because something rather similar happened to me once before and that harrowing experience probably left me oversensitive, which is why I lost my temper and assumed the very worst of you.'

Tabby was stunned into silence by that bleak, blunt confession. As she hovered, an apology brimming on her lips, Aristide took charge and urged her to the door. Something similar? *Harrowing* experience? His choice of that particular word shocked her and sobered her into deeper thought. 'Was there a child born?' she heard herself ask under her breath as they headed towards the stairs.

'No, the woman concerned miscarried,' he revealed flatly. 'Now can we talk about something else? I don't want to talk about *that*.'

Typical Aristide, she thought ungraciously. Having finally told her the truth about why he had flown off the handle that first night with her, he was still refusing to share the whole story. But then why should he? His intimate past wasn't her business. He wasn't bound to tell her about everything. Intellectually, she understood and accepted that, but she craved further knowledge of that particular episode because it had clearly left a wound.

Dinner was full of chatter and easy conversation. Demetrius asked her how she had met Aristide and she told him about that day at Traxis and the belated discovery that Aristide was not a senior accountant. He laughed but gave her a searching look, as if he was not quite sure whether or not to believe her.

As the meal continued, Aristide seemed to become more preoccupied and then, over coffee, he rose and gave her an apologetic appraisal. 'I have a visit to make to an old friend this evening. I hope you'll forgive me for leaving you for an hour or so on your first night.'

In an even more sudden movement, Demetrius Romanos stood up as well. 'Old Theo? Of course. I'll come too and pay my respects,' he announced.

And with that, the two men left the room.

'Who's old Theo?' Tabby asked Andromeda curiously.

'A fisherman Aristide knew as a boy. He's dying,' the brunette explained. 'Aristide didn't know that Theo had fallen ill until he arrived.'

Tabby nodded, surprised by the fleeting look of discomfiture on Andromeda's face, wondering if it was dealing with the old man's passing that made her that way or whether there was some other complication that she remained ignorant of.

Aristide returned in a volatile mood. Theo had been well enough to reminisce for almost an hour but then Imogen had joined them and his father had stood up to immediately leave, determined to protect his son to the last even if his son no longer needed protecting. He wasn't a teenager any more, more in love with a woman's face and body than anything else. He no longer expected perfection either, knowing there was no such thing. Everyone had strengths and weaknesses. Imogen had once been his weakness but that was over and done. In her favour, his former fiancée had been irreproachably polite and charming and had not once alluded to the past. Points to her on that score, he acknowledged, knowing his own reactions had been less presentable and his father's comments on her afterwards had been unrepeatable.

In the darkness, as he stripped and left his clothes in an untidy heap, he studied Tabby in the moonlight filtering through the room. Light shimmered over the point of a delicate ear and pale blonde hair as she shifted and rolled over, evidently in the grip of a disturbing dream. A low moan was wrenched from her. 'Daddy...*no*!' she sobbed and his blood chilled in his veins.

She sounded like a frightened child and Aristide was in that bed and gathering her into his arms before he could even think about what he was doing. His need to comfort her was overwhelming.

CHAPTER SIX

Tabby surfaced shuddering and gasping for breath, her last recollection of trying to intervene after her father had struck her mother to the floor and, while he was still ranting, returned to kick her.

'It's only a dream,' Aristide murmured softly.

'No, it was a memory of Dad beating up Mum and me trying to stop him,' she muttered shakily.

'And how did that go?' Aristide prompted in a strained undertone.

'I got kicked too,' she mumbled wretchedly. 'But he backed off after that.'

'What age were you?'

'Seven, eight… I'm not sure,' she admitted. 'I've never told anyone about that before. I was in bed and I heard him shouting and I got up. I should've known better—'

Aristide expelled his breath in an audible hiss. 'No, he's the one who should have known better when he saw his child in his way. But then he should not have been hurting either you or your mother.'

Aristide cradled her in his big, strong arms as he sat on the bed and she had never felt safer in her life. Dimly she recognised that was always, *always* what she had sought from a male: that he would be there for her when she needed him, that he would understand that she was softer inside than her prickly exterior implied. And then, most of all, that he would make those connections without thinking she was somehow *less*. The scent of Aristide, forest-fresh air with a hint of sea salt, engulfed her and she breathed in deep, firmly resisting the urge to snuggle, aware of the hard male contours of his lean, fit body against her.

'What are you wearing?' she whispered.

'Nothing. I was getting undressed and then you were crying out and I wanted to wake you out of that dream,' he murmured lazily. 'And what are you wearing? Something silky and small.'

Long fingers tugged at the hem of her shorts and she shrank inside her light vest top, her nipples tightening and pushing forward at the awareness that he was naked.

'Rather cruel and tempting considering I'm the guy you were set on sentencing to the couch,' Aristide opined huskily.

'You weren't here. I wasn't thinking of what I was wearing,' she protested truthfully. 'Anyway, I wasn't really planning to make you sleep on the couch. I was just annoyed with you.'

'You smell delicious, *angelos mou*,' Aristide breathed thickly. 'I think I'd better return you to bed.'

Rising, he threw back the sheet and slotted her into place, throwing the sheet over her. Without that physical contact, she felt cold and then he climbed in beside her and she relaxed again as he drew her into his warmth. In a sudden movement, she squirmed round and put her arms round him, her mouth instinctively seeking and finding his. And just as suddenly, she was pinned beneath him and he was kissing her breathless, heat darting to the heart of her and stirring a tight, intolerable ache.

Aristide released her swollen mouth and lifted his dark, curly head. 'You're impulsive,' he pointed out, as if she weren't already conscious of that failing. 'I was sentenced to the couch...remember?'

'I'm not impulsive—'

'You so *are*. I have to know that you want me and that this isn't some impulse you'll start regretting at dawn,' he decreed.

'I always want you,' Tabby admitted as if that was so obvious that it should go without saying.

'And I never stopped wanting you,' Aristide growled.

'Has there been anyone else or several someone elses for you since that night?' she asked, even though she knew that she wasn't being fair demanding an answer to that question when they had parted as enemies without any kind of future even seeming possible.

'There's been nobody since you,' Aristide admitted after a lengthy pause, brilliant eyes glimmering dark in the moonlight. 'But that isn't a fair question—'

'I *know*,' she agreed without regret. 'But I had to know. I'm possessive. I don't share—'

'Neither do I,' Aristide growled, returning to worry at her parted lips with his lips, the edge of his teeth and then the deep plunge of his tongue, his hunger unhidden and thoroughly stimulating.

'Did I ever tell you how much I like the way you kiss?' she asked breathlessly.

'No. You can tell me tomorrow over a late breakfast. I think we are both due a very late breakfast,' Aristide positively purred, the vibration of his deep dark drawl travelling down her taut spine, filtering intrinsically into softer, warmer places.

He settled her on the bed and leant over her, all hard profile and dominance in the low light. 'Have you any idea how sexy it is that you're carrying my children?'

As a big hand splayed possessively across her abdomen, Tabby blinked and shook her head. 'Sexy?' she queried in disbelief because, to date, pregnancy had not felt sexy to her. It had meant tiredness and nausea and the irritatingly strong rise of hormones that craved Aristide and his lean, hard body round the clock, something that torture would not have persuaded her to admit.

'It makes me feel proud, possessive, territorial, *angelos mou*,' Aristide husked. 'When I entered that bakery and saw another man fondling your hand—'

'What other man?' she exclaimed.

'The guy in the chef outfit—'

'Oh, you mean Luca, Violet's replacement baker. He's harmless,' she assured him without concern. 'He flirts with every female around him and he's ridiculously touchy-feely.'

'You need to crush that tendency in him. He'll land you with a sexual harassment issue,' Aristide forecast.

Tabby loosed a startled laugh and reached up a hand to cup his hard cheekbone. 'Aristide, all the female staff, no matter what their age, adore Luca because he makes them feel good, he makes them feel interesting. He's a genuinely nice person and you don't meet as many of those as you would like to.'

'But you won't be there any more for him to flirt with,' Aristide affixed, clearly happy at that development. 'You're out of bounds now.'

'Oh, really?'

For the next two weeks, she was thinking.

'I'm the only guy allowed to flirt with you,' Aristide told her.

'Oh, I don't think that's going to work,' she warned with helpless amusement. 'Sometimes a little flirting is what makes the day go around a little faster.'

'Not for you,' Aristide asserted, nuzzling his jaw against the soft silk screening her aching breasts. She could feel her nipples, tight as buds, straining for attention.

The warmth of his mouth enclosed a pulsing bud below the thin silk and she shuddered, sudden excitement claiming her at even that slight touch.

'And what do I get in return for not flirting?' she dared to gasp as he lifted his head again.

'Me and bragging rights,' Aristide quipped with a lazy, wildly engaging grin. 'Only you can pin me down.'

'That's you assuming that I *want* to pin you down,' Tabby murmured. 'But just like you, that first night I was only after one stolen experience, only we both got more than we bargained for out of it.'

'Why did you only want that?' he demanded.

'Think about it. I didn't want this contracted stranger of a husband to become my first lover,' she argued ruefully. 'It was a stupid, short-sighted move and I soon regretted it—'

'I don't,' Aristide imparted, lifting the vest top off over her head, quickly sliding his attention to her slender hips and skimming down the fabric there as well. 'I met you and I have not a single regret.'

'Seriously?' Tabby gazed up at him in wonder at that statement. 'But you *must* have regrets. You didn't want children—'

'It would be more accurate to say that hurt pride made me deny any desire for children of my own,' Aristide contradicted, lowering his dark tousled head to find the pert buds of her full breasts.

Just as quickly, the concept of talking vanished from Tabby's mind as the erotic invitation of his teasing mouth caught and played with her swollen pink nipples and his lean fingers joined in the torture. Her body writhed under him of its own volition. She was like a touch paper set alight, need burning through her like an arrow, sharp and unsatisfied. She had wanted him for what felt like for ever and now suddenly he was there and nothing could happen fast enough to answer that fierce craving for sensation.

Aristide was intuitive. It was as though he were inside her head, knowing the extent of her desire, working though that to a painfully slow degree down her body to find all the most sensitive spots. She couldn't stay still, racked by hunger and intense urgency. He parted her slender quivering thighs, traced the heart of her with teasing fingertips when she was already too far beyond that stage. As his touch glanced across her swollen clit, she went off like a rocket into an orgasm that shot through her like white lightning, momentarily stilling her before her body jerked and convulsed in pleasure.

Unperturbed, Aristide continued to dally there, utilising his mouth and his tongue and his long fingers with a finesse that sent her shooting a second time into orbit, a deep flush drenching her cheeks as she thought of how easily she had responded and the depth of the need that she had exposed. He had been quite correct when he had accused her of being impulsive, she acknowledged unhappily. She had not even thought about what would happen if she ended up having sex with Aristide again. But did that matter any more? They didn't need a label, she told herself. They were both single and committed only to their unborn children. Perhaps friendship would've been a wiser option but there was little chance of a platonic relationship developing while they were still so wildly attracted to each other.

He held her against him while she still trembled and gasped and struggled for breath. A lean hand ran down the damp curve of her hip and her heartbeat started to edge up in pace again. 'Do you want a break or may I continue?'

A little sensual tingle at her molten core answered and she shifted back into his long, strong body, drinking in the fresh scent of him with pleasure. 'You need to ask?'

Aristide laughed with rich appreciation, claiming her mouth again, tasting her with hungry concision. He ached for her and he crushed her parted lips beneath his, teasing her tender flesh with skilled fingers, probing her slick depths with a satisfied growl. Excitement gripped her again. He could make her want him again so easily that for a split second she felt intimidated. Reacting to that feeling, she slid a hand down over his muscular stomach and found him, velvet over steel, more than ready for her, and he groaned and nipped at the taut muscle between her neck and her shoulder in retribution.

He rearranged her like a doll but there was nothing doll-like about the zing of pure energy surging through her veins or the race of her quickened heartbeat. He slid between her thighs and drove into her with precision. He was being careful, she sensed, careful of her pregnancy. 'The babies are fine, but I won't be if you stay this cautious,' she warned him.

And he took her lead, lifting her to him and driving deep, giving her the friction and urgency her body craved. It was a wild ride from there on in, her internal muscles clenching around him, glorying in renewed sensation, pleasure flaring up like a bushfire racing through her body. Exhilaration held her, that endless ache sated, but she still craved more. He gave it to her but the tumult of sensation was rising to a peak she couldn't resist and she climaxed again with a quivering cry of delight. He came to completion with a groan of satisfaction, his whole body jolting and jerking into hers.

'I like sex with you,' she said chattily in the aftermath.

Aristide burst out laughing, pulling back from her so as not to crush her with his weight. 'Of all the things to say,' he derided. 'You're a bossy little creature in bed, aren't you?'

'I'm only discovering that side of me and I could tell that you were moving into the "treating me like a delicate flower" approach and I wasn't having that,' she confided.

Aristide tugged the rumpled sheet over them. 'Go to sleep. We're lunching with Dad and Andy tomorrow at the taverna. It's a tradition when I come home. You and I will do a tour of the island first.'

Tabby stretched out and slept, gloriously relaxed for the first time in weeks.

The next morning, after a light breakfast, they set off in a classic open-topped green British sports car. His father was a classic car enthusiast and that particular one had been a gift for Aristide's last birthday. He used it to get around the island, which wasn't that large. It took only an hour to do a loop on the single main road that ringed Anthos. They stopped off at various places, walking along the beach at one point before climbing a wooded hill to the tumbled remains of an old lookout tower. From the hill they could view the whole island, taking in the little town with its ranks of houses on the slopes and the tall steepled church above the picturesque harbour and, finally, the luxury hotel resort built at the far end, which belonged to his father.

'So, you and Demetrius don't work together at all?' she gathered.

'No, he owns a luxury chain of hotels. We'll stop off there to eat some day.'

The taverna was right down on the beach and Tabby eased through the crush round the bar to choose a seat on the decking outside. She sipped her fruit juice and watched as Aristide dropped down into a seat opposite her. A woman was walking up the beach from the water, a sarong carelessly tied at her waist, a blue bikini top cupping her pert breasts. A mane of golden blonde hair drifted round her gorgeous face as a photographer ducked and dived all around her taking photo after photo of her. She peeled off the sarong and slowly turned, showing her perfect body and the bikini from every angle. She was both stunning and familiar. Tabby stilled, recognising her from the media images forever peppering newspapers and glossy magazines. Imogen Ross, the famous supermodel in the flesh.

'I think that's Imogen Ross,' she hissed at Aristide.

'It *is*,' he confirmed in an undertone.

'Aristide,' an English voice drawled barely a minute later. 'Introduce me to your little friend.'

Tabby's head spun back to the beach. Imogen Ross was standing in the sand by the edge of the deck and smiling at her while extending a manicured hand.

'Tabitha, meet Imogen Ross,' Aristide murmured without any expression at all.

The blonde gasped as she saw the ring on Tabby's finger. 'Oh my goodness, that puts *my* old thing to shame!' she exclaimed, waving her other hand to display the fabulous diamond solitaire she wore that flashed in the sunlight. 'I have a friend who tried to buy that sapphire at the auction last month. I didn't know you got it! How does it feel to wear a jewel worth millions, Tabitha?'

'Aristide… Tabby, your seats are waiting for you,' Andromeda Romanos called with a slightly desperate edge to her voice as she stood in the doorway of the bar.

'Excuse us, Imogen…'

'You were much friendlier when I saw you last night,' Imogen said with a reproachful look, her ripe red-tinted mouth settling into a disappointed pout.

'Goodbye,' Tabby murmured brittly as she turned away, feeling a little as though she might get a knife planted in her back.

Her brain was swirling in chaos. Aristide knew Imogen Ross? Why hadn't he warned her? Aristide had once been *engaged* to that beautiful woman? Or had she picked up that hint wrong? And was she really wearing a sapphire worth millions of pounds? Was that even possible? And had Imogen genuinely seen Aristide the night before? If so, why hadn't he told her about the blonde? Furthermore, exactly how had he come from a cosy meeting with the sickeningly gorgeous Imogen Ross and ended up making love to Tabby? She didn't like that time frame or the associations it awakened. Had she been the consolation prize? What on earth sort of a triangle had he got her into? And why the hell hadn't he warned her in advance?

'Of course, she knew we'd be here today for lunch because we arrived yesterday. Imogen is well acquainted with our family traditions,' Aristide framed glacially.

'Probably lying in wait for you like some poisonous jellyfish in the shallows!' Andy remarked with angry defensiveness. 'Ghastly woman—'

'Your ex…?' Tabby glanced at Aristide for verification as they took their seats at the table.

His dark eyes flashed gold with anger. 'For my sins. Yes.'

Tabby's slight shoulders set while her temper roared and boiled beneath her carefully tranquil surface. She was furious with Aristide for not telling her that they might run into his ex-girlfriend. She was even more furious with him for daring to have sex with *her* after spending time with his ex. She could never compete in attraction or appeal with a supermodel with perfect hair, a perfect face and an even more perfect figure. Any woman would cringe at such a cruel comparison, she reflected in exasperation, most especially a woman already conscious of her steadily growing and less shapely pregnant body.

Rescuing her appetite from that mood took time but by the time they reached the main course, she was eating again and chatting comfortably with Andy. She noticed that absolutely no one mentioned Imogen again, even though she entered the taverna and sat down with her photographer, talking in a rather loud voice in English about her diet and how she simply couldn't possibly digest cream or eggs. They departed, Aristide tucking Tabby into the car with careful hands.

Tabby sucked in a deep breath and flexed her engagement finger in the sunshine so that the light penetrated the pure deep blue of the sapphire. *'Millions?'* she stressed incredulously.

'My father collects classic cars. I collect rare jewels,' Aristide responded calmly.

Well, obviously, the very valuable sapphire would be remaining with Aristide once their engagement was officially over, Tabby reasoned as the car traversed the driveway to the large villa. Unlike Imogen, she would not still be flaunting a former engagement ring in the future, nor did she expect to. After all, she wasn't looking for expensive perks or rewards from Aristide.

They walked into the hall and Iola, Aristide's housekeeper, smiled and asked them what time they wanted dinner that evening.

'You decide,' he told Tabby. 'I'll be working.'

'Seven would be lovely,' Tabby told Iola with a smile, reckoning that she didn't need a thermometer to read Aristide's mood. It was definitely bordering on chilly.

He was in the dressing room getting changed when she got to their bedroom. 'So, that's it, then, is it? You're going to act as if nothing happened at lunchtime.'

Aristide straightened and zipped his jeans, wary dark golden eyes clashing unexpectedly with her questioning, open gaze. 'Nothing *did* happen,' he pointed out.

'Obviously, I'm going to ask about her,' Tabby replied defensively.

'But that doesn't mean that I have to answer.'

'I don't see why you wouldn't,' Tabby remarked, striving to be more casual about her curiosity. 'She came up and spoke to us.'

Aristide shrugged a broad shoulder as he pulled on

a black tee. 'I don't owe you chapter and verse on everyone who speaks to us,' he countered very drily.

'No, but there's such a thing as explaining stuff to make people feel more comfortable...especially if we were to run into her again—'

Aristide straightened to his full intimidating height and the cotton tee dropped down, screening his spectacular muscled torso again. 'I can assure you that you won't run into her either in this house or my father's—'

Tabby nodded, fresh out of an alternative approach that wouldn't seem to be too much like prying. Of course, had she wanted to do that, she would have followed Andy to the cloakroom. She suspected that Aristide's stepmother wouldn't have had a problem telling her about Imogen, whom she had clearly disliked. But her self-respect cringed from the concept of going behind his back to find out information like a common gossip and his family would probably tell him what she had done anyway. She flushed with discomfiture, mortified that she had even thought of doing such a thing. Had it been Imogen who fell pregnant and miscarried? Tabby winced, grudging sympathy assailing her.

Aristide strode downstairs, marvelling at her curiosity. Surely it was obvious that he didn't want to talk about Imogen? Did he really need to say any more? But Tabby was so blunt, so open, compared to the kind of women he knew best. He suppressed a groan and sat down at his laptop to catch up with his email.

Tabby lingered in the bedroom to change as well, throwing on a bikini and a wrap to take advantage of the pool behind the villa. Seriously, he wouldn't be looking at her and actually comparing her to Imogen, would he be? How did she know when he wouldn't even open the subject with her?

Having run him to earth in an obvious office space, Tabby hovered uncertainly in the doorway. 'Why won't you talk about her?' she asked.

Aristide narrowed glittering black eyes on her as she posed there. She looked so awkward and uncomfortable in her persistence because she knew that she shouldn't be pushing him. She was so unlike Imogen in every way and he cherished that even if it did make life more challenging. With her blonde hair lying rumpled on her shoulders, her make-up-bare face soft and open, she exuded honesty and good intentions.

'I just don't. Let's say it's a period in my life that I prefer not to revisit—'

'But clearly, if you were engaged to her, it was a major relationship that must've lasted a fair time. And if she is the one who miscarried your child, it must have been even more distressing."

Aristide jerked a shoulder in dismissal and swung away.

'Do you realise how much you're annoying me?' Tabby prompted.

An unwelcome smile slashed across his darkly serious features. 'Yes, I do.'

'I'm not going to fight with you about this…'

'Good, because you would lose,' Aristide told her equably.

'No, I wouldn't!' she tossed back to him, lifting her determined little chin in the air.

Aristide sent his chair screeching back from his desk and vaulted upright. He opened his arms. 'Come here, *angelos mou*,' he urged huskily. 'I want to kiss you.'

Tabby dragged in a shaken breath. 'You can't kiss me out of this!'

'You may be stubborn but I think I could.'

And he stood there, tall and dark and drop-dead gorgeous, a curl of black hair lying on his brow above the scorching dark golden gaze suddenly locked to her mutinous face.

'Try it and see,' Tabby suggested with a dangerous spark in her eyes as she moved closer.

Aristide could no more have stopped himself from reaching for her then than he could've stopped breathing. He hauled her to him and crushed her parted lips beneath his with a suppressed groan. All the turmoil in his busy brain stopped dead. The chemistry between him and Tabby electrified him, making him splay a hand across the soft curve of her bottom, jerk loose the sarong shielding her from him and yank her into full contact with the urgent thrust of his erection.

Low in her throat, she gasped as he enforced that connection and without hesitation he lifted her up and set her down on the edge of his desk.

Her body humming, giving her messages that she still wasn't used to receiving, Tabby blinked and then noted her surroundings, dismay and reluctance assailing her before embarrassment could cover her instead. 'Not here,' she said distinctly, struggling to suppress the hungry ache he had stirred between her thighs and rise above the sensation. 'And not when we're arguing either… I'm trying to talk to you.'

Aristide gritted his teeth, registering that he had underestimated her resolve. 'Tabby—'

'No, no more excuses,' Tabby cut in, sliding off the desk and snatching up her discarded sarong to wrap it round her hips again.

Aristide expelled his breath in a slow hiss and leant back against his desk, annoyance at her rejection, so rare in his experience with women, pulsing through him in a lethal wave. He tilted his darkly handsome head back. 'Ask yourself why I would have to tell you anything private about my past when we're only *faking* our engagement.'

Every scrap of colour drained from Tabby's once animated face. That reminder hit her like a brick and a much-needed wake-up call to common sense. Why? She had forgotten it was *all* fake except for her costly sapphire ring, and the shock that she could've allowed herself to forget such a basic fact reverberated through her like a crack of doom. No, she wasn't entitled to private explanations about his past loves, not if he didn't want to make them. And yet she had pushed and pushed until he ran out of patience and confronted her with the truth that she had been avoiding.

As she left his office, Aristide wanted to smash the wall with a clenched fist. He shouldn't have said that. Indeed, that was the very last thing he should've said when he sincerely wanted their engagement to become real. He had given way to temper, a rare occurrence with his deep, reserved nature. But he didn't talk about Imogen, not to anyone ever, not even his father. In truth, legally, he *couldn't* talk about her and she couldn't talk about him either, conditions his father had considered necessary at the time for *his* protection rather than hers.

And he was glad of his father's caution, wouldn't have cared to lift a tabloid newspaper some day and read *that* particular story. He wouldn't like the way it depicted him and couldn't help wondering just how differently Tabby would see him if she ever learned what an idiot he had once been.

And wasn't that truly *why* he had stuck to the letter of the law and remained silent?

CHAPTER SEVEN

TABBY MADE HERSELF walk out to the pool at the rear of the house and lie down on a lounger.

A mere minute later, she got up and dived into the pool, forcing herself into swimming fast aggressive lengths to drain her angry pain and tension away. No point letting feelings like that fester, she told herself. That wouldn't change anything. What she really needed to know right then was why she was so hurt. Aristide had merely reminded her of the truth that they were not a real couple where she would have been entitled to cherish certain expectations of him.

And in reality, he had hit the nail square on the head. Their engagement was fake, so how had she stumbled into a kind of non-relationship with the father of her unborn children? By not using her brain and thinking first, came the answer. The situation was of her own making. But you couldn't live for two long weeks as if you were involved in an endless one-night stand... at least, she couldn't. She wasn't built that way, wasn't able to just write it off as a casual, light-hearted fun fling. Certainly, there was nothing *fun* about the way she felt now. Her heart sank when she appreciated that all along, while she had been priding herself on her independence, she had been unconsciously hoping for *more* from Aristide Romanos. But he wasn't offering more, was he?

When she had had enough of the heat and was fed up with agonising, she went indoors and phoned her mother, catching up on her news. Lucia's treatment was going as well as could be expected at this stage. Guessing that it would raise her mother's spirits, she gave updates about her pregnancy and confided that she was currently staying in Greece with the father of her children. But no, she admitted, they weren't together-together, as she phrased it. They were only being civilised for the sake of things and meeting his family. There was no need to mention the fake engagement that had persuaded her to make the trip under false pretences, she reasoned ruefully. That was entirely her own fault. Aristide had extended the carrot and she had duly bitten.

She dined initially in solitary state that evening, Aristide joining her with apologies halfway through the meal. 'I'm also sorry for what I said earlier,' he added ruefully.

'Why? It was the truth,' Tabby replied with a determined smile.

'It is…and it isn't,' Aristide countered, striving to be more honest.

The urge to slap him surged inside Tabby and she gritted her teeth, refusing to ask for clarity lest it make her seem too desperate for reassurance. She was here to oil the wheels for her children's future visits, to meet the family and let them get to know her. She was *not* here to romance Aristide. Aristide could keep his secrets. His past shouldn't matter to her because it was none of her business.

Aristide wondered how he had contrived to say the wrong thing *again* and he went back to work that evening even though he would've preferred to be with Tabby. When he went to bed, she was already there and asleep, the faint vanilla scent that always clung to her in the air. He lay awake so long resisting the urge to reach for her that he slept in long past his usual rising time. And Tabby was no longer beside him. When he got downstairs, he learned that she had had breakfast early and gone out. He frowned and questioned his security, sunning themselves on the veranda.

'She didn't want anyone with her. She said she fancied a walk.'

'You follow her to protect her even if she doesn't want company,' Aristide instructed and then his phone buzzed and an urgent business query made him turn away.

Tabby walked along the beach all the way into the little town, proud of herself for taking some exercise. When she arrived, though, she knew that she should've carried water with her because she was hot and a little dizzy, scolding herself for not thinking ahead, reminding herself that she needed to be more sensible now that she was pregnant. She walked off the beach, down the side of the taverna and into the front where a shaded terrace functioned as a snack bar. There she found a seat, fanning herself to cool down, and ordered water and a roll to sustain her on her return trip.

It wouldn't be a lie to say that her heart sank below floor level when she spotted Imogen Ross, impossibly tall and resplendent in a pristine flowing white sundress and hat, strolling towards her. Tabby turned her gaze quickly to the server who had returned with her order, keen not to catch Imogen's attention.

'No charge,' the server declared when Tabby persisted in trying to pay.

A frown on her face, Tabby returned her bag to the seat beside her just as Imogen took the seat opposite her. She noticed the server still staring fixedly at the table and, mainly, at Imogen.

'The Romanos family doesn't pay here and that ring on your finger means that you don't have to pay either,' Imogen explained in a tone of superiority.

Tabby wrinkled her nose. 'Not paying makes me uncomfortable.'

'Aristide owns most of the houses and the businesses here. What else would you expect?'

Imogen might be looking fantastic clad in her blinding white linen, glacial blue eyes deceptively languorous, but she reminded Tabby of a poisonous spider getting ready to pounce on prey. Although she had been enjoying the shade, Tabby lifted her bottle and her roll and began to rise to leave.

'Do I scare you that much?' Imogen rested her chin down on the heel of her hand, supremely poised and beautiful. 'Of course, I'm going to speak to you when I see you here. Please, sit down.'

Tabby hesitated and then, feeling foolish as she hovered uneasily, she dropped back into her seat again, her colour rising. 'What do you want from me?' she asked boldly.

'I want you to vanish and stop coming between me and Aristide,' Imogen replied with a pained note in her voice. 'I'm the love of his life and you are nothing but a pale facsimile of me. Have some pride...walk away—'

Another, more familiar masculine voice sounded without warning behind Tabby and made her jump. 'Tabby, I'm so sorry, I was held up.' Demetrius Romanos did indeed sound rather breathless. 'Let me get you into the car where you'll be comfortable,' he urged, reaching down to grab her hand.

'Aren't you even going to speak to me?' Imogen demanded imperiously of the older man.

Demetrius addressed her in low-pitched Greek at length and whatever he said made Imogen pale and look away. With that, he planted a supportive arm to Tabby's spine and walked her out to the classic Morris Minor sparkling with perfect trim and paintwork by the side of the road. 'I'll run you home. I was at the garage to collect a part I'd ordered when the taverna owner called me to tell me that you were here and that Imogen had cornered you.'

In another mood, Tabby would've laughed. All hands on deck and to the rescue, she thought hysterically. *A pale facsimile? The love of Aristide's life?* Admittedly she and Imogen did both have blonde hair and blue eyes, but Tabby's hair *was* paler and even her eyes were a deeper shade. Plus, she reflected without amusement, Imogen was much taller and skinnier as well as being breathtakingly beautiful. Competition? No, of course not, she wasn't entering any competition for a man and if Aristide wanted Imogen he knew where to find her, didn't he?

'Aristide's been looking for you all morning. He drove up and down the coast road in search but it didn't occur to him that you could have walked as far as the town.'

'It's a lovely walk.'

'Yes, but it's hot and you're pregnant,' he scolded in a fatherly tone that couldn't have offended her. 'I warned Imogen not to approach you again. That qualifies as harassment and she's legally bound not to harass any member of the Romanos family—'

'But I'm not a member of your family—'

'Yet,' Demetrius slotted in.

'Legally bound?' she dared to query.

'She caused trouble once before but fortunately she's rarely here. Her grandfather being ill put us all in this situation. Theo's not got long left.' Aristide's father sighed with regret. 'Once he's gone, however, she'll have no reason to return to the island.'

Other than Aristide, Tabby almost quipped, and it was clearly Aristide who was her target and ultimate goal.

'So, Theo, whom you went to visit, is Imogen's grandad?' Tabby gathered.

'Yes, she's his late son's kid. When her mother died, she came here to live with her grandparents. She was twelve and she got into that modelling lark very young—*too* young, I suspect—but her grandparents didn't feel able to deny her the opportunity to make something of herself.'

'Well, she's certainly achieved that. She's world-famous.'

The classic car chugged up the steep driveway and,

seconds later, Aristide stalked out to greet them, lean, strong face clenched taut with fury. 'Where the hell have you been?' he raked down at her from his vantage point on the top step.

'Don't you dare speak to me like that! I'm not a child who went out without permission and got lost!' Tabby fired back at him without hesitation.

Demetrius glanced between them, winced and climbed back into his car. 'See you both soon,' he called, unnoticed by either party, and drove off.

Tabby stalked up onto the veranda.

'I was worried about you!' Aristide exclaimed in his own defence. 'I went looking for you. I started worrying that you'd gone swimming in the sea and got into trouble. I've been frantic!'

'I walked into town.'

'In this heat? Why didn't you take the car?'

'I wasn't sure I'd be able to drive it. It has too many gears,' she complained, 'and I've only driven an automatic.'

'You should've had security with you, at least.'

'The worst thing that happened to me was meeting your ex again,' Tabby recounted, moving into the blessedly cool air-conditioned interior of the villa with a relieved sigh. 'And now I'm tired and I'm going for a nap—'

'How did you run into Imogen?'

'She approached me in the taverna and I'm not repeating anything she said. If there's ever a next time, though, she's getting a bottle of water thrown over her,' she threatened as she stomped up the stairs.

'I'm sorry. You shouldn't have to put up with her nonsense,' Aristide grated. 'She's my past—'

'Who still wants very much to be your present,' Tabby mocked.

'I think she just can't stand the idea of me moving on.'

But he hadn't moved on, had he? Not when he wouldn't even talk about his former fiancée. His father had told her more. He had shared Imogen's family relationship to the ailing fisherman, whom he and Aristide had gone to visit, and the telling fact that the gorgeous blonde had grown up on the island with Aristide. So, childhood sweethearts, Tabby could only assume. Was she right in assuming that Imogen was the woman in his past who had fallen pregnant and miscarried? Tabby was past wanting to know, past trying to talk about what *he* wouldn't talk about.

She reached the bedroom, kicked off her sand-stained canvas shoes and flopped down on the bed, rejoicing in the chill of the bed linen and the cool air.

Aristide strode in, curly black hair tousled as though he had been running his fingers through it, dark eyes fired up with angry defensiveness. 'Eight years ago, after I'd broken off the engagement, Imogen and I signed mutual non-disclosure agreements not to talk about each other. I stuck to the letter of the law with you. I suspect that was a mistake,' he breathed in a raw undertone, knowing that until that moment he had actually never *wanted* to tell anyone about Imogen. What was it about Tabby's angry, defeated aspect that tore at him to such an extent?

'When you actually *know* it was a mistake, let me know,' Tabby muttered tiredly as the phone in her pocket began an incessant ringtone. It was Violet's signature tune and, with a sudden flashing smile, she reached for her phone to answer it.' It's my sister. Can we continue this later?' she pleaded.

Aristide went into grudging retreat, more because she looked tired and drawn than because he wanted to back away. He wasn't doing such a great job of looking after her, he conceded grimly. Twice, she had been exposed to Imogen and had undoubtedly been abused or undermined in some way.

'So,' Violet began, all bubbly and upbeat and oh-so welcome in Tabby's ear, 'you're in Greece and not far away. We're holding a big flashy summer ball the day after tomorrow. Tore has offered to send a helicopter to pick you up—'

'But I've got nothing to wear!' Tabby gasped, her heart soaring at the welcome dream of being reunited with her sister, particularly when she was feeling so low and kind of hopeless about Aristide and his situation in which Imogen loomed large.

'I'll get you a dress. Can you be picked up tomorrow? Then we can have a girls' night before the ball.'

'So I'd be away just two nights?' Tabby chimed, suddenly awash with excitement. 'Yes, I think I could sell that to Aristide… It's not like there's anything much fun happening here. What time?'

The first Aristide knew about the summer ball in Italy was the sight of Tabby racing downstairs very much like an overexcited child, burbling about helicopters and dresses and seeing her sister and niece again. He was shell-shocked by the sudden rage that gripped him and burned like flames on his flesh. Tore freaking Renzetti, barging in with his offer of helicopters and fancy dresses on Aristide's territory.

'I'd only be away two nights,' Tabby bargained. 'You wouldn't miss me because you'd be working anyway.'

Boring old Aristide, slogging away at his laptop, while *his* woman danced the night away in some Renzetti-bought dress with Italian men!

'I will provide the transport and the dress,' Aristide finally cut in, burying the anger before it could betray him. 'And I'll be your partner for the ball.'

Her wide blue eyes widened even more. 'Oh...'

'I wasn't actually invited, was I?' Aristide guessed between clenched teeth.

'No. It wasn't a deliberate omission,' Tabby insisted. 'Violet didn't think. She would never be rude or unkind. Maybe I gave her the wrong impression of you and she thinks you don't go out and don't want to be put to the trouble of entertaining me here. I just feel like a break...'

Forty-eight hours and she needed a break from his private island and his company. Aristide felt as though she had punched him in the chest until he thought about all that had happened since their arrival. He had been a lousy host and a failure as a fiancé, but he fully intended to change that and level the score.

'Away...' Tabby waved an uneasy hand to indicate her need for an escape. 'Away from Imogen and the drama and the bad feeling and the arguments.'

'I'll organise it and arrange for some dresses to be flown over tomorrow for you to try. I've also got some jewellery you could borrow. You'll be the best-dressed woman at the ball,' Aristide declared with confidence. 'But before we go anywhere tomorrow, you ought to have your ultrasound and hopefully we'll find out the gender of our babies—'

Tabby's head was whirling. It had never occurred to her that Aristide would step up to make her dreams come true and wave a metaphorical wand like a sorcerer. She had even thought that that sort of glitzy occasion might not be to Aristide's taste and that he might be thankful to see her leave for a few days.

'It's too soon for the ultrasound again,' she told him. 'You're too impatient. We'll know eventually. It doesn't have to be right *now.*'

'We'll do it when we return, then,' Aristide conceded, although he could have admitted that he had already calculated every relevant date of her pregnancy, but it didn't seem to be the moment to confess that he couldn't wait to see how their twins were developing. 'Phone your sister back and tell her that *I* will bring you to their ball.'

'All right,' she agreed, unable to see how she could possibly dissuade him in their particular circumstances. 'I suppose it might look odd to your family if you let me go alone to something like that…and anyway, you ought to meet Tore, Violet and Belle as they're my family.'

'Do they know about our engagement?' Aristide enquired.

'Yes, but they know it's fake.'

'It's as fake as we want it to be,' Aristide contradicted, making her frown as she tried to work that answer out and came up unsatisfied, wishing that he didn't talk in riddles.

'I thought it was totally for show,' Tabby muttered uncertainly.

'I don't make that kind of commitment for show,' Aristide asserted. 'I brought you here to work out whether or not we could be a real couple.'

Tabby nodded slowly. 'Like a sort of try-before-you-buy trial,' she assumed in a tone of gathering condemnation as her temper began to spark.

Aristide breathed in deep and slow before he spoke in a sudden driven rush. 'Please try to remember that you're dealing with a guy who made the most horrendous error the last time he chose to commit to a woman. Maybe he's been running scared since the moment he met you…'

At that unexpected speech, Tabby gazed up at him in unconcealed amazement and her anger drained away as though it had never been. In that moment, there was something so deep, real and emotional in Aristide's brilliant dark eyes that her heart pounded and her chest tightened. Imogen—the most horrendous error? Yes, she could get behind that opinion.

Running scared? Aristide? Of course, he would be apprehensive about getting seriously involved with a woman again. Afraid of trusting his own judgement, uncertain of what he had probably once been so sure of years earlier when it came to reading a woman's character. Having got it so badly wrong once, he was much more likely to walk the other way when it came to commitment. But it also went unspoken that she had to be the first woman to seriously attract him since Imogen and that was an intoxicating idea. Or was the truth far more prosaic? she wondered. He had got her pregnant. Would she ever have seen or heard from Aristide Romanos again if that hadn't happened? That was a more sobering thought and that fast she wasn't feeling intoxicated by Aristide any more.

'I shouldn't have shouted at you earlier,' Aristide commented over their delicious evening meal served on a deck overlooking the glimmering sea at his father's opulent hotel. 'But I was genuinely afraid that something had happened to you.'

'It's a flat beach and a straight walk into town. What were the chances of anything happening to me?' Tabby countered ruefully.

'Accidents *do* happen.' He shrugged. 'My mother tripped in her heels on the stairs and broke her neck—'

'But nobody could've prevented that,' Tabby reasoned in a pained undertone at that untimely reminder. 'That was a freak accident. Most would sprain an ankle or end up with bruises but they wouldn't die from it. Your mother was very unlucky.'

'How was I to know that you didn't go down to the beach today to swim?' Aristide shot back at her unanswerably. 'You didn't tell anyone where you were going or when you expected to be back.'

'You *didn't* know,' Tabby accepted, irritable at having to make that concession, dropping her blonde head while shooting him an accusing look. 'You just can't let me win an argument, can you?'

'And you can't stand anyone telling you when you're in the wrong,' Aristide completed drily.

That was true but torture wouldn't have persuaded Tabby to admit it to him. He had a mind like a steel trap and unforgiving principles.

'And this is why we're fighting,' she pointed out quietly. 'You like the last word—as do I. You can tell you're an only child. You've never had to compromise with someone different from you. You're a perfectionist. You won't consider human error or oversight as an excuse.'

'But I can change into a more user-friendly version of myself,' Aristide quipped with helpless amusement at the way she had summed him up and delivered her verdict. 'Only it won't happen overnight. It will take practice.'

Tabby stiffened. 'People *don't* change.'

'They mellow when they *have* to. It's the only way to build relationships with others. The art of compromise doesn't come naturally to me, but you know that we will both change when we become parents.'

There was an infuriating truth to that assurance. Instinct warned Tabby that motherhood would rearrange her priorities and alter her outlook. Hadn't she already watched Violet change as she grew into being Belle's mother? She surveyed Aristide, so achingly beautiful even in casual clothing. Even more beautiful *out* of them, a little inner voice reminded her, and she reddened as a flush of inner heat enveloped her entire body. She wasn't about to allow herself to think that way any more about him. That was a victim mentality, wasn't it? To imagine that she had no real choices of her own? And she was determined to choose a path that kept her safe from emotional harm or deep regret and, when it came to Aristide, that meant avoiding temptation and keeping the insanity of crazily good sex out of it.

'You have *another* private jet,' Tabby whispered as she boarded the sleek plane with its black upholstery.

'No, we're borrowing my father's,' Aristide informed her with amusement, watching her pick a seat in a whirl of impatient movement.

A helicopter had transferred them to the private airfield where his father kept his jet. Tabby was clad in loose linen trousers and a floaty pink top, blonde hair restrained to a neat braid down her slender spine, a slick of lip gloss her only concession to cosmetics. He had never known a woman so little concerned with her appearance. She barely glanced in mirrors, selected clothes to wear and pack according to practicality and could choose a ball gown from a rail of fabulous offerings in five minutes flat.

He had assumed she would spend the entire morning choosing her gown and deciding what to pack but she had packed before she came down to breakfast and had contrived to pick her gown for the summer ball before he had even left the room.

'Why are all the dresses some shade of blue?' was the only question she had deigned to ask.

'I love seeing you in blue and I have sapphires for you to wear at the ball—'

'Matchy-matchy. That's kind of controlling behaviour,' she had complained, shooting him a mocking wide-blue-eyed glance, teasing him because it was her favourite colour. 'What if I don't like wearing blue?'

'The next time, I'll take that possibility onboard and give you more of a choice,' Aristide countered without hesitation.

'Have you met my sister's husband before?' Tabby asked, finally settling into her seat opposite him.

'I've never spoken to him but I've seen him at events I've attended.'

'Violet said he's kind of a serious guy.'

'Most titans of industry are...goes with the territory.'

'I can't wait to see Violet,' she confided unnecessarily, her eyes sparkling at the prospect of the coming reunion. 'And Belle. She's walking now. I can't wait to see that either!'

'You like children,' Aristide appreciated.

'I've always liked them. I just didn't expect to have any of my own this side of thirty,' she confided ruefully. 'But I'm not thinking about that any more. It's pointless. I'm pregnant. The babies will eventually arrive and I will get used to the idea of being a young mother. If Violet can adjust to becoming a mum for Belle, so can I.'

CHAPTER EIGHT

AN SUV MET them at the airfield and whisked them to the Villa Renzetti. As Tabby sprang out of the car, a brunette hurtled down the shallow front steps of the imposing property and the sisters collided in a frantic hug on the driveway. They were talking nineteen to the dozen as Aristide left the car to greet their host, Violet's husband, Tore Renzetti.

'You won't see Tabby again until the ball,' Tore forecast, lowering the protesting little girl in his arms, who toddled off in the women's direction. 'Violet was so excited that her twin was coming that she couldn't sleep last night and she has so much to tell her that she was making notes in case she forgot something. I propose that we make our own entertainment. I'll give you a tour of this place and the village and we'll grab a quiet snack somewhere.'

There was a wild flurry of introductions as the sisters realised that they had forgotten their men. Tabby, now clutching the giggling toddler to her chest, gave Aristide an apologetic smile over her shoulder as she followed her sister into the Villa Renzetti.

'This is a fabulous house,' Tabby told her sister as

she scanned the sculptures adorning the classic splendour of the hall.

'Tore's into historic buildings,' Violet told her as she showed her into an inviting library, fired past a formal dining room and confessed that they hadn't yet furnished the drawing room. 'The ballroom is an amazing space and fully restored.'

It was indeed amazing, Tabby agreed as she walked the length of the big room, taking in the carved stone pillars being industriously wound in decorative flower lights for the following night. Caterers were bustling round the bar and buffet niche and she moved out of their path to walk out through one of the line of ornamental doors leading out onto the terrace beyond and into the fresh air. Stepping onto the gleaming tiled floor, where a scattering of pretty table and chair seating areas were being arranged, she walked to the retaining wall to take in the wonderful view. Miles of woodland met her appreciative gaze. Below the villa, she glimpsed the first buildings of the picturesque little village that her sister had mentioned was within walking distance.

'This is idyllic,' she told her twin.

'That's good because you're going to be a frequent visitor here,' Violet warned her. 'Let me show you upstairs to your room.'

'I wasn't quite sure what your preferred sleeping arrangements would be,' her sister admitted awkwardly. 'So I played safe and put you and Aristide in adjoining rooms—'

'No, put him in with me,' Tabby surprised herself by

saying boldly, but, when she thought about it, it made sense because she didn't like Aristide too far away from her. And why was that? And when had she started *feeling* like that? Possessive? Even a tad clingy? Wincing for herself, she reddened as she caught her sister's attention lingering on her.

'You've got attached,' Violet said worriedly.

'Yes...no...well, maybe a little,' Tabby conceded, crossing the beautiful bedroom her sister had prepared for her to take a sniff at the wonderful arrangement of fragrant peonies, lilies and roses in a jug on a table. There were magazines by the bed, a soft throw and a robe and mule slippers at the foot of it. Her heart warmed and lifted at the evidence of her sister's care for her. 'I did bring a dressing gown, you know.'

'Don't believe you. You always pack light and in a rush. So...' Violet paused with a meaningful look. *'Aristide...'*

Tabby froze. 'He's been very good to me. He takes an interest in everything, particularly in my pregnancy, but he's got a nightmare ex who casts a big shadow and screws stuff up between us. It's hard for me to know how I feel because I get so angry with him sometimes—'

'Hold it there,' Violet urged. 'We'll sit in the library. Stella will take Belle. I've got some smashing non-alcoholic rosé on ice ready for you. We'll talk until we're hoarse.'

Down in the cosy library, they curled up in comfortable velvet armchairs and talked behind a firmly closed door. The last thing Tabby wanted was for Aristide to learn that he was a topic of conversation. Snacks arrived and they nibbled and shared joys and grievances alike. They video-called their mother, delighted to see that their parent was feeling well enough to dress up and put some make-up on, and she was equally delighted to see her daughters reunited.

Only when Tabby mentioned the name of Aristide's ex did the atmosphere grow fraught between the sisters.

'Imogen Ross?' Violet repeated that name in unfeigned dismay. 'But she's starring in the fashion show being held before the ball—'

Tabby couldn't believe her ears. '*What*…fashion show?'

'This is a charity event and we have to thoroughly entertain the guests to bring in the numbers,' Violet explained. 'The evening kicks off with a trendy designer showing off her range and Imogen is the leading light of her show. She waived her usual fee for the designer, who's a friend of hers.'

Tabby rolled her eyes. 'My goodness and to think we could've offered her free transport here,' she mocked somewhat bitterly. 'Seat us somewhere at the back.'

'You're the one with the official ring on your finger. Hold your head high,' Violet contradicted. 'He broke up with her and you may not know the details but it was obviously a *bad* break-up if NDAs were required. What do you have to worry about?'

The four of them dined quite late that night, conversation waxing and waning until Tore and Aristide began talking business. Violet and Tabby returned to the library but not before Tabby took Aristide to one side and warned him that Imogen would be featuring in the fashion show. 'I asked Violet to seat us at the back out of sight—'

'No way. This ball is your sister's big night as a hostess and we have nothing to fear from Imogen as long as we stand together. If there's space in the front row, that's where we will be, *not* hiding!' he countered with derision.

Reassured by his adamant attitude, Tabby returned to the library. As the hour grew late, she was constantly stifling yawns, the travel and the excitement too much for her weary body and brain. Around midnight she parted from her twin, but her room was quiet and empty with no sign of Aristide's luggage. She stared at the connecting door between their rooms and sighed. She didn't know whether he had even gone to bed yet. The men had been talking of making a visit to the headquarters of Renzetti Pharma over dinner and she wondered if he had gone there even though it was late. That Aristide and Tore were getting on so well was great, she told herself. And Aristide couldn't be in two places at once, even if she missed him. Even so, she went to bed and slept the moment her head hit the pillow.

'I arranged for a hairstylist to come this afternoon if you want your hair done,' Violet told her over breakfast the next day.

'Lovely,' Tabby replied, but she couldn't hide her surprise.

'This my first official social event with Tore and I

want to be turned out looking as sophisticated as I can,' her sister confided.

'Me too, especially with Imogen due to parade down the catwalk in the hall,' Tabby agreed.

'You have to show me your dress,' her twin carolled.

'It was love at first sight for me when I saw it and it fits like a glove so I decided it was meant for me.'

They took Belle down to the village and browsed the crafts before settling in at the café for more chat. Aristide was down at Renzetti Pharma meeting with some contact of Tore's who was looking for an investor. In the afternoon they went back to the villa to get ready for the ball.

Aristide knocked on the bedroom door, hating that that seemed necessary but, clearly, Tabby must've told her sister that she wanted a separate room and he was sentenced to polite distance whether he liked it or not. In fact, he really, truly did not like being separated from Tabby and he had barely seen her since they had arrived. As Tore had warned, she was preoccupied in catching up with her sister and her niece, their familial affection and closeness a palpable thing.

'Come in...why didn't you use the connecting door?' Tabby asked, a large towel wrapped round her middle, her wet hair concealed by another. Her pale skin, still bearing a damp glisten of moisture, gleamed and her shapely curves beckoned to him like a siren's call.

'What connecting door?' In demonstration, Tabby dragged open a door, only to discover that it did not lead directly into another bedroom but instead to a narrow servant staircase that, going by the dust and cobwebs, appeared disused and forgotten. 'My word, I wonder if Violet knows about this bit. Presumably that door opposite leads into your room.'

Aristide, sleek and dark and sexy in a black business suit, stepped past her to investigate and opened the door opposite to confirm that it was, indeed, his room. 'I didn't intend to disturb you, but I wanted to give these to you to wear tonight.' He passed her a large worn jewellery box. 'These belonged to my mother.'

'Didn't your father give them to your stepmother?' she asked in surprise.

'No, they're heirlooms from my mother's side of the family and they came to me.'

Tabby walked over to the window to sit down and open the box. A breathtaking river of large stunningly blue sapphires greeted her admiring gaze. The drop earrings were equally remarkable. 'These are antique.'

'They are. There wasn't time to have them reset.'

'They're fabulous just as they are. Are you sure you want me to wear them?' Tabby pressed uncomfortably. 'I'm not your wife.'

'I'm lending them to you for the sake of appearances.' Aristide downplayed his generosity with characteristic coolness, not encouraging her to read too much into the gesture.

'Thank you. They're absolutely gorgeous,' she said warmly, appreciative eyes skimming over his lean, strong face. The silence lagged, the atmosphere building as his brilliant dark golden eyes shimmered. He took a step forward.

And then a knock sounded on her door. It was the

hairstylist and Tabby bid a harried, reluctant goodbye to Aristide before rushing off to pull on clothes.

Feeling flat out dissatisfied by that untimely interruption, Aristide departed again. And then he wanted to kick himself because he had also sought Tabby out to tell her about Imogen in advance of the fashion show but had somehow neglected to even open that conversation with her. He cursed, aware that his own reluctance to relive those years of blindness and betrayal consistently held him back from any desire to share the gory details.

A couple of hours later, Tabby was dressed, groomed far beyond her usual level and feeling as good as she could feel in advance of watching Imogen Ross star as the leading light on the temporary catwalk sat up in the vast hall.

Her dress was midnight blue, saved from being mistaken for black by the iridescent fabric that caught the light with tiny glimmers of green, purple and blue. It bared her shoulders and much of her slender back, cupping her full breasts and skimming her tummy, which was developing a pronounced curve. On her feet she wore high-heeled toning sandals and round her neck and dangling from her ears she sported the breathtaking sapphire combination, her hair swept up to show off her jewellery. Violet was wearing a ravishing golden sheath that enhanced her diminutive slenderness and a stunning diamond necklace glittered at her throat.

The fashion show was fun, typically full of outrageous garments that only a long-legged adolescent could have worn with panache. But here and there were little gems to be seen in the cut of a sleek red cocktail dress and a fabulous summer raincoat. Tabby tensed when Imogen strode down the catwalk towards them, flashing her spectacular smile. And she could see right there and then why Imogen was so famous because even the weird outfit she wore looked fabulous on her perfect body.

Aristide expelled his breath on a slow hiss and leant closer to Tabby to declare, 'I first met her when I was fifteen. She was seventeen and already well known. I fell for her like a ton of bricks.'

'I imagine she was incredibly beautiful at that age,' Tabby muttered, looking at Imogen all those years on, still in full possession of her glorious looks.

'I changed my whole life to see more of her,' he admitted in a gruff undertone. 'I was at boarding school in England and I insisted on moving to one in Paris. I saw her every weekend and holiday for five years—'

'You were besotted,' Tabby whispered, grateful that he was finally talking to her but rather wishing he had chosen a better setting. 'Of course, you were.'

'I believed everything she told me, even when the story didn't fit. I ditched my critical thinking and intelligence. I was like a puppet on a string, providing the yacht holidays, the fancy hotels and the designer wardrobe, not to mention the photo opportunities she craved.'

'Why the self-hatred?' Tabby chided as the show took a break and refreshments were handed around.

'Because I should've known better. I grew up with women of that ilk, some of whom were my father's girlfriends, and yet I still didn't recognise those traits in her,' Aristide bit out, his lean, hard features grim.

Tabby skated a fingertip down a lean, strong thigh in reproof. 'Oh, stop beating yourself up about it,' she urged softly. 'Being young is supposed to be all about making mistakes and learning from them.'

'I may have been a fool for love once...but I will never be again,' Aristide framed in a harsh undertone.

'My goodness, you take mistakes too seriously,' Tabby told him briskly. 'You were very young and you idealised her and naturally you put her on a pedestal. I imagine you were the envy of all your friends with her on your arm and that your ego made you ignore the stories that didn't quite fit.'

Aristide dealt her a frustrated glance as if her relaxed attitude on such a subject was foreign to him. 'I trashed my relationship with my father over her.'

'And you both got over it and moved on, but now it's time to move on past the *whole* experience,' Tabby countered gently. 'You're such a perfectionist, Aristide, and you set too high standards for yourself. You were fifteen, you were still a kid when you made those choices, not an adult.'

'What mistakes did you make at fifteen?'

'I dyed my hair pink and it didn't suit me. Mum was furious and my school complained. I chose to study maths because I was good at it, not because I wanted to work in that field. I fell for the boy next door but he couldn't take his eyes off my sister even though *she* didn't know he was alive—'

'So, nothing came of it,' Aristide gathered.

'No, I grew out of him, got a crush on an actor instead. I think your problem likely was that you were a rich, probably spoiled and quite indulged kid, who had the freedom to make life-changing choices at too young an age,' she admitted. 'I didn't have those options and so my mistakes stayed small and relatively risk free.'

'At heart, you're very sensible and steady in a crisis,' Aristide remarked reflectively. 'You'll be a wonderful mother to our children.'

Just as the show kicked off again and the music fired up, Tabby looked at him and her heart pounded at the hot golden shimmer in his gorgeous eyes as they rested on her parted lips. The tip of her tongue sneaked out to moisten the sudden dryness there and with a muffled groan he reached for her, plunging his mouth down hungrily on hers. The teasing dance of his tongue against hers sent a red-hot burning shiver from her core up through her in a heated wave. A faint gasp was wrenched from her and she pulled back, her heart hammering inside her chest, her face flaming with mortified colour.

'You have no idea how much I want you at this moment,' Aristide growled in her ear before he leant back again.

And he had no very clear idea of how much she wanted him, Tabby thought ruefully, the heart of her burning, making her press her thighs together as if she could quell that wild craving. She reddened even more when she collided with her sister's amused smile and turned her attention back to the show's evening-wear selection.

The showpiece of the night was Imogen in her most unlikely wedding gown, a sort of goth-schoolgirl dress that bared her legs, those glossy brown pins of hers wrapped in ribboned white high heels. She looked spectacularly sexy, if not bridal, and the cameras flared and flashed all around them to capture her glamorous image. Her attention, however, landed repeatedly on Aristide, as if she was expecting to claim his attention, but Aristide was chatting away to Tore and looking nowhere near his former fiancée. And in that moment, Tabby's jealous insecurity fell away as if it had never been. She finally saw that Imogen might want Aristide back but Aristide was no longer interested. And though she might never hear the full story of their relationship, she no longer cared.

They moved as a party into the ballroom to allow the staff to return the hall to normal. As the music started up, Aristide tugged her beneath his arm. 'Now, at least, I can hold you close without exciting comment.'

He walked her onto the dance floor.

'There's nobody dancing yet!' she hissed in protest.

'*So?*' Aristide countered in challenge mode.

'I can't dance very well…people will notice,' she muttered shamefacedly.

Gazing to the side of his tall, powerful frame, she glimpsed Imogen beginning to strut her stuff on the floor, clad in something short, silver and very sparkly, a tall, older man in a smart dinner jacket matching her step for step. They were doing salsa or something, Tabby registered uncertainly.

'Who cares?' Aristide fielded, single-minded as usual.

'I care.'

'But why?' he replied unanswerably. 'You don't know anyone but your sister and husband here.'

'And she who shouldn't be named,' she muttered ruefully. 'She can dance too.'

'Ignore her... I do,' he said very drily.

She shuffled around the floor in the protective circle of his arms, drinking in the evocative scent of his skin, salt and musk and a hint of citrus in the combination. Slowly she closed her eyes, feeling him shift against her, realising that he was aroused and probably very much not up for any salsa dancing. That secret knowledge turned her on. Imogen was in the room and he wasn't looking in the blonde's direction and he wasn't craving her either. No, Tabby was the focus of his desire.

She shifted against him, rather suggestively. 'You're... er—'

Aristide laughed, unholy amusement brightening his gleaming gaze. 'Of course. I've been in that state since the first moment I laid eyes on you in that dress. You look dazzling in it.'

'Thanks...'

And they danced and they mingled and had some supper before gravitating out to the freshness of the terrace, where the air cooled Tabby's overheated body. She breathed in deep, appreciating the faint chill on her exposed skin.

'I swore I wasn't going to ask but, er...what happened with Imogen and you at the end?'

Aristide grimaced. 'It was nasty. She told me she

was pregnant and we got engaged. We set the wedding date and then my father came to see me. He was very upset and told me that I needed to get a DNA test done before I married her. She was the love of my life,' he bit out in a raw undertone. 'He told me that there had always been rumours that there were other men in her life but I was furious and I refused to believe him—'

'And that's when you had the big fight,' she guessed, wretched on his behalf that he had had so much faith in the woman he loved and had then had to live with the knowledge that he had been wrong in his every assumption.

'Yes. Initially I did nothing but my father's conviction that her child was not mine played on my mind. I lied to her for the first time,' he admitted uncomfortably. 'I told her that I needed a DNA test to ensure my child's inheritance rights and she insisted that she couldn't agree to one. That only made me more suspicious. I had her investigated and, sure enough, my father's convictions were proven. I confronted her. She lied and lied. Eventually she lost her temper and came clean. It wasn't my child and she already knew that, however she needed a husband for the squeaky-clean advertising campaign that was making her so much money. She couldn't be pregnant and unmarried without risking losing the contract. I was simply...the fall guy. When I heard she'd miscarried some weeks later, I felt sad for all of us because at one time I had believed that child was mine.'

'I'm so sorry,' she mumbled, ashamed that she had pressed him. He must've been devastated by the discovery that his idol had had feet of clay throughout their relationship, that she had never really loved him back or been worthy of his trust.

'It's a long time ago but it screwed me up for a few years. I found it impossible to trust any woman,' he acknowledged tautly as he reached for her hand, his thumb stroking her slender wrist. 'Now can we sneak off and have sex in a broom cupboard or, indeed, any place? I'm feeling pretty desperate, *angelos mou*...'

'Er...' Mouth running dry at those images, Tabby stammered, not quite knowing what to say, wanting to agree but nervous of being seen or reported on and embarrassing her sister.

'Forget it for now,' Aristide advised on the back of a sigh. 'Your twin is making signals from the door. Obviously she wants to speak to you about something.'

Tabby walked indoors again with Aristide's arm wound round her like an anchor keeping her safe while she tried not to dwell on all that he had told her and all that she had deduced from what he had not said. It was enormously upsetting to finally have the confirmation that she had not been the first woman in Aristide's life to announce an unplanned pregnancy. Everything that had happened between them suddenly swam into clearer light from his angry, defensive outburst that first night when her contraception had let them down to his controlled and measured response to her eventual announcement. And yet, he had not once asked *her* to go for a DNA test to prove that her children were also his...

'What's wrong?' Tabby asked the instant she glimpsed her twin's deeply troubled face.

'You're not going to believe it but... Dad's here—'

'What?' Tabby exclaimed in disbelief.

Violet grasped her arm and drew her closer. 'Over by the bar wearing a loud blue velvet dinner jacket. He arrived as the guest of one of our VIPs, Mrs Soames. He's staying in her home. Apparently this week he's teaching an art class in Florence...'

'Oh, my word,' Tabby groaned, having turned pale at the news of her father's presence.

Aristide glanced across the ballroom to pick out the black-haired older man beside the bar. He bore not the smallest resemblance to Tabby. He was small, with Violet's darker colouring and a rather heavily lined and dissipated face.

'Our father, Sam Blessington,' Violet supplied. 'Artiste extraordinaire. A drunk, a wastrel and a wife beater. He's a horrible man. Tore wanted to ask him to leave but we don't want to offend Mrs Soames, who runs the charity we're raising funds for tonight.'

'Does he know that this is your home?' Tabby prompted.

'I'm sure he does. This is hardly his sort of event but he's always keen to follow the smell of money and he must be broke right now if he's teaching an art class—'

'He can hardly expect any help from you,' Tabby responded. 'Just pretend you don't see him—'

'He won't allow us to get away with that. He likes attention. He won't let us ignore him,' Violet replied heavily. 'And if we try to, he'll cause a scene and there are a lot of journalists here tonight.'

'You can't let him blackmail us into letting him stay,' Tore said from behind his wife.

But even as her brother-in-law spoke, an almost forgotten oily male voice sounded behind them and Sam Blessington pushed forward to confront Violet with a sneering smile. 'Well, isn't this a surprise? I wasn't expecting to hear that my younger daughter is currently living in Italy with her new husband and within a few miles of where I'm currently staying—'

As Violet almost cowered, bad memories of their childhood clearly engulfing her, Tabby stepped forward, but Tore had already dropped a controlling hand down on her father's plump shoulder to steer the older man towards the door. 'Let's take this conversation somewhere more private,' he suggested calmly.

Tore directed their small party into the dining room at the back of the hall. 'Now, how may we help you?' he asked politely. 'I understand that you've neither seen nor spoken to your daughters since they were fourteen years old.'

'Then it's clearly past time for us to become reacquainted,' Sam Blessington declared, not one whit embarrassed by the truth that he had abandoned both his daughters as soon as he could. 'Particularly now when I'm going through a bit of a rough patch and could use a helping hand—'

'Not from us,' Violet sliced in thinly, lifting her chin. 'We owe you nothing.'

'We don't,' Tabby agreed, standing tall even as her father regarded her with unhidden distaste and resentment.

'You were always a bitch even as a little girl, taking

your mother's side, answering back, refusing to give me the respect I was due—'

'Perhaps that was because you were beating up her mother...and *her*,' Aristide murmured without any expression at all.

'I think it's time for you to leave,' Tore interposed icily.

A crude expletive escaped Sam Blessington. Obviously drunk and out of control, he rounded on Tabby, cruel fingers biting into her arm as he gripped her and shook her violently while he screamed invective in her face. And the next moment, a shocking hush fell and her vicious father was lying flat on the floor, silenced and left unconscious by a punch. Tabby stared down at his prone body in disbelief. Aristide had moved so fast to silence her inebriated parent that he had simply blurred out of focus as he stepped between her and the older man to free her.

Tore opened the door to signal an employee and returned to them with a serene smile. 'I'll have him driven home to Mrs Soames' villa. He was embarrassing her earlier and she'll be relieved to be free of him for an evening,' he surmised. 'I imagine that she's already regretting her invitation for him to stay with her.'

Pale as milk, Tabby turned to look at Aristide. 'You *hit* him—'

His lean, hard-boned face was taut, his dark golden eyes glittering. 'Yes. I would've preferred not to but he was in no condition to be reasoned with and I could not allow him to continue assaulting you or to cause you further distress,' he confessed in a roughened low voice.

'Thank you for stopping him,' Violet said shakily.

'Yes, that was done very neatly and quietly,' Tore interposed with approval.

But Tabby was still in shock at the knowledge that for the first time in her life someone had protected her from her father and he had done it without fanfare. Yet Aristide had had to employ violence, which she abhorred because the memories of her abusive childhood still haunted her in low moments: all the times she had tried and failed to safeguard her mother, the injuries they had both sustained during her father's assaults, the sick terror of knowing that nobody could stop him and that he wouldn't stop until he ran out of rage.

'I'm sorry about that,' Aristide reiterated as he guided her out of the room and across the hall to the ballroom, which was now heaving with dancing and chattering guests. 'I know how you feel about that sort of thing.'

'Let's go out onto the terrace again,' she whispered unsteadily. 'I need fresh air—'

'And perhaps some food?' Aristide said hopefully. 'You're very pale, in shock from that horrible confrontation. In fact I asked your sister if there was a doctor amongst the guests this evening—'

'Oh, for goodness' sake, I'm fine,' Tabby said defensively.

Aristide laced her fingers into his to raise her arm where angry purple bruises were already becoming visible. 'No, you're not fine and why should you be? That man is your worst nightmare and you never expected to see him again.'

Breathing in deep, Tabby dropped down into a comfortable seat on the terrace and he left her to bring her some food. A split second later, Violet dropped into the seat beside hers and gripped her hand. 'Are you OK?' she gasped. 'I'm so sorry. Everyone but Aristide just froze when Dad grabbed you. I wasn't expecting that but I should've done. Of course he always reserved the worst for you. You were always standing up to him—'

'*Trying* to,' Tabby corrected. 'That's why he hates me a little bit more.'

'I was like a little mouse around him, like Mum. I always hated myself for being so weak—'

'You weren't weak, you were understandably scared—'

'And tonight it was just like I was five years old again. I was terrified and I *froze*,' Violet groaned.

'He's gone,' Tabby soothed. 'And I doubt if he'll come back to visit.'

'Tore wished he had been the one to hit him but he was in shock. I hadn't warned him just how bad Dad could be—'

'Don't talk about it,' Tabby urged as Aristide reappeared and the fast beat of her heart steadied, her heart surging with sudden warmth and appreciation because he had sheltered her, even knowing that she would judge him for utilising force to intervene.

Aristide set out the food and she picked at it to please him because, in reality, she had little appetite. But the food and the tea took away the hollow feeling in her tummy and she began to relax again. The crisis, such as it had been, was over and she didn't want to make a fuss. He kept on checking her forearm, where deep purple bruising showed the indent of her father's fingers. 'I think we should get this cleaned up,' he said.

'No, the skin's not broken,' she protested, wishing he would forget the whole ghastly embarrassing scene that he had witnessed. 'Let's go and dance.'

Open surprise showed in his appraisal. She bore adversity well, Aristide reflected, made little of it, hated to be fussed over and yet that was all he wanted to do, along with wrapping her up in cotton-wool layers to ensure that nobody could ever hurt her again. He was still seething that the mother of his unborn children had been assaulted and denigrated before his eyes and that he himself had failed to see that more than a verbal attack was imminent. Sam Blessington, a man who had never learned how to control his temper, had bullied and victimised his wife and daughters until they had finally escaped his abuse.

Tabby drifted round the edge of the floor, calm in the circle of Aristide's arms. He smelled of wintry woods, crisp and clean and oh-so sexy and every time his thigh moved against hers, awareness flooded her and sent a delicious little shiver burrowing up through her.

'Was your father always like that?' Aristide asked.

'Grasping about money, yes. Violent when life goes against him, which it must be at the moment. I think he married Mum because her father was wealthy and he assumed he'd be a good bet but my grandfather was no fool and he refused to give him a penny. My father has a sell-out exhibition, spends all his money on the high life and then ends up broke again. He doesn't keep friends or girlfriends. He always turns on them and, unlike my mother, they don't take it. But give him a few months and he'll start painting again and reclaim his fame and his earnings. It's always boom or bust with him, nothing in between. Let's not talk about him any more,' she urged ruefully. 'I want to forget about him—'

'And your wish, *angelos mou*,' Aristide husked in her ear as he lifted his head to look down at her, 'should be my command.'

As her gaze clashed with shimmering golden eyes, her heart started pounding hard inside her and a heated liquidity surged at her core. 'Then take me upstairs,' she whispered softly and she didn't have to ask him twice.

CHAPTER NINE

THE MINUTE TABBY'S bedroom door was closed, she crowded him back against it and stretched up over his glorious big powerful body to find his mouth for herself.

And the ferocious hunger that engulfed her was nothing she had ever expected to feel but it was there burning through her like a brand, driving her on. The taste of him, heaven knew, she *loved* the taste of him. He tasted like a banquet after she had been starving, the heat of the sun after an endless dark night. She couldn't get enough of the hungry glide of his tongue and the soft yet hard sealing satisfaction of his mouth.

Her hands sank into his silky black hair, tugging on it before dropping to his shoulders. He was wearing far too many clothes. She tugged at the jacket with impatient fingers and it dropped away just as she wrenched at his bow tie and embarked on shirt buttons.

'You want me,' Aristide purred. 'You *really* want me…'

'Pretty obvious, that, isn't it?' Tabby gasped, shaken by her own bold behaviour.

'No. The first time we were together, you were so restrained that I felt like a trial you had decided you had to undergo. Initially, I didn't understand your attitude, not until I realised that I was your first. But this is the very *first* time you have fully accepted the attraction between us and matched it...'

'Well, if you must be pedantic about it,' Tabby acknowledged defensively, not entirely happy to have put herself out there to such an extent.

'As much as you resemble an angel, you are also my little witch and the sexiest woman I've ever met,' Aristide growled with driven fervour as he claimed her parted lips with powerful hunger.

And the room fell away from her. In fact she felt as though, in a sudden move, she was being wrenched from her own protective skin and thrown into a new reality where she could shamelessly declare her own wants and needs as she never had before. And she would be secure in the knowledge that Aristide would deliver exactly what she wanted. His shirt fell away, leaving her free to spread explorative, worshipping hands over the bronzed expanse of his muscular, hair-roughened torso.

A groan was wrenched from Aristide and suddenly he was lifting her away, turning her round, lean fingers cool against her spine as he unhooked and unzipped her dress and it fell away in a splash of glittering darkness to her feet. She reached up to detach her bra, which an ambidextrous octopus would have struggled to remove, so devoted was it to upholding her pregnancy swollen breasts. He lifted her deftly out of her abandoned clothing and deposited her on the bed, standing back from her with scorching dark eyes while he shed socks, shoes and shirt and, finally, the narrow-cut trousers doing nothing to hide his arousal from her.

More daring now, particularly after being labelled the sexiest woman a notorious playboy had ever met, she slid back off the bed and dropped to her knees, peeling away the boxers and finding him with her hands, her tongue and her lips, listening to his breathing quicken and rasp in his lungs as she sought to give him the same pleasure he had given her. Long fingers settled on her head, guiding her, encouraging her. And then with a roughened, wordless plea he brought an end to her attentions and swept her up to return her to the bed with the sworn assurance that he had no intention of climaxing until he was deep inside her.

Her body tingled at the words, the heart of her already slick and desperately ready for him. She had never been as aroused in her life as she was in the moment he came over her and flipped her round onto her stomach and then up onto her knees. Almost simultaneously he moved behind her to find her tender exposed flesh with his mouth, his tongue and his carnal fingers. A low keening cry of arousal was dragged from her. Every touch he gave her only ratcheted up her tension and her ever growing need for more.

And then he was finally where she wanted him to be, pushing in, forcing her open, her inner sheath stretching to take him as he thrust forward with a growl of impatience that matched her own. From that instant of perfect fullness there was nothing but the wild thump of her heartbeat and the ever rising surge of excitement as he gave her exactly what she craved. Firm hands on her hips, he pounded into her and as she reached the pinnacle of her climax she threw her head back and cried out loud in ecstasy as the blissful release gripped her and roared through her trembling body to leave her slumped on the bed.

'You're always the first to leave the party,' Aristide complained, turning her over and coming down to her, sliding between her thighs and driving into her again with tender confidence.

And in the midst of the aftershocks of that initial orgasm, he taught her that she could still want more. Throughout, smouldering dark golden eyes held hers and it was an amazingly intimate experience to meet his gaze while the flexing power of his lean, powerful body shifted over hers and, ultimately, he surged inside her as he too attained release and groaned out his satisfaction.

In the aftermath, pleasure still lingering within her like an addictive drug, she was surprised when he continued to hold her close. She breathed in the scent of his skin with the sudden jarring acknowledgement that she had never been happier in her life and had never felt more at home. And that was the definitive moment that it became clear to her that she had contrived to fall in love with Aristide Romanos, the father of the twins she carried. She had thought herself safe and far beyond such emotional fantasies and yet Aristide was here and the more she saw of him, literally the more she wanted of him.

He splayed a big, possessive hand across her no longer flat belly and her heart sank a little because she didn't want to be snuggled only because she was the future mother of his children. She was much more keen to be held close and savoured because he wanted her and *only* her as a woman and a partner. But you couldn't have everything, she reminded herself stoically, already far too used to a world in which she had never received what she truly wanted.

Was she supposed to settle into being Aristide's occasional lover whenever he took the notion? Or was what they had actually heading towards a genuine destination? Possibly even a destination where the attraction between them would eventually fizzle out? She supposed that only time would tell.

After all, wasn't she on a trial to see if she could become a part of *his* concept of the perfect couple? Funny how it hadn't yet occurred to him that if she was on trial, *he* was as well. Strange how it hadn't crossed his mind that telling her he would only be a fool for love *once* was off-putting, rather than being a vote winner with the average woman. Who didn't want to be loved?

Imogen had been a user, enjoying his wealth, looks and influence and all the extras those attributes had brought her. But Tabby was different, very different. Even if Aristide lost all his money and power, she would still want him. After all, what she had never had, she couldn't lose or miss. No, she wanted Aristide for the fierce emotion and intensity he kept caged up inside him and was already showing towards the children she had conceived. He had so much to offer but he wasn't yet offering it to *her*.

Everything he had given Tabby was temporary or

fake. Like their engagement and the jewellery she had worn at the ball. He was tender, caring and committed when it came to the children she carried but what about *her*? She needed *more* than lust, consideration and kindness. She was way too young to settle for anything less. And she wasn't about to change simply because she had fallen inconveniently pregnant to her one and only one-night stand. Or because she had fallen head over heels for him.

No, she wasn't going to be the adoring or slavish idiot who loved the unattainable guy regardless of whether or not he returned her feelings. She would sooner be alone and in little more than ten days she would *be* alone again, she reminded herself doggedly, back home in Violet's little flat and running the bakery. A return to normal life and the *real* world, she told herself, a first taste of being single and pregnant with nobody but her own family to fuss over her. It would do her good.

'I wish you didn't have to leave,' Violet lamented over breakfast.

'You knew I would only be here two nights. I'll see you next time you're in London,' Tabby declared with determined cheer.

'Only a couple of weeks until then,' Tore pointed out helpfully.

'But those will just be fleeting visits,' Violet sighed. 'We're thinking that we'll make this house our home base, particularly with Tore's grandparents and the Renzetti HQ nearby. It's the only move that makes sense.'

Aristide watched Tabby's face fall before she managed a smile to hide her dismay that her twin would be making her permanent home outside the UK. If he stayed with Tabby, he foresaw that it would be a necessity to buy a property in the same area but such a thought was very premature, he told himself impatiently. He was not prepared to redraft his entire future over the truth that she would be the mother of his children.

In addition, the three of them were barking mad if they imagined that Tabby would be back living in London in ten days' time. Aristide had never planned for her to return to her former life, scratching her living in that grubby little apartment while listening to customer complaints with a sympathetic smile. His care and protection of his unborn twins had begun the moment he was made aware of their conception and it naturally extended to Tabby's living and working arrangements. He didn't want her to work. He didn't want her tired or struggling alone while missing out on the best possible medical attention. That wasn't going to happen, he swore to himself. Her health and that of their twins were the top priority.

Tabby was damp-eyed parting from her sister and her niece. She and her twin had had long enough to thoroughly enjoy themselves but not quite long enough to cover all they longed to discuss in sufficient detail. Violet had recalled how weepy her late friend, Isabel, had been in the early months of her pregnancy with Belle and Tabby's brimming hormones seemed to be sending her down a similar road of emotional overload.

Her eyes had even flooded with tears while Belle was watching a sad moment in a cartoon.

'You'll see your sister again soon,' Aristide informed her bracingly. 'I'll organise it but for the rest of your stay on the island, we're going to relax.'

'I've got no objection to that.'

'You like it on Anthos, don't you?'

'I'm not sure I'd like it the same in winter. I'm used to a bit of bustle around me.'

'I have many other properties in livelier destinations.'

Tabby had no idea why he assumed she would be interested in the contents of his property portfolio. But he linked his hand with hers as he was ushering her back onto his father's private jet and her heart swelled with warmth inside her when he kept her anchored to him as they sat down. But while she was in love with him, he was not in love with her. She couldn't afford to forget those facts. She needed to protect herself. She recalled the wildness of their intimacy the night before and an inner flush of heat turned her pink as she inexorably relived certain moments, wondering if the sheer pleasure he gave her was normal, or if indeed she was somewhat oversexed. After all, she could barely look at Aristide's lean, hard features or meet those stunning eyes of his without thinking about what it was like when he touched her—*electrifying*.

Forty-eight hours later, Tabby had the ultrasound, which was done at the doctor's surgery in the village. The latest technology had been specially flown in for the occasion and was being gifted to the surgery, courtesy of Aristide. Her eyes stung like mad when she glimpsed the incredibly real 4D imagery of her babies. One was a boy, the other thought to be a girl. Aristide was fascinated, dark golden eyes ablaze with strong emotion.

'This makes them so real,' he said.

'But you do know that the gender is only a guess because it's still too early to be sure,' she reminded him.

'I read the small print just like you did.'

'We should've waited a little longer to have it done,' she reiterated.

'Why? They'll be here in little more than six months. We need to get ready for them. Rooms furnished, toys, staff hired,' Aristide counted out, galvanised by the concept of useful activity.

'They won't be needing their own rooms to start out. They'll be sleeping in the same room as me,' Tabby informed him calmly. 'A night nurse would be helpful the first few weeks but there will be no need for actual *staff*.'

Aristide breathed in deep and slow and opted to say nothing.

'Of course, I expect you were mostly raised by nannies,' she guessed.

'Yes. My father travelled round his hotels, which are all over Europe. He had no choice.'

'Well, I'm unlikely to be travelling very often.'

They dined that evening at his father's farmhouse and she got the official tour of Aristide's childhood home. Unlike Aristide's giant barn of a house, this one exuded warmth, atmosphere and comfort. Yes, sleek sophistication ruled in every corner of Aristide's imposing mansion, along with some very modern art, but it was not, by any stretch of the imagination, a *home*. Every choice Aristide had made screamed rich single male and the latest technology.

'Feel free to make changes to my house here,' Aristide told her calmly.

'I wouldn't feel right doing that,' Tabby replied, even though she was bursting with ideas to improve the ambience. What they had was temporary and it wasn't her place to change anything within his home. 'It's not my house and my taste wouldn't be relevant.'

'It's the interior decorator's taste, not mine. I didn't need to be part of that process.'

The next morning was Imogen's grandfather's funeral and Aristide attended with his father. Andy had shown Tabby some pottery she had bought at an art gallery in town and she suggested they visit it some day. One day wended into the next seamlessly and Tabby relaxed again. Her morning sickness had dwindled and she stopped taking tablets to control it. Her appetite returned once she was no longer nauseous.

'I'm inviting some friends to join us on the yacht and we'll island-hop for a few days,' Aristide informed her.

'I didn't know that you had a yacht—'

'It's chartered out most of the time. I haven't taken a lot of time off work the last few years but that'll have to change when I become a family man,' Aristide remarked.

'You won't really be a family man. The children won't be living with you,' Tabby pointed out. 'Although

I expect they'll come for longer visits once they're a little older.'

Aristide shrugged a broad bronzed shoulder. 'We can live together—'

Tabby tensed and paled at the casual manner in which that invitation landed on her. Loving him made her very vulnerable and she had to be careful so that she didn't get too badly hurt. His whole approach was too casual to persuade her that he was serious. 'No. We're not drifting into some weird, loose live-in relationship just because I'm pregnant,' she warned him. 'I'm having these babies and getting on with my life.'

Aristide dealt her a startled, searching glance from shrewd dark eyes. 'I rather thought we'd moved beyond those boundaries.'

'No, this is just a holiday, not my real life,' she stated with conviction. 'I have to get back to my own life.'

'As long as you accept that that life includes me,' Aristide responded with studied mildness of tone, although he was not remotely as blasé about her answer as he was pretending. What did she mean about her *own* life? Did she mean she was planning to go back to dating other men? She was rather firmly rejecting his ideas. He had never asked a woman to live with him before! Didn't she appreciate what a major commitment that would be for him? No, she had just breezed on past the suggestion as if it hadn't happened, utterly dismissing it. He would've liked to go into the topic more deeply right there and then but a glimpse of the anxious tension etched into her small face dissuaded him from persisting just at that moment.

'We'll have a great time on the yacht,' he forecast soothingly, backing off. He was a terrific negotiator and he knew when to push and when to soft-pedal.

He wondered what was going on with her, wondered grimly if he should've put the whole business of his becoming a parent in his lawyers' hands. Should he have made it business rather than letting emotions get in the way? Legal advice would've given him guidelines. He knew his lawyers would disapprove of the actions he had so far taken: putting a ring on her finger, fake engagement or otherwise, bringing her to Anthos, letting his family get to know her. All of that was serious stuff.

It was true that he had done the same thing once before with Imogen but that had been at the point of a gun, when he had offered marriage even though he had felt far too young to make such a huge decision, only that very thought had seemed wrong, cruel and irresponsible when he had believed she was already expecting his baby.

Aristide was even more passionate than usual that night and Tabby submersed herself in the passion and refused to think about anything serious because she was so angry with him. As if she would simply move in casually with him because she was pregnant! That wasn't for her, that would never be for her. He had to want her for *her*, not for the babies inside her. She didn't want to stray into a live-in relationship with Aristide that then broke down because it was only a fleeting notion on his part. It infuriated her that Aristide did not see her as having choices when, in reality, she had nothing but choices to make.

The next morning, she was surprisingly calm over breakfast on the veranda overlooking the cove. And there out to sea in deeper water sat a very large, opulent white yacht that was all sweeping decks and layers. 'Is that it?' she asked.

'Yes, my friends won't be arriving until the weekend so we'll have a few days alone first.'

'And then I'll be going home and all this...' she spread her arms in an expansive gesture that embraced the deep blue water washing the sandy shore below them, the fabulous house behind them and the yacht anchored in the cove '...all this will seem like a beautiful dream.'

Of course, it was different for Aristide because Anthos was home to him. But Tabby loved simply being with Aristide. He had so much power over her emotions that it frightened her. Didn't he realise that what they had found together was rare?

The following five days were a whirlwind of activity. She had packed with greater care than usual and at a slower speed, not wishing to find herself underdressed or missing anything once they were on the yacht. *Sea Breeze* was every bit as luxurious as it had looked from shore.

They sailed to Corfu, where Aristide took her shopping, strolling old cobblestoned streets between the historic Venetian buildings. She wore a classic cream sundress and the heat seemed to seep into her very bones, stealing her tension, making her work even harder to suppress the fact that soon she would be leaving the man she had recklessly fallen in love with. The day after that they landed on Rhodes, visited some ancient ruins and lunched in the medieval old town in a shaded garden. He insisted on buying her a new watch in a very upmarket shop where he was waited on as though he were royalty. The jewels on the face shone with blinding glitter in the sunshine that flooded the hotel room where he took her to literally ravish her in the late afternoon.

The uncontrollable hunger between them had not abated one little bit, in fact she thought it might be addictive so that surrendering to that overpowering desire once only made it easier to do again the next time it struck. It was like living a dream to have Aristide all to herself and to be the sole focus of his attention. As long as she didn't look into her empty future she was deliriously happy while she was still with him.

On Crete they walked the Venetian city walls, revelling in the fantastic views. On Santorini they watched a spectacular sunset and dined in a cliffside village where the views made her dizzy but the food melted in her mouth. It was idyllic and she was enjoying every moment of their time together. The boundaries between what was fake and what was real in their engagement seemed to have magically melted away.

But then she had deliberately let go of those boundaries. She had decided to make the most of their last week together and forget that theirs was a temporary arrangement. She had made the most of her happiness and his and would leave awash with wonderful memories.

On the fifth day Aristide's friends arrived, a married

couple in their thirties, an Italian industrialist and his wife. Both were charming and great fun. They landed on Mykonos, lay on the beach and swam and then dined before taking advantage of the vibrant nightlife to visit a club. They rose late the next morning, sunbathed on deck while the yacht cruised on to Naxos, where Aristide's guests disembarked to travel home, and finally they arrived back on Anthos.

They breakfasted on the veranda, where she drank in the beautiful views, conscious that she was leaving that evening to return home and would presumably never enjoy that sweeping, stunning view of the sea again. There was an odd tension between them and then Aristide's stepmother drove up to take Tabby with her to the new art gallery in the village. Aristide looked mildly irritated by her arrival but did not object.

'I'll see you later,' Aristide remarked before stalking back into the house.

'Did I interrupt something?' Andy murmured, always intuitive.

'I don't think so, but I can't stay out long because I have to pack and I don't want to leave anything behind.'

'Where are you going?' Andy enquired with interest.

'Back to London this evening. This has been a wonderful holiday but I have to get back to work,' Tabby replied.

'I rather thought that Aristide was hoping to change your mind on that score,' his stepmother admitted.

Tabby reminded herself that she was supposed to be Aristide's real fiancée as far as his family was concerned. 'Not much chance of that at the moment,' she said lightly, wondering if Aristide's father had been expecting a wedding announcement or something of that ilk before she departed again. It was best to play dumb.

'You know…' The older woman hesitated before continuing. 'Imogen left a lot of damage in her wake. He had such total faith in her and then that was ripped away from him and I suspect he has trust issues—'

'Don't we all?' Tabby countered without any expression at all but she meant it.

Aristide had trust issues, as did she, but hers had softened since Aristide had proved his reliability. But then she had already surmounted the problems of enduring a violent, unpredictable and uninterested father and her resulting innate distrust of men. Not all men were the same. Sam Blessington was just a bad apple in the barrel. But essentially she had moved on under her own power to embrace the best life she could make for herself without letting herself be restricted by the unhappy events during her childhood and adolescence. Aristide still had to make that leap and she couldn't do it for him. He needed to move forward alone, willing to change for her benefit.

They entered the gallery, Aristide's stepmother immediately leaving her side to go upstairs in search of the owner, who was sourcing a specific metal sculpture for her husband Demetrius' birthday. Tabby lingered by the pottery, which was Violet's particular love, but she could see nothing unique enough to attract her twin's acquisitive urge. The door behind her opened, the tap-tap of stilettos making her turn round and then wish she hadn't.

Imogen, clad in a very sleek black dress, aimed her megawatt famous smile at her, golden hair shimmering in waves round her slender shoulders. 'Oh, this is convenient. You've saved me from having to visit my landlord.' Scooping keys from her trendy little bag, she extended them. 'The keys to my grandparents' cottage. I'm returning them as per the agreement.'

'They're nothing to do with me,' Tabby said uneasily.

'Oh, don't be silly. You're *living* with Aristide, aren't you?' she pressed, tossing the keys, forcing Tabby to catch them. 'I wish you well of him. He'll never love anyone the way he loved me.'

Tabby lost colour and turned away. 'Goodbye, Imogen.'

Andy came clattering down the wooden stairs to the rescue and Imogen turned on her heel and stalked out, the door slamming on her exit.

'What am I supposed to do with these?' Tabby shook the keys in exasperation.

'Celebrate. She must've finished clearing the place and now she's leaving.' Andy sighed in relief. 'Now we won't be running into her all the time.'

CHAPTER TEN

TABBY SETTLED THE bunch of keys down on Aristide's desk in the room he used as an office. 'I ran into Imogen at the art gallery and she insisted that I return these for her.'

Aristide grimaced. 'I'll return them to the agent. She shouldn't have approached you with them, but I'm pleased to know that she's finally leaving and that she will have no reason to return to the island.'

'I'm going upstairs to start packing before lunch—'

'I'm heading down to the beach for a walk.' Aristide rested his truly stunning dark golden eyes on her shuttered face. 'Join me...'

'OK,' she said lightly, determined to keep up the bright, breezy front out of pride. 'But I'll have to change first into something cooler. I dressed up for Andy this morning. She's always so elegant.'

Up in their bedroom, where she scolded herself for even thinking of it as *their* bedroom, she picked out denim shorts and a halter top and stripped off her skirt with its elasticated waist, loose-ish top and flat comfy pumps, thinking enviously of Imogen's racy red stilettos and bag and of how frumpy she herself had felt in comparison. She didn't want to leave Aristide but she had to protect herself.

Aristide was already down on the beach, a tall, lean figure sheathed in black denim jeans and tee, thumbs lodged in his belt loops as he gazed out to sea, his proud profile perfect in silhouette. She followed the path down to the shore, recalling the rarity of beach visits while she was a kid and the sheer excitement of seeing her first rock pool. Her throat thickened and she swallowed convulsively as she looked at Aristide and then looked away again. Like Imogen, she was leaving and, certainly, with regard to the remaining months of her pregnancy, Aristide would be a very rare visitor... if he visited at all.

Refusing to hurry herself, she strolled across the sand to join him, her flip-flops abandoned above the waterline. 'It's so beautiful and peaceful here,' she sighed appreciatively.

'I don't want you to leave,' Aristide admitted with absolutely no lead-in.

'I sort of don't want to leave either,' she confided reluctantly. 'But isn't that always true of a good holiday?'

'Don't cheapen what we've had together,' Aristide rebuked. 'We've enjoyed a great deal more than a shared holiday.'

Tabby stiffened. 'Yes, we've had a fling and now it's over,' she opined in a tight, small voice. 'But from now on we will be friends and co-parents and that's a bit of a jump right now, but not seeing each other until the babies are born should make it easier on both of us.'

'I don't know where you get the idea that I'm about

to vanish from your life while you're pregnant. What sort of male would behave like that?'

'A sensible one. Get a little distance. Obviously if I'm ever in need of help I can phone you...or if...er, anything were to go wrong,' she muttered. 'But we're not together in the normal sense of the word.'

'I thought we were,' Aristide declared.

'Did you really?' Tabby turned to look at him, her wide blue eyes bright against her breeze-stung cheeks. 'Put it this way—if you thought we were a couple, you failed to mention it to me.'

Faint colour etched the knife-sharp slant of his high cheekbones as he reflected that that was a fair point, for he had, out of habit, played his cards very close to his chest. 'I did tell you what I was hoping to achieve by bringing you here with me.'

'Yes, that this was a trial run at a real relationship for you. One mistake, Aristide. I'm nobody's *trial run*. I didn't come here to try and impress you as an eligible match like some desperate Regency heroine. I came here because it made sense to find out more about my babies' father and his family because you and your family will soon be part of their lives.'

'You're very defensive,' Aristide growled, dark eyes glittering with censure.

'No, I'm not. For once, I'm simply being honest. We're both adults, we're both pretty practical and we're not enemies. That's a fair basis for being good co-parents in the future.'

Everything she was saying was inside her head and came from a logical place, but her heart was breaking at acknowledging the current emptiness of her future without him. She wanted him and she loved him but he did not feel the same way about her, unless she had got something terribly wrong in her assumptions.

'You've detached from me. You're talking as though you've already gone.'

'I'm being sensible. We had a great time together but now it's almost over,' she argued, conscious that he had hit the nail squarely on its head with that accusation. Once she knew that she was leaving, she had tried to move on mentally from him, but what else could he have expected from her? Nothing would ever persuade her that Aristide would have preferred an emotional scene in which she condemned him for using and discarding her.

Aristide moved a step closer and reached for her hands. 'I didn't want to do the conventional thing. The dinner, the down on bended knee and the proposal felt outdated to me when there's already a ring on your finger. I now see that I was too proud, arrogant and smart for my own good. I should've given you the frills,' he completed.

Tabby had been stunned into silence. Out of the blue, he was asking her to marry him? Where had that come from? She hadn't foreseen that, should've seen that coming from a mile away, she reasoned. She had formed her attitude to him of recent entirely on what he'd shown her. And what she realised at that point was that Aristide had shown her *nothing*. Well, at least nothing that even hinted at love.

'I wouldn't need frills from a male that sincerely

cared for me,' she muttered awkwardly, her tongue tripping in her dry mouth because the unexpected had thrown her for a loop.

'Obviously, I *do* sincerely care for you,' Aristide reasoned.

'Yes, but you don't love me.' Tabby said it for herself, the truth of that statement piercing her like a sharp, wounding blade.

'We don't need love. We have everything else,' Aristide told her fiercely. 'We have the passion, the fun, the commitment, the caring. How could you possibly add to that?'

Tabby winced at the fierce grip of his strong hands and he released her crushed fingers immediately. '*I* need love. I'm happy for you that you don't care about that but I do care about it. I will only marry a man who loves me and whom I love. It's the one thing I can't compromise on. I don't think a marriage that isn't built on love would survive the years. Love keeps you loyal to your partner even when that partner is annoying you. Relationships wax and wane and go through rough patches,' she argued. 'But what keeps a couple together is love.'

Aristide shrugged a broad shoulder, his lean, darkly handsome face stony. 'I don't agree with that. You're getting all emotional and this isn't what this is about. Marriage is primarily a legal agreement—'

'I don't agree with that either. I will only marry a guy who can tell me he loves me…and be proud of the fact,' Tabby retorted chokily, her throat convulsing. 'But you're never going to do that. You're still too bitter about Imogen—'

'I am not... Why the hell are you bringing *her* into this?' Aristide demanded with sudden anger.

'Because she's right there square in the middle of it whether you like it or not. I'm not saying that I believe you're still hung up on her but I do think that your attitude is all wrong because of your experience with her. I also won't be punished, with your lack of faith in me or in love, for her mistakes either. I deserve better. Thanks for the proposal, Aristide, but no, thanks.'

'Tabby...' he breathed rawly, hands hanging fisted by his sides.

Tabby spun back to him. 'And don't think I don't know that you're only thinking of marriage because I'm pregnant,' she condemned. 'It wouldn't even have occurred to you otherwise. And that's humiliating, Aristide. Maybe I'll never meet anyone who loves me or wants to marry me, but I need to stay free to give life a chance. If I married you I'd be closing myself off to the possibility of being loved by someone else, someone who is less of a perfectionist than you and who can care about me, flaws and all!'

As she stalked away in high dudgeon, wondering if she had dealt as poorly with him as she possibly could or whether she should have reacted differently, she suppressed her increasing emotional turmoil. Right, she reminded herself, it's time to pack. If he couldn't give her even a faint prospect of love, she didn't want him, she told herself firmly. Such a marriage would end in tears.

He might fall for someone else. And she truly did not fancy figuring as the loving wife of a male who did not love her back, who would always refuse to let the more tender emotions have space inside him. It would be like downsizing herself, reducing her to the level of a beggar seeking crumbs from the table. She would end up hating herself if she married a man who didn't love her.

Aristide was in shock. He had been toying with the option of marrying Tabby almost from the first moment he'd learned that she was pregnant. It had lurked in the back of his mind ever since. Of course, he hadn't told her that and it had never crossed his mind that a proposal in such circumstances could be seen as humiliating. He had been more afraid of recklessly talking himself into a sudden disastrous marriage that had no prospect of success. And then he had got to know Tabby properly and appreciate her and, no, he was not always looking at her and seeing flaws. Where had she got that idea from? In fact he thought she was pretty much perfect, which would no doubt surprise her.

But instead of proposing marriage at the start, or at least making his intentions clear, he had instead conned her into a fake engagement and done himself no favours, he registered belatedly. And, of course, that had been a total con on his part, knowing how attractive he still found her, knowing how much he wanted her in *his* home and *his* care and *his* bed and away from other men. In truth he was very possessive of her and the thought of having to let her go away from him and back into the wider world downright appalled him.

Not only had he let that fake-engagement business get in the way, but he had also let Imogen get in the way. He should've shared that story with Tabby much sooner. He had even let a desire to be cool and real get in the way! So, you propose on a walk along the beach on her very last day! Couldn't you have done better than that, Aristide? Waiting until the eleventh hour and going with casual had been a major miscalculation.

He breathed in deep and swallowed back his disordered emotions with difficulty. He had royally screwed up, although he was still trying to work out how a proposal of marriage could be humiliating, offensive and too little too late. And she was upset, deeply upset. She had gone pale and there had been a bleak look in her eyes he had never seen there before.

'At least come home with me tonight,' Aristide urged as his limo swept away from the airport.

It was a dreary wet night and she was back in London. She had been surprised when Aristide had announced that he was flying to the UK with her.

'I need to get back to work too,' he had told her.

'Why would I come home with you now?' she asked him baldly.

'You're returning to an unheated apartment that contains no food. It would be easier for you to return to my place instead.'

'There's a twenty-four-hour supermarket within a mile of my place. I'll manage…but thanks for offering,' Tabby told him, striving to be gracious even in the face of adversity. And it was definitely adversity when you turned down a marriage proposal and the guy just went on being charming and considerate. If he'd brooded, acted short-tempered or ignored her, at least she could have convinced herself that he or his ego had been damaged by her rejection.

She eased her gorgeous engagement ring slowly off her finger. Her fingers had swelled in the heat so it wasn't that easy an operation and when it was finally free, she extended it to him.

'I don't want it back. I bought it for you.'

'Stop being difficult!' she exclaimed. 'I'm tired, I'm hungry and on a short fuse.'

'Then why don't you come home with me?'

'Will you please stop being nice?' Tabby launched at him furiously. 'It's only making this more difficult!'

Aristide studied her flushed and mutinous face with concealed amusement laced with concern. He wanted to gather her into his arms and soothe her. Hangry was a word that had been invented for Tabby when she was tired and hungry.

'And please take the ring...' she begged, still holding it out to him.

He dropped it into a pocket. 'I don't want it.'

'Well, sell it, then,' Tabby muttered, aware that she was behaving badly and embarrassed that she couldn't control her heaving emotions just then. She didn't want him to sell her ring because she adored it, but it wasn't hers to keep and she wasn't mercenary. 'I'm sorry I left the box on the island.'

She climbed out of the limousine and went to open the door but he stole the key from her hand and opened it for her while his security men saw to her luggage, hauling it upstairs. Aristide moved ahead of her, switching on lights, and the emptiness of the rooms engulfed her along with a bone-deep sense of loneliness. More than anything she just needed to phone her sister and admit her misery and when feeling as low as this, she consoled herself, she could only go up.

Aristide looked frustrated, glorious dark golden eyes troubled, and guilt almost got her by the throat. For the first time she saw that he wasn't much happier than she was and he was showing it. Just last night she had been in his arms and as close to him as any two human beings could be and now that seemed like a far-off daydream.

'I'll see you tomorrow,' Aristide announced.

'But I'll be working—'

'No, you won't be,' Aristide contradicted. 'Violet was unable to find a replacement for you willing to take on the contract for less than a month, so you still have two weeks to fill…unless, of course, you want to break the contract and pay the costs.'

Tabby gritted her teeth. She hadn't known that her replacement was in the bakery to work a full month and she had no intention of taking any action that could damage her sister's business or add needlessly to her costs. Slowly she nodded, wishing that just once Aristide didn't know better than she did. 'Goodnight,' she said tightly.

'Tomorrow morning, I'll send the car to pick you up at eight,' he specified. 'We'll have breakfast together and we can talk.'

'We've got nothing left to talk about.'

'I'll talk. You can listen and pronounce judgement,' Aristide traded lazily.

Tabby resisted the temptation to tell him that she wasn't a judgemental person, because it would have been a lie where Aristide was concerned. She watched every move Aristide made, tried to read his every expression and was forever judging him and making assumptions. Now she was learning that, just as often as she was right, she often got him wrong. The shock of the marriage proposal she had refused was still reverberating through her.

She ordered food from a local takeaway place and ate before falling into bed, exhausted and miserable because it was very bad news that she was *already* missing Aristide.

What on earth did he think they still had to talk about? The very prospect of that dialogue made her anxious because she didn't want to argue with him again. What did she have to say to a male who believed that love was not required in marriage?

She was collected on the dot of eight and driven through the heavy morning traffic to Aristide's apartment. In spite of everything that had happened between them, the anticipation of seeing him again made her heartbeat quicken and released butterflies in her tummy. She breathed in deep as she crossed the threshold.

Aristide was elegantly dressed in a dark business suit. His lean dark face was taut and a touch remote. But he was still so hot he positively sizzled with lethally sexy vibes. His expression reminded her very much of their first meeting at her former place of employment and she shrank a little into herself, asking herself what else she could've expected, other than distance, after turning down his proposal. She doffed her coat, passed it to his hovering manservant, and took a seat at the table.

'I'm going to do most of the talking,' Aristide warned her in advance. 'Try not to interrupt me until I'm finished. I get one chance at this and one chance only. I don't want to screw it up.'

Slightly dazed by that unexpected speech, Tabby nodded and reached daringly for a croissant as her tea was poured for her. 'You're making me nervous,' she whispered, the atmosphere so tense that her stiff shoulders already ached.

As the door closed behind his staff, Aristide released his breath in a pent-up hiss. 'I grew up in a very dysfunctional household. Women floated in and floated out again. I often had no idea whether the same woman would still be there on my next visit and there were often frightening arguments and distressing scenes between my father and his partners. All of that made me decide that I would ideally settle down and marry one woman and stay with her for ever…'

'Understandable,' Tabby chipped in and then flushed, for she remembered him saying that she was to let him speak.

'I never planned on being a playboy. Imogen did that to me. I didn't trust women any more. I protected myself to the extent that, when I met you, I was as tempted by you as I was by the conviction that I should turn away and walk fast in the opposite direction… because the moment I met you I knew that you would mean *more* to me in every way. And that scared me, made me feel out of control. But I couldn't resist you…'

Tabby unfroze and glanced up, her anxious eyes warming with acceptance of that admission. 'The same,' she echoed, feeling that identical irresistible pull tug at her afresh.

A sudden slashing grin stole the gravity from Aristide's lean darkly handsome features. 'I just can't shut you up, can I?'

'Probably not,' she agreed, her cheeks burning.

'I told myself that it was only one night, but even over dinner that first evening I was toying with the idea of spending the whole weekend with you, which was groundbreaking for me.'

Tabby sipped her tea, wondering where he was heading in his journey back to the start of their relationship. It was definitely heartening to learn that long before they'd reached the bedroom he had already been interested in spending more time with her. 'And then the contraceptive misunderstanding occurred and it all went horribly wrong,' she said for him, because that subject had already been done to death and she had long understood why he had reacted the way he had that night.

'That night, if you hadn't given me the impression that you were cheating on your fiancé, I would've been in touch and apologising for my loss of temper by the next day. That's how keen I was on you,' he volunteered, disconcerting her.

'So you waited…'

'Had you investigated—'

'Came to check me out,' she filled in. 'And I told you that I was pregnant without meaning to tell you.'

'When I suggested we fake our engagement, I was already thinking of marriage. I never planned to let you go. I was deceiving you.'

'And you're admitting that?' Her eyes were wide with surprise and a certain amount of satisfaction because the idea of marrying her had been in his head long before he had actually got around to proposing.

'I'm a talented negotiator.' Aristide snatched in a deep, audible breath. 'I was so busy plotting how to catch and keep you, I didn't consider how my...er... unconventional courtship would look to you.'

Tabby startled both of them by bursting out laughing. '*Unconventional courtship?* Yes, that's a term and a half!'

'That ring was always intended for you—'

'But you didn't ask me to marry you, Aristide.' Tabby shot him a reproving look. 'In fact the closest you came to that was asking me to live with you.'

Aristide gritted his even white teeth. 'I was still committed to the softly-softly approach where our lives would eventually be so entangled you would wake up one day and realise you couldn't live without me—'

'You *hoped*,' she slotted in, unimpressed.

'And then you said no when I asked you to marry me and it all fell apart. I didn't know where to go from there. I had nothing more to offer,' he admitted in a raw undertone. 'And I can't face my life without you in it...so quite happy for you to chip in now with useful suggestions.'

'Why can't you face your life without me?' Tabby asked squarely instead, her heart beating very, very fast because Aristide was severely on edge, ferocious tension etched in every hard line of his lean, strong face.

'Well, it's got almost nothing to do with you being pregnant! I wanted you, *seriously* wanted you, long before I knew you were pregnant. That simply complicated everything and gave you the wrong impression. Why would you think I only wanted to marry you because you were pregnant?' he shot at her. 'We could've done that thing with co-parenting that you kept on throwing at me. We could've just shared a house. But *only* if you marry me are you mine and it's very important to me that you are mine and nobody else's!'

'Why?' she asked again.

Unconcealed frustration radiated from Aristide. 'Obviously because I *love* you...why else?' And after a moment's hesitation, 'Should I have said that first?'

Tabby was reeling in shock. 'But yesterday on the beach you said you didn't believe love was necessary.'

'I would've done almost anything rather than acknowledge it because, in my experience, once you tell a woman you love her you are no longer equals and she *owns* you!' he framed in raw condemnation.

Her lips parted company. 'I've got to admit that I wouldn't mind owning you body and soul,' she confided softly.

'Since when?' Aristide queried in a tone of disbelief.

'Oh, from just about the first moment I met you, and that desire got stronger every time I saw you. So, there you are, I'm your worst nightmare come true. I would own you if I could,' she confessed in a rush with a huge smile. 'I tried to fight how I felt about you too but it didn't get me very far. I'm not being facetious but my love was at its height when you punched my father and shut him down. I like how protective you are.'

Aristide almost knocked a dining chair over as he swooped on her and lifted her right out of her seat. 'I'm crazy about you, *angelos mou*—'

'Me too…about you, I mean,' she mumbled blissfully, colliding with burnished golden eyes that made her heart sing with happiness because now she could see the tenderness and the very real feeling there. 'So, let's own each other and then never mention it again. And I won't marry you until Mum's back in the UK because she's got to be part of it.'

'But we're getting married, right?' Aristide checked with a huge smile. 'All I had to do was tell you that I loved you and then you wouldn't have said no?'

'Sometimes the uncool, simple way is the best move you can make but you will always try to be clever and make it complicated, Aristide.' Tabby ruffled his curly hair with fond fingers. 'That's just the way you are.'

'Can I take you straight back to bed?'

'Only if you let me sleep late afterwards,' she bargained. 'That was too early a start this morning.'

He carried her through the hall and down into his bedroom and laid her on the bed. She looked around, remembering their first encounter in the same room and giving him a sunny smile because all that nonsense and drama and insecurity were now far behind them.

'Being owned is paying dividends I never expected,' Aristide teased. '*Thee mou*, I love you so much I can't wait to put a wedding ring on your finger. Oh, that reminds me...' Reaching into his pocket, Aristide extracted her engagement ring and slid it onto her finger. 'That feels better.'

'Why did you never ask me to take a DNA test?' she enquired with belated curiosity.

'I didn't have the slightest shade of doubt that if you were pregnant, it was my child. I knew that you were very different from Imogen. When I consider it, I was already trusting you back then without even realising it,' he murmured with wry amusement.

Tabby yanked on his tie and sat up to kick off her shoes. 'Why are you still wearing clothes?' she asked with a distinctly sultry smile. 'Well, you already knew I was bossy—'

'Be warned. I am bossy too.' Aristide stripped without hesitation, dropping everything in an untidy heap.

Tabby shimmied her hips out of her skirt and peeled off her top. Aristide's eyes literally lit up when he caught a glimpse of her full breasts cupped in lace. 'You look amazing.'

'I didn't think I'd be back in this bed today.'

'I love you,' Aristide breathed in a roughened undertone. 'I'll do whatever it takes to make you happy. You'll have no regrets.'

'You're already making me happy.' Tabby tugged him down to her and they kissed and she luxuriated in the connection of their minds and warm bodies. He felt like home. She should've guessed he loved her in the way he made love to her, she reflected. He had shown her love in so many little ways and she hadn't counted them up when she should've done. Only a male in love was so tender, thoughtful and caring round the clock. As they joined together with a kind of frantic energy, the world around her splintered and she lazed in the aftermath in his arms, feeling ridiculously happy and content.

'We'll fly over and visit your mother and set a wedding date if it's possible.' Aristide was back on target and laying down the law, his attack of humility short-lived.

'We'll see,' Tabby sighed, wondering if he would ever learn patience.

'You're always going to call me out when I get too big for my boots, aren't you?'

'Probably,' she agreed sleepily. 'But it's good for you to be challenged.'

EPILOGUE

Five years later

IT WAS A divine dress. A slinky red sheath that flattered her curvier shape since her pregnancies. Of course, it would never surpass her old favourite that she had worn at Violet's first summer ball in Italy. Aristide had persuaded her to wear it again the previous year and it had enjoyed various other fashionable outings but this year Tabby had decided to be different and wear something a little more daring, now that she wasn't pregnant any more.

Every year they attended Violet and Tore's charity ball. They were able to bring the children with them since Tore had extended the house into former outbuildings at the rear. And the kids had a lot of fun as well when they were in Italy. It was a blessing that their children were all so close in age. Tabby's twins, Elias and Eleni, were four, just like Violet's twins, Sofia and Enzo. And little Xander, their two-year-old toddler, followed the others around like a faithful puppy. Belle, Violet's adopted daughter, was incredibly sensible even at the age of six and she watched over them all, preventing the worst excesses.

Tabby had been grateful when she had had her twins,

because she had found the pregnancy tough, and Aristide had persuaded her into Xander, a pregnancy that had been a breeze in comparison to her first. Three children were enough, she had told him, although she knew he still had hopes that she might change her mind and Violet being pregnant again would probably make him a little envious.

Tabby, however, was perfectly happy with the family they already had. Elias was dark-haired like his father, inclined to be bossy and serious. Eleni was a blonde dreamer, never more content than when she was reading picture books to her dolls with a made-up storyline. Xander, with his rampantly curly black hair, was just an ever moving splash of liveliness and endless chuckles.

They had held their wedding in Greece at the village church. For the first time their giant house on Anthos had been filled to the gills. Her mother's cancer was in remission, but it had taken considerable encouragement to get her out to Greece because she hated travel and rarely left her home outside London, which she had inherited after their grandfather died, along with a comfortable income. Both Violet and Tabby were regular visitors to the UK and still saw their mother often.

The mansion on Anthos was now their home base. Tabby had found the island an amazingly relaxing place to raise young children. Demetrius and Andy were very much involved with their grandchildren and the kids had much more freedom to run wild on Anthos, much the same as Violet's kids did on the Villa Renzetti estate in Tuscany. And when the sisters wanted to get together, Tore had come up with a solution. He had gifted Tabby and Aristide a piece of land nearby where they had built a modern, comfortable holiday home. They often used it at weekends, but for big occasions like the summer ball they stayed at the villa itself because it was more fun for the kids to be with their cousins and there was constant supervision there.

Tabby had done without hiring a nanny. She wanted to enjoy her children while they were young, spend time with them, appreciating that it wasn't time she would get back and there was never a shortage of babysitters around her. Not least Violet, who adored her nephews and niece almost as much as she adored her own children. After the ball, Aristide and Tabby were flying off for a week of precious alone time on the yacht and leaving their children with their aunt and uncle.

Aristide, long since dressed ahead of her, strode into the bedroom and stopped dead. *'Thee mou,'* he husked. 'That's a killer dress.'

Tabby pirouetted in front of him. 'You like?'

Aristide grinned down at her, the warmth of his gaze heating her down deep inside. 'I will like taking it off on *Sea Breeze* even more…'

'One-track-mind male,' Tabby quipped as he tugged her back against him and dropped a careful kiss on an exposed shoulder.

'No, a very happy male. I love having you all to myself,' he confided. 'Is that selfish?'

'No. Tore and Violet do the same. We're not only parents, we're a couple and we mustn't lose that in family life. We need a break now and again.'

'Well, you do all the heavy lifting,' he conceded,

turning her round, pressing a kiss to her brow, careful to steer clear of her make-up and her hairdo. 'I want to rip your dress off you, *angelos mou*. It's incredibly sexy and it will be torture looking at you in that all evening and not being able to touch you. Maybe I am a male with a one-track mind...'

'Whatever you are, I love you,' she murmured, suddenly frustrated that she couldn't kiss him and risk messing her make-up.

'I'm absolutely crazy about you. You rock my world,' Aristide groaned. 'It only took me almost twenty-nine years to find a woman who could teach me how to be happy.'

'I didn't know real happiness either until I met you,' she confessed softly.

* * * * *

If you couldn't put Her Two Greek Secrets, *then be sure to check out the previous instalment in the Billion-Dollar Bride Swap duet,* Unveiling the Wrong Bride*!*
And why not try these other stories by Lynne Graham?

Baby Worth Billions
Greek's Shotgun Wedding
Greek's One-Night Babies
His Royal Bride Replacement
Shock Greek Heir

Available now!

KING'S HEIR ULTIMATUM

LORRAINE HALL

MILLS & BOON

For best friends.

CHAPTER ONE

King Alexandre Enzo Rodrigo Lidia had been a married man for almost a year. He had been king for almost three months, thanks to the untimely death of his father.

He knew far more about how to be a king than about being a husband.

Being a king made sense, after all. There were laws to uphold, the previous king's mistakes to fix and a country to usher into a new era of peace and stability.

Being a *husband* was something else entirely. If he was not royalty, at least. Luckily, he was.

He had not chosen his wife. Ines had been chosen for him. At the time, Alexandre had been rather grateful that his father's choice had been bearable. King Enzo had been a vindictive despot of a king, and even worse as a father, so Enzo had not chosen Ines for anything except access to her father's wealth.

She could have been anything. A pampered, spoiled, dramatic nuisance. A pompous, withdrawn, cruel snob. The terrible options were endless.

But Ines had turned out to be a wonderful princess and an even better queen. She was dutiful, modest and quiet. She was kind and pleasant, but not dull. She never behaved above anyone, and so the country of Alis quite loved her. She was a workhorse and never complained, always happy to take on the next royal task assigned.

If she disagreed with him about anything, they had calm, reasonable discussions, and he could almost always talk her around to his way of thinking.

Alexandre was hardly ever wrong.

He'd had a lifetime of preparing to be king—of preparing to undo every horrible thing his father had enacted. On his mother's deathbed, she had tasked him with fixing everything. Alexandre might have only been five, but he had taken that promise he'd made her quite seriously. For the nearly twenty-five years between her death and his father's three months ago, he had watched his father and planned to fix everything the horrible man had done to his family, to his county.

For the past three months, he had worked exclusively to undo all his father's petty, militaristic whims.

Not that Alexandre was perfect. He could not claim to be. He had failed many in his life. He had not been able to protect his mother from the wrath of his father's so-called love. He had not been able to protect her from the medical complications that had stolen her life at Evelyne's birth. He knew he had not always been able to protect his younger sister from the abuses of their father as she'd grown up.

But he had done his level best. And would continue to do so, until death took him. There was simply no other choice.

So Ines was a better wife than Alexandre could have ever hoped for, taking on her responsibilities so easily, so adeptly. She could connect with their kingdom in a more...*emotional* way than a protector could.

Perhaps the necessary heir had not come as quickly as

he might have liked, but that was hardly her fault. And now, he needn't worry about it. Thanks to an old Alis law, the heir did not need to be born from the eldest child or even the male heir. The first child born of the following generation became heir to the throne.

His sister was due any day now, and Evelyne's son would be the future king. So Alexandre no longer needed to worry about producing an heir with Ines. His sister and his best friend had done it for him.

It had been a relief.

Not because it was any trial to bed his wife. Quite the opposite. *That* was the problem. He did not have room for passion or interest or *relationships* in his life. The kind of emotion that marked his parents was the kind that ruined kingdoms.

Alexandre would not stand for it.

Ines was meant to be his wife in name only...once she'd produced an heir. But an heir had not come. Doctors had assured him that there was nothing medically preventing either of them from conceiving a child. The doctor had advised him—and her—to *relax*.

Something Alexandre could only see as the enemy. Because if he *relaxed*, he could make a mistake. One that would harm his entire country. That would have been impossible enough before his father's unlikely death three months ago.

Now? Relaxation would be the same as catastrophic. He had *years* of work yet before he could fully ensure Alis was on the right track.

So the minute Evelyne had returned from her exile after Enzo's death, pregnant with the Alis heir, Alexandre had stopped keeping his weekly...*appointments* with Ines.

They had not discussed it, but she had not mounted any

kind of argument or asked him why he no longer came to her bedchamber on the assigned evenings. She let it slide.

This was the beauty of Ines. A good queen let things that did not matter slide.

So he was more than a little surprised to find his wife in his office this morning when he arrived. He glanced at his watch. She was not one to interrupt his daily routine.

"Ah, good morning, Ines. I'm afraid I don't have time to talk just now. I have an appointment." And his concentration was already a bit scattered with the news Evelyne had gone into labor. This information had left him feeling...more on edge than he'd like.

He could remember the day Evelyne had been born more clearly than he liked. The hushed whispers. The screaming. The blood when he'd snuck himself into his mother's room and she'd tasked him with saving the baby she'd birthed, the kingdom she left behind.

"Yes," Ines agreed in the here and now. "I am your appointment." She sat in the chair opposite his desk, dressed for a day of royal meetings. A trim suit in a vibrant blue. Her brown hair with hints of mahogany was pulled back in an elegant twist. She wore an exquisitely simple gold pendant around her neck, blue diamonds at her ears that matched the color of her eyes, and his wedding ring on her finger. Her left hand rested over the right in her lap, her ankles crossed and drawn slightly beneath her chair.

She really was quite perfect. In every picture, in every portrait, in every moment, Ines looked like a queen.

He did not allow himself to consider the rare moments he saw her mussed, her lips swollen from his. Those moments tended to threaten his necessary equilibrium. His required focus.

So he supposed she was *not* perfect. She could stand

to be a *little* duller. Perhaps she would not pop into his thoughts unbidden if he did not find her quite so beautiful. But a beautiful queen was something indeed, and to wish her duller was no wish for his kingdom, so he shoved that thought away.

He skirted his desk and took a seat so they were opposite each other. A bit like strangers.

In some ways, she was a stranger to him. He might know that she preferred cream in her coffee, lemon in her tea. He might even know what she looked like beneath her clothes—far too beautiful, small, soft, perfect—and what sounds she made in pleasure—haunting, really. But sometimes it struck him that he did not know *her*.

She kept herself hidden behind a royal mask, just as he did. A good thing, Alexandre knew. A preferred thing. And still…sometimes he'd see her tucked away with Evelyne somewhere, laughing over something, and he'd have the strangest desire to want to know what it was about, what she found funny, what made her smile just like that.

But he did not have time for such things, and she was definitely not laughing this morning. "You've been avoiding being alone with me, and this discussion requires privacy," she said directly. "So I made an appointment."

There was no censure in her tone, but he felt it all the same. "I'm sure that wasn't necessary."

She regarded him coolly but did not argue. She let that lie slide, just as she did so many things. "I wish to speak to you about our…evening appointments."

Alexandre did not care for what that word *did* to him. Elicited physical responses and memories he tried to block out of any time he visited her bedchamber. Which had been far more than he'd anticipated, thinking at *most* it would take a month or two to render her with child.

He blamed the frequency on how difficult it had been to stay away, when he'd known that was the best course of action.

He did not understand the feelings she brought out in him. They didn't make sense. Nothing straightforward. Nothing black-and-white. A messiness. An uncontrollable cyclone of disparate things.

And messiness, a lack of control, these were all purviews of his father. The way his father had felt about his mother. Because no doubt the formidable King Enzo, happy to order people hung for small crimes and other such atrocities, had not known the meaning of love—although he had claimed to love his queen.

A love Alexandre had stolen from him, according to Enzo. A love that had destroyed everything in its wake.

And it was Alexandre's job to fix all his father had destroyed. His mother had told him this with her last breath, so how could it be anything but the most simple and important truth?

Alexandre had to be on constant guard or he could not be the king required of his family and his country. A king who put *them* above all else.

Was this fair to him as a person? Of course not, but it was his role, his task. The *person* could not exist if the crown was meant to lead, protect, save.

So he could not worry himself over Evelyne—he had all the best doctors with her. He could not concern himself with how the appointments with Ines used to make him feel—they were done and over.

"I'm not sure this is something that requires a discussion," Alexandre said stiffly. He did not attend such *appointments* anymore because Alis had its heir in Evelyne's soon-to-be child.

Concern jittered again in his chest, but he shoved it away. He had all the best doctors at her disposal. She would not meet the same fate as their mother had. He simply wouldn't allow it.

Ines held his gaze. Her eyes were the same color blue as the diamonds at her ears and direct. "You have skipped the last three such appointments. You have given me no reason why this is the case. Therefore I would like to discuss it."

She did not say this in any accusatory way *exactly*. But she said it in a way that felt like he had performed some dereliction of duty, and she was the general here to hand out punishment.

He cleared his throat at the strange, uncomfortable uncertainty that settled inside his chest. A king did not have room for uncertainty. Certainly not when it came to his wife.

"I apologize for not being clearer," he said, trying to trot out his regal tone and finding it fell a bit flat with her. Or maybe when discussing *sex* with his wife in the necessary…vague terms. "With an heir now secured, we no longer need to…" He had no other words. Everything became a kind of odd blank.

This was what Ines did to him sometimes. Turned him into a man he did not recognize. Who did not know how to proceed or protect. When everything—*everything*—rested on his ability to do both.

"This is not about an heir to the throne, Alexandre," Ines returned. Her tone remained businesslike, her posture straight and regal. "I wish to be a mother regardless of where our child would fall in the royal hierarchy."

He stared at her for a minute. He got the sense she'd been thinking about this for quite some time. Had practiced these words and this argument, and so it felt somehow like a betrayal. That she would upend his status quo so purposely.

"As the king and queen, it will be our duty to usher Evelyne's child into our world, into being an *heir*. We may not be his parents, but we will have a very important role. Surely this is enough."

She didn't flinch, didn't look down or away. She held herself as still and regal as any queen should. Her gaze was direct, if a little chilly. "It is not enough."

It is not enough. He blinked. Once. Before he remembered himself. Gathered himself. Armored himself. He looked down at her, as he might any recalcitrant employee. Because at the end of the day, his wife *was* a role—not a person. They were titles, not feelings.

He would forgive her for forgetting, but he would not change course.

"Ines, I'm sure you can be reasonable."

"In this I'm afraid I cannot be," she said, sounding the very example of control. "If you are not going to give me a child, then I should like an annulment."

Queen Ines Lidia regarded her husband with as much control as she had left in her. She had begun to think she didn't affect him. That any flashes of temper or passion she had seen over the past year were figments of her own imagination.

But she saw both in his eyes now. Little flickers of a man she knew existed under all the trappings of the title he was so devoted to.

"I understand how divorce is out of the question for you," she continued, keeping her tone reasonable. "But I'm sure your publicity team can work through an annulment." She didn't let herself clutch her hands together like she wanted to. She would *not* look down at her lap. She had to maintain eye contact and certainty. She'd been practicing this conversation for weeks now.

Perhaps she'd had the *tiniest* hope he would simply agree to return to their appointment schedule rather than an annulment, but mostly she had known better. He'd made the decision *not* to come to her bedroom on purpose and with reason.

Alexandre did nothing without his precious reason.

"The timing could not be better," Ines continued, keeping her polite smile in place. "Evelyne having the baby, the *heir*, in the coming days means there will be ample distraction from anything such as an annulment. Any bad press over it shouldn't last long in the face of the new heir being born."

When he didn't speak, she knew he was angrier than he let show on his face.

In some ways, she thought she understood her husband better than anyone. She too knew what it was like to be saddled with a duty far too adult at far too young an age. And she could even admit that Alexandre's duties were far more complex than hers had been. Not just to be a good king, but to be the king that *fixed* everything. It was difficult work. A constant fight. King Enzo had done deep, lasting damage to the country of Alis.

All Ines had been tasked with since she could remember was to bag an important husband so her father's wealth could buy him some influence. She had been trained since birth to be nothing more than some royal's wife.

And she'd succeeded. *Bagged a prince*, as her mother had told her somewhat drunkenly one night before the wedding. Before Enzo had died, her father had enjoyed that royal ear he'd wanted. Of course, Enzo had been chaotic and not very trustworthy, so Ines didn't think it had worked quite the way her father had hoped.

Particularly when Enzo had died and Alexandre had shown no interest in playing her father's games. In those first few months of being a princess, of Alexandre meeting every *appointment*, she'd been happy enough. Then, she'd gotten everything she'd wanted when King Enzo had died, except a child, and her father had gotten *nothing*.

But such satisfactions were short-lived when she was left with no child—and a husband who avoided her.

She would have stayed with Alexandre forever, and maybe even happily, if she had a child. But if he couldn't even bear to visit her bed, she needed something…else.

"You made vows, Ines," he said, enunciating every word like he could turn it into a dagger without any heat or ice behind it. "You knew going in what those vows meant. You cannot simply break them because…we don't see eye to eye."

She made herself breathe carefully before she responded. She'd learned as a child to hide her temper, her reaction. She knew how to keep those things buried deep down, and they would not serve her here anymore than they had served her in her father's house.

But this was more than seeing eye to eye, as he well knew, and his trivializing it was *infuriating*.

"But you are changing the nature of our agreement," Ines argued, keeping her calm even if she had to clasp her hands together to remind herself she had to be centered. "You are changing what that meant. We were meant to have a child. Now you are saying we won't."

There were other things she wanted, but she was giving

up on them. Something about seeing Evelyne so happy—with her husband, Gabriel, and with her pregnancy. It was a window into a life Ines had never believed she could have. She had known since birth her only role was to secure her father's status with the royal family. That love would never really matter.

She had done her duty, married the prince, become a queen. She had thought that would be it. And all along she told herself it would be all right because someday she would be a mother, and she would raise a prince or princess to be a good person.

Someday she would have someone to love and love her back.

Perhaps she could have withstood being unhappy forever, Alexandre always at arm's length no matter how she'd come to care for him. There was that care *and* many things she enjoyed about being queen. She got to work with charities, make sure the issues she cared about were supported throughout the country of Alis. She had power and sway and influence, and because of Alexandre's outreach programs, she got to go into the public and *help*. She had not expected to be allowed to be so deeply involved in her people's lives. She had not expected any future royal husband to actually want her input and help.

That had certainly not been her father's way. He'd rather viewed a female child as cattle to be sold off.

So if Evelyne had never returned to the palace—married and pregnant and happy—perhaps Ines would still be going along. Perhaps she would even let Alexandre strip this last dream from her.

But the friendship she'd developed with her sister-in-law had opened her eyes to a different future. Ines liked to think she'd learned a thing or two from Evelyne over the past few months. How to stand up for herself as much as she stood up for others. How to value herself, not bury herself in everyone else's value. Evelyne was not afraid, not dutiful. She stood up to her brother and to her husband.

And life had rewarded her.

So Ines had come to the conclusion that enjoying her duties was not enough. She deserved more.

She would have loved to believe she could get that *more* from Alex. She knew what a good man he was. Underneath all his layers of cold control was a man who desperately wanted to put his country to rights, to undo his father's evil. Ines loved being at his side for that.

But Ines knew she could not get under that control. If he cared about her at all, he saw her as a tool. Not a wife in the true sense of the word. Not even a friend.

So if he would not give her a child, she could not stay.

Her hands shook, so she tightened her grip on them. She did not let herself look away from Alexandre's handsome face, though the grim line of his mouth and the fire of fury danced in his dark eyes.

She had seen him furious before, mostly when his father had been alive, but he always kept it under control. And he did so now.

Perhaps that was why something that was nothing like fear fluttered low in her stomach. Because she didn't *fear* Alexandre. Sometimes she was terribly afraid she was so in love with him that, even if she did leave, she'd never get over it.

Alexandre inhaled deeply, and she braced herself because she knew he would speak once he carefully exhaled.

"Ines, I will not pretend to know what has gotten into

you. I suggest you leave at once, and we will simply… forget about this conversation."

Ines squeezed her hands tight enough for her nails to dig into her flesh. She wanted to jump to her feet and *yell*, but she would not. She would *not*. She would be like him. So cool and detached and *certain*.

For once, she would demand what *she* wanted. What *she* deserved.

"I do not want to do that, Alexandre."

"You married into a *system*," he said viciously. "Your wants and desires ceased to matter when you pledged yourself to Alis."

A system. A pawn. Yes, she'd known her role, but in the past year, outside of her father's house and rigid rules and demands, Ines had slowly unfurled. Maybe not outwardly, but inside herself.

Her role no longer felt like some fixed, external cage. It was something *she* got to have some say in. Alexandre could really only blame himself for such a change. He'd let her determine which charities she wanted a role in. He'd given her carte blanche to plan events. He had solicited her opinions on certain matters.

Yes, he was still in charge. Yes, because of years of training she almost always let him have his way, but he'd opened up a new world. He'd given her a small say, and now she understood the phrase *Give them an inch and they'll take a mile*.

Because she wanted so much more than his measly inch.

She stood and let her hands relax at her sides instead of clench into fists. Because she had stood, and because his manners were so ingrained, he stood as well. He was taller than her, but he'd placed his palms on his desk and leaned forward so they were nearly eye to eye, only the desk between them.

"I pledged myself to Alis, yes," she agreed, keeping her voice quiet enough to feel like she was in control. Because she would not raise her voice to bluster. It didn't work with him. He'd survived too many years of his father. "But I also pledged myself to *you*, Alexandre."

He looked at her like she'd taken to speaking Greek. "This has nothing to do with *me*. Your wish to be a mother is...your own."

She sighed. "It is. But it was part of our agreement, was it not?"

He was stubbornly silent in response.

Ines did not consider herself someone with a temper. She had never been *allowed* temper. Perhaps that's why when it sparked to life now, she let it. "I want a child."

"Well then, by all means. Let us simply get after it right now."

He said it with such savage distaste, she felt the need to meet his disgusted tone with a challenge of her own, to take his snide comment and flip it on its head.

"You know what? Let's. We've the time blocked off, after all." She jerked off her jacket and tossed it aside, watching the muscle in his jaw tic. A strange feeling swept through her. Perhaps it was freedom? She wouldn't know. She'd never had that. And since she hadn't, she chased it.

She began to unbutton her blouse.

"Ines. Enough."

But it wasn't. Not nearly enough. She shrugged out of her shirt, quickly unzipped her skirt and stepped out of it and her shoes. She was in nothing but her underwear. In his *office*. And she felt...

Alive. Ridiculously, foolishly alive. In charge. In control. Not once in twenty-five years on this planet had she ever felt this. Maybe a *fraction* of it a few months back when she'd insisted that Alexandre *must* interfere with Gabriel's thick-skulled abandonment of Evelyne.

But this...this was a freedom she'd never felt. She was a *storm*. Powerful. About to do *damage*.

So she did not cower, as she might once have done. She did not wilt at his icy, disapproving stare. At the way he could look like an imposing mountain, all broad shoulders and dark hair and eyes. So much larger than her. So much more powerful.

Except, whatever flickered in his gaze made *her* feel like the powerful one.

She crossed the distance between them, pressed her body to his. He held himself stiffly, even as his heat wrapped around her.

And he did not push her away, when he had all the physical power to do so. His nostrils flared, his gaze was angry, but he did not set her apart from him.

So she hooked her arm up around his neck and pulled his mouth down to hers.

And then she kissed him with all this newfound wildness, as she'd never once kissed him before.

She expected cold dismissal. Perhaps even a kind of pleasant response before carefully setting her back and telling her *no*. She expected so many things.

Except that he shudder out a breath when she pulled his bottom lip between her teeth.

Except that his hand clamped on her hip, strong and steadying.

Certainly not his other hand moving up her spine, the strong, hot weight of his palm a drug in and of itself.

Then his fingers were in her hair, tensing into a fist. The pressure a delightful frisson of pleasure that twisted into violent want and need when he pulled enough to get her mouth away from his.

The slight prick of pain in her scalp fused with a dark pleasure of his kiss, his body, so that her knees grew weak, her body *pulsed*. She thought it would take nothing at all for an orgasm to sweep through her.

She had enjoyed sex each and every time they'd engaged in it, but *this*? This was something else entirely. The word *enjoy* had no place here. It was too tame. Too small.

He held her back from his mouth, his eyes dark and wild, his breathing as ragged as hers, his hands still a fist in her hair. She watched him try to fight for some control, some sense of the usual *Alexandre*.

But he couldn't find it.

CHAPTER TWO

It was insanity. The pulsing, sexual haze that surrounded him was utter insanity. It was a spell, and he had to be strong enough to break it.

She had tested his control and resolve before, but only in the bedroom, only in his own mind. Never with demands. Never with wants of her own.

Nothing like this.

He held her there, a terrifying thrill of power flowing through him. She was in his grip. She was *his* to do what he wished with. She was such a tiny little thing in stature, but the curves she carefully downplayed in her royal outfits were on plain display in nothing but her underwear.

Ivory skin. Soft. Warmth. *Life*. Her cheeks were flushed, her breath as ragged as his. Her blue eyes wide, but there was nothing like *fear* or *concern* in that gaze. No, it was all want.

Underscored by the fact her hands were carefully undoing the buttons of his perfectly pressed shirt, all the while she looked right back at him.

She was just so warm. She smelled as she always did, some alluring mix of citrus and vanilla. It existed in her skin, deep in her hair, everywhere. Now it wound around him like some opiate haze.

Her hands pushed the shirt open so that his chest and

stomach were bared to her. She leaned forward, and his hand in her hair allowed the forward movement. As she pressed an open mouth kiss just over his heart.

Then lower. She undid his belt, the button of his pants, his zipper, and he watched her as if outside himself. She tilted her head up, and he still did not let go of her hair, but he let her continue to move down his body.

She held his gaze the entire time she sank to her knees, even as she wrapped her hand around the base of him, guided the hard, throbbing length of him into her mouth.

He hissed out a breath.

They had never done this. They could not be doing this. *This* did not beget children, which was the only reason he'd ever been with her in the first place. Heirs. Duty. To be sure, it had always ended up being pleasurable, but not solely for the sake of pleasure.

This was.

Her mouth hot and sweet. Her eyes that vibrant blue that held him in some kind of vise. Her hands on his still-clothed thighs as she took him as deep as her inexperience allowed.

He would come undone in mere seconds if he let her continue such a thing. He would stop this. Here. Now. A lapse in sanity. A momentary weakness.

When King Alexandre was *strong*.

He pulled her away from him by her hair, the sound she made—a keening kind of moan—arrowing through him, tearing all his determination to ribbons.

He released her hair and pulled her up from her knees and in one swift move deposited her on his desk. He kissed her, deep and rough, wildfire in his veins. Pounding through him so hard he couldn't hear any more of his thoughts.

He unsnapped the enclosure of her bra and filled his palms with the perfect weight of her breasts. They moaned together this time. The warmth of her skin, so human, so real, so soft. His. *His.*

The desk was at the perfect height to spread her legs wide, to step in between them, to slowly, torturously rub against where she was wild and ready. Her desire ripe around them as he kissed her deeper and deeper.

There was some distant alarm in his head. His office. His desk. His *control* tattered on the ground, but he could still pick it up, salvage this mess.

"Alex," she panted into his mouth. She almost never called him Alex. Not even in the throes of passion. Usually only when she was angry with him.

Now she panted it. Angry? Maybe. But not *only* angry. His name was as much demand as it was *plea*.

He thought himself a better man, and it only took his arranged bride to undo all of that.

And then he was inside her, and she *moaned*, erupting around him in great, clenching waves. Wanton and careless. He'd known he could push her here, and yet he always held himself back.

Wild was the enemy.

But it had won today, because he moved inside her chasing all that wildness. All that desperation. She moved against him, held on to him, chanted his name in pleading, pleasured glory. She touched him, and somehow she made him feel like a person—hot-blooded and real—instead of what he had to be: an icon. A statue. An immovable force of good.

She kissed him—her mouth was soft, reverent. Like she might care for him beyond all he had to be.

He had no space for that, even as it wound inside of

him like a drug. Even as he stopped holding back from his own crashing orgasm.

The moment was intense. It made him feel like someone else. Like a man. Any man. Not a king. Not the man tasked with undoing his father's horrid mistakes.

Just a man. The weight of it enough to make him unsteady.

And even in his brain-melted state, he knew unsteady was the enemy.

He removed himself from her, blinking back into reality even as his body still pumped in sluggish pleasure.

His office. His *day*. He did not have time for *this*. He'd be late. For all the tower of things that must be done.

God knew he hadn't even locked the *door*. What if someone had come in and seen him in such an animalistic state? It would have been a disaster in a million different ways.

And she dared to sit on his desk, naked and mussed from *him*, looking…sated. *Smiling*. It stoked a fury in him that he knew was the tainted blood of his father. But he would not ever cross a line into violence, into fury.

That did not mean he had it in him to be *kind*. "I hope you're happy."

Ines *was* happy. Oh, it wouldn't last, considering he was about to ruin it all, but that had been…

Glorious. Wondrous. Altering.

Except it hadn't altered him. Well, for a moment it had, but now they were back to stone cold King Alexandre. Maybe with a little more panic, but he was reining it in, even as she sat on his desk—*naked*—still trying to catch her breath.

But now, in a stark kind of clarity, she understood why

she'd believed he could never return her feelings for him. He always saw to her pleasure during their *appointments*, and she knew he found some of his own. But it was always…a kind of detachment. He never caused her pain, was always gentle and attentive, and obviously came to his own…conclusion. Or there would be no expectation of a baby, after all.

But never this wild, fiery thing. Never this loss of control. Never seeing who he was underneath all those brick walls he built for himself.

But now?

She reached out to touch him, and he sidestepped away from her hand. He bent over, picked up her discarded clothes and handed them to her.

She didn't take them at first.

"We didn't even lock the door, Ines."

He sounded so disgusted. She thought she should feel some kind of shame as he did, but she could not find any inside of her. Perhaps when the aftershocks of it all wore off, but she rather thought it was hardly the end of the world to get caught up with one's *spouse*.

She took the clothes. "I do not know that anyone would be all that shocked that a man and his wife might share a morning *appointment*." She slid off the desk and began to pull her clothes back on—because the door *was* still unlocked.

"Perhaps they would not be shocked, but people have *phones*, Ines. Would you be quite so casual if pictures of your naked body were sold to tabloids around the world?"

Ines blinked, his words like a bucket of cold water. She shivered against them. "Perhaps not," she managed to say. "But it seems you are reaching for the worst-possible scenario."

"Yes, that is my *job*. My duty."

She sighed. She knew he felt that way, but she did not know how he lived under the weight of that. She kept trying to save him from the weight of that, but he never listened to her. Never considered her. Not when it came to *them* as people. "It does not always have to be about duty. Not *always*." She stepped forward, wanting to reach out and touch him, knowing he would only avoid it again. "Sometimes it could be about *us*, if you'd let it."

He made a dismissive sort of noise. "I am going to be late for my meeting with the French diplomat. A meeting I cannot afford to be late for. You must leave at once."

He did not look at her. A million feelings crashed around in her chest. She even gave half a thought to causing another scene. Be the storm. Be in charge.

But for the moment she was a bit too bruised. She wanted to retreat, and wasn't this whole thing about getting what she wanted?

So she followed the impulse. She left his office saying nothing else. She tidied herself up and met with all her appointments that day, but neither her heart nor her head were truly in it.

They were both back in his office, reliving that moment over and over in her head.

She wanted it to mean something. She wanted it to mean *everything*. She even fantasized about it.

If she pressed for the annulment, would there be a repeat performance?

Or would he relent and give her what she didn't want but thought she probably needed?

She was too terrified of the second option, but she did not know how to continue like this. She wanted to be a *person*, not *only* a queen. A *human being*, not only a statue.

He wanted the opposite. Whether he *should* or not did not matter, because it was what he wanted.

Almost a year of being his dutiful wife had not changed anything for him. Her *goodness* had not suddenly made him any different. Even that unexpected loss of control and blazing passion had not changed anything for him.

She had realized sometime in the past few weeks it never would, and today only confirmed that. So how should she proceed? How could she save herself from the relentless weight of wanting to be a mother? Wanting him to love her—knowing he never would?

If he would not give her the annulment, what then?

A knock sounded at her bedroom door where she sat at the mirror getting ready for dinner. Before she could respond, it opened, and Alexandre stood there. He did not cross the threshold.

"Evelyne has had the baby."

For a moment, the words couldn't arrange themselves in a way that made sense. His sister. Baby. *The baby.*

Her nephew had been born. Ines knew she should feel elation, but for a moment there was only a sharp stab of pain at the idea that she could not seem to find love and a future for herself. "Oh."

"She would like us to come meet him."

Ines gathered herself. There were some things that no matter how she was feeling, no matter how much she wanted to *change* them, she still had to put on a queen's mask and face. This was one of those things.

Not because it was *business*, but because regardless of what went on between her and Alexandre, her nephew had been born.

Will he be my nephew if Alexandre allows an annulment?

That thought ached. But she shook it away because

no matter what Evelyne was her *friend*. They would remain friends.

She rose. "Yes, of course."

She crossed the room, but Alex did not move. He stood in her doorway, a disapproving, concrete mountain.

But he hadn't been that in his office this morning. Certainly not when she'd lowered herself to her knees and—

"Before we go down to her room, I would like you to know I've given your request the necessary consideration." He stood there, stiff and formal, hands clasped behind his back. He *appeared* to be looking at her, but he was not *truly* meeting her gaze.

She studied his dark eyes, fascinated by this slight change. This slight sign of…cowardice.

"An annulment is unlikely, though not fully out of the question. This delicate situation will require time and thought and careful planning," he said, his voice toneless. "I do not wish to use my nephew's birth as a distraction for anything so…distasteful. Since it will take some time, and you no doubt do not wish to remain in the palace, I will arrange somewhere for you to live. Out of the way. Private."

Her mouth dropped open. She had not expected him to simply sign off on an annulment. She had definitely expected refusal. But this was…

"You're…sending me away?"

"Not immediately. You will stay put until we know…" He glanced down at her stomach. As he so often had in the past year. They never said words like *not pregnant* or *no baby*. It was all code words and glances at the parts of her body that seemed honor-bound to betray her while offering no medical answers for *why*.

Stay put. He wanted her to stay put. But if she was *not*

pregnant in a few weeks, as would no doubt be the case considering the past eleven months, he would send her into *exile*. While he and he alone worked out the *details*.

She forced herself to breathe normally as she began to see spots. Perhaps it was rage. Perhaps it was a rage *stroke*. She wasn't quite certain. But he turned on a heel and walked away.

To see Evelyne. To meet the baby.

And she would *stay put*, while he adjusted everything to suit himself.

No. No, she couldn't allow that. The certainty of that was like a tsunami of purpose, but an argument would be pointless. He was the king.

So she said nothing. She followed him to Evelyne and Gabriel's wing and tried very hard to force a believable smile for the pair as they entered the bedroom.

Evelyne was in bed, a bundle in her arms. Gabriel's hip rested on the edge of the bed, looking down at both his wife and the baby.

Ines did not look at Alex. She stayed on one side of the bed, while he went to the other.

Ines looked at the baby. Just the tiniest thing. His eyes closed, his round face relaxed and content. It brought a wave of love and envy. Joy and pain. She blinked back some tears, looked up at Evelyne.

Luckily her sister-in-law's eyes were on her son, so she would not see the tears in Ines's own eyes. She just looked exhaustedly at peace.

Ines *felt* the love and joy she so wanted to experience. She felt a wave of love for this little bundle who was her nephew.

Or not, depending on how Alexandre *worked things out*. Details *he* got to choose. Instead of doing the *sane* thing and agreeing to return to their *appointment* schedule, he was going to send her away.

No. No, he didn't get to do that. He didn't get to decide. If anything made it clear it was this new *life*—a life that brought Evelyne and Gabriel so much joy in the moment. She wanted that.

If Alexandre wouldn't give that to her, she would not be his pawn, his tool, his *anything*. She would not be *sent away*. She would not live her life at *his* whim.

She was the storm.

For the first time in her life, *she* was going to decide.

CHAPTER THREE

IT TOOK NEARLY forty-eight hours to realize Ines was missing. Alexandre had been avoiding her, and he'd been so wrapped up in diplomatic meetings that also required meetings with his bloodthirsty general he was still trying to get rid of without starting a bloody *coup* that he had simply assumed she was avoiding him as much as he was avoiding her.

He had heard no rumblings about missed appointments. He had heard nothing of her not being where she was *meant to be*. And since *he* had avoided meals with her, no one had bothered to inform him that *she* had not been taking meals at *all*.

Apparently because she had planned it quite carefully. Her assistant—also missing—had quietly and carefully rearranged all of Ines's appointments—canceling, rescheduling, taking care of them via *email*.

Then there was the fact no one even knew what car she'd taken or even what day Ines had *actually* left the palace. Since he had gutted his father's insane border patrol with checkpoints everywhere, leaving only what was necessary, it would be easy enough to slip out of the country unnoticed.

And so she likely had.

But it *would* require planning, and the conclusion Alexandre had come to was that it had also required *help*—from more than just her loyal assistant. There was no way disappearing for *days* without being found out could have happened without the most *personal* intel.

So he went in search of his sister, doing his level best to maintain the roiling anger underneath an outer wall of frigid calm. He'd had such practice at hiding his feelings, it was second nature.

Why didn't it feel like second nature today? Why did it feel like he'd been split open and his insides were pouring out of him? Why did the anger feel akin to grief? Why was everything so damn confusing?

Ines.

Perhaps she was the punishment his father had wanted for him after all.

When he found his sister, Evelyne was sitting alone in one of the parlors. She was sipping tea with her eyes closed. She looked tired. In any other situation, he might have reconsidered making demands of her.

But his wife had *run away*, and someone had *helped her do it*. Evelyne had survived labor, and though he worried about her sitting here alone in silence, the doctors had assured him everything had gone exactly as it should, and Evelyne was as healthy as could be.

And his wife *was missing*. He gritted his teeth together and stepped into the room.

Evelyne's eyes blinked open. "Oh, hello, Alexandre." She closed her eyes again. "I'm a bit busy right now."

He looked at her dubiously. She was curled up on the settee, drinking tea, no baby to be seen. Eyes *closed*.

She opened them again, narrowed them. *"Shoo."*

He stared at his sister for a full minute. "I beg your pardon?"

She sighed heavily. "Sorry." She did not sound the least bit apologetic. "I have thirty minutes of alone time to sit with my tea in silence while Gabriel takes care of Gabriel." Her irritable scowl softened into a smile. "I suppose there are some downsides to naming your child after his father. It gets rather confusing, but we can't decide on a nickname. *I* think Gabby is quite nice. Gabriel thinks Gabri. They're near the same, are they not? So why not just go with mine? *I'm* the one who had to push him out of my body, aren't I?" She waved a regal hand in dismissal. "*Anyway*, this is my quiet alone time. You're not invited."

He let his sister prattle on, but he did not pretend to care about what she was saying. "Where is she?"

Evelyne's eyebrows drew together. "Who?"

"Ines," he ground out.

"How should I know?" She gave a careless shrug, then after a moment seemed to take on at least some of the gravity of the situation. She studied him, tilting her head slightly. "You've lost your wife, Alexandre?" she tsked and shook her head. "What a shame, though I can hardly blame her the way you stomp about."

He did not trust his voice right away. He breathed through the fury and some other feeling he did not know how to label.

Evelyne must have recognized *some* note of seriousness in his expression, because she sobered. "Alex, I haven't seen Ines. I've been exhausted and out of sorts, what with having a *baby three days ago*. And... Well, to be honest, I thought perhaps she was feeling a little tender over the baby, and that's why I haven't seen her. So I haven't asked after her. Perhaps she's in the library."

"She has been missing from the palace for nearly three days."

Evelyne blinked, looking well and truly shocked. But his sister *was* a good actress. "She ran away?"

"You're telling me you had nothing to do with this?"

Evelyne's gaze got a little cool. She leveled him with a hard look, but there was a softness in her eyes. "I would help Ines in a lot of ways and support her in more, but I wouldn't do either at the cost of you."

It hurt, because he knew she was telling him the truth, and he did not fully deserve the high opinion she had of him. Yes, he'd tried to protect her, and yes, he had tasked Gabriel with saving her from having to marry the awful General Vinyes last year, but there were also so many ways he'd failed her since she'd been a baby.

And still she saw him as a hero, even when he wasn't one in the least. Father had still hurt her—physically, emotionally. No matter what stumbling blocks Alexandre had managed to erect, he had not been fully capable of protecting Evelyne.

"What will you do?" Evelyne asked gently. In the here and now. Married to a man she loved. Mother to a child she would love—better than anyone. It was not his doing that she had managed to find a good life. At best, he'd helped her survive. *She* was the one who'd figured out how to thrive.

While his wife had *run away* from him. Like *he* was a monster. Like *he'd* done something wrong, when all he'd done was work hard to do what was right, needed.

What would he do?

His reply was not gentle. "Find her."

The days stretched out long, uncomfortable and nerve-racking. Ines had never rebelled before in *any* way—not against her father, not against Alexandre—her two captors, more or less.

Well, she supposed asking Alexandre for an annulment was *kind of* a rebellion. An easing into it. Asking permission to be allowed to rebel? It hadn't felt so much scary as exhilarating, necessary, groping for *change*.

The way he'd reacted hadn't exactly *scared* her. It had given her hope. That maybe here in the life she hadn't chosen was something she *could* choose.

Him.

Then disappointment. Because he'd never choose her.

But now, running away, she felt like she'd taken a dive into an icy ocean. She was cold and scared and lost at sea.

If not for Jonet, she would have turned back. To the comfortable and familiar, even if it was a little miserable.

Jonet was Ines's cousin and oldest friend, who Alexandre had allowed Ines to hire as her personal assistant. Jonet's loyalty was not to Alis or Alexandre, but to Ines. So when Ines had asked her to make the runaway arrangements, Jonet had jumped to do just that.

Jonet was handling all the travel. Keeping Ines out of sight as much as possible and doing all she could to keep her moves from being easily found out by Alexandre.

He was a king with endless resources, so no doubt he *would* find her. She was not so foolish to think this was permanent, but if she could make it *hard* on him…

Well, maybe it was childish to want to punish him. Maybe she was childish. Maybe the *new* Ines could be childish and brave and terrified—all at the same time.

After a few days of crisscrossing Europe, keeping a low profile while Jonet handled things, they were now walking up a quaint, dirt walk to a small cottage in the middle of a forest. Ines did not know what country they were in, and she would not ask.

She did know they were meant to stay here for a while, as Jonet was satisfied they had not been followed.

Jonet marched forward, shoved a key into the lock and opened the door. She stepped inside, and Ines followed.

Inside it was dim, and all the furniture was covered. It was a bit musty, but nothing alarming.

"Home sweet home," Jonet said brightly.

It reminded Ines a bit of a fairy tale. Like Princess Aurora's cottage, and Jonet was her little fairy godmother flitting about making everything okay and safe. It left Ines feeling a strange kind of exhausted. She simply wanted to find a bed to sleep in for perhaps as long as Aurora had slept after pricking her finger.

"Jonet, I will never be able to repay you."

"Let us not worry about repayments just yet." Jonet moved into what Ines realized was the kitchen area. "It's a bit rustic," she said. "I know you're not used to that, but luckily for you, I am." While Ines's father had always had money and they'd always lived in luxury, Jonet's mother had married a man considered *beneath the family's* means. She had not grown up poor exactly, but there had certainly been lean times for Jonet's family—and Ines's father had refused to help his sister monetarily.

That was the kind of man her father was. Selfish. A little mean. But Ines had always lived comfortably. She knew her guilt over what Jonet had dealt with as a child was unwarranted, and certainly unwelcome, but she felt it all the same.

Jonet fiddled with the stove and started a fire in it, while Ines stood in the middle of the small cottage feeling more at a loss than she ever had in her whole life. Was running away any better than staying? Was having Jonet handle everything really the mark of a brave woman taking charge of her own life, her own wants?

Jonet looked over her shoulder at Ines. "Why don't you pull off all the furniture coverings? We'll get settled in."

Right. Something to do. She wasn't a queen here. She was a person like any other. She was *herself*, just like she'd always wanted to be. She tried to move toward the living room to remove the furniture coverings, but her legs wouldn't move.

Ines couldn't fathom why, but the only thing she could seem to do was stand there and sob as though she'd just lost *everything*.

CHAPTER FOUR

ALEXANDRE WAS NOT his father. He reminded himself of this as he made plans to find his runaway wife.

He would not track her down like prey. He would be civilized.

They would be civilized, even if her running away was decidedly *not*. Even if every time he thought about her *sneaking out of the palace* with that *cousin* of hers, something hot and mean erupted inside him.

But he would control it. All of it. He summoned Gabriel to his office so that it was clear it was *official* business. So that he could have a reminder that he was a good, calm, controlled king here in his minimalist office—the opposite of his father's gaudy, gilt one that Alexandre had gutted and turned into a soft, feminine office for Ines.

History be damned. His father be damned.

Gabriel came into the office, settled himself on a chair casually. "Evelyne told me Ines has…disappeared."

"Yes, I'd like to hire your company to find her, but this cannot be official business—for the palace or for you." Perhaps it *was* royal business to track down the country's queen, but Alexandre didn't love the optics of that.

Gabriel ran a security company for many royals and wealthy people. He had contacts all over the world. And maybe finding a runaway wife wasn't *security*, but it was something Gabriel's outfit could no doubt handle, especially now that he wasn't just Gabriel Marti, but *Lord* Gabriel Marti, the title he'd been given upon marrying Evelyne.

"Luckily my company specializes in off-the-books," Gabriel replied.

"Yes. Well." *Off-the-books* left him feeling a bit…*oily*. It was not how he operated, but…sometimes a king had to go against the grain. As long as it was for good, for the right reasons, it had to be okay. As long as it was handled *appropriately*, and not at all like his father.

"I'll need to ask you a few questions before I can decide how to proceed," Gabriel said, watching Alexandre carefully.

And since they had been friends since they were boys, Alexandre knew Gabriel saw too much. Still, he ignored what was in his friend's expression. Concern. Perhaps, worse, understanding.

"Why would Ines run away?" Gabriel asked, his voice very neutral. None of Evelyne's commentary on his *stomping about*, as she called it.

"I have no idea."

"Alexandre." Gabriel sighed, leaning his elbows onto his knees. "I do not know your wife nearly as well as I know you, but she has never once struck me as someone to just…fly off the handle. Even if she was, there would still be an inciting incident." His gaze was direct. "It would help if I knew it. It's easier to find where someone has run away to, if one knows *what* they're running *from*."

Alex supposed it was his friend's directness, and lack of blame, and the fact that they understood each other as few others did that allowed him to relent a *little*.

"There was…nothing. A small disagreement, I suppose, about what our future was to look like. But there were no…dramatics." Unless wild sex on this very desk counted. But much as he might like to convince himself *that* was what had sent her packing, he knew it had been his reaction to it.

Much as he'd like to pretend it was the opposite.

"I…" Gabriel shifted in his seat, a sure sign of discomfort that Alexandre found *very* off-putting. "I did hear you and Ines arguing the day Gabri was born."

Alexandre could only blink. He had argued with Ines briefly before it had turned into…well, something he hadn't quite been able to put out of his mind, particularly with how often he was required to sit at this very desk.

He shook his head. "The matter was settled. She made no threats. There was no discussion of leaving." Just him sending her away…

"Perhaps *you* thought the matter was settled, but this points to…well, her feeling otherwise. Don't you think?"

Alexandre shook his head because it did not make *sense*. "I simply could not give her what she wanted. She understood this. She said—" No, she had never come out and said she understood. He had taken her usual quiet distance as her customary agreement.

"So you disagreed on…personal, marriage matters? For your future?"

"Yes, I…" Alexandre cleared his throat. If there was anyone he could be honest with, it was Gabriel. Gabriel knew that the marriage had been arranged by his father for the most part. And if explaining the truth would help find Ines, help fix this whole situation, there was really no harm in Gabriel knowing.

Besides, Ines running away because of *this* was… She was in the wrong. "I did not think we needed to pursue having a child since the heir has been taken care of. She…disagreed."

Gabriel did not say anything to that. For a moment, his study was done in utter silence, and Alexandre could not see through it. Could not read his friend's expression. Something he had always been able to do…

At least, before Gabriel had fallen in love with Evelyne and married her. Something about that seemed to open up another dimension of Gabriel that Alexandre could not fully comprehend.

Didn't want to.

"Perhaps she simply needed a break from the palace and its fishbowl quality after such a disagreement," Gabriel said. "It's quite possible she will return all on her own after a nice holiday. Still, I will handle tracking her down, quietly and carefully."

"I…" Alexandre was at war with himself. What did he want out of this? He *wanted* to drag her back to the palace, lecture her for such a dereliction of duty, demand… something. Something.

But all of these reactions felt like ones too close to King Enzo. And still, he could hardly let his country know his wife had found fault with him and run away. Queen Ines was *beloved*. Alexandre had not yet been hailed the hero to his people that he'd hoped to be.

Because he would *not* be his father. "I want to be assured she is okay and safe. I do not wish to…" He did not know how to find the words, but Gabriel stood. He put his hand on Alexandre's shoulder.

"Understood."

And Gabriel had to understand. He had also lived in fear of King Enzo as a boy. He had helped Alexandre save Evelyne from one of his father's plots.

So Alexandre sat back and let Gabriel handle this. He did not ask for updates. He did not demand *action*, though days dragged on with none of those things.

It took nearly a month—between Gabriel carefully choosing the right man to track Ines down to making sure the investigation was quiet, careful and involved no threats.

Finally, Ines had emailed Evelyne at one point to assure her she was fine, and it was the break Gabriel's man needed.

They'd traced her to a small Italian village, living out of town a ways in a *cabin* with her traitorous cousin.

"I can have someone bring her home," Gabriel said, his voice devoid of any emotion, but Alexandre knew there would be judgment based on how he responded.

Alexandre shook his head. "No."

"Evelyne and I could handle things here for a day or two if you'd like to collect her yourself."

"Not yet."

Gabriel's eyebrows rose. "You want her to…stay there?"

He did not. He wanted to drag her home, lecture her, demand to know what the hell she had been thinking.

He wanted his *mouth* on her—and this was the main thing that made his decision for him.

All of these overly emotional responses were not acceptable. So perhaps it would be best if she just…stayed where she was. This was, essentially, his plan. Get her away so he could *think*.

So let her hide. Let her think she'd done some great runaway. What did it hurt? It got him exactly what he'd been planning on anyway—though *he* would have done it with more tact and a PR plan in place. Still, it wasn't so different.

That idea *almost* got through the red haze of anger.

"Yes, for the time being. Let her have her runaway. As long as I know where she is, what she is up to, that is enough for the time being." He could rest. Relax. And be safe from losing his hold on everything with her an entire country away.

While he got everything sorted—determined if an annulment was even *possible*, this was better.

"All right." It was not approval. If anything, there was a tinge of disapproval in his tone.

But Alexandre knew this was the right way to handle it, whether Gabriel approved or not. Ines would be too far away to tempt him, to needle him. But he would know she was safe and he wouldn't worry that she would chafe under his demands. She would think *she* was in control.

Let her.

"I need someone to watch her though. Completely hands-off. Just keeping tabs."

"I'll make sure of it."

"Thank you."

But Gabriel didn't leave. He hesitated, which wasn't like him at all. So Alex braced himself for whatever Gabriel would say.

"Eventually your country is going to want to know why they haven't seen their queen for so long," he said softly, gently even.

"Yes," Alexandre agreed.

But today was not *eventually*.

Nor would tomorrow be.

Ines was miserable in so many different ways she couldn't even catalog them all. She'd stopped worrying about Alexandre finding her. Maybe it was foolish to let her guard down, but she couldn't seem to muster the mental energy.

She was tired. Achy. Nauseous. A flu that came and went, ebbed and flowed, but never disappeared. At least, she kept telling herself it was the flu. Even though she began to suspect something else.

She couldn't let herself engage in that possibility, though. It was too hopeful a thought. Too *awful* a thought. All mixed together into one big fat mess.

Impossible messes were not new to her. She'd been in what had felt like a few in her life. Being promised in marriage to a man she didn't know, a prince she had no concept of, had been her duty. That had felt like a potential sticky mess at the time.

Then she'd been introduced to Alexandre. He'd been so handsome and kind. Not as aloof as he could be now. No, in the beginning he had been almost *warm*. He had at least always tried to put her at ease, tried to engage in *some* charm.

Now that she'd been around him—and his father—she understood what Alexandre had been doing. Maybe his father had picked her out, thanks to her father's fortune, but Alexandre did not wish to make *her* a victim of King Enzo.

Alexandre was not like King Enzo. Sometimes she wondered if she only loved Alex because he was the bright spot of good in King Enzo's kingdom. But she'd watched Alexandre both under King Enzo's rule and since the old bastard had died.

Alex was a man who put others' needs before his own. He was a man who endeavored to be all the good his father had not been. He could be cold. He certainly kept his *real* self hidden behind a mask.

But sometimes, very rarely, she'd seen underneath the mask—not when he was being kind or even sweet—like in the early days before the wedding when they'd take walks in the garden and he'd made some attempt to get to know her—what she liked and didn't, her hobbies, her interests. The true Alex didn't show up in all that planned *warmth*.

No, the true Alexandre came out in darker moments. When he'd sent his sister away to save her but worried over her. When Evelyne had returned married to Gabriel and very pregnant and Alexandre had been conflicted about his best friend's role. After his father's death when he'd felt guilt over not feeling grief—and he'd let her comfort him.

In his office, when anger had finally snapped some band of control, and he hadn't held anything back.

Her heart ached thinking about him, considering that the one moment he'd lost control might have created... She shook her head, refusing to engage with the thought.

She would soon find she wasn't pregnant at all. It was just the stress. Or perhaps these physical issues were simply about not acclimating to the water at the cabin or some such.

If you think that's the case, why won't you see a doctor? Jonet had demanded that a few days ago when Ines had once again been miserable.

Ines had not had much of a response to that. She'd made noises about being afraid Alexandre would find her if she sought medical attention, but it wasn't true.

If he hadn't found her by now...he wasn't trying to find her. Perhaps he hadn't even noticed she was gone. Didn't care. Perhaps he'd told the whole kingdom she'd simply disappeared, and they were all better off.

None of that really made any sense, but she didn't have the energy to figure out what *did* make sense. She just sank into the certainty he didn't want her.

And that was fine, because she didn't want *him*. Not... not the way they'd been doing things. A wall always in between them, except when something terrible happened or when he deigned to visit her bed.

On the verge of tears again, Ines looked up as the front door swung open. Jonet marched into the cottage, carrying bags from the market, interrupting Ines's pity party. *Thank goodness.*

"I've brought you something from the market," Jonet announced loftily. Something about her hard expression had Ines's stomach fluttering in concern.

"I hope it's more ginger ale," Ines offered with a pleasant smile. It did nothing to change Jonet's expression.

"There is that. Also this." Jonet pulled a box from one of her bags and walked it over to where Ines lay on the couch.

Ines took the proffered box and tried to read the label. Her Italian was patchy at best, but she read English quite well, and underneath the larger print of Italian, in smaller print in English it read *early pregnancy test*.

She looked up at her cousin. How had Jonet come to the conclusion Ines was so desperately trying to avoid?

"You need to know," Jonet said firmly. "You cannot keep wallowing. We need answers so we can decide what to do. Go on then."

Ines opened her mouth to argue, but Jonet was clearly determined. "If you are not pregnant, you will need to see a doctor to see what is wrong with you. If you are, you will also need to see a doctor to make sure you and a potential baby are healthy. So this is the only step to take." She pulled Ines to her feet and then into the bathroom. "Do not come out until the test is done."

Then she left and closed the door smartly behind her.

Ines blew out a shaky breath. She looked at the offensive box. She could…lie. To Jonet. To herself.

And where would that get you?

Well, wallowing. Which she had to admit, she'd been… *enjoying* wasn't the right word. But it felt nice after years of denying herself every emotional reaction to swamp herself in this one. She was not required to think or act or know. She could just feel.

But now she needed to know. As much as she'd rather continue the wallow, Jonet pointing out she'd need a doctor either way was… Well, it was one thing to deny concerns about her own health, another to deny what might be going on if…if…

She looked at the box. Why was she avoiding this so much?

Because you know.

And the test confirmed all her suspicions.

After a year of desperately trying and having *no* luck, they'd engaged in reckless, angry sex in his office and conceived a child.

She leaned against the sink, eyes closed, emotion swamping her. How could this *be*? Why couldn't it have happened months ago? Everything would be different. *Everything*.

Jonet tapped on the door and then opened it. She stepped in, looked at the test on the sink, then nodded.

"Would you like to call Alexandre?" Jonet asked gently.

"God no." Ines couldn't imagine explaining this to him over the phone. Or at all. Not in this moment, anyway.

"Return to the palace?"

Ines shook her head. Go back there? With this news? After he'd… He didn't want a child. He didn't want *this*.

"Then what, Ines?"

"I don't know." A baby. Finally. This thing she'd wanted for so long, and now it was here at the worst possible time. She slid a hand over her flat stomach. She was elation and joy and dread and disappointment, all in one body.

She swallowed at the wave of nausea. Proof there was a *baby*. A baby *she* wanted, even if he didn't. The thing she'd left him over. How could she listen to any of the negative thoughts when this was everything she wanted?

"I will need a doctor," she said, finding some strength in the idea of a baby, a child. Hers. *Hers*. Yes, Alexandre's too, but he'd rejected this possibility. Which meant it was *hers*. Hers to decide. Hers to protect. Hers to consider *everything* for.

"Yes," Jonet agreed.

"There's no point in letting Alexandre in on this until I know for sure," she said. "Until I have a medical opinion. Until…"

"Until you decide what *you* want."

Ines blinked at Jonet. Yes…yes. What *she* wanted. For herself. For her baby. She would have to tell him, but she got to decide how and when. It didn't have to be right away. She had a right to determine how *she* wanted to handle this before she involved someone who'd made it clear they didn't want this.

Ines nodded. "Yes, I'll tell him once I have figured everything out. For right now, though, we'll just…stay put. Okay?"

Ines ignored the questions and indecision on Jonet's face and took her cousin's *Okay* at face value.

CHAPTER FIVE

THE FIRST TIME Gabriel informed Alexandre that a man had visited Ines and Jonet's cabin—and said man was a doctor—Alexandre had felt a panic unlike anything he'd ever felt before.

He thought of his mother. Of blood. Screams. The doctor at a loss while everything crashed and died around him.

He had not given in to the panic, the memories though. If he gave in to panic now, everything in his kingdom would unravel. And, since no one was taken from the cabin in some kind of emergency vehicle, no bodies emerged, Alexandre knew that whatever was *wrong* was…fine.

The second time, a month later, he might have flown off the handle if Gabriel hadn't pointed out it was exactly a month from the first appointment—down to the date and time, so likely some kind of follow-up. Nothing new to be concerned about. Not an emergency of any kind.

The third time… Well, he might have stormed over to Italy that very second if Evelyne had not delivered a calm, direct question.

"Is there any way she could be pregnant?"

He had stared at her sister, sitting on the floor with baby Gabri, who seemed to grow at an exponential rate, all the while remaining impossibly small.

Sometimes Evelyne handed him to Alexandre, and Alex felt like he was five years old again, holding baby Evelyne because Father refused to let the nursemaids *coddle* her.

He didn't care for the reminder of such a helpless feeling—knowing he needed to be strong for Evelyne, for his lost mother. And not having a clue as to *how*.

But this question, this *possibility* that Ines might...

Evelyne looked up, seemed to note the shock on Alexandre's face and explained herself.

"She told me there was nothing medical in the way, according to your doctors. So unless you...hadn't been together." Evelyne pulled a face as she gazed down at the baby in her lap. "A monthly doctor's appointment *could* point to a baby. Perhaps more likely than some monthly illness if the doctor's visits are happening exactly a month apart."

Alexandre supposed he heard the words, absorbed them, but they left him in a strange in-between world. He did not know how to move forward from this simple question.

Is there any way she could be pregnant?

There was precisely *one* way, but surely... Surely it was an impossibility that after almost a year of trying she would finally fall pregnant when...

Alexandre felt a bit like his brain was short-circuiting. He couldn't seem to follow any thought to completion. It was all...*feeling*. Complex, confused, irrational *emotions*.

Surely she would have told him. If it was true, she would have returned. She would have *told* him.

And why the hell would she do that?

"What are you going to do?" Gabriel asked.

The question was asked with a gentleness Alexandre

could not engage with. No one should be that gentle with a *king*. He was in charge. He was the one thing keeping everything together. So there could be no *gentle*.

Only decisions. Only leadership. Only moving forward with certainty and surety.

"I am going to this cabin, and I am going to bring her home."

"Alexandre, perhaps…perhaps you should let me or Gabriel do it." Evelyne smiled at him encouragingly, but he could see underneath that smile was a worry that he would not conduct himself as he should.

"I will be reasonable." Would Ines be? Well, she would have to be.

Reason was the only way out of this.

"Of course you will," Evelyne agreed, still with that kind of encouraging tone that made him want to grind his teeth together. "But it wouldn't hurt to have a friendly face—"

"I am her *husband*."

"Discuss what's going on before you—"

"Before I what?"

"Make demands and proclamations or say something you might regret."

You might regret. Like *he* was the problem here? "I am the king of Alis, Evelyne. Everything I do is a proclamation. I cannot regret this."

Evelyne sighed. "But you will," she muttered.

Alexandre ignored her. He went to his office. Then he stood there, frozen with an indecision that made it hard to breathe. He had to decide. He had to take charge. He had to *know* what was right or everything would crumble.

"If you're looking to do this under the radar, I can fly you."

Alexandre did not look behind him at the sound of Gabriel's voice. He couldn't face a man who knew him so well—who would read the panic when Alexandre could not allow *panic*.

So he would not consider Gabriel's words until he could *breathe*.

He had to breathe. Decide. Act. Protect. Ensure.

He blinked a few times, centering himself in the here and now. Ensuring he could speak clearly before he attempted it. "Yes. I will need to attend my meetings this afternoon." Because he could not shirk his duties, no matter the circumstance. "Can you get away early tomorrow morning?"

"Of course," Gabriel said.

He would act. Not regret his actions. He would go to this *cabin*, he would explain what would happen now—she would return to the palace, they would go back to the way things were, and now she had a child, likely, so there was no need for an annulment.

Everything could be as it should. It was a *relief*. The panic eased, but something else swept into its place. Because it struck him then, wholly and painfully. If she'd had a doctor come out three different times, she'd known.

She'd known and stayed away. Purposely. Not just for a few days of adjusting to the information. She'd stayed away on purpose, knowing this truth, for *months*.

Why hadn't she come back? If the annulment request was just about having a child, and now she would have one, why would she stay away?

He rubbed at the pain in his chest and forced it down with the rest of his feelings. Deep under a wall of reason. Sense. *Action*.

It didn't matter why she'd stayed away. Because now it was time for her to come home.

Whether she wanted to or not. Whether he wanted her to or not. Everything would go back to the way it was, to the way he'd planned.

And that was that.

Ines had decided to wait for the second trimester. If the pregnancy was in good shape then, she would call Alexandre and inform him. She would lay out a plan where she stayed here. He didn't have to give her an annulment if that was a no go. He just had to let her *be*.

Because that was what she wanted. Or needed. Or something. She refused to allow herself to hope for some...change of heart from him just because she was pregnant. Because he did not want this, and *she* did.

So.

She made it into the second trimester in the sweet little cabin, enjoying the quiet days with Jonet, even if she was a bit bored without all her royal commitments. But she still replied to emails and sometimes even attended virtual meetings for some of her responsibilities. She missed going to meetings, visiting the orphanage and the children's hospital, the adaptive park she'd helped spearhead.

She tried not to think about Alexandre or the future and instead focused on caring for her changing body, her new home and her cousin.

When the doctor arrived for her four-month appointment, he went through the exam in the cabin as he had the past few times. They listened to the baby's heartbeat. He assured her everything was well.

Every time an appointment came, motherhood felt real and impending, and then the doctor would leave, and everything would feel like a dream again. Like she made it up.

But she was firmly in the second trimester of her pregnancy, which meant she needed to start planning for what happened on the *other* side of pregnancy. Which meant she needed to tell Alexandre, as she'd promised herself.

But she did not call Alexandre that night. She did not make plans to return to the palace. She knew it was wrong. Guilt swamped her every time she thought of him.

But so did fear. And anger. And a million other emotions.

When Ines crawled out of bed the next morning, tired and still vaguely nauseous, she figured she could give herself another month. Just to feel steadier. She didn't want to approach Alexandre when nausea still seemed to rule her life. She needed more…traction. Physically. Telling him in a month would be fair.

There was nothing he could do as a king or as a father at this stage in her pregnancy, so it wasn't *wrong*.

And if she still felt as emotionally confused and wrung out as she did now when the physical symptoms settled? Well, she would cross that bridge when she came to it.

She went into the kitchen hoping for some breakfast to soothe the unsteady feeling in her stomach, but Jonet stood in the living room, peering out the window.

She glanced at Ines over her shoulder. Grimaced. "Ines, we have a problem."

"What's that?" Ines moved over to the window, expecting to find some kind of wildlife conundrum. Instead, she saw a car parked in front of their cottage. It was black, sleek and *expensive*. It was certainly not the physician's car—their only visitor out all this way.

Then a familiar figure stepped out of the driver's side.

He was dressed as casually as she'd *ever* seen him, like he was trying to fit in with the *commoners*. Jeans and a sweatshirt. Boots befitting the forest around them.

But there was nothing common about him. So tall. So *severe*. That preternatural control in everything he did—including striding toward the front door. Like he knew exactly what was on the other side.

He didn't *look* angry, but she knew he would have to be. If he was here, if he'd left his precious kingdom behind for even a moment... Yes, he was angry.

She had convinced herself if the king of Alis had not found her in all these months, he was not trying to find her. Had she been wrong? Had Jonet done such a good job of making them disappear that it had really taken him all this time to track her down?

She didn't know what to do with that thought, even if her heart fluttered a bit. She didn't know what to do with *any* of this.

"Ines. Do you think he knows?"

Ines shook her head. If he knew, he'd... No, how could he possibly know if he was just showing up here now? "No. And he...he doesn't have to know," Ines heard herself say. Her body had changed *some*, but not much. He certainly wouldn't notice any thickening by the baggy clothes she wore.

She would send him away, and he wouldn't have to know. She could keep living in this space, where the baby was hers, and she did not have to deal with Alexandre's resentment.

"Ines, I'm not sure..." Jonet bit her lip. "You know I'll support you on anything. I'm on your side. But...he *is* your husband and the father of the baby. And, perhaps most importantly, a king."

The hard *rap* of knuckles on the door caused Ines to jump. She didn't have time to think. To plan.

"We can pretend we're not here," Jonet whispered.

For a moment, Ines held on to that thought. They could avoid this. All of this.

But this moment was a stark reminder that *hiding* did nothing but delay the inevitable. She could not pretend she wasn't here—because he was. She could not keep this pregnancy from him any longer—because it *existed*.

She had gotten her months of running away, wallowing, indulging in feelings and emotional responses, but she had known, deep down, that it could never be *real* life.

Not with a baby on the way.

So it was a crystalizing moment. Alexandre on the other side of this door, knocking. Tracking her down. No doubt here to *fetch* her.

She'd run away thinking she was in charge. She wouldn't let him *control* her. She would live her life. For a while, it had felt like finding freedom after a lifetime of men controlling her.

But this wasn't living. It was hiding. It was avoiding the hard things because they hurt to deal with. If she wanted to build a life for herself, rather than go along with what she'd always been told, *hiding* was no answer. Maybe it was better than cowering or acquiescing, but it still wasn't what she wanted.

She wasn't fully sure *what* she wanted. Except to be a good mother. Something she'd never had. Her own mother had been negligent at best, dulling whatever pain she felt with alcohol or pills.

Hiding.

Ines would not hide and let her child deal with the fallout. No, she would always be the protector. The *mother*.

The pounding on the door started up again. Ines didn't flinch this time. It was time to make a choice. Time to start being a *mother*, not just a vessel.

"I'd like to speak to Alexandre alone, if you don't mind, Jonet."

"Of course. Shall I go to your room and pack your things?"

Ines inhaled deeply, let it out. "Yes, thank you."

CHAPTER SIX

ALEXANDRE HAD THOUGHT he'd braced himself for seeing Ines again. He had expected to feel a spurt of rage over what she was keeping from him, but he'd also expected some *time* to prepare. He'd *assumed* Jonet would answer the door.

Not his wife.

Her hair was pulled back, but not in her usual slick, elegant way. It was messy, strands falling out of the band. She wore something baggy and soft—not quite pajamas, but certainly not the kind of outfit a queen should wear in *public*.

It did nothing to undercut this moment of seeing her in the flesh for the first time in *months* and realizing how much he'd *missed* her. Looking at her across the dinner table. Listening to her chatter with Evelyne. The way she'd felt like such a seamless partner when they'd go over their schedules and determined who would handle what.

So for the past four months, essentially, he'd been alone again. Like before their engagement. When he'd felt his entire life was trying to mitigate his father's violent whims—toward Alis, toward Evelyne, toward Alexandre himself.

It had been quiet and empty, and he had never *realized* that his life was mostly made up of those two things—

not until Ines had been there by his side for a year and then not at all.

He curled his hands into fists to keep from reaching out to touch her. Assuring himself she was real. That she was what he was missing.

Because he was missing nothing. He was a king. He had a kingdom to serve. His own wants mattered not at all. He was a king, not a husband. Not a man.

No matter what Ines made him feel sometimes.

He was missing *nothing*. Except a good night's sleep and the ability to be home, handling the responsibilities of his *kingdom*. Because of *her*.

"Good morning, Your Majesty," she said, with that old bland warmth that she'd trotted out before they were married. Sometimes even after. Like they were friends, but on a surface level. Acquaintances. Coworkers, maybe. She even gave a little curtsy.

He did not know what was wrong with him that it hit him like a bolt of lust. Luckily, anger swept in with it. That she could be so *casual*, with no sign of any kind of apology or even defiance.

Just *Good morning*, while everything inside of him raged and crashed around—emotion against bones. The only things keeping him from cracking apart were years of experience and the knowledge that emotional outbursts were the enemy.

Case. In. Point.

"So, to be clear, you disappear into thin air for nearly four months and you consider *Good morning, Your Majesty* the appropriate greeting?"

"Would you rather I be on my knees?"

He *knew* what she meant—begging forgiveness, but

it was not the image in his head. No, that image was of his office and her on her knees for far different reasons.

She must have realized that, because her cheeks began to redden.

Which was *dangerous*. "We will return to the palace at once. Pack your bags." He braced himself for the argument—the anger, the emotion, the push and pull. He would not give in to it like he had three months ago. He would be strong, calm and cold in response to it.

He would be the *king* he had to be, not the man underneath that he could not be.

Jonet stepped out from somewhere in this rustic little cabin, carrying a collection of bags, pulling a suitcase behind her. "They are already packed."

Alexandre blinked. He looked from Jonet to Ines. Her expression was serene. For a moment, he had no words. She was just…agreeing with him? He thought there'd be refusals, arguments, shouts. Maybe even tears. She had stayed away all this time.

But she was just… She already had her bags packed.

He opened his mouth to say something, to question this, then thought better of it. Questioning could lead to an argument, and he wanted—needed—to avoid that.

He moved past Ines, doing everything he could not to touch her as he did, and approached Jonet.

She looked a little startled. "You don't need to—"

Over her objections, he relieved her of all the bags except the one she was pulling. He then carried said bags outside to his car, putting them in the trunk, not looking at the two women. He was just going to move forward as if he'd known all along they would follow his every command.

He *was* their king after all.

He opened the back-seat door for Jonet. She did *not* look comfortable. She shot Ines a questioning glance. Ines nodded her head regally, and Jonet slid inside the back seat. Ines made a move to follow, but Alexandre closed the door before she could. He moved to the passenger-side door, opened it and gestured her inside.

He watched the inner argument chase across her face. Be defiant, or go gently? He kept expecting defiance, but she simply slid into the passenger seat.

Since he did not know what to do with the ease at which this was going, he could only continue to move forward. He closed her door, then got into the driver's seat.

Ines was frowning at him. "You're driving?"

He glanced at her. "Yes."

She looked away. "How modern," she murmured.

Modern. He felt about as modern as a caveman at the moment. But he drove away from her little cabin, away from her betrayal, and back to the private airport Gabriel had arranged for him to fly in and out of without detection, something that could be done with Gabriel piloting the plane himself.

Gabriel must have been surprised at their quick arrival, though he did not say anything. He simply greeted Ines and Jonet and helped Alexandre load the bags onto the plane while the women settled themselves into their seats.

Everything continued to go easily. They flew back to Alis. Gabriel drove them back to the palace. Gabriel took Ines's and Jonet's bags. The staff knew they had been gone, but the more they handled this clandestinely, the more whatever stories Alexandre came up with to explain the past few months would be believable.

He dismissed Jonet to return to her own quarters. He

said nothing to Ines. Ines said nothing to him. But they both walked through the palace to their residential wing.

As they began to approach her set of rooms, she walked in front of him. Down the hall toward her door. As though she was just going to go inside, go back to their old lives, without a peep.

He should rejoice at that. In fact, the entire trip back he'd conceived a plan to let it all go. Let it play out. See what she did. See how she handled all this. He'd determined it was the best course of action to simply *let things be*.

She reached her door, lifted a hand to the doorknob, but he couldn't keep the words inside. All his plans fell to ash around him, just like always seemed to happen when it came to her.

"When were you planning on telling me?"

She stopped, her hand frozen on the doorknob. For a moment, she said nothing, keeping her back to him. Stiff. *Caught.* But she did not give in right away. "Telling you what?"

"That you are pregnant."

Ines stood there in the hall, her back to Alexandre, heart beating hard against her ribs.

He knew. *How* did he know? How could he have found that out? Certainly not by *looking* at her. Perhaps she was heavier than she had been, her curves a bit more pronounced, but she wore clothes that hid that, she was almost certain.

"Unless you are sick, and that is the reason for these monthly doctor's appointments, but you certainly do not look *ill*."

She inhaled, trying to work through that. So he didn't

know for *sure*, but he knew a doctor had been to see her... And suddenly it all made sense. It wasn't that he *hadn't* found her for months and now suddenly had.

He'd known where she was. Known everything. He simply hadn't *collected* her for all these months. She closed her eyes, surprised at how much that realization hurt. Almost as bad as his never looking for her in the first place. He knew, and he hadn't come to fetch her, fight for her or even let her go. He'd just...kept watch.

"You were just...keeping tabs on me all this time?" Why did she sound so winded? How could she be so hurt? She *knew* him. Of course he had been doing just that. Why had she expected different?

"I could hardly let my queen gallivant off unprotected."

"Gallivant?" She laughed bitterly, turning to face him. She leaned against the door behind her and studied him. "I ran away from you, Alexandre."

If he had any reaction to this, it was hidden behind that forbidding expression. "You did not do a very good job," he said flatly. Just standing there, somehow looking regal in his casual attire. Looking disapproving and detached.

Because he'd known for all this time where she'd been. He hadn't come to fetch her until he'd heard there was a *doctor* involved. A *child* involved.

"Answer the question, Ines," he ordered, as he always did, with complete certainty his order would be followed. It was funny how even now it didn't prompt her to want to be contrary for the sake of it. His demand for the truth was a fair-enough one, and she didn't have energy for anything other than the truth.

"When was I planning on telling you? I don't know. I promised myself I would after the three-month appointment. And then I gave myself another month to feel more…to be stronger. Physically. Being pregnant is not for the faint of heart."

She saw a flicker of worry cross his face. Watched as he took a few steps toward her and then stopped as if remembering himself.

How could these two polarities exist inside him? Worry and kindness and warmth versus that cold, demanding detachment.

King and real man underneath? Mask and truth? It didn't feel that easy. There was something messier at play, and she wanted to dive in and not fix it—there was no fixing the complications of humanity—she simply wanted to understand. To make sense of him.

"But you are well," he said, his voice a little rough. He phrased this like a statement, like she had to be well because he said so.

But it *was* a question, no matter how he put it. And it softened her when it shouldn't. Like it might concern him that she was well. That this was not a totally one-sided connection, no matter how much he might like it to be.

"I am well. The baby is well."

His gaze dropped, just for a fleeting moment, to her stomach. He could not see the soft swell of her belly under the draping of her shirt, she knew, but she felt *seen* just the same.

"We have much to discuss," Alexandre said roughly, then made no move to discuss it.

"Yes, I suppose we do, but I am tired. And hungry."

"I shall have a tray sent up. Some breakfast cake and tea. That's usually what you prefer this time of day, yes?"

"Yes." She stared at him, wondering if it was foolish to be touched that he knew that about her, or was it his robotic need to make everything *correct*? To know what she ate and when. Was it control? Interest? Concern?

Maybe it was all three. Maybe his feelings for her were as mixed up as hers were for him. Because she should be angry and defiant and contrary, and she *did* feel some anger. But she also ached to touch him.

She'd *missed* him. His steady presence. He was such an *anchor*, even when they were doing little more than sharing a meal, she felt safe with him. In ways that were new to her because growing up in her father's house had always meant being concerned how she would be used next.

Alexandre didn't *use* her. Even when he was controlling, even when he was so worried about their *optics* and his kingdom. She wasn't a pawn so much as a useful *tool*, and that meant he valued her in some way.

But he frustrated her and concerned her and infuriated her and... And he was standing close enough right now that she just wanted to kiss him. To feel what she'd felt in his office all those months ago. An uncontrollable heat—something so big, so important, so soul-deep that even perfect, controlled King Alexandre couldn't resist.

Because now she knew there *was* some hidden Achilles' heel to him. Was it her? Was it anger? She didn't know. The only thing she knew for certain was that for a year she'd held back. And when she finally hadn't, she'd gotten what she wanted. Because she wanted this baby with all she was—*regardless* of him.

But he was still a factor, because she wanted to touch him. And she was done pretending she didn't. Done holding herself back.

Like Jonet had said back at the cabin, now it was about what *she* wanted.

So she stepped across the space between them, moved

to her toes and pressed her mouth to his. Just because she could. Just because she wanted to.

She'd come back with no promises. Which meant this return was like…a fresh start. Not the clinical agreement they'd made when they'd married. No, she was someone else now.

So this time around, she was going to take what she wanted.

And for one sweet, blissful moment, he kissed her back with such *desperation* she could almost believe he'd missed her as she'd missed him. That there was something between them—an emotional connection they could work through, they could grow and tend to. Believe in.

A moment, a *flash* of that hope and joy, but he locked it down and away quickly this time.

His hands curled around her upper arms, and then she was being pulled away. Put back. His gaze was hard, even if she could see the unsteady rise and fall of his chest.

"You will behave yourself now that you are home, Ines."

It made her angry, but there was something more than anger now. She looked up at him, feeling like crying. Why would he kiss her like that and then push her away? Why was it all push then pull? Why did none of it make sense?

"I don't understand you."

For a moment, so clear and intent, she saw exactly why in his eyes.

For a strange, disorienting moment—likely for both of them—she saw clearly that he didn't understand himself.

But that was quickly swept away, into ice and distance and control.

"Get your rest, Ines. Your food will be up shortly. Try

not to run away again. It will not be tolerated a second time, particularly while you carry my child."

My child. How did he pull her in two totally different directions? Love and affection and *care* that he didn't know himself, that he tried so hard to be good. And a cold, cutting fury that he could say things like that to her.

My child. When he hadn't even wanted a child. He'd wanted an *heir*, until he hadn't needed one. And then he'd...cut her off. Cut himself off. And she could believe that it was this simple. He didn't want her.

But he *did*. He kissed her like a man starving. The way they'd come together, angry and wild, those months ago was not an uninterested man.

It was a tortured one.

The way he strode away now, quick and purposeful, was a bit like a man chased by *something*.

So maybe it was that... It wasn't the child, the pregnancy. It was her. He *wanted* her but didn't want to. He *felt* this thing between them but wanted to control it.

Because it was uncontrollable. Because it was unpredictable. Because it did not fit into the neat little order of his life he'd created trying to be the antithesis of his father, the savior of his country and his people.

But he was Alexandre, so he didn't understand *middle ground*. He had been raised by a monster, and while he had somehow turned out good in spite of it, he didn't understand his own humanity.

Which meant Ines knew what she needed to do now.

CHAPTER SEVEN

ALEXANDRE IMMEDIATELY WENT back to work once he'd ordered Ines a tray of her preferred morning snack.

He had *wanted* to track down the doctor who'd checked out Ines and demand to know every detail. It seemed a better action item than standing there cataloging all the ways her body had slightly changed in all these months.

Better than wondering how he'd lost control of all this and wanting to beg her forgiveness for wrongs he *hadn't* committed.

Because he was a king, and he was right. *She* was in the wrong. No matter how at ease she seemed with *everything*, down to growing a child.

A child. *Their* child. His child.

He was to be a father, and he knew what that meant: be the opposite his father in every way. But he didn't know what that meant in terms of being a *king*—his most important role. His *only* role.

Except Ines had upended all of that. Pregnant. Growing a child. So many dangers in that simple, age-old cycle.

But she'd said she was well. The baby was well. And Ines was not like his mother. She had no reasons to hide the truth of her health from him like his mother had hidden the truth from his father. Leading directly to her death during labor.

Sometimes Alexandre thought of that and wondered if she'd signed her own death sentence on purpose. Just to escape. Just to leave it all to *him*.

And since he was thinking about *that* awful time, and apparently blaming his poor victimized mother for anything, he kept his afternoon appointments, conferred with his assistant over a few requests and approved various action items. He skipped lunch and got out of his head, out of his past *and* his future, and into the present.

Until it was time for dinner. Something he might have skipped too, but he was not a coward. Ines was back, and everything would go back to the way it was. If it did, he would know how to handle this new role she'd thrust upon him.

Which meant he would not *hide*.

If he could get through to Ines to stop kissing him and such, everything would be *fine*.

Besides, he'd stopped that, hadn't he? Perhaps it had been difficult to set her away instead of sink into her, hold on tight and assure himself she was real and back and *here* and that meant all was well.

All *would* be well. Without kissing. Without any changes. They would go back to the way things had been. She'd had her time to run away, and she'd gotten the child she'd wanted. There was no reason for anything to change. She would be a mother. He would be a king. Easy.

So why did his heart beat in odd, anxious flutters in his chest as he walked to the dining room this evening?

Ines sat at the table—not in her usual seat, but everything else about the scene was usual. Her hair was sleekly pulled back instead of haphazard. She wore a dress more befitting her station. She did not wear the earrings he'd given her as a wedding present, or the necklace she usually wore on casual days without appointments, but she was wearing his ring.

Because everything was back the way it should be, or so he kept assuring himself. But Alexandre did not know how to get rid of this unease sitting on his chest. She was giving him exactly what he wanted. Returning everything back to normal, *just as it should be.*

He couldn't seem to relax and trust that this was true. Which was when he started to pick up on that which was *not* normal. Like the fact that table was only set for two—right next to each other.

"Where are Evelyne and Gabriel?"

Ines studied him for a moment before answering. "They are eating in their rooms this evening."

"That is highly unusual." He studied the table arrangement. He did not want to sit *right* next to her. They usually sat across from each other. But she was next to *his* seat, and it was set for him, and...

"I asked for some privacy as we discuss what's next."

His gaze went from the table setting to her. "What do you mean, *what's next*?"

"How things will go on now that I am pregnant."

"Nothing will change. Everything will go back to the way it was, except we will now follow the plans we'd previously made for a child. You will scale back your old responsibilities of course, but for the most part, everything goes on as it was."

She sighed. "Yes, I had a feeling you'd say that." She shook her head. "This does not work for me."

"I beg your pardon?"

She sighed. "Sit, Alexandre."

He balked at being told what to do, but a staff member appeared with the first course, and Alexandre had no choice, he felt, but to take the seat next to Ines. To continue on as normal for *him*, even if she was determined to make things difficult.

She gave his hand a little pat as the course was served, like she was *placating him*.

"I have missed the palace food," she said, smiling as the bowl of soup was put in front of her. "Jonet has kitchen skills I do not possess, but nothing like this."

Just normal conversation after saying their *plans* did not work for her—even though she'd been a part of making them. Or, at least, agreeing to them.

Once the staff had left them to the first course, Ines spoke again.

"We have only a few months between now and when the baby is born. For those next months, we will do the following." She picked up one of the portfolio-notebook combinations she was always using for business. He hadn't noticed it there on the other side of her, but now she handed it to him.

He took it.

She began to eat, so he opened it and saw a list in Ines's beautifully perfect handwriting. Neat. Organized.

Alarming.

Because as he read everything in her neatly printed list, his unease grew.

On weekends, we will eat meals together privately, in our own quarters, unless there is an event. They had never eaten meals together *privately*. They always ate here—with or without guests or his sister.

We will walk the gardens once a day together—you may have your assistant schedule a time or choose spontaneously. Spontaneously? He was trying to rebuild a *country*, and she wanted him to accompany her on *walks*.

We will return to our appointment schedule—with the additional requirement you spend the night in my bed on such evenings.

"What is this?" he demanded, frustrated that even *reading* the word *appointment* seemed to elicit a physical response in his body.

"Well, this is what normal married people do, Alexandre. They have private time together. They are intimate. They build a relationship outside of their roles in public. I realize we are not normal, and it occurred to me that you might need spelled out for you what I require to remain in this marriage."

Remain? "You are pregnant. You are the queen. There is no getting out of this marriage, Ines." He closed the portfolio and handed it back to her, but she did not take it. "You made certain of that whether you wanted to or not."

She held his gaze calmly, even as he felt the scalding heat of frustration poke at him.

"These are my terms, Alex. This is what the next few months will entail if you'd like me to stay put."

Alex. Alex. Why did it matter if she shortened his name? Why did it feel like she was talking to some version of himself he wished existed but didn't?

He cleared his throat, forced himself to focus. "And if I do not agree to this plan?"

"I will continue to run away," she said evenly, her gaze direct. "Every chance I get. You will have to lock me in a dungeon to stop me."

"And you think I won't?"

"No. I don't. You'll want to, God knows." She put down her spoon, took a sip of water. "But it will remind you of your father. And you won't be able to go through with it."

"You'd be surprised."

"No, Alex, I wouldn't be," she said, with absolutely no hesitation. "You have too much nobility in you to ever sink to your father's levels in anything more than thought."

"Perhaps I just haven't been pushed far enough yet."

She watched him, that blue gaze of hers as steady as ever. When she spoke, each word somehow felt like a curse. "If you haven't yet, you never will be."

The staff of course chose that moment to clear the first course and replace it with the second. Alexandre sat there in a seething silence, trying to get ahold of his temper.

If you haven't yet, you never will be.

He did not know how to believe that was true, but she said it so matter-of-factly, as if there was no doubt.

Once they were alone again, she kept prattling on in between greedy bites.

"Nevertheless, I will take that chance. If you refuse to abide by my rules, I will involve the press. I will embarrass you, if I must. But if you agree to my terms, and the baby comes and nothing has changed—you have no feelings for me, want nothing from me except to be some excellent queen mannequin—I will release you from my horrible attempts to give us a real marriage. I will go back to the way things were, remain as your wife, your queen, the mother of your child in this detached, joyless, loveless abyss."

He could only stare at her. *Detached, joyless, loveless abyss?* Is that how she saw her life? It felt like something banded around his lungs and squeezed. It felt like *guilt*—when he'd never promised her anything but just what she laid out.

"But you must give me a chance first."

"A chance for what?" he asked, truly baffled by this

woman who had been *perfect* for nearly a year and over the past few months had taken all that perfection and ease away.

She cocked her head, studying him. "To show you what living feels like."

Living. What else did he do every day but live? Meet all his lofty goals, turn this country back into what it could be? "I breathe. I live."

"You breathe. You *exist*. You deserve more. *I* deserve more. Our baby deserves more."

He could not even grasp these words.

"So do you agree?" she asked. She had cleared her plate. He had not touched his food.

Agree? He could not agree to this. It was pointless. A waste of time. It was...a ransom of sorts, and he did not deal with terrorists anymore, now that his father was dead.

But he *did* have experience with these kinds of tests, didn't he? Hoops to jump through to prove himself. His father had given him nothing but tests and hoops and challenges. Of course, there'd been no winning those.

He could win this one. Ines was honest and fair, even if this was utterly ridiculous. She wouldn't change the stakes.

What was a few months? She would be pregnant the entire time, and if he could suffer through these months of her pretending they could be more than their roles, their titles, their *responsibility*, on the other side of it was everything he wanted.

A partnership with his queen. A detached, joyless, loveless abyss as she defined it. Yes, *that* was what he wanted.

And she would have her child—the best doctors in

the world would ensure she and the baby were healthy through this—so she would get what *she* wanted.

And all would be well.

He just had to resist his wife through a few months of *intimacy*. He'd survived nearly a year before. He could do this. He would do this.

For Alis. Even for *her*, though she would not see it that way.

Ines thought her acting was superb this evening. Alexandre had to believe she was nonchalant and unaffected. That she would happily trot away to wreak havoc on his life if he did not agree to her terms.

She *would* do it, but it would hurt. Even when she was furious with him, she would take no joy in trying to ruin his reputation. He cared so much for it, and she understood why. She didn't want to continue to run or go to the press.

She wanted what she'd outlined. A *marriage*.

And it had occurred to her, after she'd eaten her morning cake and taken that long nap this afternoon, that he didn't even know what that might look like. If he didn't know himself, didn't understand his own feelings, then why should he know what a functioning relationship looked like? His only example was likely his parents—and while Alex almost never mentioned his mother, knowing King Enzo meant Ines knew it could not have been good.

Not that she had any fine example of marriage in her life, but she had solid relationships that weren't romantic. With Jonet. With Evelyne. She understood how to care for someone without needing to protect them. Without the threat and terror of abuse in every corner.

Alexandre loved his sister. He even loved Gabriel. He was *capable* of love, but Ines did not think he understood it except in the role of protector or savior. He only knew how to exist in a world where people owed him for being the good one in relation to the evil one—King Enzo.

With his father dead, he was only protecting everyone from his memory. Something no one needed. Especially her. He did not need to be her protector in anything, so he did not know what to do with her except keep her at arm's length.

There would be no more arm's length. She was sure—*almost certain*—that if she could get him to behave as a real husband, as though they were in a real relationship, he would see that it was possible. Neither he nor his kingdom would crumble if he was allowed to be the real man underneath the cold, detached crown.

"Fine. I agree to your terms. Dinners. Appointments. Et cetera." He waved these away like they were inconsequential.

But they wouldn't be. Ines wouldn't allow them to be. She beamed at him, showing only her pleasure that she'd won—not the wave of relief that he hadn't made her hurt them both by running away over and over again. "Excellent."

When dessert was served, she ate her fill. A well of hunger had begun to displace the nauseous feeling. *Or you're just happy to be home.*

She looked around the luxurious dining room full of history—some of its furnishings particularly ugly—and did not know for sure when it had begun to feel like home. Early on, she supposed, when she'd decided that marrying Alexandre meant marrying Alis, meant marrying his *goals*.

If she could be a good queen, if she could belong to and serve Alis, then she could be something. More than the pawn her father had used her as.

But she wanted to be more than a useful tool now. She wanted to be a person too. Who loved her husband and her child. Who had a family. They would always be beholden to their country, but they all deserved a place to go to just be themselves.

She would have to build it, to show Alexandre it was possible.

With dinner finished, Alexandre stood and helped her up out of her chair as he always did. But she did not let his hand go. "Shall we take our garden walk? And then, tonight would be our normal appointment, would it not?"

He stiffened, as she'd known he would. He even cleared his throat. "Surely you are exhausted from your travel."

"Funny how a short drive and an equally short flight on a private plane did not quite exhaust me. Besides, I took a nap between lunch and dinner. Do you have any other excuses you'd like to trot out?"

His face became a storm. "They are not excuses, Ines."

"Then what are they?" she asked, feigning innocence.

But he had no answer for that. Just a disapproving expression. "Very well," he muttered. "We will go for our walk."

She noted he did not mention their *appointment*, but she let that slide for now. He tucked his arm into hers and led her out of the dining room, through the palace, and then out one of the terrace doors that would lead them down to the gardens.

The night was warm, the scent of flowers and midnight wafting around them. The gardens were extensive and one of Ines's favorite places in the palace. Some long-gone ancestor of Alexandre's had planted them, and the gardeners tended them, and in every season there were different delights to discover if a person perused the winding, meandering pathways.

Ines often did just that, alone, instead of with her husband. But tonight, they walked, her arm tucked into Alexandre's, and she felt something ease inside of her that had been tied tight these past four months.

Perhaps she'd known all along that running away wasn't the answer, but she was glad she'd done it. Learned something from it. And now she was glad to be back, fighting for something good.

"This reminds me of our wedding."

"Why?"

The bafflement in his tone made her smile, because the memory was not *with* him. It was before. "My hair and makeup was done, but they hadn't put me in that monstrosity of a dress yet."

She watched his face illuminated by moonlight, surprised to see his mouth curve ever so slightly. "It was a bit of a monstrosity."

Neither of them had been allowed any say in it. Their wedding had not been for *them*. It had been for King Enzo to show off his wealth—well, her father's wealth combining with the king's power. But still, they had said vows, married and consummated said marriage.

And here they were over a year later. Walking the gardens. A baby on the way. It should be enough, but it wasn't. Not yet.

"I needed some air while they dealt with how they were going to get me into such a thing. So I came out here. I sat there on that bench and looked at the gardens. I listened to the birds. I told myself that it didn't matter if I hadn't chosen this, there were things I could choose. Like being a leader and a good princess. That even if your father was a scary monster, there was...you."

He eyed her warily as they walked through an archway of blooming trees.

"Do you know what I thought when I first met you?" she asked him. Because they never discussed *them*. They never discussed anything but work, and that needed to change.

He did not say anything, and that slight curve to his mouth flattened.

She kept talking. He would not silence her. "You were so handsome, but so severe. And I had no reason to trust my father's choice in suitor, and, of course, I knew what a despot your father was. Even though people around the palace seemed to speak highly of you, I could hardly take it at their word. And then we met in that reception room. Do you remember?"

The wariness in his expression had only intensified. "Yes."

"And what did you think of me?"

He took a moment, no doubt searching for the *right* answer in his mind, not the actual answer. "That you were very small."

She rolled her eyes. "Are you always looking for ways to protect, Alex?"

Something flickered in his eyes. She was beginning to think he actually *liked* it when she shortened his name. Few people did it. Evelyne or Gabriel sometimes, but not often.

The longer name suited who he was better, but there was a man inside who was more than his long, royal name.

"You were very polite. We talked of birds. Do you remember? I said I liked birds—just a nervous blurt because you were being so silent and foreboding—but then you spoke, and you very kindly told me there were great places to watch birds in the gardens."

His gaze lowered to hers, his eyebrows furrowed as if he didn't quite understand what she was saying.

"And then the next time I came, you showed me. Every time, you always looked after my comfort. You were always gentle. Nothing in my life had ever been *gentle* before. Pampered, yes, but not gentle. Does that make sense?"

He looked at her, not detached now. Maybe a little confused. He didn't answer, but she thought it did make sense to him. She thought if anyone could understand the difference it was him.

"I went into those first few meetings with you always waiting you to show your true colors. But after a while, I began to understand. You were different than the men I'd known in my life. Not perfect, certainly. Abrupt and aloof and…cold, at times. But you had a goal—to see your kingdom and your sister survive your father. And to be nothing like him. And when I realized that, I began to trust you."

Alexandre stopped—not quite abruptly, but the stop wasn't smooth either. "We should return. You do not want to overdo it."

"A walk is hardly overdoing anything." But she let him lead her back inside. Up to their wing. She could feel the stiffness enter his body, like knots tying in slow succession—tighter and tighter, until he stopped at her door.

He opened his mouth, no doubt to dismiss her. To find some excuse to put her off.

But this was the deal.

She opened the door to her set of rooms, curled her other hand in his sleeve so she could pull him in behind her.

He could have stopped. He was certainly bigger and stronger than her, but he didn't pull back. Still, he looked uncomfortable as she closed the door behind him. Like he didn't want to be here.

But here he was. He had *agreed* to this.

In the past, whenever he'd arrived for one of their *appointments*, it was usually late. She was usually already in bed...waiting, waiting, waiting. She'd always let him set the tone, and he'd always set it...carefully.

Seen to her pleasure, his. It had been enjoyable, but it had not been like that day in his office because they had both known what it was about. Not pleasure. Not enjoyment. Not intimacy.

An heir.

This was different. It would be different. This was them—beyond their roles and their masks. Though, he would try to hold tight to his.

She faced him now, in the entry of her rooms. He stood stiffly. But stiff wouldn't do.

So she wrapped her arms around his neck. His expression was cool, but she knew she just needed to learn where to look. He was *not* passionless. He was *not* unaffected. She would find the signal somewhere in him.

But right now, she would keep talking. She would talk and talk and talk. Let all those scary truths inside of her out until he saw her, until he trusted her enough to show himself. His true self.

"I was terrified of our wedding night," she said, reveling in the feel of pressing her soft body to his hard one.

"Ines."

It was a warning, but she was done heeding his warnings. "But you were gentle and kind. You promised you would do everything in your power not to hurt me, and I believed you. Because you had shown me nothing but kindness."

"Yes, kind. I am kind. I get the picture."

She laughed at the disgust in his voice. Because he was so many things aside from kind, but that was what had allowed her to find some *ease* in this marriage in the beginning. "I was so relieved. You could have been anything." She moved to her toes, pressed a light kiss to his mouth. "Cruel." She kissed his chin. "Abusive." The corner of his mouth. "Arrogant and cutting." She kissed him on the mouth, deeper this time, and his arms came around her. "Dismissive. Horrible. You could have smelled like rotted fish."

"I am a *king*, Ines."

She smiled against his mouth. "You were a prince at the time, and I'm quite sure both could smell awful if they've a mind to. But you don't. And didn't. You were something *good*, and I promised myself in that moment that no matter what difficulties we faced, I would be grateful for that."

His hold tightened for a moment, and not in any kind of sensual way. "So grateful you ran away?" he demanded gruffly. A little flare of temper in his eyes.

The edge in him thrilled her. She knew how hard he worked to keep that temper hidden. That she could bring it out meant something.

It simply *had* to mean something.

"The thing is you can't live your life being grateful for crumbs. This is something I only began to realize when I saw there is more out there to have, more than just roles and games and being someone else's pawn. I came to realize I wanted so much more than the crumbs."

"You are a *queen*, Ines."

"Yes, I am your queen." She stepped back, trying not to grin when it clearly took him a minute to realize he needed to release her. When he did, she reached for the hem of her dress. It was a soft, stretchy fabric, easily pulled up and over her head.

His eyes raked over her as she dropped the dress to the floor, though he stayed stiff and still and where he was. A statue. A crown.

But underneath that beat the heart of a *man*. She wanted to show it to him. Again and again and again, until she got through to him. It would take time. He'd spent years building these walls. Hardening his heart. Protecting himself just as much as he protected everyone else.

But she had time. Months. She would get through to him. Not just for herself. Not just for Alexandre. For their baby. For their *family*.

"I have no regrets, Alexandre. You have been more than I could have ever hoped for when my father said he had found me a husband." She crossed to him, reached up and began to unbutton his shirt.

"Why are you trying to make me out to sound—"

"Good? Noble?" She met his gaze.

His breath shuddered out as her hands slid over the expanse of skin she'd exposed by unbuttoning his shirt. "Yes. That."

She pressed a kiss to the underside of his jaw. Always in search of some spot he might have missed with his ruthless razor. But he was always perfect, wasn't he? She let her hands explore the hard, tense muscles of his chest and abdomen. "Because you are both. You are also bad and selfish. And obnoxious and bossy. And honorable beyond reason. Handsome. Strong."

"Ines." He caught her wrists with his hands.

She looked up at him. "Because we're all a mess of lots of things, don't you think?"

His gaze was hard, his jaw clenched tight. "I most assuredly do *not*."

She smiled at him, even though he was disagreeing with her. Because he was wrong, and she would *prove it*.

"If we are to do this," he muttered, pulling her hands off his chest, "let us go to your bed."

She shook her head. "No. No, I don't think so. I know how that goes."

His eyebrows drew together, as if he honestly didn't know what she meant by that.

"You turn off the lights. You try to turn off…everything. Just get the job done." She took his palm, pressed it against her stomach. "The job's been done. This, tonight, and for the next few months isn't a *job*. It is just us."

"It is an action item on your to-do list, Ines." He said it with his trademark cool disdain, but his warm palm remained on her stomach. And in his eyes, she saw that hint of something…hot over cold. Intent instead of detachment.

So she moved his hand down, to touch her where she ached for him. His gaze followed his hand, and then she did not need to guide it because he stroked, over the fabric of her underwear but exactly where she wanted to be touched.

Yes, she had missed this. The fires he could stoke within her. Because he was relentless in all things, even this. His fingers slid under the fabric to find her. The core of her. He knew just where to touch, where to apply pressure, how to find that first, throbbing peak.

She held on to his shoulders, her body a shuddering mass of what he always brought her. But he was still standing there in control. Maybe there was the flicker of something triumphant in his dark gaze. Maybe she could see the outline of his arousal against his pants. But she had not broken through that wall.

She would. She *would*. There was no point to being back here, to accepting that her runaway had done *nothing*, if she did not get through to him.

"Come, Ines." It was not the dirty order she might like. He was trying to lead her to the bedroom. He wanted lights off, heart off, and she *refused*. So she did not let herself be pulled.

She unbuttoned and unzipped his pants quickly. She was trembling and desperate for more. More of him. More of everything. Once she managed to get his clothes off him, she pulled him to the ground. Here in the pretty sitting room she took appointments in. The light on. So she could see him. The ridges of muscle that tensed, contracted, jerked under her hands. Under her body as she straddled him.

His breath was ragged, but there was still distance in his eyes. It faltered when she gripped him, guided him to her. She wanted to see more than a falter. She wanted an obliteration.

So she moved against him in shallow, teasing strokes, not meant to do anything more than stir.

A hand came to her hip, clamped down, pulling her so that she had to sink down, sighing in contented pleasure to be filled by him once more. To be *here*, fighting for something rather than running away from all he couldn't give her. And if he never did—

She stopped that thought in its tracks. She would only think in positives. And for now, the positive was the pleasure wrapping around her body. The intimacy of two bodies moving with the same purpose.

Intimacy—except, he was holding himself back. He was being so *careful*. Yes, he would give her pleasure. Yes, he would find his own. But there was that old wall between them. Like they were *only* bodies, nothing more.

She could not abide it. Not now that she knew there was some part of him that she could find if she broke down that wall.

She leaned forward, pressing her body to his, even with him lodged deep inside her. She pressed a kiss to his mouth, then dragged her lips to his ear.

"You do not have to be anyone but yourself with me," she murmured there, before nipping at the lobe with her teeth. "Gentle. Rough. Sweet. Dirty. Whatever you are, I want that, Alex. Because *I* am yours."

CHAPTER EIGHT

IT WAS AN ONSLAUGHT. Too many emotions, feelings, sensations. Too much *her*. There were proclamations he'd given himself, and he didn't know where they disappeared to.

Because it wasn't like the last time. It wasn't *wild* per se. It wasn't frustration bubbling over.

I am yours.

How he wanted her to be. Needed her to be. Couldn't *let* her be.

But she was moving against him, soft and sweet. It didn't have to be about her words. It was two bodies. That was how he'd always seen it. How he'd prepared himself every time he'd come to her room. That this act was separate from who they were and what they must do.

Nothing felt separate, and all his old proclamations to himself were deserting him. She was making it so difficult to hold on to them. To separate duty from need. Because there was no duty here now. She *was* pregnant. So this was all…something else. He could not pretend it was duty. He *wanted* it to be proof that he did not need such soft things.

But in the moment, he felt as though he needed her or he might never breathe again. All those careful fortifications that kept him separate, that kept him protected, that kept him *sane* felt more of a burden than necessary when she nipped at his ear. When she said those things. When she shuddered and came apart around him with his name on her lips.

He moved up, tangling his hands in his hair to find that wildness that was dangerous and he should avoid, but with her it only felt elemental.

You do not have to be anyone but yourself with me.

It was a dangerous, insidious thought. Too good to be true. Things that felt this good were only ever harbingers of doom.

She met every thrust, every wild desperate move with one of her own. She used her teeth on his bottom lip, and he emptied himself in a shuddering, mind-blanking moment that seemed to echo on and on until he collapsed onto the floor.

A *floor*. In a room where she took appointments with palace staff. In a room not meant for *this*. But she snuggled in, her head tucked into his shoulder, her naked body tangled with his. She had a *smile* on her face.

On her floor. While she carried his child. No, this would not do.

He bundled her up in his arms. She made a low, contented sound in her throat that was both a dagger to his heart, and a salve to some part of him he tried to ignore existed. He carried her through the doorway to her sitting room, then another door to her bedchamber.

It was dim in the room, but he had navigated it in the dark every time he'd come for one of their *appointments*, so he knew the way.

He deposited her in her bed, ready to leave, *needing* to leave, but she held out her hand as if to invite him into her bed. Because he was meant to stay, when he had never once allowed himself that before. To stay here in warmth and sated pleasure was akin to taking some kind of drug. He couldn't allow it.

But it was on her list. A list he'd agreed to. Because he would prove to her this changed nothing. *Nothing.* So he got into the bed, and she curled up against him again.

Perhaps it was the deal, but if she fell asleep... Well, he had every right to leave, didn't he? He'd tell her he was called away. That she did not get to have first dibs on a *king*. He could go along with some of her little list, but not all. Not all the time. Just enough to hold up his end of the bargain, but not enough so that she *won*.

He'd just wait until she slept, and then he would slip out. Everything would be—

But the next thing he knew, he woke up with his wife in his arms and morning light filtering into the room.

He looked down at her sleeping form and wondered if letting her run away again—or throwing her in the dungeons—might be a better option.

Because he did not want to get out of bed. He was tempted to stay right here, watching the morning light gild her beautiful face. He wanted to feel the soft, even rise and fall of her chest.

You do not have to be anyone but yourself with me.

What a ridiculous statement. Because he always had to be a king. He always had to be a man who would put his country above his ego. And what was this damnable lust except some version of ego? Selfish desires. This *yearning* was all the things he'd taught himself to reject.

He slid out of bed. He was careful to be quiet, collecting his clothes and pulling them on. With each item of clothing, he managed to build back a layer of armor. Of *kingly duty*. Maybe these months would not be so bad.

If he could wake up and find King Alexandre again… he could survive this. Give her what she wanted, then the baby would be here, and she would have that. She would not have a need for…this.

Everything would work out all right. He would make as certain of that as he did everything else.

"Good morning," he heard her murmur, sounding sleepy and satisfied. He didn't dare turn around to see what that looked like on her face. He had met her demands, and now he would get a respite from them.

"You will meet with the palace doctors after breakfast," he said, sounding stiff and formal to his own ears. "You will follow all their directives."

She didn't say anything at first, and he didn't dare look at her, though he could hear the rustle of sheets, the sound of feet meeting the carpet. "Your health is paramount," he continued, pulling on the rest of his clothes. "You will not hide anything from them. Pregnancy and childbirth is a dangerous time for a woman, if you are not aware."

He felt her approach but did not look. Had she pulled on clothes or something to cover herself with? Was she naked? How much time could he spare to tumble her back into that bed and—

No. They had *appointments* for a reason. Lines. Boxes. Carefully constructed protections.

"I hadn't thought…" She trailed off, somewhere behind him. She didn't say anything else.

"Hadn't thought what?" he demanded, feeling irritation scratch along his skin.

She slid her hands down his back, then around him, hugging him from behind. Her cheek pressed to his spine. "I *knew* your mother died in childbirth, but I did not really put it together. That you were old enough to understand what was going on. That it might have marked you."

He froze. When he spoke, he felt as brittle as thin ice. "It did not mark me. It simply made me aware that pregnancy can be a dangerous time if one does not take care of themself."

"You were so tense the day Evelyne went into labor. So...wound tight. It's why you lost control, no doubt. You were terrified."

He had not considered...but that was ridiculous. Yes, he had some concern for his sister, and learning that morning that she had gone into labor had left him worried. But only because she'd been away for so much of her pregnancy and had dealt with some stress during it. That didn't mean he was...*terrified*.

"I will go to whatever doctor's appointments you like. And I will give them permission to tell you everything."

He pulled her arms off him, stepped away and fixed a glare on his face. "Ines, I am—"

"The king, yes, I know." She was wearing a brief, silky robe that covered enough...and yet not enough, because he wanted to rid her of it immediately. But she beamed up at him, so happy and...different than he'd ever seen her. Relaxed? Like any walls she'd kept up were gone, and she was certain she could break down his.

He couldn't let that happen.

"You could have all the information anyway, but I want you to know I'm *giving* it to you."

He stared at her, wondering how all this positivity and sweetness and acquiescence felt like little daggers being shoved into his heart.

So he left, while he had some semblance of sanity left.

* * *

Ines was in a marvelous mood.

Being home? Relaxing in a way the cabin just had never fully been.

Being able to immediately storm through all Alexandre's defenses and have him in her bed—and meeting room—that very night? Incredibly satisfying.

She had not expected to be getting through to Alexandre on what was only the first day of Operation Real Marriage, but she *had*. There were still mountains to climb, but they felt…scalable this morning.

She had an hour before her meeting with the doctors, so she went in search of Evelyne. She hadn't seen baby Gabriel since he'd been born.

She found both of them in the playroom. Evelyne was stretched out on the floor with the baby laid on a little mat connected to a kind of arch that had things dangling from it. Evelyne reached out and sent one spinning, and the baby on the mat kicked his legs and gurgled.

The boy had grown by such leaps and bounds in four months, Ines's heart gave a jerk. She'd missed so much. It was another wave of being happy to be home. Being happy to be part of this family. If there were things she had to fight for, so be it.

Her child would have a family. Not just a loving father, but an aunt and an uncle and a cousin—probably more than one. Her child would *never* be anyone's pawn or bargaining chip. And it wasn't just *her* who would make sure of that. It was the entire family.

"Good morning," Ines greeted.

Evelyne looked over her shoulder at Ines. She didn't smile. She didn't really do anything. Her expression remained a strange kind of neutral as she got to her feet and hefted Gabriel onto her hip.

"Gabri and I have an appointment," Evelyne said, and for the first time in their entire acquaintance the stiffness in her voice reminded Ines of Alexandre. Because usually Evelyne was bright and vibrant and…warm. Welcoming. No matter *what* was going on around them.

Now she walked past Ines without a second glance. Said nothing else. Ines watched her walk to the door and had the sickening realization something was not right.

"I… Are you angry with me?"

Evelyne didn't turn to face her. But she stood still. For a moment, the stiff posture reminded Ines so much of Alexandre she assumed Evelyne would simply walk out of the room. That she had messed something up and would constantly be met with the cold detachment of the people she cared for.

Instead, the woman slowly turned. Her expression was grave. "You ran away, Ines. Without telling anyone. Not even me. You do not get to waltz back into our lives as though nothing happened."

Ines looked at her sister-in-law, who'd become a friend. But she was still Alexandre's sister. "I emailed you. If I'd told you what I planned before, you would have told him. And he would have stopped me. And…" She didn't know what would have happened then. Maybe it *would* have been better. But she could not go back and undo what was already done.

Evelyne said nothing to this.

Ines took a careful step forward. "He's…your brother. I wouldn't have blamed you for telling him. I know how much you feel like you *owe* him, so I couldn't tell you."

"You shouldn't have run away from him," Evelyne returned. "He doesn't deserve that."

Ines's heart gave another jerk, more painful this time. Something close to guilt, even though Evelyne did not know everything about their marriage. She might be Ines's friend, but Ines had always been careful not to make out Alexandre to be the bad guy or the ogre.

She did not want to do so now, but part of the entire past few months had been about realizing...

"What do *I* deserve?" Ines asked quietly.

Evelyne blinked once, clearly surprised by the question. And unsettled, because she offered no answers.

So Ines continued. "To haunt his life like a ghost and be happy with the crumbs he tosses my way on occasion? To never... I will not get into all of our private matters, but I deserve something too. I cannot simply exist to be whatever *he* wants without ever considering what *I* want. Not anymore."

Evelyne couldn't quite meet her gaze after that, but she didn't leave the room.

"Evelyne. Please. I cannot..." She had taken for granted that Evelyne would always be her friend simply because they both lived in the palace. The thought of losing that friendship...

"Please, don't be angry with me."

"It isn't that simple, Ines."

No. Nothing was that simple, and she had to be careful to remember that just because she'd found some happiness didn't mean simple was in the offing. She and Alexandre had a long way to go, and apparently she and Evelyne did as well.

But when Ines thought about it, she knew all her actions stemmed from something very—if not simple—

straightforward. "I love your brother. Do you know that? Perhaps you don't. I don't think *he* knows it."

Evelyne frowned at her. "I didn't think—"

"I did not marry him for love, and God knows he didn't marry me for love, but you of all people know how good he is. How could I not fall in love with him over the past year?"

"Why would you run away from someone you love?" Evelyne asked. "It's not like if you stayed you would have hurt him."

It didn't surprise Ines that was Evelyne's only thought to running away—because Gabriel had run away from *her* for that reason months ago. But there were so many reasons to run.

"No, I would not have hurt him, but it hurt *me* to stay. Because he does not love me. Or at least, doesn't want to. Because I want so much more from him, and he is so unwilling to give it. But…this baby changes things." She put her hand over her stomach. "Running away doesn't work with a baby. So I'm back to deal with it, and him, and make him fall in love with me. And make him realize that doesn't have to cost him…his kingdom."

She hadn't realized what a tall order that was until she'd said it out loud. Sure, in her mind love should make it easy, but Alexandre—and Evelyne—were working against years and years of not having *any* love, any stability. They had spent their entire youth in survival mode.

Still, Evelyne had found Gabriel. Which meant *she'd* learned how to do more than survive, so Alexandre was capable of it too, wasn't he? Ines didn't know anything of Evelyne's and Gabriel's interior lives, except that Gabriel himself had been afraid to love, afraid of *himself*.

What was Alexandre afraid of?

Ines could only think there were too many things to count.

The baby reached out for Ines, and her heart tripped over itself. She had missed so much of his growth, and he was reaching out for her. But Evelyne would have to relinquish her hold. And she still hadn't said *anything* in reply.

But she let Ines take the baby. Still saying nothing. Just standing there, watching her.

So Ines looked down at Gabriel. "Aren't you handsome? And you'll have a cousin playmate soon enough." Ines looked up at Evelyne. "They'll be friends *and* cousins, like Jonet and I. They'll have each other. What a gift for the both of them."

Evelyne's mouth curved, and she stepped forward, wrapping an arm around Ines holding Gabri. "Yes. How lucky they'll be."

Yes. Lucky. Ines liked the sound of that.

CHAPTER NINE

ALEXANDRE SAT BEHIND his desk and looked at the sociopath before him. General Vinyes was a problem, and while Alexandre had excelled at handling almost all the problems his father had left behind, this was one he hadn't quite worked out yet.

Vinyes was canny. It made him a more difficult foe than King Enzo, because while Vinyes was bloodthirsty and cruel, he did not fly off the handle. He had not quit in a rage when Alexandre had cut military spending. He had not voiced a true opposition to any of the peaceful measures Alexandre had enacted.

Vinyes went along, voicing *concerns*, but never disobeying a direct order. So Alexandre had no real reason to get rid of him, and keeping him on board had managed to appease some of the members of the council who might not have *liked* King Enzo but had liked the power supporting a dictator had given them.

So Alexandre was always on the lookout for *anything* that might make getting rid of Vinyes a just, acceptable choice. Just as he felt Vinyes was always on the lookout for a way to depose Alexandre if he made the slightest mistake Vinyes could leverage.

"I have heard rumors your wife has returned from her...*holiday*," Vinyes said.

Alexandre held himself very still. He did not like Vinyes mentioning *any* of the women in this palace. There was something about the way he spoke that always made it feel like a threat.

But Vinyes hadn't *acted* on anything that was or felt like a threat, leaving Alexandre with a frustrating impotent feeling.

Alexandre made sure his voice was devoid of any reaction before he spoke. "I'm not sure *holiday* is the appropriate word, as she maintained many of her duties while away."

Vinyes made a noncommittal kind of sound. "Highly unusual, that."

"I wanted Ines away from the stressors of the palace for a bit." Alexandre tried for a smile but wasn't sure he managed.

"No trouble, I hope?"

Alex held the general's gaze. Flat. Cold. "None." *Clear.* "Are we done here?"

"You have not given me an answer on the necessary training stipend."

"Yes, I have. Quite a few times, in fact. My answer remains the same. Your men do not need training on weapons Alis will not be purchasing. We are not a military power, as I have explained on numerous occasions as well. I understand you disagree with that, but it is my choice and my choice alone."

"Your people do not matter to you, Your Majesty?"

It was asked with such feigned concern Alexandre wanted to rage. But he sat behind his desk and regarded the general with cool disdain. "I cannot fathom what this has to do with my people, Vinyes. They have been quite vocal in their support of my peaceful measures, since the petty wars my father tried to enact were detrimental to our safety, our standing in the world *and* our economic wellbeing."

"I do not know of any people happy to be left unprotected."

Alexandre wanted to rub his temples, where a dull pain pounded. He remained in his seat, behind his desk, looking at the general who had refused a seat so stood there in a military stance, stoic and commanding.

Except, he could stand there and look disapproving all he liked—Alexandre was in charge. Alexandre had every last say. Vinyes was nothing without Alexandre's approval. And the man clearly knew it.

"The fact I maintain you and an army is protection, General. I have considered being rid of you both altogether." Which he should have kept to himself, but he was *tired*. And he knew who to blame for that.

He would *not* be tired if he'd slept in his own bed last night. He would not be *tired* if his wife was following the perfect balance they'd created in the beginning of their marriage. Instead, she was making everything more difficult, and he was bound to make a mistake because of it.

You cannot allow mistakes.

"Get rid of me?" The general laughed, low and bitter. Bitter enough it put Alexandre on edge...and filled him with hope that the general would finally *break* and give Alex something to fire him over.

But the door swung open instead, distracting both Alex and the general.

"Alex, we need to discuss—" Ines appeared, then came up short as if surprised to find him with Vinyes.

"I beg your pardon. Your assistant wasn't at his desk, and I did not know you were in a meeting." But she didn't leave. She smiled regally at Vinyes. "Good afternoon, General."

"Good afternoon. It is so good to see you after such a…long time."

There was something about Vinyes looking at Ines that made Alex's blood *cold*. So his words were equally so. "It is customary, General, as I'm sure you are aware, to bow to one's queen on her arrival."

A muscle in Vinyes's jaw ticked, but he gave a perfunctory bow. "I apologize, Your Majesty."

"Of course," Ines said sweetly. "Manners aren't everyone's strength."

It was a subtle dig. Alexandre wasn't sure Vinyes even picked up on it, but Alex did. It made him want to laugh. He might have, but Ines wasn't leaving.

He should dismiss her. He *knew* he should. That was the right thing to do. The thing that would appease Vinyes, at least a little bit. Send the woman away so the men could continue their meeting.

"I think that will be all, General," Alex said instead. Because he'd damn well rather be around his confusing, confounding wife than spend another minute having the same pointless argument with Vinyes.

General Vinyes looked at him, temper straining in his eyes. "I wasn't finished discussing this training."

"I was," Alexandre replied.

The general looked from Alexandre to Ines, then said nothing—gave no bow or anything else that would be considered protocol *or* acceptable behavior—and stalked out, clearly angry.

Alexandre should do something about it. Smooth it over. Fix it.

He didn't.

Ines closed the door behind Vinyes. Then flipped the lock casually. But the sound of it echoed through the room. Perhaps through *him*.

"I hope I didn't interrupt something important," she said, crossing to where he sat.

But he could only think of the locked door, even as she came around the back of his chair and began to rub his shoulders. She dug her fingers into his tense muscles.

"You *are* stressed, aren't you?" she said, a slight censure in her tone. "What was he on about now?"

"Just another attempt at strengthening the army, which I refused."

"I understand there's no good way to dismiss him, but I so wish you could."

"As do I. It never occurred to me he'd last this long without some kind of outburst or attempt at revolution." His eyes closed, head bowing forward as her fingers did wonders to loosen the tension in his shoulders. But it wasn't just her hands on him. It was her understanding of the situation.

Evelyne and Gabriel were a little more bloodthirsty. They did not quite understand the full range of diplomacy needed to right the ship of Alis, and they had a more personal hatred of Vinyes since he'd wanted to marry Evelyne and had threatened Gabriel.

In an ideal world, Alexandre could simply sweep out anyone who had supported his father, anyone who had made threats to his friend or wanted his sister as some kind of possession. But life and kingship weren't that simple.

Ines understood this. Her role. His. The caution required in such situations. And her hands were doing magic at the tension in his neck. He even sighed.

"I truly did not mean to interrupt. I assumed the front desk being empty meant you were alone, and I wanted to let you know the doctor's appointment went well. All is as it should be with baby and myself. They want to do an anatomy scan next, but since it will tell us the gender, I want you to be there, so we'll need to arrange a time. We'll also need to work out how to announce it to the kingdom. My clothes are getting tighter at an alarming rate. I won't be able to hide it much longer."

Alex didn't stiffen, if only because her hands were doing wonders on his tense muscles. But the word *gender* prompted visions of a *child*. He had seen Gabri grow from tiny little *lump* to a slightly bigger lump with a burgeoning personality.

And in mere months, there would be another baby in the palace, existing, growing, living. Becoming a *person*.

His child. A child he would not allow to face any of the challenges laid on Alex himself at a young age. Neither Gabri nor his own child would suffer under the weight of his duties. He would need to find some plan for this, some way to ensure…everything.

"But I'm glad to have cut that meeting short," Ines was saying. "You would have tied yourself into even tighter knots if it had gone on any longer." She made a tsking sound.

Her scent enveloped him, and he leaned into the vanilla notes of that instead of the baseline fear of thinking about *children*. He let himself sink into the way it felt for someone else to take care of the state of his tension. Rubbing, kneading, easing it away. Her thumbs pressed up the back of his neck, and some *noise* escaped him. Not quite a groan. Just simple pleasure.

She slid her arms over his shoulders, letting them dangle there over his chest. He could feel her breasts pressed to his back and her breath against his skin as she leaned her head close to brush a kiss across his cheek. "I locked the door," she whispered in his ear.

"I know." He reached back, pulled her in front of him. She smiled down at him, taking a seat on his desk, facing him. She wore a typical outfit for an afternoon of meetings—a blouse under a trim jacket that matched the color of her skirt—except instead of the usual style that hugged her hips, this one was looser. With enough give that he could push it up her thighs.

Which he did. Taking his time. Falling into this lull of relaxation she'd created for them. He pushed the fabric of the skirt up to her waist, then hooked his fingers in the waistband of her stockings, and she toed off her heels so they fell with a thump on the floor between them. She lifted so that he could pull the garment off.

It wasn't *exactly* like that morning all those months ago. He was too relaxed to feel anger and frustration. Desire pumped through him, but it was warm and sluggish instead of sharp claws of destroyed control.

That had been a break.

This was a yield.

How he'd thought of her here in his office. How he'd relived that day over and over, against his own will.

This would be compounding the mistake, to do it again.

Or just enjoying a mistake already made. He did not tolerate mistakes, but making them with her took his mind off impending fatherhood and all that lay on the other side of *that*.

Or he just wanted her, and it was like a drug so that nothing else mattered but her.

Still in his chair, he tugged her jacket off her shoulders, but not all the way off her arms. It held her there, a kind of handcuffs if she did not shrug her arms out of the sleeves.

She did not.

Desire pumped through him, drugging him into forgetting everything except her, this moment, the blood pounding in his own ears. He could not be a real man in any sense of the word. He had to be a king. He *knew* this, but it was like she took away all his brain power so that knowledge was gone completely and utterly and replaced with only desire.

He wrapped his hands around her wrists so she couldn't even shrug out of the jacket, restricting her movement if she wanted to. He needed some control. Some ballast.

"This will count as my next appointment," he told her. Because that would make it okay. Acceptable. Not another mistake. Just a duty done.

She was completely at his mercy. She couldn't move if he didn't let her go. And this was not out of the bounds of their agreement. It was simply...a little spontaneous.

But her eyes held his. Calm and direct. "I'm afraid not. If you want me here and now, you can have me. But you will *also* make your next appointment. You don't get to substitute on a whim." Her mouth curved into a smug smile. "But you may add whenever you like."

He should argue with her. He should stop. He should refuse. Let her go.

This would not be an *addition*. She did not get to determine that.

Instead of arguing, he kissed her. Deep and wild and hungry, holding her arms still so she could do little more than kiss him back. She made greedy little noises, squirming there on his desk. He put his mouth to her neck, scraped his teeth down the taut tendons there. She moaned his name.

He wanted to remove her shirt, but that would require letting her go, and he didn't seem to know how, so he only used his mouth over the fabric, and bit gently just where he knew it would send her arching back, gasping in pleasure.

He felt nothing but an ache, a need, and she alone could solve that. Which meant it was a problem *he* did not have to solve.

Finally, he released her hands—not that she moved. Because he needed more. To spread her legs wide. She still wore her underwear, but he didn't even bother to pull them down, just moved the offending fabric out of the way and set his mouth to her. He tasted her, as deep, wild and hungry as the kiss. She cried out—and if anyone was listening outside his door they might hear. They might know.

He didn't care. Not as he drove her to a blooming, shuddering climax with his tongue. Her hand fisted in his hair as an anchor.

He pulled her off the desk and into his lap. The chair was just big enough she could straddle him. For a moment, his gaze was hooked to the swell of her stomach, the tiny evidence of his child growing there.

His.

He itched to reach out and place his hands upon it, *feel* it, the life she grew inside of her, but there was a terrible ache inside of him—one he was afraid would never go away if he did so.

So he kept his hands to himself and looked up at her on his lap. Her cheeks were pink, her hair tousled now, and her hand worked on the enclosure of his pants quickly.

It took nothing at all, just a few tugs, a little rearranging and she was shuddering around him as he moved inside her. So responsive. So perfect. Like she'd been made for him instead of the curse he knew she had to be.

And though he had no time, he took it, building her up again. And again. And again. Reveling in the sounds she made, the way she felt against him. It shouldn't be here, but *here* ceased to exist. There was only her. There was only the way he felt with her.

A man, not a king. Helpless and out of control and *hers*, not his country's. The relief of that was as staggering as she was.

"Alex, *please*." It was the *Alex*, her voice, the sheer perfection of everything she gave that had him finally giving over to his own release.

Then she simply melted into him. Their breathing ragged, but she didn't get up. Didn't remove herself. She held on to him, and he found himself holding on to her, sitting in his chair. When he had responsibilities and meetings and duties outside that door.

"What are you doing to me?" he heard himself rasp. He should not have said it, but he did not *understand*. He could not seem to fight the temptation she was. She gave too much, and how could he be who he needed to be if she kept showing him some inner part of himself that had no place in the reality of his life?

She pulled back, still in his lap. She framed his face with her small hands. Met his gaze. Looked so *earnest*. "Loving you."

It was as if she'd thrown ice water on him. He went from a sluggish, sated confusion to ice. He felt ill. Actually, physically ill. Something old and dark poked at him, but he shoved it away. Set her off him and got to his feet. He moved away from her and these horrible words.

He knew what love could do. To kings and queens. His parents had claimed love, but all it had ever done was destroy. Not just each other. Him. Evelyne. Perhaps some people could wield the weight of love, but not a king.

Not *him*.

"Alex."

Her voice was quiet. Plaintive. "No." He roughly righted the state of his pants and didn't dare look at her. They had not discussed…*love*. Whatever this was, whatever they did… She could not fool herself into that.

"Darling, what's the matter? I—"

"Enough," he said harshly. Her words echoed inside him like icy tendrils of something he refused to acknowledge. Love. *Darling*. Something old and sharp clawed through him. Something he didn't let take up space in his head. Ever. "Put yourself together and leave. At once."

"Alex."

"Go *away*, Ines."

"Why? What is *wrong*?" she demanded. But she didn't sound demanding. She sounded soft and worried.

He *hated it*. It was exploding inside of him, building and building, and what would he do if she did not *leave*? Fall apart himself? Impossible. "I said go away." He swept a hand across his desk, sending anything in its path crashing to the ground.

A terrible loss of control. *She* made him lose control. *She* made him someone else.

His blood is in you, Alex. Always in you. You must always fight it.

He would. No matter what. He would. But if throwing things got her to scurry out of this room, it was worth it.

***

Ines was shaken, and it wasn't the sex. That was becoming almost normal. The wildness and the joy that came with it. The way she'd found she could make him lose his famed control. She was almost used to the heady knowledge that *she* did something to *him*.

But the aftermath of today was different. There was no triumph. She'd never seen him look so... She didn't even have words for it. The way he'd dismissed her had not been cold or detached or even cruel. It had reminded her of a wounded animal roaring.

There had been a naked kind of hurt on his face that she neither understood nor knew how to soothe. He'd tossed the contents of his desk at the ground, not at her, but the out-of-character outburst still left her shaken to her core.

She stumbled out of his office, grateful that his assistant's desk was still empty. Because she was about to *cry*. Even as her body still ebbed with the echoes of a pleasure too big, too wonderful for even Alex's horrible reaction to stop.

She had known he wouldn't react *positively* to the idea of love, but she hadn't anticipated it...hurting him. She couldn't fathom it. No matter how she tried to make sense of any of that, it didn't make sense.

She blinked back tears as best she could, but some fell anyway. She'd mostly put herself back together, though she'd left her pantyhose behind. He wouldn't be pleased about that. But she needed to get to her rooms. Get herself together and figure out...

"Ines?"

Ines stopped in the hall. She hadn't expected anyone to be in the common living room they sometimes all had tea in together, but apparently Evelyne was in there and had seen her pass the door.

Ines pressed a palm to the wall, squeezing her eyes shut. She breathed in deep, then out. Quickly she wiped the tears from her cheeks then backtracked. She stepped into the room with a smile on her face.

Maybe it was brittle, but it was a smile. Apparently not good enough because Evelyne's expression quickly morphed into concern.

"Are you all right?" she asked.

Ines nodded, trying to swallow the lump in her throat. "Where's Gabri?"

"Napping. I'm trying to get some emails dealt with this morning, and it's horrible. Come. Distract me." She grinned at Ines.

Ines tried to look cheerful in return, but she knew she failed.

"You look…" Evelyne's gaze of confusion turned into a wrinkled nose "…rumpled."

"I—"

"No, that's okay. Don't tell me. I do *not* want to know." She waved it away with a laugh. "In the middle of the day, huh? What *are* you doing to my brother?"

Ines's lump grew bigger. *What are you doing to me?* he'd asked. Like he didn't know. Like he didn't want it. Like she'd caused him pain when she'd thought it was something good.

And the way he'd dismissed her…

Evelyne's expression went back to concern, she reached out and took Ines's arm and led her to the couch, then nudged her into a sitting position. Evelyne lowered herself next to Ines.

"What is it?" she asked.

Ines shook her head. "I—I'm not even sure I know. It wasn't a fight." Because it wasn't. She hadn't fought back. Alex had reacted, and she had gone away like he'd ordered.

Just like she'd always done. Obeyed. She couldn't even be mad at herself though, because her heart felt bruised. Because he was scared and hurting, and Ines couldn't *understand*. And God knew he'd never tell her, but Evelyne...

Ines studied her sister-in-law. A woman who had grown up in this palace, with Alexandre her protector from their awful father. A woman who had fallen in love, married, had a child despite all that.

Evelyne wasn't *hurt* by Gabriel loving her. She'd *fought* for it. For him. It wasn't the same, but she'd grown up with Alex. Maybe she could make sense of this for Ines.

"Evelyne..." Ines knew Evelyne's loyalty would always be to Alexandre, but this wasn't about getting Evelyne on her side. It was about...understanding. She studied her sister-in-law's face. "Did it ever scare you to love Gabriel?"

Evelyne took a deep breath as if thinking that question through very carefully. "I suppose it did a little, but that wasn't really the predominant feeling. It was more relief. That love could exist." Her eyebrows drew together as she studied Ines's face. "What's going on, Ines?" she asked gently.

It was private. Alex would probably want this to remain private. Or at least rather that she discuss it with Jonet, not his *sister*. But Evelyne had to have *some* insight, didn't she? She knew her brother. She was married.

"I told Alex that I loved him, more or less. He did not react...well."

"Well, you've come to the right person," Evelyne said with a brightness that didn't quite read as genuine. "You should have seen Gabriel's horror at me loving him in the beginning."

Ines wanted to smile. It had worked out for Evelyne, but this was different. It wasn't fear, it was something deeper. Something more substantial. Hurt. *Hurt* to be loved? It made no sense.

"I don't understand why it would…hurt him so. Gabriel was not hurt that you loved him. He was afraid. Of himself. I think I could understand that in Alexandre, but this is *hurt*. You were not hurt by Gabriel finally admitting he loved you."

"No," Evelyne agreed. "But Alexandre and I are not the same. Never have been. Both in personality and in how we were raised. As much as I love him, I don't understand…the deeper level he keeps hidden."

"But you were raised by the same man, in the same place. You were both hurt by your father."

"Yes, but our lives were not the same. From *birth*. Starting out, he had five years with our mother. He remembers her. He won't talk about her much, except in vague, glowing terms, but that means he remembers her enough that it *hurts* him to. I know she can't be quite the saint Alexandre makes her out to be when he *does* mention her, but she was a good person, other people have told me that. So Alexandre had that mother's love and then lost it. That's different than never having it."

Ines supposed that was true. Not that one was easier or better, just that it would mark you differently. And he was marked by the way his mother had died, even if he didn't acknowledge that. Everything she had today was because he'd been so worried about Evelyne he'd lost control all those months ago.

"The thing is, Alexandre was the boy, the heir. I was..." Evelyne shrugged. "I'm not really sure what I was to my father, but it was different for Alexandre. And I think, looking back, Alex made sure I didn't know the depths of that difference. He never let on that my father might be harder on him than he was on me. Alex always wanted me to..."

Ines waited, but Evelyne was clearly struggling with what to say. Ines didn't think it was out of loyalty, though, so she waited.

"I don't know how to articulate this as well as I'd like, Ines, but I think he feels like, sometimes, we deserved the way Father treated us. Like we *should* be punished for something. I don't think it's a *conscious* thought. More like being brainwashed by Father. He knows Father was awful, wants to be *nothing* like him, but his mind was still affected by the things Father would have told him, taught him."

Ines pressed a hand to her chest where an ache centered, spread. "I can see that," she managed to say, without even crying, though it was a hard-won thing. Alex held so much on his shoulders. So much *responsibility*. That no doubt stemmed from some kind of guilt the horrible king had instilled on him.

Because she knew Alex had not loved or respected his father in any capacity. That he'd dedicated his life to being different, to changing Alis for the better was clear in everything he did. She'd assumed that meant that he'd rejected everything from King Enzo.

But maybe there were deeper wounds he didn't know

how to reject. Still, Ines could not figure out how that could connect to her loving him being such a *blow*.

"That doesn't explain why me loving him would be something that *hurt* him though. Shouldn't it be something…positive? Even if he didn't feel the same. Love is a good thing."

Evelyne nodded. "I'm not sure I could explain it. I'm not sure I *know*. What I do know is that anything positive, loving anything or anyone in this palace, would have only ever made him a target to my father. Perhaps it's an old echo of that. Fear that it will be taken away?"

Ines sighed. It didn't seem that straightforward. That sensible. But maybe Evelyne knew better than she did.

"The thing is, I only ever saw Alexandre handle Father expertly. He knew how to calm him, distract him, sometimes even stop him. But that had to have come from a place of… By the time I was old enough to be truly aware of things, Alexandre was a pro at handling Father. But he wasn't born a pro, I can't imagine. Perhaps our mother taught him. Perhaps he learned all on his own."

The hard way, no doubt. Because Ines knew from her months of being married to Alex before King Enzo had died that Alex did not agree with Ines's assessment. He did not think he was a *pro* at handling Enzo. He had felt like he was always just barely hanging on, just barely escaping disaster for himself and everyone around him.

He'd been the most tense she'd ever seen him the day of their wedding, because Enzo had promised Evelyne to General Vinyes. Alex had blamed himself for that, for not seeing it coming. So no, he wasn't a pro in his own mind.

Evelyne smiled reassuringly. "That just means you need to be patient with him."

"Perhaps," Ines said, diplomatically because she did

not think *patience* solved the hurt on his face. She did not know how to *wait* for something to change when it was clearly a deep-seated trauma.

Evelyne grabbed her hand. "Don't give up on him. He won't see it, wouldn't admit it if he did, but he needs you."

Ines let out a long slow breath. She wished she agreed, but she wondered if it was quite the opposite. If by loving him and having his child, she was making everything harder on him.

The ache in her chest settled deeper, tears battling it out again. She would do anything to make life easier on him, except… Except she was pregnant with his child. Their child was growing and would be here eventually. She could not sacrifice all their child might have for Alexandre's comfort or ease. No matter how she loved him.

Which meant she had to find *some* way to get through to him. She forced her mouth into a slight smile. "I won't give up on him," she told Evelyne reassuringly.

Now she just had to figure out a way to get *through* to him.

CHAPTER TEN

ALEXANDRE KNEW HE could ignore Ines's missive. He was not beholden to meet her for a walk whenever *she* wanted. Even her list had acknowledged that *he* was the one who determined the time.

But he had skipped lunch and dinner with her. He'd convinced himself it was for work. The work he'd neglected because *she* had upended his morning.

She needed to get it through her head that he was a king first, second and last.

He would tell her that now.

Outside the sun was low in the sky, the air getting cooler. The gardens were an explosion of blooms and chirping birds. He never took walks in the garden—who had the time? There had to be a reason for such things, and the last time he'd had a reason was when he'd been wooing Ines.

But now she was wooed. The end.

He thought of the way she'd recounted their first meetings. She *had* blurted out that she liked birds, in a kind of desperate rush. It had eased something inside of him. If *she* was nervous but willing to take on the mantle of his bride, then... Well, it couldn't be so bad, could it?

So he'd endeavored to make her feel better about it.

And she had held on to that kindness as some kind of sign that he was good...

There is only good in you if you make it, Alex.

There is no good in you. I will make sure of it.

He wanted to press his hands to his temples and squeeze the old voices away with it. He had not thought of those early days in some time. Did not allow himself to remember, wallow.

And the only difference in his life between all these years of shoving that turmoil away and having it live in his damn head was *Ines*. He did not blame her for his weaknesses. That was hardly fair.

But he blamed her for existing. For somehow reaching into his psyche and bringing those turbulent times back to the forefront. When his parents had argued, violently and viciously.

Over him. Used him as a pawn. A weapon against each other. And love with it.

In so many ways he had been some kind of linchpin in their marriage. His existence had caused problems. His mother's love for him. His father's love for her. She had not wanted that second child, had not taken care of herself because no matter how much she'd loved Alexandre, she'd known children were the death of her marriage.

Sometimes he wanted to believe that he'd been so young he'd simply misunderstood the things his mother had told him. He'd confused things.

But he knew he hadn't. Love had been a bludgeon—and so he'd been used as one. And where had that gotten any of them? His mother dead. His country in turmoil. So many mistakes he now had to set to rights.

And Ines would dare claim she was *loving him*. Ines

was now convinced she *loved* him? No. Something had to give.

Loving you is such a curse for us all, Alexandre. I am so sorry.

No, he would not go back there. His mother had died years and years ago. His father was dead. There was no use reliving the past. There was only the future—of Alis.

He walked through the garden, growing more and more irritated he couldn't find Ines, when her message through his assistant had said the north side of the garden. The side of the garden he avoided. Did Ines know that? How could she? He had certainly never told anyone what he avoided or why. He rarely even thought of it.

He stood at the fork in the walkway. In order to get to the northern section, he would need to take a left. He would need to face that which hurt.

Well, what else was new when it came to Ines? Always forcing him into hurts that were better left buried.

He could return to the palace, refuse to take part in this ridiculous intimacy ruse, but then she would run away again, and he wasn't sure what little hold on control he seemed to have could survive it. Particularly with Vinyes making comments about Ines's *holiday*.

Plus, it was necessary to prove to her *and* himself that he was stronger than what strange feelings worked their way between them. These few months of torture would be followed by getting his *life* back.

He was used to those kinds of bargains, wasn't he? Years of dancing around his father's threats and whims had made him well acquainted with a devil's bargain.

And he always won. Because here he was, the king. Alive and well and fixing Alis, one step at a time.

He walked along the path, knowing every step would

lead him to where he did not wish to go. But when had he ever had any say in where he went? A good king was not beholden to his own whims. He was beholden to his *country*. This he had learned from watching his father only care for himself—his ego, his temper, his wants.

His *love*.

Alexandre would be the best king, which meant rejecting all those things. No matter how Ines tested this. No matter what she was up to being in this part of the gardens.

The burial ground for one.

His mother's grave was not in the Lidia family cemetery on the other side of the palace grounds—where generations of Lidia royalty including his father were buried in the shadow of a chapel. If any god truly sanctified such an institution, it would have certainly burned to ash at his father being buried on its grounds.

Instead, the chapel survived.

Mother had originally been given an elaborate mausoleum in the capital city's cemetery. Buried far away from the family and Alex himself.

Alexandre had argued against this, even as a child. He'd been slapped and locked in his room for two days for the *audacity* to demand something other than his father's plan. He'd then been dressed up and trotted out for the funeral at the city center, surrounded by strangers.

The building, the stone, the memorial had been meant to show off the king's wealth and power, but it had left Mother separated and alone. A symbol and nothing else.

Just like you.

Luckily, Alex had been ill and didn't remember much of the funeral itself except feeling outside himself. But he had carried that day, that betrayal with him all his life. And he had always vowed to fix it when he got the chance.

So one of the first things Alexandre had done once Enzo himself was buried was to quietly have his mother's body moved here—not to the chapel but to the gardens. Not that he ever visited. But he'd wanted her safe and protected, as he had not been able to make happen in real life. She was still alone here, but she wouldn't be forever. He and Evelyne's family would be buried here. And Evelyne came to visit. She even took Gabri sometimes.

Alexandre could not fathom why Evelyne would subject herself to such a morbid exercise, but maybe it was different for her since she did not remember Mother. She had no memories of her voice, her perfume, the way she had snuggled him into her bed and told him stories of all the good he would do. Be.

Better than your father. Because you have all my love, and he has none.

Alexandre pushed the memory away. These memories only lead to one place. The bitter, bloody end, and that simply would not do.

Ends were over. He had beginnings to work out.

He spotted Ines in the distance. At the foot of his mother's grave. She was kneeling in the grass, the light fading around her as there were many trees here to create shade.

So many emotions battered at his insides, he could not even find some anger amidst them to hold on to, to use as an anchor. Or armor.

He approached her like a man approaching his own death. "What are you doing here?" He had meant it to come out sounding like a clear-cut demand—not a rusty, unsteady plea.

"Thinking," Ines said. She began to get up, and he

rushed to help her to her feet. He did not look at the stone or the flowers she'd laid across the grass.

He might see that old flash of her dead body. Bloody. Desecrated.

Because she had dared die on the king, and even in death he had used his fists to make it worse.

Ines did not look up at him, instead kept her gaze on the stone. Alexandre breathed through the sickness roiling around inside of him.

But it meant he was looking at Ines. She was wearing the same outfit she'd worn in his office earlier—and even though it had been *hours*, she still looked a bit rumpled and mussed. Not her usual put-together, elegant self. Her eyes were a bit red and puffy. Almost as if she'd been crying.

Luckily there were so many pains inside of him vying for purchase this one did not cut him off at the knees.

"Would you tell me about her?" Ines asked quietly.

"I hardly remember her," Alexandre lied.

"By all accounts she was wonderful. The antithesis to your father. I would like to know about that. My mother… Perhaps my mother was not always the way I know her. But for as long as I can remember she dulled everything with whatever substance she could find. And I think my father preferred it that way." She finally looked away from the stone, up at him. Her blue eyes a vivid blue—that the tears in them seemed to bring out. "I want a role model to look up to."

He did not know what this was. He understood she might be upset with him for his behavior in the office this morning, but what did that have to do with his mother? With their child?

"What do you remember of her?" she prodded. The

tears, the emotion in her didn't seem to disrupt her determination.

"Very little."

She sighed heavily, and she sounded *tired*. "Alex."

Darling, what's the matter? She'd asked him that as though she could fix it. Everything that was the matter. But she would fix nothing. And neither would he if he leaned on her.

It would all end in blood and death and bludgeons needlessly used against each other.

"I do not wish to rehash my memories of the mother I lost, Ines," he said curtly. "Why are you pushing this?" Always pushing at the things he needed to stay locked away.

"I want to understand."

I don't understand you. She'd said that when he'd brought her back here. When she'd kissed him outside her room after running away for *months*.

But he figured that was only fair, since he didn't understand her at all.

Except he wasn't poking into *her* pain. "You think you will find some...childhood trauma that you will—what? Fix?"

She shook her head sadly. "No, of course not."

"Then, I do not see the purpose of this."

"I can't want to understand you?"

"There is nothing to understand beyond the fact I am the king of Alis." He had truly believed she'd understood this. For almost a year she had, and he could not fathom what had changed. What he had done wrong for all of this to come crumbling around him.

Except he had done nothing, changed nothing. *She* had been the agent of all change. If she had not pushed for an annulment, if she had not run away, if she did not continue to push at him to behave differently than he knew he *should*—walks in gardens, spending the night in her bed, sex in his *office*—they would not be having these conversations. He would not be in *turmoil*.

"I know you wish that were true, but it isn't," Ines said quietly. "You can't *be* a crown, Alex. You are a man. A man with a wife and a child on the way."

"A queen and a prince or princess."

Her expression hardened at that. "We are not our titles. However you see yourself, you will not reduce me to a *title*. A *pawn*."

"Fine, but *I* am a title. I will always be. This is fact. Not a point to be argued."

She blew out a frustrated breath. Good. Better frustrated than soft. Better they argue about titles than his *mother*.

"Do you want our child to be raised the way you were?" she asked him.

He could see it so clearly. Standing in that doorway as his father pounded his fists into his mother's dead body, Evelyne crying down the hall as the nurses tended to a child without a mother.

But no one had tended to him, so he'd watched a nightmare.

"No," he rasped out. He did not want that for his child. Didn't she see he was trying to protect them *all* from that?

"I do not want them raised the way I was either. I want something different for our child. But we are responsible for building that, Alex."

"He or she is not the heir, so it will be different."

Her mouth tightened. "That is not what I meant, Alexandre. And you know it."

Perhaps he did. But he didn't care. It would not be his concern. She would raise the baby. His job as father was simply to guide the child in the ways of the palace. Because a king was a father to many—not just one.

Perhaps it was not *everything*, but it would be better than anything his father had ever done for him.

His gaze moved, without him fully realizing it, to the stone with his mother's name. And what had she done for him in those few years he'd had her? *If I didn't love you so much, everything would be different.*

His father sobbing over an already-dead woman he was desecrating with his *feelings*.

"I mean *love*, Alex," Ines said quietly, as if she could hear his memories echoing around him. Using that weapon when he was at his weakest. "Our child will be loved. And I will love *you*. It is what we all deserve."

Perhaps they did all deserve something so destructive, but he would not abide by it. Or her words. Or these memories.

Because he was the king, and nothing would be destroyed on his watch.

So he left her there.

And didn't look back.

Ines stayed in the encroaching dark. There was something peaceful about this spot. Or maybe she was tired of crying, and she was afraid if she went into her bedroom, she'd just end up sobbing until she fell asleep.

It was silly to feel this crushed. She could not expect to get through to a person like Alexandre in one or two conversations. It would take time. To get through to him, to get to the source of his pain, and even once she understood it he would need time to heal from whatever it was.

Could he heal? She gave a little derisive snort. She should be worried about getting through to him at *all*. Healing was so far off it shouldn't even be a consideration.

But they had a *child* to think about, and he still didn't really acknowledge that. Maybe she didn't either. Though she had symptoms, it still felt strangely not real. That a child should be growing inside of her.

And she still had months to accept the reality. To bring it on board. For *both* of them.

Trying to shake the disappointment and sadness and worry away, Ines made her way back to the palace. So she could not get through to him regarding his mother—which was no doubt at least *some* of his pain, which seemed to be brought on by the idea of *love*.

God knew Enzo had not loved his son. So the only love he could have gotten was from his mother. There had to be *something* there, but he rejected letting her in. Letting her know.

He rejected everything when it came to her. Except sex. And even that she thought he'd reject if he could. But the powerful attraction between them was just a little too much to resist. She'd once seen that as a positive sign.

Now she wondered.

Once in her bedroom, she did as she'd feared. Cried herself to sleep and woke up feeling exhausted and achy, a headache from all yesterday's tears drumming at her temples. She felt so poorly she didn't even bother to get ready for the day. She simply trudged into the sitting room in her pajamas where tea and breakfast waited. And Jonet. Which wasn't a great sign.

"Good morning," Jonet greeted her brightly. A sure sign something was very, *very* off.

"What is it?" Ines asked. She had no polish, no strength to be anything but straightforward today.

Jonet shifted in her seat. She poured Ines a cup of tea. She took her time speaking.

"I have gotten a memo from the king's assistant. The king has, uh, been required to travel into the city and attend an economic conference."

"And I am being told this because...?"

Jonet blinked, clearly surprised by the acid in Ines's tone. Ines might have been surprised too, but she was too tired to work up to conveying it.

"He will be staying in the city, and so he wanted you to know he would not be attending any meals or walks or appointments for a few days."

Ines wanted to laugh—bitterly—but she didn't have any energy for that either. "Of course," she said instead. She looked at the tea, then waved it away. "I'm going back to bed."

"Ines..."

But Ines simply walked away, back to her bedroom. The next few days passed in a kind of blur. Jonet kept Ines on track, but it was the first time since joining the royal family that Ines needed to be told what to do and prodded into doing it. Usually, she took all of her tasks quite seriously, but she couldn't seem to now.

Those who knew she was pregnant blamed that. Those who did not know whispered behind her back—about her long absence and now her detached behavior. Ines couldn't even bring herself to care. Because, funnily enough, she thought both sides were right. Part of this exhaustion and emotional turmoil was brought on by pregnancy and hormones and growing a child.

And part was just plain old heartbreak.

"Are you giving up on him?" Evelyne had asked her last night.

Ines hadn't known how to answer that. She did not want to give up on him. She did not know how to get through to him. It left her in a terrible kind of no-man's-land, just waiting for the blow to take her out.

The morning Alexandre was supposed to return—in time to go to her anatomy scan—Ines forced herself to get ready in a way she hadn't been doing lately. She made sure she looked elegant and put-together, as befitted a queen.

Alex had missed their meals and walks, but tonight would be their previously agreed-upon appointment night, and if he thought he was getting out of it…

Well, they would just see about that. Even if she didn't particularly *want* to have sex with him right now or sleep in the same bed or even see his obnoxious face. He wasn't getting out of this because of the bad mood that *he'd* put her in.

She held on to that little blaze of anger because it felt like *something*, when most of the past few days had felt like nothing. Just *gray*. She'd take anger over that.

But the ultrasound technician had arrived with her equipment, and the palace nurse had ushered Ines into the room that was set up for the scan to take place.

The technician gave her directions, and Ines followed them, settling herself on the bed. The technician was ready to start, but there was no sign of Alexandre.

"My husband is supposed to be here," Ines said, her confidence slipping. What if he just avoided her from here on out? What if he was calling her bluff—daring her to run away? What then?

The door swung open, and in strode the king.

"I apologize," Alexandre said, closing the door behind him. He didn't even glance at Ines. His apologies were for the technician. "You may proceed."

"Um, well, of course." The woman smiled down at Ines reassuringly. "This is quite easy, I promise. You only need to relax, Your Majesty," she said kindly. "I'll be looking for a variety of things, but once I can confirm the sex of the baby, I'll let you know. Unless you were wanting to be surprised?"

"No," Alex said, his voice very regal. The one-word answer a command. "We will know the sex."

"Of course, sir," the technician murmured. She got to work, and Ines didn't look at Alexandre. She watched the screen as the woman made the occasional humming noise as she clicked on this or that, zoomed in, hit another button. Anxiety tightened in Ines's chest.

She glanced at Alexandre helplessly. He was frowning at the screen, his own expression one of tension. She wanted to reach out for his hand, but he was just absent. And had been late. And what was there to reach out for if he would always walk away from her?

"Everything is measuring just as it should. Heartbeat, size, et cetera, all in line with your current due date." She smiled down at Ines. "Congratulations, Your Majesties, a princess is on the way."

A girl. They were having a girl. Every feeling in Ines's body simply whooshed out of her. She felt boneless. Empty. *Terrified* and...somehow overjoyed all at the same time.

She looked at Alex, tears spilling over her cheeks. Happy tears, a joy she couldn't fully understand. A *girl*, a *princess*. Something about this tangible thing to hold on to felt real when so little else had.

Alexandre clearly did not agree. His expression was blank. He held his hands behind his back, just as he had when he'd entered. There was *nothing* in him that gave way to any kind of reaction to the news.

"I've sent the results to your medical team. You'll only need to go to your follow-up appointment in a few weeks, unless there are any concerns. They'll contact you. I'll leave you two alone to...celebrate." The woman's smile was tight but polite, and she curtsied to both of them before exiting the room.

Alexandre stood there in silence, and Ines still lay on the bed, tears drying on her cheeks.

A daughter. She was to have a daughter. Who would be a princess. Who would be Alex's daughter.

He seemed very unimpressed, and it made her sad and angry at the same time. *Better than nothing, right?* She wanted to believe that, but it all felt so awful.

Except... No. She wouldn't let him ruin this. They were to have a daughter.

"We will need to discuss names," she announced, finally pulling her shirt back down over the swell of her stomach.

"Names," Alex echoed.

Ines got off the bed. She stood to face him. He didn't look at her, which made her angry. "Yes, our child is a person who will need to be named, Alexandre. I can handle it on my own, but I thought the *king* might have an opinion."

He looked down at her now, a bit like she was a bug to be wiped off his shoe. He had *never* used that expression against her. It made her feel worse. Everything about him made her feel worse.

"I'm sure you will choose appropriately."

She stared at him, fury turning her mute for a good minute or two. He wasn't even going to make a suggestion? He was going to leave it to her?

Fine. *Good*, even. Because she was done with this. Done with *him*. Her daughter would not live like this, hoping for *something* from her father only to get *nothing*. Ines didn't know how to accomplish that just yet, but she'd find a way.

I am the storm.

"Just so you know, you do not need to attend any meals, walks or *appointments* today. I do not wish to see you or be anywhere near any *kings* at the moment. I will let you know when that changes."

And with that, she marched off.

CHAPTER ELEVEN

Alexandre sat at his desk, trying to focus on his ever-growing to-do list. Instead, he kept thinking about Ines.

And a *princess*. A daughter. His. To protect.

He had protected Evelyne. Not perfectly, but from the *worst* of things. He still counted it as a partial failure, but this would be different. It had to be. He could protect his princess.

Your daughter.

He was an adult now. The king. He did not have to try to stop the whims of someone else, so she would be... She would be fine.

Names. Ines wanted him to have a say in a name, and he could barely wrap his mind around a *baby*. A girl. His.

All the ways he'd failed Evelyne felt bigger in his head now. Alex would never lay a hand on his daughter as Enzo had, but that didn't mean he would be *good* at this. He was a *king*, not a father. Didn't being a good father require him to be more than a title? He couldn't be.

He was a protector—of *all* in his kingdom, not someone to think of names and futures and...

A *daughter*. What was he supposed to do with this? It felt like a terrible unfurling in his chest, painful with claws. It was hard to breathe. Impossible to think of anything beyond that staticky picture on the screen. It hadn't looked like much more than a blob to Alexandre, but the technician had confidently seen something.

A girl. *His* daughter.

Gabriel strode in unannounced, but Alex heard his assistant huffing and puffing from behind him. "We have a problem," Gabriel said seriously, ignoring the flustered assistant.

Alexandre wanted to rap his head on the desk. He had more problems than he could begin to count. Instead, he waved his assistant away. "Hold my calls until we're done," he told him.

The assistant frowned at Gabriel but did as he was told, leaving and closing the door behind him as he did.

"General Vinyes is up to something," Gabriel said once the door was closed.

Alexandre wanted to shout—something he rarely felt toward Gabriel, but he didn't have time for this nonsense. He had to figure out what to do with a *daughter*.

And a wife...who'd looked at him like he'd slapped her when he'd told her he trusted her to handle the names. He winced at the memory. Sometimes he behaved in ways he didn't understand how they hurt people—but he'd known this would hurt her.

He'd hurt her on purpose. And what did that make him? Not the man he claimed to be, certainly. Fists weren't the only way to hurt someone.

Still, he held his temper at Gabriel's interruption. By a thread. "This is hardly news. General Vinyes is always up to something. Do you have proof of said wrongdoing?"

"Not exactly. But I'm hearing whispers and—"

Alexandre pinched the bridge of his nose, hoping to pinch away the lick of temper with it. "I have told you there's nothing I can do about *rumors*, Gabriel. I need something real to be able to get rid of him for good without causing more problems than his existence does."

"It is a big *something*, Alexandre," Gabriel said seriously. "And it sounds credible enough I'm considering sending Evelyne and Gabri off to Italy and my parents until we sort out what the threat is and how we can stop it."

This poked through some of Alexandre's frustration. That *was* big. Gabriel might have no love lost for the general, but if he was worried enough to send Evelyne and Gabri away... "You think it is *that* dangerous?"

"There have been whispers of revolution. I haven't been able to get to the bottom of them yet. But everything I know points to Vinyes, and if he *is* at the source, it's more than possible. And it's more than dangerous."

"I need proof, Gabriel."

"Then I'll need your permission to do more than *listen*."

Alexandre knew how protective Gabriel was of Evelyne and Gabri, but he was not a man prone to exaggeration. If he thought it was this serious, it was. And as much as they might not see eye to eye on how to handle Vinyes, Alexandre trusted Gabriel. He would not behave outside of what Alexandre wished.

"You have my permission to get to the bottom of things, but all action must go through me."

Gabriel nodded. "Of course. You might consider sending Ines with Evelyne and Gabri as well."

"Why?"

"Revolutions have the tendency to get...bloody if not handled correctly."

Revolution. God, he hated that word. "Why...why would anyone revolt *now*?" There had been attempts against King Enzo here and there over the years, but Vinyes had ruthlessly stopped every one.

Those Alexandre had understood. Perhaps even rooted for from time to time, even if he himself would have ended up on one of their pikes. He couldn't blame those who hated his father's reign.

But him? He'd done everything to *solve* the problems his father had created. Maybe it was taking longer than some people liked. Maybe it wasn't *perfect*. But to revolt now when there was actually progress being made?

"Sometimes people love a cage, Alexandre," Gabriel said quietly. "Vinyes certainly knows how to make them believe they aren't in one. Most of the people are behind you. You know this, but it only takes a well-connected few to threaten that. A general is pretty damn well connected. A bloodthirsty one? Well, he doesn't need the will of the people. He only needs the might of a few, and access to a king."

It made more sense, honestly, that Vinyes was pretending to be a dutiful general who listened to his king while secretly planning some kind of revolution rather than just trying to keep his job, but it didn't make it any easier to hear.

What would Alexandre do if the general used his own army against him? Surely not all the soldiers would heed Vinyes's commands. Vinyes was no loved leader, but Gabriel was right. People loved a cage that felt like safety. And people would do a lot of things out of fear.

Fear. Ines. His *daughter*. Safety.

Here in this palace while someone planned revolution. No, that could not be. He had to protect them. Always.

"I cannot imagine Ines would want to go, but…" Well, she wasn't happy with *him*, was she? She didn't even want to see him. All the things on her *list*, all her determinations they should try to be a couple wiped away earlier.

She wanted nothing to do with him right now. *Kings*, she'd said. As though it was different. A person. A king. As though she was *disappointed* in him being a king when she'd known all along what she'd signed up for.

You do not have to be anyone but yourself with me.

But he *himself* could only be a king. The protector. The brick wall between chaos and pettiness and whims and personal vendettas and the right thing for the good of the people.

There were *not* two people inside of him—no matter what she thought. And maybe she'd finally realized it. She didn't want to be around him tonight. She understood. He was only a king.

An idea that he had held as a talisman that had gotten him through the worst. That *should* continue to but…

He shook that thought away and the discomfort with it. He should be happy he'd finally gotten through to her.

Why couldn't he feel anything but another weight around his heart?

"I will ensure she heads to safety as well," Alexandre managed. He would order it. Command it. And it didn't matter if she went willingly or with an argument. It would be done.

"Will she put up a fight? I'm preparing for your sister to. Evelyne will not want to go if we are planning on staying behind," Gabriel said.

"I am the king. I can hardly leave my kingdom."

"Yes, I know. And I will not leave you. I have connections with some of the soldiers. We will work to nip this in the bud before anything happens, but we do not want to risk anything. It will take some doing, but I don't think Evelyne could stand to be away from Gabri long enough to send just him to safety. I don't particularly love the idea, but…"

"But we must keep them safe. When is this to come to a head? Do you know?"

Gabriel shook his head. "Soon, I am led to believe. I will need to dig deeper to get a better idea, but I'd like Evelyne and Gabri off palace property by tomorrow."

Tomorrow. So soon.

Ines didn't want to see him right now. Maybe that would help their case. "It might go better if you or Evelyne discusses this with Ines."

Alexandre could not meet Gabriel's gaze. It would see too much. So he focused on some papers on his desk.

"What exactly is going on with you, Alex?"

Alex. A distinction this question was friend to friend, not lord to king.

"Nothing is going on. I am dealing with…impending revolutions and an impending child. It is a lot."

"It is, but these are not unexpected things. You've been preparing for both for months now, haven't you?"

Yes. He had known revolution was a possibility at the transfer of power, at the changes he'd instituted—though, he'd gotten a little complacent in thinking that dangerous between-time had passed.

And yes, the plan had originally been for Ines to have his child, but…

Not like this. "Ines has…developed ideas."

"Ideas?" Gabriel returned equitably. "Or feelings?"

Alex scraped a palm over his jaw. "She is simply confused. Perhaps…hormonal." He winced a little bit at that, because he knew both Ines and Evelyne would take great offense at that suggestion, and they'd be right to.

But he needed a reason that Ines claiming she loved him was something temporary. Something he could *fix*. Her loving him would only end in pain and suffering. That was what love did, in his experience.

Gabriel sighed gustily. "It's beneath even you to blame *feelings* on *hormones*, Alexandre. Ines has been a wonderful queen to you and—"

"And I am a king. I have an entire country's fate resting on what I choose. How I handle this revolution. I cannot be concerned about *feelings*. Hers. Mine. Anyone's."

Our child will be loved. And I will love you. It is what we all deserve.

A princess. A daughter.

Names.

"You are more than a king, Alex."

But Alexandre could not take that to heart. Certainly not *now*. Why could no one understand that?

Because they had never been tasked with this. *You cannot save me, Alex, so you will need to save them. Do not change course. Do not let anything in. Be better than him.*

She'd been dying. Right before his eyes. Nurses and the doctor tending to the newly born Evelyne. No one had noticed him sneaking in. No one had noticed...

You must save your sister. You are her and Alis's only hope. If I loved you less...

Alis's only hope. He had held that close his entire life. His one duty. His mother had wanted it of him, so it would be done. She had not gotten to live a long, happy life. She had been brutalized, living and dead, by a man's selfish whims and uncontrollable, unpredictable feelings.

This was all he had to offer her memory.

So he could only be a king. *Only.*

"If there is to be a revolution, I cannot be more or less

than exactly that. I am the king. Period." This was the clearest truth he knew, and getting Ines out from underfoot would help him remember that.

He had made a promise to his dying mother. Nothing would get in his way of protecting Evelyne. Of protecting Alis. Certainly not his own wants. Feelings. Self.

"Not all that long ago, you interfered when I was keeping my distance from Evelyne and my marriage," Gabriel said.

Alexandre managed to meet Gabriel's gaze now. "You were afraid of yourself. I am not afraid."

"Aren't you?"

Alexandre frowned at Gabriel. *Fear* was not what he felt. He was making decisions out of experience and determination. Not *fear* of hurt. "I would never hurt Ines. I am not worried about that."

"I know. But love has always terrified you. Even when it comes to Evelyne and me, you keep a careful distance. That is why you save people, saved us. So you don't have to deal with the love you feel. You can convince yourself the protecting is enough."

Alex did not have words for long ticking moments. Then he shook his head, because Gabriel didn't understand. For Gabriel, love could be life. A foundation. A country, a legacy did not rest on Gabriel's shoulders. So he could be more.

Alexandre was different. He was a king. He had a mission. And yes, he protected people, but that was because of the title he'd inherited.

Besides. "Love is little more than a weapon," Alexandre muttered.

"I think that means you're doing it wrong."

Alex knew Gabriel wouldn't understand. Gabriel and

Evelyne were...different. They might have titles, but they didn't have to save a country. They didn't have to walk that tightrope.

Alex had made sure of it.

Things would be different if I loved you less. How often had his mother said that to him? Like this giant love was a gift—even though it had taken everything from her.

She loves you more. You took her from me. His father's words. He'd turned from the queen's dead, bloody body looking like a monster covered in that blood. Eyes wild. Because for all the evil inside King Enzo he had mourned when Mother died.

He'd pointed at Alexandre then. *You took her from me.*

Alex had run then. But just because he'd escaped that beating didn't mean more hadn't come. No, it had only meant that for the rest of his days Father had blamed Alexandre for the love lost between them. Evelyne for Mother's death. Alexandre for her lack of love.

Always blame. Never responsibility.

That was love.

So Alex had taken on every responsibility. Even his mother's death.

Alex had always felt if there hadn't been a *kingdom* in the way—power and titles—these things might have been surmountable, but the palace made everything soft, complex, *messy* insurmountable.

The people would always come first. Had to. It was his role or he was no better than his monster of a father. Or he would fail the mother who'd loved him most at the cost of everything, even her life.

"Talk to Ines," Alexandre ordered—and it was an order, king to lord, not friend or brother. "Or have Evelyne do it. But I want Ines to go with Evelyne. If she is difficult, I will command it. But Evelyne should be able to get through to her."

Gabriel's expression was disapproving, but he nodded with a somewhat sardonic bow of protocol before striding out of Alex's office.

Ines stared at her sister-in-law while her gut churned with worry. She held little Gabri in her lap, because the boy seemed to like it here, and there was some comfort in the sweet, warm baby in her arms. She would have one of these in a few months. A girl. A *princess*.

Could she hold strong and wait and hope the reality of a baby changed Alex's mind? Or would that hurt everyone? She shook her head. More pressing problems at hand right now.

"They really think there is to be a revolution?"

Evelyne nodded grimly. "Neither Gabriel nor Alexandre are ones to overreact. They want us to leave tomorrow morning, if possible." She got to her feet, began to pace. Not just worry. Temper flashed in her eyes. "Protecting the womenfolk," Evelyne said disgustedly. Then she stopped pacing, looked at her son in Ines's lap and sighed, softened. "The problem is I don't want to be separated from Gabri, and you *are* pregnant. A dangerous situation is no place for us right now, even if I won't admit it to Gabriel. Or Alexandre."

Alexandre. Just the thought of him made worry the secondary feeling in her chest. She was just so…angry. But it wasn't the kind of angry that had prompted her to leave the castle all those months ago. It was something different. More complicated.

Probably because of the child she carried, more than anything else. Ines had more to think about than herself, her own wants and frustrations with Alexandre. She had a child to think about.

And he didn't even want a say in her name? He saw himself more as a king than a father? She wanted to think he'd change his tune when the baby arrived, but she knew the depths of Alexandre's stubbornness.

He'd just avoid the both of them—his wife, his daughter. Out of sight, out of mind. He'd never actually have to deal with *love*. It made her somehow both sad and angry, compassionate and full of righteous blame.

But for right now, if there was to be danger, he wouldn't rest until she was out of the way. Maybe a different version of her would feel Evelyne's temper, but pregnant and angry and hurt—yes, hurt mostly—she did just want to be away.

Not that she wouldn't worry. No amount of anger and hurt could turn the love off. And revolution could only be dangerous. Particularly when the man she loved was the king—and would be the target of any revolution.

She felt sick to her stomach just considering it.

She put a hand to her belly in some hope that might still the nausea, but it only reminded her she had another life to concern herself with. Her baby.

"I don't necessarily mind leaving right now," Ines told Evelyne. "But I wouldn't feel right invading Gabriel's parents' home. Jonet and I can go—"

"Don't be ridiculous. Gabriel must stand by Alexandre's side because they are basically brothers, and he has the knowledge and connections to hopefully stop this in its tracks. So you and I must do the same. Stand by each other. Together. Jonet, too, of course. Anyone you like, really. But we aren't separating. We are family."

Family. Fierce and determined. Nothing about the

kingdom or titles. "Why doesn't Alexandre feel that way?" she asked, then wished she hadn't when Evelyne looked at her with something too close to pity in her eyes.

"This is about more than us leaving, isn't it?"

Ines nodded. She refused to cry all over Evelyne, but it took effort. "We had the ultrasound this morning. Did he tell you?"

Evelyne's mouth firmed, clear irritation. "He did not."

"We are having a girl."

Evelyne sat with a thump, then wrapped her arms around Ines. "That's *wonderful*. I can't wait to buy something frilly and pink."

Ines wanted to laugh, but she was afraid it would come out like a sob.

"He said he trusted me to name her. As though he didn't even want a say. As though he doesn't even…"

Evelyne pulled back and her expression was conflicted. Between the truth and her love for her brother. "He does care, Ines. I know he does."

"I know he does too, but it is so deep down I do not know how to reach it. And I worry he'll just keep burying it and our child will only ever know…a king instead of a man. Instead of a father."

Evelyne took a deep breath and let it out. "He is nothing like—"

"I know, Evelyne. I wouldn't be here if I didn't know that he's nothing like your father. He means well. I think that's what makes it worse. How do you get through to someone who thinks they're doing the right thing? Who is *trying* to do the best thing but is just so misguided?" She shook her head. It didn't matter. This wasn't about her marriage or even Alexandre right now. "Will they be…in danger if we leave them behind?"

"I hope not. But I think it's possible if Vinyes is behind this, which of course he is. Father had uprisings when I was little. I don't remember much of them because I didn't understand what was going on, but Vinyes always swept through and took care of any protests. So he would certainly know how to whip one up."

"I cannot understand why anyone would follow Vinyes. Alexandre has done everything he can to undo all your father's harsh policies. Why wouldn't he be celebrated?"

"Change is painful. And complicated. And not easy. Violence is an easy promise. At least, that's what Gabriel tells me. I kind of think these are all problems made up by men."

Ines snorted. She couldn't disagree. Though the words landed deeper than the problem of men and revolutions.

Change is painful. Yes, it was. Could she turn her back on Alex because he needed to change and he resisted because of all that pain?

"But leadership comes with risks, and so we must let our husbands take those risks, not because they are *men* but because they are the leaders. We are leaders in our own way, but not *this* way."

Ines studied her sister-in-law. "You are such a good princess, Evelyne."

Evelyne blinked once, as if surprised by the compliment. But then she shook it away. She reached out, stroked a finger over her son's cheek.

"You'll come with us, won't you? We can keep each other from having nervous breakdowns worrying about our husbands."

That was the worst part, Ines knew. Even when she was mad at Alexandre, even hurting and despairing and not knowing how to get through to him, she would love him. Worry over him.

So no, she could not run away like she had before. Not that she wouldn't go. But she deserved something. Her daughter deserved something. Maybe she couldn't get through to Alexandre, but she was going to keep fighting. She was not giving up.

"Yes, all right. I'll come. On one condition."

"What's that?"

Ines lifted her chin and met Evelyne's eager gaze. "Alexandre comes and asks me to leave himself."

Evelyne wrinkled her nose. "Oh dear."

Oh dear, indeed.

CHAPTER TWELVE

ALEXANDRE HAD TROUBLE concentrating on what still must be done because his mind was focused on revolution, on *protection*. But there were still the day-to-day responsibilities of running a kingdom, and Gabriel thought it best as if they went on like they weren't aware of any *whispers*, so Alexandre had to be in his office, acting normal.

Alexandre agreed with this plan, but it didn't make his day *easy*. Particularly when only a few hours after Gabriel had swept into his office unannounced and, against his assistant's wishes, Evelyne did the same.

"You and your husband seem to think my office is yours to enter and exit as you please," Alex said, waving his assistant off, because he would not kick Evelyne out no matter how much he wanted to.

That was the purview of his father, and Alexandre was a better man—even when his sister was being ridiculous.

Evelyne rolled her eyes. "You must go talk to Ines."

He turned away from her to the papers on his desk. It was not a shock Evelyne would stick her nose where it didn't belong, but he had no time or patience for it. "Why would I do that?"

"She's on the fence about leaving with me and Gabri. You need to talk to her, convince her she should."

"On the fence?" Of course. Why would Ines just make

things *easy*? He couldn't understand what had *happened* to her. Nearly a year of obedience and—

He went a little cold at the word. *Obedience* felt…ugly. He didn't want her to be *obedient* necessarily. Just…easy. Just… She should *understand* his bidding and do it without it feeling like orders against her will, because he was doing the *right* thing. They should go back to the way things were when she always agreed with him, always understood he made good decisions.

Which was clearly a lie. He frowned at that realization. It wasn't that she'd changed. She'd just stopped pretending. Why had she pretended in the first place, though? Evelyne never did.

Because Evelyne knows she's safe with you, no matter what, and Ines had to learn that.

He didn't know where that thought came from. He wanted to reject it. But the conversation with Ines about when they'd first met, about how she'd come to believe he was *good*, was all too close to wave it away as easily as he might have.

He looked up at his sister, bowled over by the thought that…he had always tried to protect her and felt he'd always failed, because it hadn't been enough. She'd been abused anyway.

But was the simple act of trying enough?

Ridiculous.

"I am busy, Evelyne." And in a terrible, knotted pain that made it hard to get a full breath. But he kept his voice devoid of that. Detached. Cold. "Tell her to be reasonable."

"If there's anyone I shall tell to be reasonable, brother, it is *you*."

He glared at his sister, but he recognized that look in

her eye. Stubborn. Period. He was in no mood for the stubborn whims of his little sister. Particularly if just her existence brought on startling realizations he didn't want.

"I have a revolution to stop, if you haven't heard. Perhaps the two of you could concern yourselves with *that*."

"You have a wife who loves you. I cannot begin to fathom how you've made a problem out of *that*."

Alexandre stiffened in spite of himself. What had Ines told her? Why was she bringing other people into it? "That is not your concern."

"My *God*, Alex. Be a man."

He straightened, temper stirring when he almost never let it stir with Evelyne because it was too much like Enzo. But *this* was a step too far, even for her. "I am a king," he reminded her. "*Your* king."

There was no room for a *man* in that equation. He'd learned that as a *child*. How had she not?

She looked wholly unimpressed by that. "You're an ass."

He stared at her in shock. Not that she was never rude to him, but it had been quite some time, and usually she wasn't taking someone else's side when she did it.

"An ass," she continued, using that offensive word once again, "who must *ask* his wife and the mother of his future child himself if he wishes her to leave him so he can fight a revolution alone," she continued, clearly not backing down.

Alexandre could blame Ines for this too, that Evelyne would stick her nose in this. Because if there was no Ines, Evelyne and Gabri would just be on their way to safety.

"I will not be fighting anything alone."

"No, my husband and the father of *my* child will stand beside you. Something Gabriel and I discussed. Together. Because we both love you and each other."

He did not have time for this. He did not *have* to do this. He was the king. Only his command mattered.

His breath caught when he realized...that way lay the way of his father.

But that did not mean he couldn't find—wouldn't find—his own way. He looked his sister in the eye and asked her very plainly, "Evelyne, what do you want from me?"

Evelyne's expression softened a little—a very little—but her words did not.

"I want you to go talk to your wife. Really talk to her. I thought I knew you so well, or that Gabriel and I did, but I don't understand. She *loves* you. Why would you run away from that? You're the best man any of us know. There's no reason not to enjoy love when it's offered."

Best. But it was a constant battle. Did no one understand how *hard* that was? To be better than his father, *best*—for his country and his family. And Ines...she was a threat to all of that. Love or not. Maybe especially with *love* involved.

If I loved you less...

Love was a weapon. A bludgeon. It was pain and suffering and *selfish*. Love destroyed. He could not be those things and save his country. Hell, he could not even be those things and somehow save his wife from the revolution that now threatened.

And people expected him to talk to her. Face-to-face. When all that ever did was end in...confusion. He had no time or space for that, but what else was new?

"I will talk to her," Alexandre agreed because it would get Evelyne to leave and stop talking about...whatever this was.

It would be easy enough to go to Ines and tell her she must leave for her own safety. And the safety of the baby.

Girl. Princess.

Alexandre squeezed his eyes shut as Evelyne came over and gave him a hug. "I know you care for her too, Alex. I know you *could* love her if you let yourself. I may not be able to understand why you won't or can't, but I know what it is like to be in love and be loved. It can be scary and hard, but it is hardly an enemy."

Alexandre awkwardly patted his sister's shoulder until she released him. He said nothing because there was nothing to say.

He wasn't concerned about love being *scary* or *hard*, he was concerned about it being used as some kind of bludgeon. Not against *him*.

Against Ines.

Against their daughter.

He had seen one lifeless, bloody body in his life, and he would not witness another—literally or figuratively.

Love was the root of too many mistakes. The kind Evelyne and Gabriel did not have to worry about because an entire country didn't rest on their shoulders.

And good for them. They should enjoy that. They should have all they'd built. But he could not.

He could not.

He held himself very still until Evelyne left, then finally allowed himself to sink into his chair. One minute, just *one minute*, to pull himself together. He raked his fingers through his hair as his breath seemed to clog in his lungs.

Had he condemned Ines to this fate when he'd married her? He supposed he had, and for the first time he realized how unfair that had been—because she did not understand. She did not see the world as he did.

Maybe when this was all over, revolution thwarted, he

could explain it to her in a way that would make sense. In a way that could turn something to good for her.

For your daughter.

He didn't know why that kept poking at him. Any child of Ines's would be well cared for and loved, and perhaps she would be a princess, but not an heir with that kind of responsibility.

No, that would fall to Gabri.

Pressure tightened in Alexandre's chest. He did not wish this on his nephew. He did not wish this on...anyone. He had only ever been concerned with *his* role, but he would not live forever. Someday, this all would be someone else's mantle to bear.

That little baby.

Who will be loved by Gabriel and Evelyne, and it will be different. You will make it different.

But if he could make it different for Gabri...

He shook that fear, that concern, that possibility away. Everything would have to wait until this trouble was solved. Even that.

So he went in search of Ines, because that was a tangible. He would find her, tell her she must go. She must be safe. The end.

He found her in her bedroom. There was a suitcase on her bed, open but full. Alexandre frowned at it, then her. "You've packed."

"Yes," she agreed, putting a little bag on top of the neatly folded clothes. She didn't look at him.

"Then I don't... Why am I here if you've already agreed to go?" Had Evelyne misunderstood something? What a waste of—

"I haven't *agreed*, exactly," Ines returned equitably. "I thought it best to discuss it with you first."

Frustrated and not at all understanding her, he fell back on icy detachment. "You know my thoughts."

"You wish to send me away, yes, but I wanted to be certain it was for my safety, not for your convenience." She sat on the edge of the bed, all regal elegance, and met his gaze with a direct one of her own.

Convenience. Temper licked, but he could not let it win. Not today. Not with all this *love* talk in the air.

"Ideally, there is no violence," he said, a bit through gritted teeth but clearly nonetheless. "I think Gabriel and I can stop this before it becomes something, but on the off chance there *is* some kind of skirmish, the children should not be anywhere near it."

Would Gabri face this when he was king? No, Alexandre would solve all these problems before he had to pass them along. That was the purview of a *good* king, and he would be that—revolutions or no.

But he had to stop this dustup first, and he could not be thinking about any of the things the women in his life seemed determined to poke into.

"Then I will go."

"Why could you not have simply agreed with Evelyne and let me be?" he demanded.

She rose from her seat on the bed and crossed to him.

"I am so angry with you for so many reasons I can't even count them all." She moved to him then, reached out and put her hands on his forearms. "But I still love you, and I will miss you and worry for you. And I didn't want to leave without saying that. To your face." Her blue eyes were shiny and earnest.

He stepped back from her before he realized it would be viewed as some kind of retreat. There was no retreat here. He had to stand up to her.

"Why does that hurt you, Alex?" she asked, such *pain* in her voice. Which wasn't fair. He did not wish to cause her pain—she was causing it herself. If she would just do as he said, feel as he felt… *Understand.*

"Do not concern yourself with what you perceive as my *hurt*. If you are quite packed, I will take your suitcase down myself."

"Do you feel nothing for me?" she asked, her voice quiet, tight, hurt.

The question made such little sense he didn't know how to respond to it.

"I thought perhaps things had changed," she said, her voice still vibrating with emotion. "That the thought of losing me might have opened your eyes, hence that morning in your office. And then again when I returned. Was I wrong? Was it all about avoiding an annulment? For the crown? Is that all it ever was?"

He should tell her *yes*. He should form that word. It would be so easy, and everything would be all right. "I never promised you anything to do with *love*, Ines," he managed.

"No," she agreed, looking solemn and regal and perhaps a bit shattered. "Nor did I to you. But it's there."

It was too much. This insistence. The hurt in her eyes. He had not done this. He was not pushing this. *She* was. *She* was using love as a weapon, and this was why he would not engage. He would not love. He would not *harm*.

"I have had enough."

"What about what *I* have had?" she demanded, temper flashing.

"What *you* have had?" he repeated, frustration reaching its boiling point. Everything he did was for *her*, for his citizens. And she complained when she was the one who had dismantled all they'd built?

"You have *destroyed* me," he shot at her. "Does this make you happy?" he demanded. "Satisfied? This love you speak of has only ever been used against me like a weapon. You are not the first. I hope to God you are the last."

It was too much. He knew it was too much. A break. She was always causing a damn *break*.

She looked at him like he'd lost leave of his senses. If *only*.

"A weapon? Love isn't a weapon," she said, shaking her head. "What would make you think... Your father didn't love you, Alexandre. The way he harmed you and Evelyne was never love."

She said this with such certainty, as if she worried he saw the warped version of his father's attention or, even worse, his father's abuse as love. "No. Never. He never loved *us*." But Enzo *had* loved.

And Alexandre had enjoyed an unwanted front row seat to what that meant. What kind of adversity it caused. The stress, the blows, the end. Violence and grief and destruction.

All for love.

"Your mother also loved you." She said it like a statement, but it felt like a question, and it stirred up too many things that needed to stay in the past. His mother *had* loved him. She had tried to save him. She had been good, wonderful. Everything he did was for her memory and for Evelyne.

He was the protector in the face of all the ways he'd failed as a boy.

He turned away from Ines. "I will not speak of her. I have made that clear. You must go. It is for your *own* good, but you are making me glad of it."

"She did love you, didn't she?"

Ines wouldn't give up. She wouldn't *see*. "More than anything, Ines," he said, exhausted clean through. "Why must you belabor this point?"

"If she loved you more than anything, and your father did not, I do not understand why you feel so...threatened by me loving you. By me wanting you to love our daughter. If you would explain anything to me, maybe I could understand."

He remained mute for a wide variety of reasons while she sat there looking at him, seeking answers he didn't have. Even if she deserved them.

"I am trying to understand, and I cannot," Ines said, quietly but with deep, haunting emotion in her voice. "I know you want to be nothing like Enzo. I don't think you *could* be anything like him, but this is not that. So what happened to you, Alex?"

Alex, Alex, Alex. Always *Alex* with her. Always poking under all the walls he'd needed to erect to be the perfect king. The *opposite* king to his father.

"Happened to me? Nothing. Don't you see? Nothing happened to *me*. My mother died because of *love*. My father used her dead body as a punching bag. Because of *love*. My father violated the trust of his citizens and his duty to them. Evelyne suffered abuses her entire childhood that I could not stop, but I stand before you, all in one piece."

Ines's eyes were wide and bright and full of tears. She looked pale. "Perhaps in one piece, Alex, but no less marked. No less...warped."

"You dare call me *warped*?" he demanded. The shock of the blows just kept coming. "Just because my father didn't love *me* doesn't mean he didn't *love*. Oh, he loved. My mother most of all. Until I was born and ruined everything. Because she did not have room for both of them, only me. And he blamed me for that. *She* blamed me for that."

If I loved you less, I could be what he wants, but I love you too much for that. How often had his mother whispered that to him, as if it were some mantra to save herself?

But it had only felt like blame.

It wasn't her fault. It wasn't. It was *his*.

If she loved you less, everything would be the way it was. There is no good in you or for you, I will make sure of it, so she never knows your love. How often had his father taken his rage on not getting exactly what he wanted on Alex—a punishment for love.

Love was Enzo's weapon. His bludgeon.

And his mother's excuse.

And Alexandre had built himself to be everything his father was not, but he loved in spite of himself...and he would never, ever use it against another.

The silence was heavy, throbbing, but it was Ines who broke it first.

"And you'd never wield a weapon your father did," she said, with such quiet surety he felt as though she'd used her own weapon to cut him open. But in all that pain, he found some semblance of nothingness. Detachment. A bit like watching his parents fight when he'd been but a boy.

Over *him*. And he'd learned the only way to survive it was to retreat within himself. Through the fights, the abuses, the blame, the death. Even watching Enzo beat his mother's body. He'd learned how to exist outside himself. So that reality couldn't touch him.

Ines had upended that skill for a while, but it was back

because this hurt badly enough he needed it to be back to survive.

He turned to face her then. He felt nothing but ice and was relieved. Because she understood, so maybe he could *survive*. "No. I will not. The car will take you and Evelyne and Gabri to the airport first thing in the morning. You will be ready." He did not pose it as a question.

She studied him, her hands clasped together over her heart as if she could feel his own pain radiating inside of her chest. She looked broken. Appalled.

But there were worse things in her eyes. Worse even than the tears. Something too close to pity to be considered anything but.

He was a *king*. He was not meant to be pitied.

"We can go back to the way things were." There were tears in her eyes, but they didn't fall. There was a shake in her voice, but each word came out clear. "I will make it all as easy on you as possible. I will go while you fight this threat, and when I came back, it can all go back to the way it was."

He had no words for this strange turnaround. No way to fight the shocking *pain* those words elicited, when he should feel nothing but relief. Or the calm detachment of disassociating.

"But I will love our daughter," she continued fiercely. "With all I am. And I will prove to you that it will not warp me. It will not be a weapon. Because what your father called love, and perhaps even your mother, was nothing more than *control*, Alexandre. And you of all people should know that. You are not your father, but you have certainly learned how to control the world around you. You do it for good, but that does not make it good."

He had no words. He couldn't even breathe. Was she

accusing him of being, if not as bad as his father, still not *better*?

"I love you," she said firmly, never looking away from him. "That's not a weapon. It's only a fact. It is only a *promise*."

But he felt stabbed clean all the same, as though it was nothing more than a dagger shoved into his heart.

"When you are ready to heal from these horrible things you saw and felt, I will be here." She pressed her palm to her stomach. "We will be here."

"I will never be ready." Because there was nothing to *heal* from. He had endured. Survived. He was a *king*, and his kingdom would remain in one piece no matter what he had to do in the coming days.

Men might need healing. King's were only the weight of their crown.

"Then, I guess we will all be miserable," she said, as though it was *he* who was the one damning them to that fate.

Before he could find words, or perhaps more likely before she could do anything else, someone cleared their throat behind them.

Alexandre looked back to find Gabriel standing somewhat awkwardly in the doorway.

"I apologize for the intrusion," Gabriel said, his expression apologetic, the set of his mouth grim. "We've moved up the timetable. The car is ready. I'd like everyone to get out now."

CHAPTER THIRTEEN

THINGS MOVED QUICKLY THEN. Ines might have sunk into a depressed grief, but the threat of danger had her heart beating heavily in her throat as Gabriel packed up the car and gave instructions to a driver Ines didn't recognize.

Because the man was some kind of security guard who worked for Gabriel and not the crown, so he could be trusted not to fall into any traps of revolution.

Gabriel then said his good-byes to wife and son. Ines knew it was a private moment, but she watched the embrace, the soft whispered words, the lingering kiss from Evelyne, the last tight squeeze of Gabri, and ached.

Where was her husband? What was he doing? Off somewhere believing that this was a weapon. Believing he could only be a king—not a man. Save his country while sweeping his wife and unborn daughter out of the way.

She wanted to be angrier than she was, but how could she be angry at a boy who'd seen and felt and endured such terrible, terrible things? Life had never taken him by the hand and taught him different.

Of course he was afraid of love.

But understanding him now solved nothing, because there were no magic answers in his trauma. She had no answers, no ideas, only a terrible kind of grief welling up inside her.

The women piled into the car, Jonet helping Evelyne strap Gabri into his car seat. Ines sat in the back of the car, pressed in between Jonet and Evelyne, as it pulled away. Evelyne was silently crying. Ines felt too much fear to cry, but she pulled the handkerchief she kept in her purse out and handed it to Evelyne, who wiped her eyes.

"Are we doing the right thing?" Ines managed to ask. Because it didn't *feel* right. It felt awful.

Evelyne's gaze was down at the sleeping Gabri in his carrier. "Yes." It was clear that *yes* was for her son, not for herself.

Ines put her hand over her stomach. *Yes, for you. Everything is for you. No weapons. No bludgeons. Only love. The good, soft kind. The real kind.*

They drove to the airport and got on one of Gabriel's private planes that would fly them to Italy and his parents' estate.

The truth was, Ines didn't know how to fight what Alexandre had said. He was wrong, but he wasn't. He was living based on an experience that had shaped him, and he didn't know how to believe there could be a different one.

Perhaps there was only time and dedication to the task of proving something to him, but when their daughter came into the world, would time and dedication only hurt her?

Ines *would* love Alexandre no matter what. It was not something that seemed to shrivel up and go away. It was like some necessary organ inside of her. There was no deciding it didn't exist, didn't serve some necessary function to life.

So she would try very hard to give him the life he wanted just as she'd told him. She wouldn't pressure him for more. She would try to abide by his policies and decisions.

But not at the cost of their child's happiness. That would be where she had to draw the line.

Ines worried that there was no way to make everyone happy or even content in this situation. She worried, as she'd told Alexandre, that they would all just spend their lives in misery if he didn't come around.

She rested her hand on her ever-expanding bump. *I will not let that be the case for you.*

She had to find some way...some way for that not to be her child's fate. She could live with her own misery, as long as this baby was happy, loved, satisfied.

Once in the air, Gabri awoke, and Evelyne had him cradled in the crook of her arm as she fed him a bottle. She gazed lovingly down at her son, and Ines could picture it, more and more every day. This life inside of her being a child in her arms. A child to care for.

It would change everything. She wanted to believe it would even change Alexandre, but she worried he was ruled by such *fear* it would only drive him further into this determination to protect.

Not anyone else. *He* thought he was protecting those he loved, but Ines could see it for what it really was now.

Protecting himself, from the pain he suffered as a child. Protecting himself from confusion and control and cruelty disguised as love.

She ached for him because she too had suffered, but not in the same way. Not with such a mantle of responsibilities on his shoulders. She had been a pawn in her father's plans—but he'd never pretended it was about *love*. He'd never pretended much of anything. A child was to be the parents' tool.

She had learned love from her friendship with Jonet,

seeing her aunt and uncle together, reading books where hope had more power than cruelty.

She rubbed her stomach. *You will never be my tool. You will be your own. Love will never be a weapon.*

"What did Alexandre say to make you amenable to coming?" Evelyne asked softly, interrupting Ines's distressing thoughts.

"Nothing." Ines laughed, and it wasn't bitter exactly, but it wasn't cheerful either. "I didn't want convincing so much as an opportunity to say good-bye face-to-face. So I told him I loved him and would miss him, and I wished he would tell me why that hurt him."

"Let me guess. He got very quiet and commanding."

Ines almost smiled at Evelyne's very correct guess. "For a time, but I must have worn him out. Or worry over this revolution did. He got a little angry and began telling me things…" Ines shook her head. "Heartbreaking things. About how he sees love. *A weapon*, he said. Because that is how your parents used it."

Evelyne frowned. "My father never loved anything but himself."

"Alexandre claims Enzo loved your mother. That it became a bone of contention between them. I do not think it was love, but they called it that, so Alexandre thinks it was that."

Evelyne was quiet contemplating that.

Ines realized Alex had not discussed what he felt for his sister, how she fit into his views of love. Someone to protect, yes, but he also loved Evelyne. How did he view that if not as a bludgeon?

"But…he loves me. And Gabriel," Evelyne said softly, coming to perhaps the same conclusions Ines was. "They are like true brothers. They know each other better than anyone."

Ines wondered if Gabriel knew what Alex had told her this afternoon. She very much doubted it. "I don't know. I don't know how he justifies it. I only know he told me love is a weapon."

"He said that to Gabriel too," Evelyne murmured. "Gabriel told him he was doing it wrong then."

Ines almost managed a smile. "Do you think he believed Gabriel?"

Evelyne sighed, looking down at Gabri again. "No."

No. There was just something too complicated and complex, and at least some of the change or healing or whatever it was had to come from Alex wanting those things.

Maybe she understood that his awful childhood *had* marked him, but she could hardly make sense of all the different ways. Besides, he was an expert compartmentalizer. Evelyne probably had her own little compartment in his mind, more about protection than love.

"How do I get through to him when he's spent over thirty years believing that love is a weapon? I just worry that I cannot."

Evelyne sighed, leaning back in her seat. Gabri finished his bottle, and Evelyne shifted him onto her chest, where she began to rub circles on his back until he burped. She made it look easy, but Ines knew she had been gone for those months of the adjustment to motherhood, so she could hardly assume Evelyne had easily and perfectly adjusted to her new role.

"I cannot speak for everyone, but I do know something about deep-seated issues. They *are* possible to overcome, and I think love is one of the best things to help accomplish that," Evelyne said. "But sometimes so is giving them what they deserve."

Ines knew that when Gabriel and Evelyne had been having their problems, Gabriel had determined he was a threat. Instead of fighting him on that, Evelyne had agreed with him and let him go—not because she actually agreed or wanted him to go, but because he had to come to terms with himself...himself.

Gabriel had come crawling back, though it had required a little interference from Ines and Alexandre. Not that Alex had wanted to interfere. But Ines had made her case, that it was Alex's duty to get through to his friend.

Alex had done an excellent job of setting up a situation in which Gabriel would have to face the truth about himself. Ines had looked back on that moment as a bit of a triumph. Moving in the right direction. He'd listened to her. Interfered in his friend's personal matters that involved love.

She'd thought change was in the offing, so how had they ended up here instead?

"I don't suppose Gabriel could create a ruse in order to prove to Alexandre that love is no weapon?" Ines asked, somewhat miserably. Because she did not know how to fix childhood trauma.

Evelyne smiled wryly. "If he could think of one, I would have made him do it months ago. But this is..."

Different. Complicated. *Alexandre*—the king of Alis *and* being stubborn.

"I've done exactly what he wanted. I've run away. I've demanded he be a husband. I've given up. I feel like I've done it all. And he's still..." Well, he wasn't the same, was he? He'd broken down and told her the things that held him back. That was new. Maybe it was even progress?

But it was hard to see what the end result of progress would be when there was the ticking clock of this child, of the love *she* would need from her father.

Evelyne reached over with a free hand and squeezed Ines's arm. "He does love you, you know."

Ines let that settle inside her. Did he? Did she know that? "I think I do know that, but sometimes I worry I'm kidding myself. How do *you* know?"

Evelyne smiled, a little sadly. "He has spent his entire life trying to protect people, solve problems, undermine the bad in this country, all enacted by my father and General Vinyes—and then fix it once he had the chance. I have never seen him... You don't make sense to him. By which I mean that you are something good for him—as a man, not as a king. He doesn't know what to do with that. I think it is new for him, and so it feels like a threat."

"A threat. Yes. Perhaps he thinks of it as a...curse, instead of a positive. What if he sees love only as that weapon? How could I ever be the one to show him otherwise if he uses that crown like a brick wall battlement between us?"

Evelyne clearly didn't know what to say to that. She opened her mouth, but no words came out.

Ines sighed deeply. "Yes, that is the problem."

Alexandre had been able to set aside what had happened in Ines's bedroom. It was easy when things were moving at a quick clip. When the danger Gabriel had been concerned about seemed to snowball.

Vinyes had disappeared, along with a small group of soldiers. No doubt planning some kind of...threat.

Gabriel had been talking to all the soldiers he knew and not coming up with much, until a young soldier—

who could not have been in service for any more than a year—had asked for a meeting with the king.

The man, little more than a boy, stood before him now in his uniform, explaining what he knew of Vinyes's treason. Where Vinyes was hiding and the number of soldiers he'd taken with them.

"You're certain?" Gabriel asked after the young man had outlined General Vinyes's plan.

Alexandre looked at the young soldier—wide-eyed, a little pale, hands shaking. But he stood there before his king and Gabriel and nodded. "I'm certain. And I am certain it isn't *right*, Your Majesty."

"Your information is appreciated," Alexandre said, somewhat stiffly. "We can offer you a safe place to wait until we've dealt with the Vinyes threat, or you may go back to your post. No one besides the two of us will know what was said here today."

The boy straightened, chin jutted. The signs of nerves were gone now. "I will return to my post, sir."

Alexandre nodded. "Very well. Should you change your mind, you only need to contact Lord Marti in the same manner you did before."

The soldier bowed, then walked out of Alexandre's office. Alexandre stared at the door as Gabriel closed it again. Gabriel looked at him, waiting for instructions.

Alexandre felt…at a loss. He was not *surprised* the general had handpicked a group of soldiers to storm the palace and try to enact martial law. What surprised him was how little fury he felt. It wasn't a detached calm either.

It was a kind of…exhaustion at the games men played when they could simply have a damn discussion. Just like his father. They could never talk, strategize, decide. It always had to be action. Feeling. Emotional outbursts, really.

"It was true bravery on his part," Gabriel said, "to stand there and do something he knew might cause him harm but was right. For the kingdom."

Alexandre eyed Gabriel suspiciously. He didn't know what Gabriel was going for, but it felt...metaphorical. "Are you drawing some kind of parallel, Gabriel?"

"He will make an excellent general someday, with some experience under his belt. I'd keep an eye on that one for possible promotions. No doubt you'll have to do some reconfiguring of the army once this is all done," Gabriel returned, not answering Alexandre's question. As though he wanted Alex to *sit* with the metaphor and figure it out himself.

Alex grunted.

"Was there some parallel you *think* I was trying to make?" Gabriel asked, settling himself into one of the chairs opposite Alexandre's desk. He was not relaxed, though he was clearly trying to appear it.

Having Vinyes's plan was a good start, but now they had to decide what to *do* with it.

"No."

"Ah. Perhaps you are just distracted," Gabriel said. "I admit to missing my wife and my son. You seem to be missing...someone yourself."

Did he miss Ines? She'd been gone all of a few hours. She should be arriving in Italy soon, and she was with Ines and Gabri and *safe*. Missing her would mean admitting...

It hardly mattered. This problem wasn't about their families. It was about Alis.

"It is no hardship to love your family, Alex. It is not so different from loving your country and wanting to do the right thing by them. It is not so different from being a king."

Alexandre sighed. Because if all it required was for him to be *king*, he would know exactly what to do and how to proceed. But to be a person within the title...

All he could seem to see were the shells his parents had turned into, on account of *love*.

Ines had called it control, not love, and maybe it was. Who was he to say? He'd been a boy.

Did semantics matter? What did it matter what it was called if the end result was the same?

That poked at him in ways that had nothing to do with revolution and everything to do with Ines. If he didn't call it love. If he didn't call it control. If he just accepted these feelings and tried to—

Gabriel's phone chimed. He looked down at the screen. "They have arrived safely with my parents." He let out a slow breath, clearly one of relief. "My men are in place to keep an eye on the property. I cannot imagine Vinyes will trouble himself or his men with them, but we'll keep an eye out just the same."

Because there was danger. Real danger in front of them, and Alexandre had to determine what to do. About revolutions. About traitorous generals. And brave young soldiers ready to stand against them.

"I know what my father would do with Vinyes and the rest," Alexandre said. He'd send an army into Vinyes's hideout and slaughter them all. Without a second thought.

"Have them all killed?"

"Yes." It would be swift and efficient and end this issue, but Alexandre was aware of what all his father's violence had wrought—more violence, anger, division and festering distrust Alexandre still hadn't been able to climb out from under—clearly.

Alex wanted something else. Not just power. Not just

might and whatever *he* wanted. Alex wanted a solid Alis not just for the present day but for the future. For Gabri, the future king. For all who lived here and came after.

For your wife. For your daughter.

"We could go that route," Gabriel said carefully. So carefully even Alexandre wasn't sure if that would be his recommended position or not.

So he met his friend's careful gaze. "You know I cannot."

"I know. You will want to do the opposite."

But what was the opposite of violence? Forgiveness? Peace? It couldn't be *that* easy. "Vinyes will no longer have his position. The soldiers that followed him will face some penalty, but heaping violence on violence solves nothing."

"True. The problem is the opposite of evil and violence isn't always goodness and peace, Alexandre. We cannot simply give leniency and hope it fixes itself." Gabriel spread his hands as if to encompass the entirety of the problem. "The safety of our families rests on a stronger response."

Stronger. What was strength in this situation? Alexandre found he didn't have an easy answer. That might have concerned him, but his father always found the easy answer. The violent, reactive answer.

So taking his time wasn't *wrong.* Reasoning this out, looking at different angles could only be right.

The problem was, one of the angles *had* to be chosen. He could not simply refuse to act. Gabriel was right. The safety of too many people rested on action.

"What do you want to do, Alex?" Gabriel asked.

Alex.

Yes, Alex the man. Not the king. A man who wanted

what was best for the future. For his kingdom, his family...and maybe even himself.

Alex. When this was a *kingly* duty. Except he was also protecting his family. And thinking of his kingdom. His past, his father's legacy, his own. The soldiers who would stand for him and stand against him.

Maybe there was not *only* room for a king in this situation. Maybe there had to be room for...all the roles he played, all the versions of himself he inhabited. Maybe he finally had to be one and be unafraid that it might crumble everything.

"We know where they are now," Alex said, thinking it through. If this had happened a few months ago, his actions would have been clear and precise.

But he was starting to understand middle ground. Complex ideas of duty and goodness. He could not be his father, but the opposite of his father, as Gabriel had stated, was not automatically *goodness*.

Ines had pointed that out to him as well.

Alex wanted to be *good*. He wanted to be *correct*. A king had to be. A man made mistakes.

Except his father had only ever been a king—only cared about money and power and military might. Not his children. Not his legacy. He had been a crown—a cruel, violent, controlling one.

The opposite of that was a kind, peaceful, compassionate crown...which was not necessarily *good*. Better, but not...good.

So what was the answer? It seemed he had to come up with his own view of what that meant. That he had to be not the opposite of this father, but his own *man*.

Ines believed he was a good man. Not because he was a king or the opposite of his father, but because of how he'd treated her before they'd married. And after. Up to this rather conflicted point of a few months.

And still she loved him. How did it make sense?

"We could send soldiers in," Gabriel said. "Not to attack, but to arrest. But we would need to determine how to get a message to the soldiers who would support you and see if they are willing to storm in and arrest Vinyes and his men. This is almost certain to lead to violence, a fight."

Alex didn't want violence or a fight, but he also could not let this stand, so where did it leave him?

"No." The plan took shape in a strange way. Gabriel's words about the opposite of evil. Ines's words about love and standing true. "We cannot avoid violence at *all* costs, but we can mitigate it. I want a special team to arrest Vinyes—as quickly, quietly, and without violence as possible. Then I want the soldiers supporting him brought here. I would like to address them."

Gabriel's expression was unreadable. "That could be… dangerous. Even without a leader they might not feel beholden to our laws if they don't now."

"It could be dangerous, yes, but I need to know. What is it they're against? What does Vinyes offer them? This isn't about right and wrong. We all think we're right. It's about finding the best way forward, and we can only do that by discussing it."

Gabriel still didn't seem entirely sure, but Alex knew this was the right way forward. Not might. Not kingly disassociation.

Connection.

Just like Ines had given him.

CHAPTER FOURTEEN

When Ines woke the next morning, there was very little news. Evelyne had passed along Gabriel's assurances that everything was okay, a plan was in place, and ideally Vinyes would be arrested by nightfall.

Gabriel's parents were kind and attentive and did their best to take Evelyne's and Ines's minds off things. They arranged a picnic in their pretty vineyard while they took care of Gabri, and Jonet joined the two women and attempted to chatter about all matter of things that had nothing to do with Alis or revolutions.

Ines tried very hard to set aside her trepidation and enjoy the sunny day, the pleasant company. To think of it as a holiday instead of running away from *revolution*. Instead of worrying if she wouldn't even get the *chance* to stand by Alexandre. To get under all his walls, all his traumas.

The day passed with no news. Ines grew more tense, but she thought she hid it well. Evelyne on the other hand... Well, there was nothing hidden about her nerves, her worry, her anger.

After dinner, they sat in the pretty, cozy living room—Gabriel's parents and Jonet having retired to their own bedrooms. But Evelyne paced while Ines rocked Gabri, finding the rhythmic movement and the baby's warm weight soothing. Ines knew Evelyne was concerned because Gabriel hadn't sent an update, but no doubt arresting a general took some time and careful doing.

Or he's leading a successful overthrow and Alex is somewhere hurt and—

She squeezed her eyes shut, trying to shut out the anxiety loop of her own thoughts. It was pointless. There was nothing she could do from here. There'd be nothing she could do at the palace. This was military and such.

This was a *king's* duty. Not a man's.

The fact that she understood that distinction better now than she ever had before was painful. Not only because she understood, but in understanding she had no idea how to get through to him. How to convince him he deserved to be a *man* too. Not when so much rested on him being a king.

He thought love a weapon, and his title armor. How could she ever foment her own successful revolution against *that*?

Footsteps sounded quietly in the hall, and then a man appeared in the entryway.

Evelyne stopped her pacing, then in the next moment crossed the room at a jog and flung herself at Gabriel, who caught her and held on tight. They murmured words to each other, too soft for Ines to hear—but it was not a moment for her.

Ines stood—Gabri still in her arms, her heart in her throat.

There was no Alex with Gabriel.

"Everything is well," Gabriel said loud enough that Ines was able to hear this assurance. "Vinyes has been arrested. Alexandre is currently interviewing and figuring out punishments for those who followed him. Vinyes will remain in jail until his court-martial. With the evidence stacked against him, his punishment will no doubt be swift and just." Gabriel, still entwined with Evelyne, moved over to peer down at Gabri.

The baby wasn't asleep yet but was getting there, with drooping eyes. Still, Ines handed Gabri over to his father with a shaky smile. All was well. Alexandre was busy, but safe. Safe. That was all that mattered now.

Gabriel held Gabri close with one arm and Evelyne with the other. Safe. Everything all right.

Except Ines felt very, very alone.

She pressed a hand to her stomach, reminding herself she wasn't alone. Perhaps her child was not born yet, but the baby still needed her for right now to take care of herself. And soon to hold and nurture and *love*.

"We will spend the night here and return to Alis in the morning," Gabriel said.

"Will Alexandre be all right?" Evelyne managed to ask the question which Ines hadn't been able to find words for.

Gabriel nodded. "Vinyes did not have as many followers as he would have needed to truly enact his plan. He believed more would follow than did. Many he thought would follow stood with Alex instead."

Ines felt her knees go weak, but she locked them. Her husband *was* a good king. He deserved such loyalty. If only he could take that on board. His goodness, his strength, all grown in spite of what he'd been given. If only he could see how *amazing* he was.

Instead, he hid behind a crown.

Evelyne let go of Gabriel and squeezed Ines tight. "Let's get some rest. We'll get up very early and head back home."

Ines nodded and even managed to keep her smile in place as the small family left to go to their room. Ines found her way to hers. She dressed for bed, then simply lay down in the guest bed, her phone in her hand.

She stared at the screen. She could call him. She could reach out and take that step. She so wanted to, and yet the fear of hearing that clipped, detached tone of his had her staring at the phone in her hand until she fell asleep.

She awoke to the bustle of everyone getting ready to travel back to Alis. Gabriel and Evelyne were cheerful, though baby Gabri was grumpy—which gave Ines something to focus on. She helped Evelyne and Gabriel try to cheer him up in the car and on the plane ride back.

When they returned to the palace, Ines excused herself and went to her rooms immediately. As much as she was desperate to find Alex, to hold on to him as Evelyne had held on to Gabriel last night—just to assure herself he was alive and well—she knew she wasn't steady enough for any kind of rebuff.

So she settled into a warm bath and tried to wash away all the worry and stress and focus on what came next.

She couldn't *make* Alexandre believe in love. Perhaps with time she could, but the misery she'd spoken of before they'd left the palace wasn't something she could stand. She had spent her entire childhood unloved, unwanted. A pawn. Perhaps she'd even thought it her due.

Until this new life had taught her otherwise. But it hadn't changed her parents. It hadn't changed anyone. *She* couldn't. People had to change themselves.

Just as she had made the decision to change herself.

Perhaps she would always be a little miserable Alex could not believe in love, but she could hardly condemn her daughter to the same fate. But what other options were there? She was a queen. Their baby would be a princess. What would Ines do if not this?

For the first time she thought she fully understood why Alexandre had worked so hard to be only a crown. To eschew anything that was *more*. By marrying into the royal family, she had made everything so much more difficult.

Trying to be a person within a title was complicated, difficult, and had no easy, perfect answers.

Or maybe that was just life—for everyone. A title was just a more concrete inanimate thing to blame the complexity on.

When she got out of the bath, Ines considered simply putting pajamas on and spending the day in bed, but the day after an attempted revolution would no doubt require the queen's presence. So she dressed to be seen.

Maybe she was reluctant to see Alex face-to-face today, but she still supported him, and anyone who came into her orbit would know it. Once she was happy with her hair and makeup and had found a skirt with an elastic enough waistband to wear over her ever-expanding middle, she forced herself to leave her bedroom.

She came to an abrupt stop as she walked into the sitting room to find Jonet waiting for her. Jonet had her phone in one hand, a tablet in the other, a clear sign she was in assistant mode.

Nerves jittered in Ines's stomach.

"I have received a message from the king's assistant," Jonet said, her smile somewhat apologetic. "He has an announcement regarding your pregnancy he'd like sent out today, if you could approve it."

Approve…

Alexandre wanted her pregnancy announced *today*? After everything yesterday had been, he was thinking about this?

Jonet held out the tablet. Ines took it dutifully, read the short statement.

King Alexandre would like to share the happy news with all of Alis that he and his queen will be welcoming a child to the kingdom in the coming months.

Ines found herself frowning at the words. *Happy news?* He had yet to act particularly *happy.* Of course this statement wasn't about Alex. This was royal business. "Yes, that's fine," Ines said handing the tablet back to Jonet. "I think I'm just going to go back to—"

Jonet cleared her throat to cut her off. "The second part of the message was that the king would like to see you now."

A message through *assistants*. She didn't have the wherewithal for that. "I'm exhausted, Jonet." She had only slept in fits and starts, and she knew she would need strength, true strength, to deal with Alexandre. Especially if this was how he was summoning her.

"Yes, but his assistant did say it was an urgent matter. I can put him off—"

"No." She might as well get this over with. Alex wouldn't claim something urgent if it wasn't. "I'll go." Maybe she didn't know what to say, but if he had an urgent matter, then they would deal with that, and maybe she could get away with not knowing what to do for the time being.

She walked through the palace. It had changed in the months since King Enzo had died. Alexandre had allowed Evelyne and Ines carte blanche to redecorate whatever they saw fit, and they'd mutually decided to move away from austerity and military, while keeping the historical integrity of the castle.

So Ines walked down carpeted hallways, taking her

time and enjoying the art on the walls—landscapes and royal portraits, instead of bloody war scenes.

And, okay, yes, she was stalling. She wanted to find some center of strength—like Alexandre always seemed to have. She wanted to put on her queenly mask, but she was afraid the moment she saw him she'd throw herself into his arms. Relief that he was okay.

She just didn't want to be pathetic. Not because she cared so much about herself, but she had to start thinking about what her daughter was going to see. Alex had been incredibly harmed by what he'd seen as a young boy. She wouldn't do the same to her child.

So that was her center of strength. "You," she murmured, spreading her hands over her belly as she finally made her way to Alex's office.

His assistant nodded at her approach. "You may go right in, Your Majesty."

"Thank you," she murmured. Nerves battled, reminding her of a time early on when she'd been so nervous to be alone with him. Nervous because she didn't know how to read him. Nervous because she thought he was ridiculously handsome. Nervous because she had been afraid one wrong move would ruin everything.

But he'd always made sure she knew she could not *ruin* things. At every step in their courtship, he'd always assured her she was exactly what he wanted, even if he hadn't chosen her.

Oh, how that had changed. Now he'd accused her of *destroying* him.

She tried to fan the little flicker of irritation. Anger would stand against him better than *nerves*. Anger was better than pathetic, desperate love.

Or was it? Perhaps anger was the weapon, the bludgeon.

That thought left her feeling hollowed out, bereft all over again. She stepped into his office not knowing how to be, because she so badly needed things from him he wasn't ready to give, and she wanted to punish and save him from that reality.

When had life gotten so damn messy?

He stood behind his desk, hands clasped behind his back. Tall. Severe. Just like the first time she'd met him. His dark eyes unreadable.

But she had seen them clouded with passion, direct with fury, lost, sad. She had seen every emotion in his eyes, no matter how hard he'd tried to hide them. So she wanted to rush over to him as Evelyne had done on Gabriel's arrival last night. She wanted to cry—at least that she could blame on hormones.

But she stood across from him, frozen to the spot because he surveyed her with that detached calm that left her feeling travel-frazzled even after her bath.

I am so glad to see you in one piece. I am so proud you handled this the way you did. Your country will love you because you are a good king, but I love you because you are a good man.

All words she might have tried to say if her throat wasn't so tight.

"Good morning, Ines. I am glad you are back."

She blinked. Those were not exactly the words she'd been expecting. They hadn't exactly left on happy terms, so it worried her that he was *glad* she was back. Had he come up with some horrible new plan that would crush her?

She cleared her throat. "I am glad to be back. Gabriel's parents were more than kind, but I prefer..." *Home.* Not just this place, but a place she knew he was. Safe and sound and *home*. "I have approved the pregnancy announcement."

"Excellent. It will go out at once."

Ines nodded, feeling little more than adrift. Why was she here? She wanted to scream that at him. And yet all she did was stand here, waiting for him to speak.

He picked up something from his desk. A little notepad. She could see he'd written some things in his blunt but elegant hand. He crossed to her and held it out.

"I have made you a list, Ines."

"A list..." He'd successfully stopped a revolution, and he had a *list* for her. A list when he'd told Jonet, or rather his assistant to Jonet, this was some *urgent* matter. She took the outstretched pad of paper, but she couldn't quite make herself look down at it.

She couldn't take her gaze off him when he was whole and in one piece and something was just off. Something she couldn't put her finger on.

"It is a list of things we must accomplish before the baby is born," he said regally, perhaps noticing she wasn't reading.

He was giving her a...to-do list. Perhaps to keep her busy and away from him? Maybe that was for the best. But she couldn't seem to look at it. Not when he was within reach. Not when...there was *something* in his eyes she didn't recognize, didn't think she'd ever seen.

It terrified her. What if this was it? The end of the line. He'd stopped a revolution and now he'd stop her.

No. He doesn't get to stop you loving him.

"I have also thought long and hard about it," he continued, though Ines had no idea what *it* referred to.

"There was a queen of Alis many generations ago named Phillipa. She was highly regarded as brave and intelligent, no small feat for a woman to be given any credit in that time period."

Ines stared at Alexandre, wondering if he was suffering from some sort of sleep deprivation, because why was he talking about old queens? A history lesson?

"It is history, family, but it is also a symbol," he continued, his gaze steady and serious, but something was lurking in their dark depths that Ines couldn't quite identify or understand.

"I believe it would be a nice name for a princess."

Princess. Ines's mouth dropped open. Something cracked open inside of her. "You thought of...a name." Her eyes filled with tears, but she blinked them back. She didn't know what that meant.

"Before you cry, read the list, Ines." His voice was... soft. She could not remember his tone ever being quite so resonant like that before.

So she finally looked down at the list in her hand and began to read.

We will breakfast together every morning. If I must miss a breakfast, I will make it up at the other meals of the day, and if I must be away for the entire day, you may punish me accordingly.

Punish... This didn't make sense, so she kept reading.

There will be no more separate bedrooms. You will move into mine—you may adjust the decor accordingly.

But that seemed to mean... Ines shook her head. Maybe this was a very elaborate dream.

We will continue to walk together at least once a day, per your list.

Her...list. But they weren't doing that anymore. Did he think she would hold him to it? She wasn't sure she could. Except...he had a list. One with another line to it.

Once our baby is born, we will revisit our lists and adjust accordingly to ensure we are both happy.

"What…is this? What…" It read like everything she wanted. Like a marriage. Like *love*. But she didn't know how to absorb that. Maybe she was hallucinating.

"This is to be on top of your list, of course. Except we are getting rid of *appointments* since you will be in my—in *our* bedchamber."

She swallowed at the lump in her throat, finally worked up the courage to look at him. Was he really offering… all this? She couldn't quite trust it. "What brought you to change your mind?"

He sighed, closing the distance between them. His hands were gentle on her face. His eyes direct, maybe a little sad. But sad was something new. It wasn't detached. It wasn't walls. It was simply true.

"It is not that I have changed my mind, Ines."

Fear scrambled through her. And anger. "Then what is it?" she demanded, even as a tear slipped over onto her cheek. He brushed it away with his thumb, his gaze never leaving hers.

"A change of *heart*," he said, very seriously, very gently.

She inhaled sharply, held her breath there, staring at him trying to believe this was…really happening.

"Brought on by…everything. You. Our child. Gabriel pointing out that being the opposite of my father is not exactly a guarantee of *goodness*, and you had said the same. I have to be my own man, driven by my own core principles, and that man cannot be ruled by the kind of fear my father employed. The kind of fear that turned love into control or a weapon or whatever it was."

She couldn't quite find the words. Her mind seemed

to be struggling to catch up to whatever this was, while her body reveled in his hands on her face.

"I met with the soldiers who followed Vinyes. I listened to these men tell me why they followed the general over their duty. For many, it was out of fear, bitterness. Things born out of feeling unseen, uninvolved, unimportant. And I realized that as a king I could not solve this for them—the fear, certainly, but I could not fix the things in their lives that led them to these feelings, because these feelings were not about them as soldiers, but about them as men."

She did not know why anger welled up inside of her when he was finally breaking through his walls, finally *giving, compromising, believing*. The idea that she'd told him all this and he hadn't *listened* but some rebellious soldiers would get through to him absolutely infuriated her.

"Well, I'm glad facing your men got through to you where I could not. Perhaps they can keep you warm at night." She tried to turn away, but he held her in place.

"Ines." His voice was so gentle. Almost *amused*, and her hands curled into fists, tempted to punch him—not that it would do any damage.

But his gaze was still direct. His hands still gentle on her face. "None of this would have happened if you had not done the fighting for me first. I was able to see this for what it was because of *you*."

The lump in her throat was back. A softening waved through her with such vigor she was afraid of it and tried to maintain her anger. "So, what? You're *grateful*?"

"Yes, grateful. But much more importantly, I love you, Ines. Not as a weapon, but as simply a…feeling. That we get to decide how to wield."

Surely he didn't mean… "I don't understand," she croaked.

"Don't you? You're the one who has been trying to get through to me." He brushed at the tears that fell over her cheek.

"You're just…suddenly in love with me because you stopped a revolution?" she asked, her voice squeaky.

He shook his head. "I have been in love with you for a long time. I think I began to fully realize it when you told me I needed to interfere with Gabriel and Evelyne's problems. When you stood up to me and showed me who you were underneath your mask. I'm sorry it took longer for me to be brave enough to look under my own. I'm sorry it took palace turmoil to realize that dedicating myself to the crown and only the crown makes me no different than my father, not really."

"You are wholly different than him," Ines said fiercely. Because no matter how confused or afraid or happy she felt, this was simply a truth they all deserved to know, to believe. But especially him.

"Perhaps *different* isn't the right word. Perhaps the point is… I should stop measuring myself against what he was or wasn't and measure myself against who I want to be. And I want to be the best king I can be. But I also want to be a man. Your husband. Our child's father."

Her heart was beating so hard against her chest, maybe she wasn't actually hearing him. But he still held her, still looked deep into her eyes like this mattered. Like they mattered.

Like they *loved*.

"Are you sure?" she whispered.

"Yes." He spoke without hesitation. "I love you. I will not stop. I will make mistakes, but I will endeavor to fix them rather than…" He grimaced. "I will do my level best not to try and *control* them but instead deal with them. Because that is what my parents did not do. They hurt each other to control, not to love. What they felt I cannot say. I was a boy. But I know they did not handle themselves as they should. As I will endeavor to."

He shook his head, as if irritated with his own words. "No, that is not right. I don't want to be in opposition to them or the memory of them any longer. I want to build something myself. I want *us* to build something. No measuring sticks. Just us trying to do our best with this love. For our kingdom, for each other, for our family."

Ines absorbed those words, and in them she heard the promise of a future—not perfect, not healed. But the journey *toward* healing. The journey of life with highs and lows, peaks and valleys, but love through it all.

"I will want to get rid of that hideous comforter on your bed," she managed to say, though her throat was tight and her words came out raspy. "And those curtains are an atrocity."

He smiled, the curve of his mouth so rare, and so wholly for her. "If you are with me every night, you have free rein, my queen."

She gripped his wrists, his hands still on her face. She met that serious gaze with her own. "I *am* yours," she said fiercely, because she would be fierce about this. About love.

"And I am yours." One hand slid off her face, smoothed down over her stomach. "Both of yours."

EPILOGUE

King Alexandre Enzo Rodrigo Lidia worked very hard to be a good king. He served his people and endeavored to make the right decisions for his kingdom. He still tried to fix his father's mistakes as king. No matter what happened, he would always wish to leave this kingdom to Gabri much better than he found it.

But, regardless of the outcome, he did not measure himself against the poor choices of his father.

He measured his success as a king against the quality of life of his people—lowered poverty and crime. Better health and education outcomes. Peace.

When it came to being a man, Alex didn't think of his father at all. He worked equally as hard to be the kind of man deserving of a wife as loyal and strong and wise as Ines, and a daughter as bright and happy as Phillipa.

Balance was not always easy or possible, and it still was not comfortable to sometimes need to pour more into being king and sometimes needing to pour more into being husband or father. But life was perhaps not meant to be easy.

Life was meant to be love.

And the palace that had once been filled with violence and anger and the pathetic whims of a morally bankrupt man was now filled with that love—Gabriel continued to work as Alex's closest adviser while Ines and Evelyne worked together to head charitable organizations and movements within the kingdom. Gabri and Phillipa grew like weeds—and Evelyne was due to bring another baby into the royal family soon.

"Pada!"

Alex got up from his desk at the sound of his daughter running into the office. She could not seem to decide between *papa* or *dada*, so she called him a mix of both.

It never failed to make him smile. She rushed over to him, and he hefted Phillipa into his arms as she nestled her head into his shoulder. She had her mother's blue eyes and his black hair. He swept a hand over the flyaway of it now—it often came out of the bands Ines lovingly placed each morning.

His darling Phillipa was not displaying sweetness for the sake of being sweet this morning. She was becoming quite the master escape artist. Something Ines was telling him he needed to discourage.

Alex couldn't quite bring himself to do so. Not when she escaped Ines's or Evelyne's or Jonet's or the nanny's watchful eye and came for him. Every time.

"Of course," Ines said, sweeping into the room with narrowed eyes. "There you are."

Phillipa dug in deeper.

"Picking her up is a reward, Alex," Ines chastised, coming over to stand next to them. "You'll regret indulging her escapes when she is a teenager trying to do the same."

Alex made a noncommittal noise, drawing Ines into him with his free arm. He pressed a kiss to her hair. "Let us all escape. This afternoon." He was still not a particularly spontaneous man, but sometimes love swept through him and he wanted to indulge in it. Away from the palace and responsibilities. Just him and his family.

Ines raised a brow. "Don't you have meetings tomorrow?"

"They can be rescheduled."

"As lovely as that sounds, there is something we best determine before we travel anywhere."

Confused, since usually Ines rewarded him quite heartily for spontaneity, he frowned at her. "What's that?"

"I haven't quite been feeling myself the past few days, and it *is* possible..." She slid a hand over her stomach.

He frowned a little with worry. "We haven't been trying for very long." Considering how long it had taken with Phillipa, Alex had assumed it would be another long wait to bring another prince or princess into the world.

"Apparently with the second one it is quite common to come a little easier. It's possible it's nothing, but let's be sure before we make any escapes, hm?"

Alex nodded, pressed a kiss to her temple again. Phillipa was wriggling between them, but it was just about nap time so she didn't lodge any of her usual complaints about not having her parents' undivided attention. "You've already made an appointment?"

"Yes, I was on the phone setting up a test with the doctor when she managed her little magician's act." Ines reached out, skimmed a finger down Phillipa's cheek.

His family in his arms, all this love. All this hope for a future that he had thought impossible for a man like him. But here it was.

"I love you, my queen," he murmured.

Ines beamed at him. "I love you too, Alex."

* * * * *

Did King's Heir Ultimatum *sweep you off your feet?*
*Then, you're sure to enjoy the first installment
in the Babies for Royal Brides duet,*
Secretly Pregnant Princess*!*

*And why not explore these other stories
by Lorraine Hall?*

Princess Bride Swap
The Bride Wore Revenge
A Wedding Between Enemies
Pregnant, Stolen, Wed
Unwrapping His Forbidden Assistant

Available now!

MILLS & BOON®

Coming next month

HIS FORCED SICILIAN BRIDE
Jackie Ashenden

'That's why you took me, isn't it?'

Caterina's pointed chin lifts, her expression half defiant, half imperious. 'So you could finish the job you started twenty years ago?'

So, the little *gattina* remembers me. I wasn't sure if she did.

'If I wanted to do that, you'd be dead already,' I observe. 'But you were right back there in the cathedral.'

Her long, thick black lashes flutter as she blinks rapidly. 'You kidnapping me, you mean? Oh...' Understanding dawns. 'I'm a hostage.'

I give her a slow smile, because I do like an intelligent woman. 'Excellent answer. Ten points to you.'

'My father will—'

'Your father,' I interrupt, 'is irrelevant, no matter what he will or won't do. I'm afraid, *gattina*, no one is going to save you this time.'

The delicate bow of her mouth, highlighted by some kind of shimmery, pink lipstick, compresses into a line, and fear flickers briefly in her eyes.

I expect her to cower in her seat, but she doesn't.

Instead, she stares back at me, undaunted despite her fear. 'So? I'm going to be your prisoner?'

'No, *gattina*,' I correct her gently. 'You're going to be my wife.'

Continue reading

HIS FORCED SICILIAN BRIDE
Jackie Ashenden

Available next month
millsandboon.co.uk

Copyright ©2026 Jackie Ashenden

COMING SOON!

We really hope you enjoyed reading this book. If you're looking for more romance be sure to head to the shops when new books are available on

Thursday 23rd April

To see which titles are coming soon, please visit
millsandboon.co.uk/nextmonth

MILLS & BOON

FOUR BRAND NEW BOOKS FROM
MILLS & BOON MODERN

Indulge in desire, drama, and breathtaking romance – where passion knows no bounds!

OUT NOW

Eight Modern stories published every month, find them all at:

millsandboon.co.uk

TWO BRAND NEW BOOKS FROM
Love Always

Be prepared to be swept away to incredible worldwide destinations along with our strong, relatable heroines and intensely desirable heroes.

OUT NOW

Four Love Always stories published every month, find them all at:

millsandboon.co.uk

OUT NOW!

Available at
millsandboon.co.uk

MILLS & BOON

OUT NOW!

Available at
millsandboon.co.uk

MILLS & BOON

LET'S TALK
Romance

For exclusive extracts, competitions and special offers, find us online:

- **f** MillsandBoon
- **X** @MillsandBoon
- **◉** @MillsandBoonUK
- **♪** @MillsandBoonUK

Get in touch on 01413 063 232

For all the latest titles coming soon, visit
millsandboon.co.uk/nextmonth